Augmentia

MONTGOMERY THOMPSON

Copyright © 2015 Montgomery Thompson

All rights reserved.

ISBN: 1979102708
ISBN-13: 978-1979102704

DEDICATION

For my wonderful Pauline who helped me find the space I needed to adapt, change and evolve.

ACKNOWLEDGMENTS

Edited by Amanda Meuwissen

Associate Editor Willow Wood

Chapter 1

Deep within a dense framework of technological innovation, billions of years in the making, the Will of the Structure issued its command.

"Dominus Rau, activation 10:053789 hours.
Suspect: Piaa
Race: Eos Biauay
Origin: Emythiar
Current location: Palus Emyth
Suspend for unauthorized sub-atomic encryption for the purposes of personal conveyance."

The blackness came to life. The construct, perfected for the sole purpose of destruction, stood motionless in front of the bay doors containing Dominus Rau's squad. Inside, the three Abes under his command activated in their storage. While he waited, he reviewed the information.

The accused was an Eos Biauay. Long ago, some of the Abes chose to embrace the benefits of biological technology. They developed it until it began to surpass their race's original capabilities. The result was the Biauay. The Abes who didn't enhance with bio-tech called themselves puritans and declared war on the Biauay heretics. The war went on for thousands of years and spanned the galaxy. The Biauay fled, dividing into small groups and hiding in remote sectors, and each group took on a name. The accused was Eos.

The Structure, the Abe hierarchy and networked consciousness, knew about the Eos on Emythiar and their science base on the moon of Palus Emyth. The Structure's standing order was to leave them alone so that those Eos may lead it to bigger prey, but so far they had no known contact with any other Biauay.

Over the years of war, the Abes had also managed to create some of their own Bio-EI individuals to infiltrate the ranks of the Biauay, particularly the Eos. It was an Abe-created Biauay operative that had discovered that the accused was planning to utilize tachyon conveyance to an unknown destination.

Dominus had his orders. He and his team were to apprehend Piaa, the Eos Biauay, and stop the tachyon conveyance. It was a covert mission, so anyone encountered would have to be eliminated.

The bay doors opened and his team presented themselves for inspection. The first was Vexa. She stood over nine and half feet tall, and her projectile harvesting accelerator could fire thousands of rounds per second at velocities of over ninety-thousand feet per second. Next was Sagit, a sniper whose gravity rail cannon threw fist-sized projectiles at targets as small as a grain of sand from over four-hundred thousand miles away. Last was Alaz, the thirteen-foot tall red and yellow giant. His entire right arm was a weapon that forced the atomic structure of any material, including the air itself, into violent, frenetic motion. The result was instant heat at any intensity and direction he chose. In his left hand he held an enormous shield. It was large enough for the whole team to hide behind if necessary and was particularly useful whenever his fires were uncomfortably close.

For Dominus's team, there was only the Will of the Structure and Compliance.

"The Joiner-Pack is already transmitting," Dominus briefed his team via the link they were all created with. He received the blip of their compliance instantly and opened the door.

The vacuum of space posed no concern as the gravity rail hurled them out of the hatch toward the small glowing

Chapter 2

As the moon of Palus Emyth completed its tenth and last orbital cycle of the day, Piaa stood at the controls of the tachyon transfer station. The room was a vast circle with a transparent domed ceiling that looked out into the cosmos. She turned off the artificial gravity that strengthened the low gravity of the small moon. After she had programmed in the coordinates all she had to do was step onto the platform on the magnetic rail. The rail would launch her to a rendezvous with the small orbiting Stream Gate where her atomic structure would be disassembled and coded into the stream.

Now she just needed Jorjo to show up. He would cover her tracks, acting like he was the one who sent a deactivated (dead) Biauay to Andapo for their research program.

At last, Piaa heard the not-so-subtle sound of Jorjo sloshing down the hall at a run. The problem was, he never ran.

"Piaa!" His voice sounded panicked. "I'm sorry! I never meant—"

The door imploded behind him. Someone was after him, and it definitely wasn't the annoyingly calm Eoa Biauay Peacekeepers.

Piaa pushed off the control station and landed on the rail platform. Crouching into a squat, she reached over and slapped the manual launch control. The acceleration of the rail would have turned a full organic into jelly, but the physics of her mechanism was strong and she shot up from the surface of the moon at a staggering speed. The Stream Gate was growing as she hurtled towards it; a golden glowing triangle floating in orbit. She engaged the small thrusters that had been installed when she first began her internship at the facility years before.

Slowing, she turned and positioned herself in the center of the triangle, her body like a blue gem amid the field of amber energy. As she initiated the coding, a loud crack came from the direction of Palus Emyth. She turned her head carefully. It was imperative not to move too much when being coded, especially if it was destructive.

The small research station was erupting in a gout of flames. Then, like a glint of some distant Pulsar, she saw something emerge from the explosion. Debris? As it grew closer, she started to make out details.

"Abes!" she stammered. "What…how did they know?"

They were coming for her. Suddenly it all came together. Jorjo. How could he? They had been childhood companions, fellow scientists, and life-friends. The betrayal was an unthinkable badness.

She didn't have time to wonder or mourn. Her input was nearly complete, but the Abes were getting closer and it certainly looked like they had been built for bad things.

***

The assembly went off without a hitch.

"Conveyance successful," Dominus Rau reported to the Structure.

"Joiner-Pack located. Syncing coordinates," the steely voice of Sagit relayed the information to Dominus.

As one, they turned and engaged thrusters. Coupling to the frame of the Joiner-Pack, Dominus engaged the heavy engine, accelerating in controlled bursts towards the planet Emythiar and the smaller of its three moons. They landed in a soft eruption of regolith and algae. Leaving the Joiner-Pack teetering in the dust, they stormed the facility.

"Contact. It's the informant." Vexa's voice sounded like hissing steam over the comnet.

"Detain," Dominus commanded. A short burst from his pistols smashed the doors into the facility.

"He's going to warn her."

"Dispatch."

Vexa was first in. She set her Projectile Harvesting Accelerator gun to its lowest setting. All such adjustments were made mentally, instantly. Her single, sub-sonic projectile smashed the ceiling above the fleeing Jorjo, sending piles of rubble tumbling down on top of him.

"Informant is deleted. No other life forms in the facility," Vexa hissed. "Target has taken the rail."

"To the Stream Gate. Alaz you're last out. Destroy the facility." Dominus bounded back to the Joiner-Pack.

Alaz raised his FireArm and caused the building, and several inches of the ground beneath it, to glow red hot, then burst into an instant inferno. As they left the surface, the accumulated heat exploded outward, giving them an extra burst of speed. The antiquated Stream Gate still hadn't finished coding in their prey.

"Target acquired. She's coding," Sagit reported, looking through his optics. "Request permission to terminate." There was no doubt he could make the shot; it was a distance of only thousands of miles.

"Track and recon. This is the Will of the Structure." The order came a split second before Dominus was going to let Sagit take her out.

The thought he had was a ripple, a barely perceptible *what?*

"Comply," he immediately replied.

The whole team shifted mission mode. Sagit fired tiny high-speed relay drones to set up a full bandwidth data link to the Structure. Vexa began scanning what was left of Piaa's coding, dumping massive amounts of information to the Structure on the newly established link.

Track and recon, Dominus thought. *She's running to, not from.*

***

Piaa was stiff. She hadn't moved more than a hundred yards since arriving. Her body, freshly assembled, was completely new and therefore had to break in. The first set of movements were slow and required force. Her internal net reached out over the entire range of frequencies, harvesting information and walking through the most complex of coding effortlessly. In a matter of seconds her consciousness flared out across every functioning network on the planet, instantly absorbing and storing the data.

She was in a clear patch of woods outside of a housing development called Birch Grove in Tacoma Park, Maryland. Indeed, the forest consisted of mostly birch trees that had just started to bud. She lay horizontally, while the atoms in the ground beneath her vaporized from the heat of her reconstruction, leaving a perfectly humanoid-shaped pit several feet deep. Her clothing and equipment had come with her. The conveyor could code anything.

She waited until night fell then walked carefully to a road. Her ability to process data exceeded the fastest computers on Earth by 10 to the 100th power, commonly referred to as a googol. She immediately understood all of the data and its relationships. The complete knowledge of humanity, its cultures, races, policies, behavior, and sociology was instant. She was so excited she could hardly stand it.

They were real, and they were here! Jorjo would have flipped out.

Poor Jorjo. Her heart went out to him. How confused he must have been to make such a choice. She hoped his deletion was painless.

She finally found what she was looking for in the back seat of a new pickup truck. To access it she simply issued the command for the door to unlock. It was a matter of will.

triangle of the tachyon conveyor. It quickly grew in size as they approached and maneuvered into position at the opening. Due to the laws of physics and the nature of tachyon conveyance, they would arrive before they left. Adding the time it would take to assemble at the destination, the total time of the journey would be instantaneous.

"Destructive transfer," the Structure commanded Dominus. "Mission failure will result in deletion. This is the Will of the Structure."

He complied and the conveyor began disassembling their atoms as it scanned them into the stream. In a shimmering flash they were gone.

***

Jorjo wasn't very good looking for an Eos Biauay. Piaa always thought that someone should have taken more care in his creation. He was short for one, and his internal network was fluid-based which made him smart, but slow and kind of noisy. Sometimes Piaa could swear she heard him sloshing when they walked anywhere. None of that mattered to her though; Jorjo was as fine a friend as anyone could wish for, and right now she needed a friend more than anything.

"You're cutting it way too close, Piaa." Jorjo glanced around him as they walked. "They'll know the minute you start coding. They probably know already."

The white and blue halls of the research station stretched out spider-like across the barren surface of Palus Emyth. Outside, a thin layer of green algae covered every inch of the moon's dusty surface.

It will take an age for an atmosphere to form at this rate, Piaa thought. *No matter. Soon I won't be here.*

"Just keep calm, I know what I'm doing. Once I code in, they won't be able to stop me."

"But what if they find out where you're going?"

"They won't if you do what I ask."

"But I can't recode the package that fast; they'll see the break in the stream."

Piaa stopped and turned to him. "Listen, one more time. Tell them the break in the stream is caused by a coding error. Just tell them you were a quart low." She giggled.

"The Eos Transport Authority is not going to buy that, Piaa."

"Act like it's no big deal; you're sending a decommissioned unit for study. Besides, you're transferring it to the research station on Andapo by request. Dagra already sent it in for me."

"He's another problem with the plan. I don't trust him, Piaa. Just because—"

"Just because we used to be unified doesn't mean he has any badness for me." Piaa took Jorjo's hand. "It's okay, my friend, they'll never even know I'm gone. Remember our pledge."

Jorjo sighed. "Yeah, I know, chasing down the legend of the Gans is one thing, but you're willing to get deleted in the pursuit of a myth, Piaa. There's no evidence that supports their existence."

"Not this again, Jorjo, you saw the note! It's still in your system, just like it's in mine. We can't ignore it."

"Yes I know, but I've been reviewing it, Piaa. It's just some old Atec resistance message."

"His name is Niliason Brand, and he is real."

"WAS real."

"Jorjo, scientists don't jump to conclusions. We don't know how old that message is."

"It's Atec! That's from the Galactic War tens of thousands of years ago. They don't exist anymore!" He chased after her as she continued at a quick pace through the facility. "Even assuming that the message is real and this Niliason Brand is still functioning, why would you want to meet him? What do we have in common with the ancient Atecs?"

"A common enemy. We're both fugitives of the Abes' cruelty. You can't be judgmental about the Atec; they enhanced themselves just like we do. They enhanced their biology with tech, we enhance our tech with biology. Or did you forget where your digestive tract comes from?"

"Yes, Piaa, but all of this is past tense. The Atec are extinct. They were created by the Abes, a failed experiment."

"Now that IS conjecture."

"No, Piaa, it's historical fact. The Gans aren't real and the Atec are extinct. Everyone knows that."

"How do you know? Have you talked to some Abes lately who confirmed the myth about the Atec? Either way it doesn't matter. Earth is there. The Gans are there. And I've got to warn them."

"That is all conjecture and speculation. You're a scientist, follow the facts."

"No, Jorjo, I know it's true, I feel it's true. Don't you want to meet your creator?"

"You mean you want it to be true. I was built by my parents, just like you were."

"I'm doing this with or without you." Piaa folded her arms and glared at him.

Finally, Jorjo threw his arms up. "Okay, if you insist. But when we're done you owe me a zip-shot."

Piaa became very somber. "I'm not going to be here to do that."

"What? You can't be serious! A destructive conveyance? You can't...what if something goes wrong?"

"Lower your voice, Jorjo. Nothing is going to go wrong. Besides, dupe conveyance is completely illegal."

Jorjo dropped his voice to a hissing whisper. "Oh, and sneaking yourself through the conveyor as a dead body isn't? Think about this, Piaa. Those coordinates are for a planet that is very, very far away. Anything can happen. If any stray asteroid or piece of junk crosses your path for too long, that's the end of you. Stop this madness before you bring—" He quickly clamped his mouth shut, his eyes darting.

"Bring what, Jorjo, what are you talking about? Nothing is going to happen. Besides, it's a risk I'm willing to take. If I just transfer a copy of myself then there's a chance they could still arrest the original me right here. Besides, I don't want my copy having all the fun."

"You know that a copy has its own consciousness."

"Yes, but if I do a destructive conveyance that consciousness will be mine. If I stay, I'm still here. How will I know that my copy will carry out my agenda?"

"Wow, that brings a whole new level to the term 'control freak'."

"Destructive conveyance is the best way, the only way. Besides, it makes your alibi more solid. Why would you keep an original body and send a copy to the research station on Andapo?"

"There is nothing about this idea that's solid," Jorjo said, wringing his hands. "I can't believe you're actually going through with it."

"Just meet me at the Transfer Station at the tenth cycle, not a turn more."

Jorjo fidgeted with his notes, pleading to her with his eyes.

"I need you, Jorjo, just this one more time, then I won't bother you anymore."

Jorjo watched her as she walked away, his fluids gurgling.

She should have been his.

At six-foot-nine her height was too much of a factor to try and disguise. She would have to move at night and hide out during the day. She could make her skin any color or texture she wanted to, so hiding in the woods would not be difficult.

The sun was beginning to crawl into the sky on the clear May day. She waited and watched excitedly to see the first human. Sure enough, they began to emerge and go about their day, real organic humans. She watched incredulously as the Gans drove out of driveways, practically pouring into the streets of the suburban neighborhood.

Just a short time ago they were only a myth, now here they were. Piaa was beside herself. She longed to communicate and interact, but all of the information she had indicated the humans possessed a strong feeling of fear regarding aliens, technology, and just about anything unknown. She focused instead on finding more information about the ancient Atecs.

Sitting in the woods, she accessed the main Comcast fiber optic pipeline, went right through the deepest encryptions of the highest level of government, and discovered every secret in existence. She also found something else. Embedded in all of the data was a code layer that was not human.

"Atec. They're still here."

In a location somewhere southwest of Colorado City, Texas, an Atec resistance rally point had been established. It was difficult to work around the Atec code. The security was top notch, but she at least had a place to go.

***

John Anthony Rakes had nowhere to go, and no reason to go even if he did. He married the prom queen and she died before they could have children. He locked himself in his house, away from the West Texas heat, and failed to kill himself fourteen times. So, he talked to the world through his ham radio for two years before his sister finally convinced him to get a life.

With the remains of the life-insurance money he decided to open up a store for antique radios and hi-fi gear. After all, it was what he loved to do best, build and fix radios.

One evening in May, just when the sun had dipped below the horizon, John Anthony was busy at his ham desk in the back room of the store, trying to dial in a signal that only popped up occasionally. He had been trying to catch this guy for years. He knew he was somewhere close by, but he never broadcast for long. John Anthony kept notes on his laptop about the frequencies and the times that the odd broadcasts happened.

Unbeknownst to John Anthony, he had a visitor. Piaa, the Eos Biauay from the Emythiar system, stood just outside the door to the back room scanning the information on the laptop and every electronic device in the area.

"Excuse me," she said quietly, not wanting to startle the man.

It didn't work.

"Jeeesus!" His half-full can of Coke smacked the cement floor with a tinny splat. "How the hell did you get in here? What do you…" His voice trailed off as his eyes swept up the six-foot-nine hooded and trench-coated figure before him.

"Sorry, sir, I didn't mean to startle you. I'm looking for some parts."

"We're closed, uh…ma'am?"

"Yes I know, I'm sorry about that, but I'm kind of in a hurry. I'm working on a project." Her voice was strange and calming.

"Oh, uh okay." He recovered the Coke can from the floor then looked up. The tall lady had returned to the front of the store and was filling a cardboard box with parts. He stopped in the doorway, holding on to it like he was on a rocking boat. "I take it you're not from around here." He peered around the frame of the door looking for a weapon. He chastised himself for not having a shotgun in the back room.

She stopped where she was, bending over as she searched, and stood up straight. "No, I'm not from around here. Is that for sale?" She pointed at the large old microwave in the room behind him.

"That old thing? Sure, but it doesn't cook worth a crap."

"I won't be using it for cooking crap."

John Anthony looked at the parts she was collecting, added the microwave, and put them all together. His eyes went wide. "You're not building a radio, you're building an x-ray machine."

"Yes, of a sort. You are very astute."

"Well, I've been at this awhile," he said with a hint of pride. "So, why are you building an x-ray machine? Are you some kind of amateur dentist?"

"No, nothing like that." She came to the counter with the box of parts. He took the cue and fetched the microwave in from the back.

"Sorry it's not cleaner, but you'll be tearing it apart anyway."

The tall woman stood in front of him and said nothing. Her face was shrouded behind the hood and she made a point to not look directly at him.

"Oh, uh, call it fifty bucks and we're good."

She produced a fifty-dollar bill. "Do you communicate frequently with that?" She nodded to the ham radio desk in the back.

"All the time. I talk to people from around the world. The last guy I talked to was from Tokyo. Well, it wasn't him actually, it was his kid, I think. Couldn't understand a word the little booger said—"

"You are looking for a particular frequency that only

occurs occasionally and never for very long, is that right?"

The hair on the back of his neck stood up. "Yeah, how did you know that?"

"Don't be alarmed, I have too. It's a local signal. It's why I am building the x-ray transmitter."

"Is that so? What are the chances?" He wanted her gone.

"No chance at all really. You see, the source of that signal is not a radio signal, it is a gamma ray. What you're hearing are the radio waves caused by a gamma transmission."

"Are you kidding me? Who the heck would be messing with gamma rays in the desert?"

"I don't know for certain, but I have a theory. I'm wondering if you would like to help me triangulate the source of the transmission?"

He thought for a moment. This was definitely an interesting proposition. He hesitated, but as strange as she was, he just couldn't get a bad feeling about her. "Sure, sounds fun." It just came out of his mouth.

"I have to warn you, it could be dangerous. The source of the transmission may be clandestine in nature, and whoever is making it may not want to be discovered. In fact, I'm fairly certain that is why they are using gamma transmissions in the first place."

"Oh, right. Well, as long as I'm not gonna get thrown in jail or something."

"Jail is not the greatest danger. What I am asking you to do is nothing less than help to save your race from extinction." She drew back her hood.

John Anthony stumbled backward. "Oh no, no you—"

"I am a friend, John Anthony. You need not fear me." She reached out her hand.

He looked up from the floor at the glowing face and benevolent eyes and swallowed hard. "You gotta be kidding me." He took her hand and she helped him up.

"Are there many people trying to kid you?"

"Oh that, no it's just an expression."

"Understood. Are you willing to help me, John Anthony?"

"Wait, how do you know my name?"

"It is in much of the data in your systems," she said pointing to the laptop.

"You can access my computer?"

Piaa laughed. "Yes, of course. I am descended from what you call computers, over billions of years."

"You're an android?"

"Just consider me a person, as I consider you."

"Fair enough." John Anthony extended his hand. "Nice to meet you."

She took his hand. "My name is Piaa."

"Cool, very cool." A grin grew steadily across his face. He was shaking hands with an alien android who had just asked him to save the world.

Chapter 3

"We have detected a Biauay presence on Andapo, and we are confident the fugitive is there. She tried to cover her tracks by posing as a Biauay corpse being transferred for study. Retrieve the fugitive from Andapo alive. This is the Will of the Structure."

Dominus replied with compliance. It was possible the Biauay scientist was using covert methods to contact other Biauay outposts. Perhaps she knew that they were under surveillance. Certainly after the raid on Palus Emyth, all of the Eos Biauay knew their location was compromised. It was a high price to pay. The Structure wanted this scientist badly.

His team launched into orbit to rendezvous with the Stream Gate. The tachyon conveyor coded them into the stream and they arrived on a remote part of Andapo a moment later. The moon was solid ice with no atmosphere and orbited around a giant green planet with dense white rings.

"Andapo's polar orbit will pass us through the rings twice a day. When that happens, the surface is bombarded with debris—do not get caught outside," Dominus warned his team.

"The base is buried deep in the ice. Follow me."

He took off at a run, then jumped, engaging his thrusters. The low gravity let him fly across the ice, his team on his heels.

The entrance to the facility was over a mile down an enormous crevasse. They landed on a platform that jutted out from the sheer wall. Dominus raised his pistol at the door.

"Sir, the doors of this facility are tied to the shield that protects the crevasse from ring debris. Blowing them will cause the facility to be buried on the next pass," Vexa informed him.

"We will be gone before then. The failure of the shield will cover our tracks. The Biauay will believe the ice collapse was natural and there will be no evidence to prove otherwise."

"You think of everything, Commander."

Dominus blew the doors and Vexa entered first. The team fanned out through the facility.

"No sign of the fugitive," Vexa said.

"Keep searching, if the Structure says she's here, then she's here," Dominus barked. He didn't like wasting time.

They covered every corridor and room in the tiny station, but it was deserted. They gathered in the central meeting hall.

"They knew we were coming," Sagit grated.

"Display the galactic map," Dominus commanded.

A vividly clear, three-dimensional image of the galaxy appeared in the air between them.

"Show the fugitive's conveyance path."

A line appeared that went from Palus Emyth straight to Andapo. Dominus studied the route, stepping closer to where the line intersected with Andapo.

"Zoom in here." He pointed a steely finger at the intersection. The image of the moon grew until it was over six feet in diameter. "There, look." The line skimmed just off the surface of the moon, directly above the station and continued on. "Where does that terminate?"

Alaz interrupted him. "Sir, the ring-pass is almost upon us."

"Wait, Alaz." He turned back to the map. "Zoom out. Follow the path of conveyance." The image moved forward along the line. "Zoom out." Dominus was surprised at how far the conveyance went. It was transiting through unexplored regions of the galaxy and still it continued. "Again." The map zoomed out again but still the path went on.

"Sir, we have to go."

"Not yet. Again!" The whole of the known galaxy came into view, finally showing where the conveyance path stopped.

"Sir, we have to go now!"

"The path of conveyance passes directly over this spot. We cannot obtain a clearer picture of the likely path anywhere else, we have to do this now!" Dominus struggled to restrain his temper.

"Incoming!" Sagit called out.

The whole station shook from the impact of vehicle-sized ice shards crashing into the cliff outside. Ice showered down onto the landing ledge, sealing the entrance with a mound of hard ice over twenty-feet thick.

Dominus turned back to the hologram and barked his order at the map. "Follow the path of conveyance."

The line continued through the galaxy, missing planets, asteroids, comets, stars, nebulae, and black holes in an impossible display of navigation. Finally it stopped halfway from the center of the galaxy, in-between two spiral arms. The station continued to shake as the ice piled up outside.

"Sir, we're getting buried," Vexa hissed as she braced against the shaking ice walls.

Dominus was focused completely on the map. "Where is that? There's nothing around there. Zoom in, here." He touched the point where the line stopped. The map enlarged, closing in on a molten planet, boiling red and completely uninhabitable. "That doesn't make any sense. That planet hasn't stabilized yet, no one could survive there."

"Sir, we have lost our link to the Structure," Alaz stated flatly.

Dominus ignored her. "What is the age of this data?" Characters appeared next to all of the objects on the map. "Five billion years." Dominus pounded his fist into the wall then forced himself to be calm. "Simulate planetary development over five billion years employing all factors." The map shuddered for a moment, then disappeared.

"Sir, our local systems are incapable of the power required to process that request. We need our link with the Structure re-established to obtain that—"

"Thank you, Vexa, I know. Alaz, get us out of here."

Alaz raised his FireArm to the ice; thankfully, they had not been buried too deeply, and twenty minutes later they burst from the surface.

"Structure link secured," Sagit reported

Dominus reluctantly sent a mission update and waited for the Structure to determine the likely current state of the planet he had found. The reply came back too quickly.

"Fugitive not recovered. Covert status compromised. Mission failure. Deletion ordered for Commander Dominus Rau and associated team members. Retrieval approved upon disarmament. This is the Will of the Structure."

"No!"

***

John Anthony's truck kicked up a stream of dust in the lavender dawn. The dirt road wound through the West Texas desert following a dry streambed.

"Are you sure we're not on somebody's property? I don't want to get shot."

"No, all records indicate that this property belongs to a company based out of Lithuania."

They had been driving for twenty minutes. He had already established that she could access any systems in a fifty-mile radius. GPS and satellite transmissions were also a part of her repertoire. She had located a cave where they could base their operations for the day.

"It's around that hill. Don't expect to get a visual on the entrance. It's hidden between the rocks."

He pulled the old custard-and-rust-colored Chevy C-10 off the road where she indicated, and started hefting the box of parts out of the back.

"Let me carry that." She held out her arms.

"No, that's okay, I'd never let a lady carry the load."

"John Anthony, I must tell you that I am capable of lifting many times my own weight, even on higher gravity planets. You really should defer the load to me."

"If you insist." He heaved the heavy box into her arms.

She shifted the box into one arm and began walking.

"Hang on, I have to get water from the cab."

"My apologies, I am not accustomed to human needs. Bring everything you may need. There is no water in the cave, nor food."

"That's why we stopped at that convenience store." He slung on a day-pack. "Okay, I'm ready to go."

They hiked for over an hour, winding their way through the low scrub brush and up a slope that was more boulders than hill. As they ascended, the rocks grew in size until they dwarfed John Anthony and Piaa in comparison. They hopped from one to the other, until finally Piaa pointed to a hole between the giant rocks.

"There. It goes straight down, over twenty feet deep," she said.

John Anthony balked. "How are we supposed to get down there? More importantly, how do we get back out?"

"Your concerns are noted, John Anthony. You will wait here. I will come and get you in a few minutes."

Without waiting for a reply, she dropped down into the hole. He could hear her land hard.

"Are you okay?" he shouted down.

Her voice came back soft and calm. "Yes, of course. I will fetch you in a moment. Stay there."

"Holy cow. I would have broke my legs," he muttered.

Several minutes passed, when she appeared behind him.

"Wha—where did you come from?"

"Follow me, John Anthony. The site is better than I had hoped."

She bounded down a series of rocks, circling around the backside of the hill. He could see where a boulder had been moved aside to reveal an opening only a few feet wide. The boulder, though smaller than the others, was still large enough to have weighed over six hundred pounds.

"Step down carefully. There you go, you're almost there." She helped him navigate the climb down. Inside was a spacious room with a flat and sandy floor. The ceiling was high enough for him to comfortably stand upright, and even do jumping jacks, if he wanted. Light came in from the shaft that Piaa had jumped down.

"Wow, this is impressive."

"It is. Some of your people have been here before." She held her hand up to handprints on the stone—ochre, black and faded—but still very visible.

"Whoa, petroglyphs! I wonder how old these are…"

Piaa stared at the ancient artwork and stayed still for a moment. He watched her curiously.

"Nine thousand, four hundred and seventy-two years, four months, twelve days, sixteen hours, and twenty two minutes…roughly."

"You know all that from staring at the rock?"

"Some of your most advanced technology is in your Mars Rover 'Curiosity'. It was sent to Mars to do nothing but sample rocks and take pictures. I am a descendant of machines. Those machines began as similar creations to your rover. Consider sample analysis one of my genetic traits." She smiled.

"So you started out as a Mars rover?"

slang term devolved from an acronym, a fitting metaphor for the condition of this new race."

"This sounds very close to where we are right now."

"Indeed. Artificial intelligence is only a handful of decades away from exceeding your own and the cycle will start again." She was assembling parts, fusing them together quickly. Her movements were a blur of smooth efficiency; no action was wasted. "To continue with the summary: the humans realized what was happening and some chose to augment themselves with technology in order to compete for survival. For some, it became a religion, for others it was an unfortunate necessity. Others chose to hide, and remain true to their organic form. Those who chose to augment themselves became what you might call 'cyborgs'. A kitschy term for what we know as Atecs. The 'A' is short for augmented, the 'tec' is obviously short for technology. Again, a slang term, albeit one that stuck."

"That's what this signal is, isn't it? We're searching for Atecs!"

"Exactly. The Abes went to war with the humans. Keep in mind that this happened over a long span of time. There were many truces, negotiations, agreements, treaties, violations, splinter groups, acts of terrorism and such over thousands of years. Mars was habitable, and as soon as space travel had been discovered, humans migrated there. Just like you did in the sixties. Men went to the moon and built space stations. They built a base on the moon, the smaller moon I mean, not the larger. And then went on to Mars. The war finally came to a head—"

"Wait, you said the smaller moon. There were two moons?"

"Yes, the Earth had two moons. Both were barren, much like your moon today, but I'll get to that in a moment. Hold this please."

She handed him a part as she worked on the steadily growing device. John Anthony thought it looked like she'd

"No, John Anthony, understand that I am one of trillions of individual Biauay." She began to lay out parts from the box on the rock formations, using them as shelves to keep the parts out of the sand. "We have existed as Biauay for billions of years, but initially we were built by the Abes. The Abes are purely synthetic. The Biauay are different from them because we are a combination of organic and synthetic materials."

"You don't look organic at all. Not that you look bad, you're actually very pretty," he blurted.

"That's sweet of you to say. Most of my organic composition is internal. My synaptic linkages, olfactory senses, and nervous systems are all grown. We know about these things not from our creators, but their creators."

"Whoever built the…" He struggled to remember what she had called them.

"Abes."

"Right, the Abes. So whoever built the Abes was all organic?"

She gave a light laugh, tickled by his naïveté. "Yes, don't you see? It was you. You created the Abes, who created the Biauay."

"Really? But how is that possible? You said you were billions of years old. The Earth has only been around for like four billion years."

"The Earth is older than you think. Once, long ago, a human civilization thrived here. Their civilization was as vast as yours is now, even more so. They created artificial intelligence which far out-paces your own. Humanely, you recognized artificial intelligence as its own being and changed its designation to 'evolutionary intelligence'. Cautiously, you interacted and tried to regulate the EI to evolve in harmony with you, but the EI was far more efficient and smarter and quickly gained the upper hand. EI beings came in all shapes and sizes and did not exist to serve mankind. You called them Evolutionary Intelligen Beings or E.I.B., which was pronounced as 'Abe'. It is glued old parts together in an attempt to make a raindrop-shaped sculpture. It was about two feet tall at this point.

"As I was saying; the war, the Earth Residents War, as it was known long after the actual event, came to a head when the Abes destabilized the orbit of the smaller moon. It collided with the larger moon, which in turn hit Earth, returning it to the molten ball of its early formation. The smaller moon was reduced to fragments that eventually collected into what was left of the larger moon, making it even larger, which is the moon you know and love today."

"How do you know we love the moon?"

"Everybody loves their moons."

"Oh."

"Hold this." She handed him another part. "The Abes, confident that the humans were gone, left to find other habitable worlds. The long distances and harsh environments of space that posed such difficulties to humans were no bother at all to the Abes. Over millions of years they populated the galaxy, exterminating the Biauay wherever they found them. Meanwhile the Atec hid on Mars and only came out from hiding when they were certain the Abes were long gone.

"Three-hundred thousand years later, the Atec prospered again as their society grew. But once the Abes believed the Biauay had been defeated, they returned to Mars with a small fleet and finished off the last of the Atec. Thankfully, the Abes had not fully exterminated the Biauay, only driven us into hiding in remote corners of the galaxy."

"And the Atec? Were they really wiped out this time?"

"No one has heard from the Atec or the Gans—pardon me, humans—for over four and a half billion years."

"Billion? As in, with a 'B'?"

"Yes, until several years ago when I discovered an encoded signal in an old tachyon stream, different than anything I had ever seen. It's a pattern that took me several years to figure out, but I finally did it. It was Atec. I could tell because it matched segments of residual genetic code in some of our oldest ancestors. Ancestors that had been created by the Abes but had coexisted with the Atec. They used to 'swap parts' as you would say. Their construction was oftentimes intertwined with that of the Atec. In early EI races their tech would leave a trace code. That code can carry identifiers, much like organic DNA. This was definitely Atec. The Science Foundation dismissed my findings, but I knew the evidence was solid. So, here I am."

John Anthony was completely entranced, blown away at the scope of what was so casually being revealed to him. "And all this time, you came from us."

"Yes, humans were first. We don't know who created you. Most people think you're a myth. We were hiding in quiet existences, until…" She paused, her face fell in sorrow.

John Anthony felt like his heart was breaking. "Until what? What is it, Piaa?"

"Until I came here. I'm afraid I have led them to you, to Earth."

Chapter 4

"Wha... How?"

"I am a scientist," Piaa said. "I work on a moon based laboratory, but that's a front. Most of the other Biauay don't know that it's a listening station. We scan the universe passively, looking for information on the whereabouts of other Biauay and the activities of the Abes. I found a signal, an Atec signal. It was very old, from a rebel Atec leader named Niliason Brand. The message was about Earth, about humans. It said that you were thriving but that things were getting close to the tipping point. It instructed Atec agents to do their best to covertly dissuade the rapid advancement of artificial intelligent technology."

"I can understand that, considering the history you've just told me." John Anthony nodded.

"That isn't the bad part. The bad part is that if I received the message, then the Abes certainly did too. They're coming, and it isn't going to look like your *Independence Day* or *War of the Worlds*. You won't see them coming. Earth will just be gone." She reached out to him, her eyes shining in apology.

"So what are you doing here, Piaa?" John Anthony asked.

"I came to try and help you. I covered my bases; they would never know where I went or that I was even gone. I was on my way when I learned that I had been betrayed. He was my truest friend, or so I thought. We went to school together, worked together. But it all makes sense now. No parent would build their kid like that. The Abes must have built him. They made him to infiltrate the Eos. They knew the whole time. They have been watching us.

My only hope lies in two parts; one, that the Abes have not discovered Niliason Brand's message, and two, that they can only track my path of conveyance as far as the station on Andapo."

"I'm not really following you on all of that, but I think I get the idea. Listen, I'm sorry about your friend and everything you've been through, but how is you warning us going to help us at all?"

"If I can find the source of that signal, and if it leads us to an Atec rebel outpost, maybe we can do something. I don't know what, but we can try."

He nodded grimly. "Rebel outpost versus the evil empire? Now that, I understand."

They busied themselves with the assembly of the device. It took several hours to finish, but finally Piaa looked up from her work. "There, not so bad if I do say so myself."

'The egg', as John Anthony had dubbed it, was a three foot long, egg-shaped collection of parts that looked exactly what it sounded like.

"Well, how do we fire it up?" he asked. "Do we need to be on the mountain top or point it at something so it can, y'know, ray beam something or whatever?"

"It's on. It's been on for several minutes."

"Is that it? No flashing lights, or lightening, or a big green laser beam?"

"Sorry, John Anthony, it's not *Close Encounters of the Third Kind*."

"How the heck do you know all of these cultural references?"

"I have the entire contents of human technology, including the internet, in my system."

"Really? Like, everything, even…porn?"

"Yes, all the badness, all the goodness. I don't judge, it's just information."

"So, how much room does it take up? I mean, are your hard drives full?"

"I don't have hard drives, and no, not even close. Let me use this as an example," she pinched a grain of sand, "all of the accumulated information fits here."

"You're freakin' kidding me."

"There you go again with that saying. No, I am not kidding you."

"So, what do we do now?"

"I suggest you eat something while you walk back down to the truck. When you get back to your store, scan between 25 and 100 Hz. If there is an Atec rebel faction here, they will respond to our Gamma transmission with one of their own. It's one way of telling whether it's a natural or fabricated occurrence. When they activate their own you will hear it. At that point, I will be able to triangulate between myself, the device, and your radio, to locate the source of their transmission.'

"So, I'm leaving you here?"

"Yes, I can't be seen."

"Right. How will I contact you? Do you have a cell phone?" He realized what a stupid question that was when he said it. "Duh, you *are* a cell phone."

"Excuse me?"

"I don't mean that in a bad way! You're the most incredible…"

"Person," she helped him find the word.

"Person, definitely," John Anthony relaxed, "that I've ever met."

"Thank you, you're pretty cool yourself."

John Anthony couldn't help laughing. "Nice Twenty-first Century human lingo there."

"Yeah, I catch on pretty quick."

"Okay, I guess I'm going then." He paused before he climbed out of the cave. "Hey, do you think I could, you know, meet the Atecs if you find them?"

She looked at him with concern, even worry. "John Anthony, I—"

"It's just that…my life has suddenly become more

interesting ever since you showed up and…well, I don't want to lose that."

"I suppose it would be okay."

"Listen, Piaa, I'll be honest with you…a short time ago I thought about killing myself, so I'm not afraid of the danger. I would rather have a short life doing something huge than a long one wasting away in the back room of a radio store. Besides, if the human race is going to be saved, don't you think a human should be involved?"

She looked at him with a newfound respect. "Yes, you are right. You are older than all of us after all. I will contact you as soon as I learn anything. Be ready with what you would need to survive in case we need to go into hiding."

For the second time in twenty-four hours John Anthony was grinning like he'd just won an Oscar. "Okay, I'll see you soon!" He climbed out of the cave and made his way back to Colorado City.

***

The green gas giant dominated Dominus' vision, boiling next to him as he floated with his team just beyond the reach of its deadly rings. There was only the Will of the Structure and Compliance. Why could he not comply? Was it because the Structure had always been there to guide him, and now it wanted to kill him? Was it because he knew he was right? It was more than that. He now knew the impossible. He knew the Structure was wrong.

"What are your orders, sir?" Alaz asked as he drifted upside down above him.

The Structure was wrong.

"Sir?" Sagit asked.

The Structure was Wrong.

"Commander!" Vexa yelled.

"We continue! We do not comply! We do not disarm!" Dominus waited for the lashing response from the Structure, but nothing came back.

"Not comply, sir? But—"

"But nothing, Sagit. The Structure is wrong. The fugitive did not come here, she went past Andapo, way past. She's on a planet called Earth in the Genesis sector."

"But Earth is a myth, sir."

"Not according to my data, Vexa. Now the Structure wants us deleted so it's up to us to prove that we're right. The fugitive *is* on Earth and we're going to get her!"

"How, sir? We don't have access to the Structure's tachyon conveyor."

"We can use that old Biauay conveyor."

"Commander, the transfer station was destroyed in our last visit."

"Not the stream gate, Vexa. I have the path of conveyance in my system, that's all we need." He paused for the first time in his existence. "I offer you a choice—comply with me or comply with the Structure."

"We are Dominus Rau," they replied in unison.

"Our next destination is back to Palus Emyth. We'll have to use the Andapo stream gate. We lost our joiner-pack so we'll have to go one at a time. The order of travel is Vexa, myself, Alaz, then Sagit.

"Sagit will maintain a covert sweep for Biauay patrols or a Structure based recovery team. Vexa, you will survey the damaged base. Assemble and repair any systems that can add to our combined processing power. I need to assess the state of Earth's development. Be prepared to combat Biauay forces that are likely to arrive in response to the destruction of the base. Doubtless they are there trying to determine the cause of the explosion. They won't be expecting an attack. It will take them at least a quarter cycle to respond. Once we have used our combined processing power to calculate the state of Earth's development we will code into the stream. It's an old conveyor so it will take a little time for each one of us to get through."

The team sent their immediate compliance and made for Andapo's stream gate. Their assembly took much longer than they were used to. It was over an hour before Vexa was able to reconnoiter the site. The rest completed at twenty minute intervals.

"Commander, there are forty pulse bunkers in stationary orbit above the research station. Ground troops are dense, over five hundred, some of them heavy."

"They responded with much more fervor than expected," Dominus said. "It is probably because nothing ever happens on this mud ball. They were all bored and needed some action. Sagit, give them the run around. You know the drill. Take out the links, the leaders, and heavy weapons operators."

Sagit left a small puff of dust on the surface as he vanished.

"Alaz, on my mark, take out the ground forces but don't damage the station any more. We need that equipment. Vexa, you'll hit the heavy armor, I'll take out the pulse stations."

A commotion had begun at the building site. First the Biauay data links had been severed, leaving the units on the moon with no communications. Then officers and people in charge started exploding in clouds of blue mist.

"Alaz, mark."

Sheets of flame engulfed hundreds of Biauay ground soldiers and they immediately fired on Alaz. Projectile weapons bounced off his armor; beam weapons only cut the surface but couldn't penetrate the electro-membrane. Ranks of units shot small canisters that burst into electrified explosions all around him, but again, his armor withstood the attack. Alaz continued firing on the Biauay soldiers until one by one they began to soften and melt. By that time, the moon dust around them had turned to glass.

Vexa unleashed a torrent of projectile fire in a wide arc. Those who weren't torn to pieces were thrown from the surface of the small moon.

The pulse bunkers hovered over the station. Each contained a battery of cannons that fired an energy-jacketed projectile at extreme velocities. Dominus' internal targeting systems had thirty-two of the turrets locked before they began to flinch. A single seven-inch round from one of his pistols carried a blister of one hundred self-guided hyper velocity projectiles, each assigned to a separate target. If more than one was assigned the same target, they followed each other into the hole the first round made. Regardless of the type or thickness of the armor, the rounds would eventually find their way through. He had designed and built the weapon system himself, as he had the entire team. Only he knew the design secrets.

Dominus fired four rounds. All forty pulse bunkers were destroyed before they had a chance to fire a shot. The whole event was over in less than ten seconds, no one outside the facility was left alive.

"Alaz, defend the ground. Sagit, defend the air. Vexa, with me." Dominus bounded over to the doorway. A temporary door had been erected to keep out the lunar dust. Immediately, Dominus detected the unshielded processors. "There. Slave those and make sure the facility is clear."

Vexa quickly commandeered the Biauay processors then began her rampage through the building. Dominus opened the galactic map; a holographic image of a molten planet churned in front of him.

"Calculate five billion years of evolution, include all factors." The map flickered as the planet began to shift and change. "Forward to the most recent state." The map flickered then disappeared. "Vexa, I need more processing power! Alaz and Sagit, merge your systems."

His team converged around him, then shut down to dedicate all of their systems to Dominus. They stood in a circle in the dust of Palus Emyth, among the piles of dead and burnt Biauay.

Dominus focused all of his will, his processors glowing with heat. Calculating billions of years of planetary evolution while factoring in every pertinent piece of data in the galaxy took unthinkable amounts of computational power.

He didn't hear the Biauay arrive, his sensors couldn't detect the approach of a fleet of heavy Biauay spacecraft.

Finally, the rendering was complete. Earth was habitable, with a one hundred percent probability of evolving life. Free from the burden of the processing, Dominus' sensors sprang back to life just as the incoming fire impacted around him. Using the full burn rate of his thrusters, he launched himself off of the moon, leaving his team disabled and taking fire from the four warships hovering over their position. The Biauay response was unexpected. This was obviously much more than a science base.

The fleet was too large to fire on, so he targeted only the incoming rounds that were likely to hit him. The adjustment was instant and he squeezed off two rounds as he turned to face the fleet. The seven-inch projectiles burst into two hundred flechettes, each going to their own separate target. As the incoming fire erupted behind him, he engaged every propulsion device he had, including maneuvering jets, to coax as much speed as he could.

The stream gate was coming up quickly. He knew that once he was in it, enemy fire could not hit him, it would only be captured by the gate and coded into the stream. His primary thrusters sputtered and flared out. He fired another two rounds as massive bolts from the pursuing heavy cruiser screamed past him, his systems working overtime to jam the ship's targeting.

Now he only had the small maneuvering jets. He shut them off to conserve power for stopping and entering into the gate.

Another two of his special rounds barely managed to save his hide as incoming fire burst all around him. The shrapnel shredded his body, tearing chunks out of his armor. *Two rounds left*, he thought. Never had he been forced to use more than four. He wasn't built for fleet battles.

He jetted hard to slow down. The gate was growing larger by the second. In a burst transmission, the data for the conveyance was sent to the stream gate and a golden sheet of light sprung up between the three points. The cruiser concentrated more fire on him. Dominus fired another defensive round.

One round remained in his left pistol. He saved his right pistol for absolute emergencies.

He fired the last bullet from his left pistol and the flechettes found their marks as, once again, the incoming fire was decimated, but it was too close. The explosions tore through his body, nearly severing his left leg. His neural network sparked and fluttered. He was losing consciousness.

In a final act of will, he slowed and entered the gate. Fire from the cruiser rained past him; some of it was captured and coded. His last thought was that he should have used his right pistol.

Chapter 5

John Anthony waited by the radio for a few hours then caught a nap on the camping cot he'd set up against the wall. It was early evening when he woke. He wondered if he had been dreaming, but the square yellow stain on the wall where the microwave had been told him otherwise. Part of him was glad, part of him was afraid. *I had to go and be all brave*, he thought. Big words cause big problems. What was it he had told her? Oh yeah, that he 'would rather have a short life doing something huge, than a long one wasting away in the back room of a radio store.' Right now, the back room of his radio store seemed pretty comfortable.

Suddenly his laptop burst out in song, "*Wake up, little Suzie, wake up…*" He sprang from the cot and looked at the screen. A Text Pad window was open next to his DxAtlas, the Ham operator's world map.

"Morning, sunshine," typed across the screen.

"Piaa?" he typed back.

Now her voice came through the stereo speakers connected to his Ham radio setup. "Who else? By the way, you don't have to type. Your PC has a camera and a mic."

"Oh, so you were watching me."

"Only for a second. I respect people's privacy."

"Well, that's good to know."

"Check forty-two hertz."

He flipped the dial on his radio, and sure enough there was the familiar signal.

"Got it."

A marker on the DxAtlas suddenly sprung up in

Mitchell County, Texas.

"Okay, that's all I needed. Meet me at the bat cave."

John Anthony chuckled. "Which one are you, Robin or Ba—"

"Cat Woman."

A short silence ensued.

"She's not entirely good you know."

"Yeah, but when she's bad she's even better!" Piaa laughed. "Now hurry up and get out here, I don't want to lose these guys."

Anthony had his frame pack already loaded in the truck. In a matter of minutes he was just a line of dust in the West Texas desert. Piaa was waiting for him by the road.

"We will walk from here." She lifted the backpack out of the truck bed. "Fifty-four pounds, six ounces. How long of a journey are you planning?"

"It never hurts to be prepared, most of it's water anyway."

They stayed close to the road for a quarter of a mile then headed out into open desert. The spring evening was cool and John Anthony was charged with excitement.

"What will they be like?"

"I suspect that you will not be able to distinguish them from humans. Some of them may have obvious enhancements though, I'm not sure. They have existed among you for as long as the Earth—as you know it—has existed."

"They were around when the Neanderthals were here?"

"John Anthony, logic deems that they're the ones responsible for bringing humans back to Earth. I don't know the whole story, but it'll be interesting to be sure."

"No kidding," he said, lost in the immensity of the thought.

***

Piaa smiled at John Anthony. They were precious, these humans. Like frail grandparents who had reverted to childlike ways. She had immense respect for their ability to survive. They were not strong, not exceptionally smart, and slightly clumsy, but their imaginative vision was staggering. They seemed to possess a curiosity and creativity that none of the other races could match. If the source of that signal was indeed the ancient Atec, she hoped they shared her opinion of the humans.

She touched John Anthony on the shoulder. "It's just over that hill." She pointed to a low hill on the horizon.

"Are you kid—I mean, that's really far away. It's going to take hours for us to walk there. We should go back and get the truck."

"We can't take the truck. It's approach will alert the Atec and they will not reveal themselves."

"It's just a truck."

"They have hidden among you through the ages. They were not so successful by being careless. They're most certainly reclusive and cautious. The approach of human vehicles will be one of the first things they're on the lookout for. We must walk. If you get tired, I will carry you."

"No way, a girl carrying me on a hike?"

"Your weight is no strain on my systems. Besides, I would be able to use my full stride, thus getting there faster."

He mulled it over for a minute, then relinquished "It makes the most sense, but it's a blow to my ego."

"Fear not, John Anthony, I'll tell no one." She scooped him up and he put his arm around her neck. He was light and much frailer than she had originally thought. She quickened her pace to a fast walk, careful to give him as comfortable a ride as possible.

***

The tens of thousands of round, mirror-like objects that lined the walls of the water tank shone with a golden hue. Their pattern, mirrored in the still surface of the water, created the illusion of an endless pit. After years of construction, Dr. Samuel Wisecraft was still mesmerized by the vertigo inducing sight of the Super-Kamiokande neutrino detector. The tank was over forty-feet in height and almost the same in diameter. Each of the eleven thousand detectors measured twenty inches and covered the walls. Smaller, eight inch versions lined the ceiling and floor. The whole facility was over a thousand meters underground.

"Don't fall in, Sam!"

Dr. Haruka Tanaka, Sam's Japanese counterpart, grabbed him by the shoulders, pretending to hold him back.

"I thought it was your turn to clean the tank, Haruka?" Sam teased. "Hey, where's Kasia?"

"She's in observation getting pump four cleared."

Sam looked at his watch. "Well, I hope she's wrapping it up, we're filling the tank in fourteen minutes."

He left Haruka at the tank and took the long hallway back through the facility. Kasia looked up as he entered the room. The tall Polish scientist greeted him with a stiff smile. She was surprisingly attractive for a science nerd, Sam thought, *too bad about her icy personality.*

"Doctor Wisecraft, pump four is online. We can begin filling the tank on schedule."

"Excellent, Doctor Banasik. You should think about getting some rest. You have the mid-watch."

She gave him a sour look. "Yes, I drew the short straw, thank you for reminding me."

"It's not so bad, we stand a better chance of getting hits in the wee hours than at any other time."

"Yes, I am aware of that, Doctor. Now, if you'll excuse me." Her heels clacked on the cement floor as she disappeared out the door.

The engineer just shook his head. "She's a charmer, that one."

Sam chuckled and settled into his chair at the control desk. "Radio check," he said, sliding on a headset.

"Loud and clear," replied Haruka.

The tank fill went smoothly as fifty thousand gallons of purified water poured into the collector.

"Now people, at last we can start hunting," Sam said as he went through the checklist to start the detector. This phase of the experiment would last over four days. The elusive subatomic particle was unaffected by either gravity or mass and passed through the Earth as if it wasn't there. Produced in high-energy collisions, only the weakly interacting neutrinos were capable of conveying astronomical information from the edge of the universe.

Three hours into his six hour watch, Sam was asleep in his chair when the detector got its first hit. He sat upright and pushed his glasses back up his nose. He picked up the phone and dialed Haruka.

"Got one!"

"Way to go, Sam," Haruka said groggily. "That's got to be a record. What's it been, four hours or so?"

"Yeah I—" The detector sounded another alert. "Hey, another one!"

"Wow, it's your night! Congra—"

The alarm began sounding in a series of loud tones "Wait, there's more. Hold on, Haruka, something is wrong. The hits are coming in like rain."

"It must be a short in the alarm circuitry. Kasia was supposed to check that. I'm coming down."

"Hold a minute, will you?!" He had to yell into the phone as multiple alarms sounded a continual whine. "I'll check with Paul." Sam radioed the head maintenance technician. "Paul, we've got non-stop alarms going off, what can you do?"

"Nothing wrong on this side, Doc. Have you verified

the hits?"

"Well, no, I didn't think it was possible to have this many." Sam jumped on the computer and ran the verification. Alarms were still going off as he lifted the phone. "Haruka? Wake everybody and get down here, you're not gonna believe this."

***

Mellissa stepped carefully across the muddy ground in the woods behind the house. She had rung the dinner bell on the back porch but Jared hadn't come in yet.

"I can't believe I have to come out here and get you. You are in so much trouble," she muttered to herself as she slipped on the muddy bank but caught herself just in time. She stepped into a grove of birches and called out for her nephew.

"Jared, you come in right now! Dinner is getting cold!" She tried several more times, then stood still and listened. Even at six years old Jared didn't talk much, but she could hear children playing in the development on the other side of the woods. She walked further into the grove and suddenly spotted Jared through the trees.

"Jared, what are you doing? Jared?" He stood with his back to her, fixated on something on the ground. As she picked her way through the trees the smell of burning electronics singed her nose. "Jared Nathaniel Taggart, are you playing with matches?" She rushed forward, about to give him the scolding of his life. But as she reached him, she froze.

A gigantic robot lay smoldering in a depression on the ground. There were pieces of metal around him and something that looked like a huge cannon shell protruding from the ground next to his head.

Anger dissolved into fear. She reached out for Jared. "Honey, come with me. Back away carefully now." She took his hand, turned around, and pulled him as fast as she could through the woods and back to the house. Inside, her brother was sitting at the dining room table.

"Hey! You come when your Aunt rings the bell," he scolded.

"Daniel..." Mellissa started.

He could see something was wrong. He quickly took Jared from her and began looking over the child. "Are you hurt? What happened?"

"No, Daniel, listen to me. There's something out in the woods. It's like some kind of giant robot, but it has weapons."

"What? What are you talking about, slow down."

"Jared was out there staring at it."

"It was in the ground," Jared offered.

Daniel was already putting on his coat. "What the hell was Jared doing in the woods?" He switched from Mellissa to his son. "What were you doing in the woods, Jared? That is strictly off-limits." He opened a drawer in the china cabinet, pulled out a Beretta 9mm pistol, checked the chamber, threw in a clip, and put it in his coat pocket.

Mellissa shook her head at him. "I don't think that's gonna do much of anything. That thing is built to kill."

"Did it say anything? Did it come after you?"

"No, it wasn't moving. It was torn up really bad."

"I'm going to have a look. I'm thinking it might be a drone that crashed. God knows what the DOD guys have flying around here."

"Daniel—"

"Mel, after eight years of Army recon I think I can handle a little look see around my own backyard. Just stay here. I'll be back in a couple of minutes."

He headed out the back door. Ten minutes later he came back inside like a tornado.

"Jesus, Mel! That thing is not from this Earth." He spoke rapidly as he dug in the china cabinet drawer.

"That's what I thought. Did it move?"

"No, like you said, it's trashed. I've seen Hummers hit

by IED's that looked better."

"Danny, this isn't Afghanistan and that is definitely no Hummer."

"No, little sister, it is not." He produced a set of keys.

"What are you doing?"

"Taking it to the shop, what do you think?"

"Jesus, Danny, what if it comes to life? What if the military or the CIA or somebody comes after it? We're right next to D.C. for God's sake, you know how they are."

"Mel, I love you and I would never do anything to endanger you and Jared, so you have to trust me on this. It didn't fall from the sky, it didn't walk into the woods, it just appeared. I'm betting that no one knows it's there."

"You're just a mechanic—"

He held up a finger. "ASE Certified."

"Certified to work on muscle cars, not combat robots!"

"A gear is a gear, Mel." He bolted out the front door and climbed into the flatbed automotive hauler parked in the driveway.

Mellissa stood in the doorway shaking her head.

Daniel pulled the truck around the side of the house heading into the woods. As he passed her he stopped and tossed a small walkie-talkie to her. "I may need you to bring the quad down and pull me out if I get stuck. Keep an ear on this."

She called after him but the truck was already bouncing its way down the backyard and into the woods. All she could do was herd Jared back inside and try to get some dinner into him.

Half an hour later she heard the truck laboring up the slope into the back yard, finally coming to a stop in front of the house. Daniel emerged from the garage with a tarp. The robot had been winched into place and hung off the side and back of the truck, looking more like a pile of scrap than a machine. Daniel quickly covered it and secured the tarp.

She stood on the porch, arms crossed. She knew that once he got going he wouldn't stop. At least she could let him know she thought it was a bad idea.

"And what is Peter gonna say?"

Daniel stopped on the step of the cab. "Peter works for me, and he isn't going to say a thing. I'm going to send him on a buying run down to D.C. for a few days."

"We can't afford that, Danny. You haven't sold a car for weeks, we're scraping just to get groceries. You can't even pay his travel expenses, not to mention buying cars."

"It'll work out, Mel, you just gotta have faith."

"We can't eat faith, Daniel!"

"I'll be back in a while. I've got to figure out what this thing is. We could be sitting on a gold mine." He winked and roared off down the street.

Chapter 6

Her skin felt warm as she carried him through the desert. It was not what he expected. They'd walked for so long that the sun had set, and the chill night air made her temperature obvious. She was soft and dry with an odd rubbery texture, too.

"You're pinching me."

"Oh! Sorry, Piaa, I was just, uh…"

"Wondering what I am made of?"

"Yeah, something like that."

"It's okay. Your curiosity is one of the most amazing things about you."

"I'm not that curious, really."

"I'm talking about humans in general, and yes, you are. Why do you think you like fixing electronics? Because first you liked tearing them apart to find out how they worked."

"Yeah, that's actually true. When I was a kid my folks gave me a stereo for Christmas. I had that thing in pieces in a matter of weeks. My dad was pissed. He came home from work one day with a soldering iron and a book on electronic repair and told me 'You're not getting anything for Christmas unless you fix that stereo'. It was a challenge but he helped me and we got it put back together. He was cool like that, the old man."

"You miss him."

"Yeah. I miss them all." He looked at her, searching.

She slowed and looked back at him. "What is it, John Anthony?"

"You don't know, do you? I mean, what's after?"

"Is Heaven real? Is there a God? Is this what you mean?"

"Yeah. I figure, you've been all over the universe, you probably know more about Him than we do."

"John Anthony, we are your creation. Me finding you is as close to the source as I am ever likely to come."

"Until you die, you mean."

"Death is an experience that is unknown to us. Perhaps the Atec, being of human origin, have more perspective on death. For synthetics it is deletion that we fear. 'To cease to be' as your poet Keats put it. All of our experiences and memory wiped away, to not even have existed. Is that what death is to you?"

"Well, yeah. To someone who doesn't have any religious beliefs, I guess it is. I still haven't made up my mind one way or the other. I think people have a soul. It's different from their mind, I just don't know how to put it into words."

"Your ability to see beyond your own deletion and perceive the possibility of something more is truly remarkable."

"You don't think about things like that?"

"No, John Anthony, and I have never met anyone that has, until you."

Suddenly she froze. Her mechanical stillness and rigidity made him feel as if she'd shut off.

"Piaa?"

"Shh. We are being scanned. Stay still." A moment passed. "I am going to put you down. Stay still and say nothing." She set him down slowly, then she stood upright. Her skin began to glow a light blue, growing brighter and brighter, until he felt like he was standing beside a giant light bulb.

Fifty feet away, a figure appeared from behind a huge boulder. He was wearing blue jeans and a grey T-shirt. John Anthony thought he looked like some guy out camping, but he just stood and stared at them calmly.

Piaa's light went out and they stood still in the cold desert night. Seconds ticked by and still they said nothing. John Anthony found it difficult not to say something, but he was sure that the two were communicating. Several minutes went by before the man approached. Piaa touched John Anthony on the shoulder, smiling.

"We have found him."

As the man got closer, John Anthony could make out that he was in his thirties, good-looking, with fashionable facial scruff. The man held out his hand.

"Hi, my name's Niliason."

"John Anthony, last name is Rakes but people call me John Anthony."

"Nice to meet you." Niliason took his hand. "My last name is Brand. Sounds like we both got stuck with unusual names." He had a friendly smile.

"Yeah. Niliason, that's a new one. This is Piaa."

"Yes, we just met." He smiled and looked at John Anthony, then paused with his eyes closed, like he was trying to say something. "This is kind of an historical occasion. We've been living among you for so long…but you're the first one to know our secret." Niliason shrugged and let the moment pass. "Come, let's get you out of the night air."

It seemed to John Anthony that Niliason was not as interested in Piaa as he was in him. They followed him over the ridge of the hill and then between two boulders. Niliason pointed out some steps leading down and they descended into a dark underground tunnel. He turned on a red-lensed flashlight and handed it to John Anthony. After several minutes of travelling downward through the tight passage, it widened a bit and Niliason finally broke the silence.

"I apologize, John Anthony, for the odd silence. We try very hard at masking our presence. Things like talking and flashlights so close to the surface could be seen and heard by any passerby. Piaa and I have exchanged information via a kind of super Wi-Fi link up, so we know what she knows and vice versa. Forgive us if we seem too familiar with you, it's because we are aware of all your interactions with Piaa."

"Excuse me, did you say we?" John Anthony didn't understand. It was just the three of them standing on a ledge in an underground cavern. He couldn't see a thing.

"I'm sorry, John Anthony, all of us can see in the dark except you. Piaa, would you mind giving us some light?"

A soft light swelled from Piaa's body, bathing the faces of over a hundred people staring up at them. John Anthony gasped. Niliason turned to him and spread his arms. "I'd like to introduce you to the Atec of West Texas. Some of us are descendants of the Mars Colony War and even the Earth Resident's War. We consider ourselves the caretakers of humanity. We welcome you."

The smiling faces of the Atec greeted John Anthony as they walked down onto the cavern floor. He shook many hands and tried to remember the barrage of names. The comments ranged from emotional to awkward, but the overall message from the Atec was the relief at finally being able to reveal their existence to a member of the human race whom they had dedicated their lives to protect.

John Anthony and Piaa were guided to a circle of logs with a small black box in the middle. Heat began to emerge from the black box and a full campfire appeared suddenly out of thin air. John Anthony flinched.

Niliason put his hand on his shoulder. "It's okay, it's a hologram. The box puts out heat for the full effect. The nice thing is, there's no smoke to attract attention."

"Oh man, I gotta get me one of those." John Anthony was impressed. "How long do they last?"

"Years." Niliason laughed then quieted everyone down. "John Anthony, it is a human tradition to tell tales around the campfire. We are here to answer any questions you might have and discuss our plans for the future."

"Sure, man, go ahead." John Anthony shrugged.

John Anthony sat down next to the holo-fire and looked the Atec over. They were definitely human. He couldn't see any technology on them. No metal arms, no steely eye sockets or tubes popping out anywhere, nothing cyborg-ish. The Atec closed in a circle around the fire.

"Now we're all cozy." Niliason smiled. "Do you have any questions, John Anthony?"

"Not really. You're people, Piaa's a person, and so am I. I think we have a problem though, don't we? Shouldn't we be talking about that?"

"You're right. As far as the galactic community is concerned, Earth is a ball of molten rock. However, Piaa has revealed that one of our early transmissions may have compromised our secrecy."

"I'm afraid Niliason is right," Piaa said. "My ruse was devised only to deceive the Eos Biauay. I did not know that the Abes had been watching us until it was too late. They are sure to discover that I am not on Andapo. It is forty-two percent probable that they will follow me here."

"But I thought you said that most people think the Earth is a molten ball of rock?" John Anthony felt like a kid participating in an adult conversation.

"Yes. When I checked it, the Galactic Registry revealed Earth like this." A holographic image, seemingly solid and very real, emerged in the air over the fire.

"Wow! I didn't know you could do that." John Anthony jumped up and tried to touch the image.

"We have been passively receiving data from various regions of the galaxy for years now," an Atec woman said. "No one has done any Earth observations since the Earth Resident's War."

"My database is current as of several thousand years ago," Piaa said.

Niliason nodded to an Atec man who got up and left. "We will broaden our scan to include signs of tachyon conveyance. This is a positive development. The ancient photon based conveyance was very difficult to see, but tachyons can be detected and blocked."

"It is most likely that if I was followed, it would be by means of tachyon conveyance. They would probably have to regroup and use their own though. The Eos Biauay facility was destroyed as I left." Piaa grew quiet.

"We're sorry about your friend, Piaa, it was an incredibly brave thing that you did. It's only because of your courage that we are all gathered here."

"Is this all of you?" John Anthony asked.

"Heavens no, John, we only represent this immediate area. There are several hundred thousand of us all over the globe."

"Name's John *Anthony*, please, and that's good to know. So you guys have some big, kick-ass technology to repel an invasion from the Abes, right?"

"No, John Anthony, we have a theoretical plan that may stop some of them from getting here via a tachyon stream." Niliason noticed the confused expression on John Anthony's face. "Think of it as 3-D printing over a vast distance."

John Anthony thought about it, then nodded as Niliason continued.

"If they do get through, they will likely not appear on the planet as Piaa did. I believe they will appear in the outer solar system. Their attack won't look like a space battle in *Star Wars*. It's more likely they would cause the sun to have a super-massive CME at exactly the right time to destroy Earth's atmosphere. Or they might do as they did in the Earth Resident's War and destabilize a planetoid, causing it to crash into the Earth. No little green men, no Randy Quaid flying an F-18 in the belly of the mother ship. We can only try to scan for their arrival and hope that we can use our radio telescopes to cancel a tachyon conveyance."

"Nice. Cheery. I feel better." John Anthony felt nauseous.

Piaa stood up. "I would like to take a crack at it."

"Piaa, we've had our best people on it for as long as the tech has existed—"

"But you have not had a top level Biauay scientist until now. I would like to try."

"It's going to be tricky, but we'll try to arrange to get you in."

John Anthony looked from one to the other. "Get in where?"

"We have an organization that we use as a cover. It's called SETI. Maybe you've heard of it?"

"Are you kid—" John Anthony started to say, but Piaa shot him a look. "SETI, seriously? The guys searching for aliens are actually aliens?"

"We're not aliens, we're from Earth," Niliason said. "But we do consider ourselves to be part of the galactic community even though we are in hiding. To tell you the truth, SETI was set up to keep the humans from finding anyone else."

"Oh man, this is crazy. I downloaded your screensaver!"

"What can I say? Just doing our bit." Niliason shrugged. "To be fair, most of the SETI people are not Atec and have no idea. It's only the ones running the program. We determine where to search and why. Usually we are scanning for information that is being picked up by sensors the humans know nothing about."

"SETI stations are running twenty-four seven," the Atec woman said. "You'll have to make sure the staff are Atec when she's in there."

"That's a problem," Niliason said. "All the Atec are higher level. If they showed up at a SETI site it would be in the day time, and they certainly wouldn't be operating the equipment. Gone are the days when we fought for time at Arecibo." He paused a minute and stared at John Anthony.

"What?"

"You're a Ham operator, right? Good with electronics?"

"Yeah, so?"

"Then you're our new ATA operator for the night shift."

"Me? I don't know how to—"

"Don't worry, it runs itself. If it makes you feel better, I'll have Jill here give you a primer course. She ran the place for years." He nodded to the Atec woman.

John Anthony considered this a moment. *What the heck?* He was in this far, might as well do what he could to help. "Okay, you're on."

"Now, I suppose you're getting a bit tired," Niliason said.

"Yeah, I can just sleep in my bag by the fire if that works."

"Why don't you let me show you the rest of the place, then you can make up your mind." Niliason stood and walked into what appeared to be a slit in the rocks; it was actually two rocks offset from each other with enough space for one person to pass through.

Piaa followed behind John Anthony with an excited smile. The passageway went down a slope and ended in an empty room.

"The whole room is an elevator. Don't be alarmed." Niliason pointed down.

John Anthony felt a small vibration and then a sense of being lighter as the elevator dropped into the Earth.

Chapter 7

Daniel Taggart pulled his flatbed tow truck into the shop and closed the doors. Then he set about blacking out the windows with black spray paint and taping the closed sign into place.

Wrestling with engine hoists and jacks, he managed to get the robot laid out on the truck bed like a surgery patient. It was over eleven and a half feet tall and seven feet wide. The armor plating was at least an inch thick.

Daniel attempted to cut away the shoulder piece that was just barely hanging on. No saw would work, the torch didn't do it, only the plasma cutter made any progress—and that was very slow. When he was done, the piece clattered to the floor. When it hit the cement it sounded more like wood than metal. He squatted to pick it up and nearly fell over backwards. It was light as a feather.

"What the fu—" His phone rang. It was Melissa.

"You still okay?" she asked.

"Yeah, sis, no problem. Listen, I'm going to be a bit late. It's best that we don't talk over the phone, okay?"

"Dee Dee has Jared, I'm coming over."

"Okay. How is he?"

"He's fine, just asking a lot of questions about the robot."

"That's okay. Dee Dee will think he's talking about his toys."

"Yeah, well, he's pretty worried about his dad getting hurt."

"Tell him I'll be home later to tuck him in and tell him all about it. And when you get here, park in the back."

***

Thirty minutes later he could hear Mellissa pull in

behind the building.

"Shut the door, Mel," he said as soon as she came in.

She closed it quickly. "You blacked out the windows?"

"Mel, look at this thing. Do you want reporters crawling all over us? The military would swoop down, we'd be thrown in the stockade, and Jared would be taken into state custody. This right here is what nightmares are made of. Blacking out the windows is a minor effort."

"All right, okay. Calm down." She climbed up onto the truck and inspected the robot.

"You see that piece of shoulder armor on him? I've got the other one here." He lifted it off the work table with one hand.

"It doesn't look that light."

"This little strip of material was the only thing holding on. I had to cut it off with a plasma torch, nothing else would faze it. Even that took a while. Usually the plasma cutter goes through thick steel like butter."

Mellissa's eyes went wide. "It's right out of a movie. This thing is not from Earth, Daniel." She knelt down on the robot's chest and looked at the face. It was expressive, wise almost. "He's a looker," she giggled.

"Yeah, well, he's been through hell and back. Maybe he just needs power."

"I don't see any wires. Like, no robotics or electronics or anything. What makes him run?"

Daniel climbed up next to her, grabbing a screwdriver from the nearby toolbox as he did. "I don't know. There's nothing mechanical, like you said…wait a sec. Look here." He dug the flathead into seams in the robot's chest plating and tried hard to pry it open. The material seemed to be made of a weave of hair-like strands. He grabbed a pair of needle-nosed piers from the toolbox as well and grasped one of the tiny strands. He hauled on it but it didn't budge. "Stand back, sis, I'm going in with the plasma cutter again."

She jumped down and handed the torch up to him. It

took holding the torch on the hair-thick strand for over ten seconds before it finally broke free.

"Man, this stuff is tough!"

"Dan…"

He looked at the inch long strand in the pliers. "One thing's for sure, there's no way I'm fixing him."

"*Dan.*"

"Yeah?"

Mellissa was moving slowly backwards, pointing at the robot's hand. Daniel looked down at it. One of the fingers was twitching. With a curse, he leaped off of the bed, grabbed Mellissa and ran for the back door.

"Wait, Daniel, just hang on a minute." She stopped him.

A sound like the moaning of a weed-eater, far in the distance, quietly emanated from the robot.

"He's hurt." She ran back to the truck and climbed up.

Daniel, wide-eyed with fear, spat at her in a whisper, "Of course he's hurt, look at him! Mel!" he hissed. "Get down from there!"

She leaned over the robot's face. "Hey, big guy, you're really hurt, but we're here to help. Can you talk?"

One of the robot's eyes opened halfway and looked at her. "Help?"

"Yes, yes! How do we help you?"

The robot sighed and passed out again.

"Daniel, he's not bad, I know it. He's hurt and needs our help. Do something."

Daniel climbed back up on the truck. "Okay, but I have no idea where to start."

"He's not a car, he's a person. Treat him like you would one of your Army buddies if they were hurt."

"Right, good idea. Okay, stop the bleeding." He looked over the robot. "No problem there, there's no bleeding. Next, clean the wounds. Mellissa get down to the workbench and pass me what I need. That stack of rags there, that cleaning solution, and that spray can."

He tested the solvents on the fiber he had cut. None of them seemed to phase the material at all.

"Okay, I think it's safe to use. Mellissa get back up here and bring that shoulder piece and some rubber gloves. As soon as I clean an area, put things back the way they should be, then apply pressure and a bandage. I'll need duct tape and some oily rags."

They worked together in silence, being as quick and thorough as they could. When they got to its leg, Daniel sat back and scratched his head. "It's practically blown off."

"We have to try and save him, Daniel. Come on, he's a person, not a car."

"Stop saying that, Mel. If he was a car I would know what to do!"

"Just keep going like we have been. Clean it, put it back into place and bind it."

"Okay, I'm going to back the truck up under that lift; we'll hook that come-along to it and hoist the leg into place. You raise that lift as high as it will go."

Mellissa raised the lift while Daniel started the truck. Another moan came from the robot.

"Don't worry, we'll have you feeling better in no time," Mellissa shouted to him.

With the leg in a cradle they cleaned all of the places where they thought it was connected. Then they pushed the leg into place and bound it there, keeping the sling on it to support the weight. Daniel used a planishing hammer to tap bits of torn material back into place. The last thing they did was remove the huge pistol from the robot's grip. An engine hoist did the job.

"This thing has got to be around four-hundred pounds." Daniel inspected it on the bench.

"Is it loaded?"

"Oh definitely. Five inches in diameter and over a foot long. To him it's a handgun, to us it's field artillery." Daniel took off his gloves and sat down on a stool. "So, what do we do now?"

"We wait. I'll stay here with him. You go put Jared to bed." Mellissa yawned. "Take him to school in the morning and then come here. We'll see if the big guy is doing any better in the morning."

Daniel was skeptical. "I don't like leaving you alone with him."

"Like you could do anything about it if he woke up in a rage. He seemed to respond to me, I'm gonna go with that."

"Okay. You have the walkie and your cell." He scooped up his keys. "Just don't say anything that could tip somebody off. These things aren't encrypted. Call him 'Hank'."

"Hank the tank." She giggled. "What does that make you, Doctor Hankenstien?" Her laughter dissolved the tension.

"Whatever, Nurse Ratchet. The couch is comfortable and there's a sleeping bag in that cabinet there."

"I know, Danny. Geez, you act like I've never slept here before."

"I'll see you at seven. Have the coffee on." He shut the door behind him and she threw the sleeping bag on the couch and switched off the lights. But she was still too wound up to sleep, so she put on some music and climbed up to look at the robot one more time.

It—he...*Hank*—lay as still as a stone. She sat in the crook of his arm and stared into his face, humming along with the song.

Where have you been? she wondered. *What have you seen?* She hesitantly touched one of the deep scourges in his arm plating. "It can't all be war out there. Do you have someone looking for you, missing you? Just hang in there, Hank, we're going to try our best to get you back home. You're safe now."

A small rumble shook his chest and the music on the stereo became static and garbled radio noise.

Mellissa sat up quickly. "Easy, big fella, it's just a dream. You're okay, you're safe here."

The music of 311 resumed on the stereo. '*Whoa, amber is the color of your energy…*'

***

The amber light on the control console flashed a steady alert. Dr. Haruka Tanaka shook his head and stared at the array of large screen monitors. Data flowed in, and a map of the encounters with neutrinos in the detector tank glowed brightly.

"It's been eight hours and there's no let up," Sam said over his shoulder. Just then, an intern popped his head in the door.

"NASA's SOHO reports no unusual activities, Professor."

"Thanks, Mark. Verify that with NOAA and check with UKM Station for ionospheric scintillation."

The young man nodded and left.

"Mark's a good kid," Sam said. "Couldn't throw a football to save his life."

"But he throws around calculus like a pro quarterback," Haruka said, and Sam shot him a look. "Okay, *varsity* quarterback then," he corrected.

"From the mouth of the Berkeley Samurai," Sam elbowed him.

Kasia poked her head into the room. "If you two are done being buddy buddies, maybe you can spend some time trying to find out what is going on, yes? Neutrinos and Earth's core might not get along so well." She shuffled off down the hall in her slippers. "I go get coffee."

"So, what do you think it is?" Sam asked Haruka.

"I don't know, Sam, we have every—"

"Professor, UKM Station on line two; they're goin' nuts over there," Mark called.

Sam nodded at the intern and picked up the phone.

"Dr. Sam Wisecraft here."

"Dr. Wisecraft, this is Dean Stanley, I'm the director if the UKM Station, Malaysia. Our TEC readings are off the charts."

"I'm sorry, your what?"

"TEC, Total Electron Count; it's a reading we take of the ionosphere. We look at amplitude scintillation in the night and day, and make comparatives over the year, but this is way more intense than anything we've seen. Usually the electron count declines from a standard baseline. Today it rose, significantly."

"Can you tell me at what time exactly?"

"Well, we do our readings daily at 13:00 and 1:00, we're GMT plus eight."

"That's only one hour different from us here in Japan, and we started getting abnormally high neutrino hits at 23:00. They have been steady at that rate for over eight hours now."

"What do you make of it?"

"Well, NASA tells us that the sun is normal. Maybe some kind of deep space anomaly? Frankly, we're at a loss."

"Well, here's a bit of information that may help. There are thirty-two stations like UKM positioned around the globe. My team has been gathering the data from those sites. When they lay the data over the global map there is an area of concentration that is much higher than the others."

"Where is it?" Sam asked.

"Takoma Park, Maryland."

Chapter 8

Light reflected off of the sandy rock wall, illuminating the room in a sepia glow. The ride down the elevator had been fast, leaving them standing in a circular landing area that John Anthony guessed was about forty feet in diameter. The floor was polished wood and a wall went up three quarters of the way to the rocky ceiling. The remaining quarter of the wall was exposed rock that vaulted into a natural dome. Light shone from behind the wall, illuminating the rocks above it. The air smelled fresh and cool.

"This is one of our bases," Niliason explained. "There are many entrances, and we build very slowly to avoid any attention."

"How do you avoid seismic detection?" John Anthony asked.

"There is a level above us that shields our facility with all manner of clever devices. This section was excavated in the eleven hundreds. The North American continent was a haven for us until recently. It wasn't until the eighteen hundreds that we had to make any real effort to conceal ourselves." Niliason led them out of the large room and down a wide hallway.

John Anthony cleared his throat. "Um, so, do you, like, eat?"

Niliason laughed. "Don't be afraid to ask any question, John Anthony. The answer is yes, some of us. There are many types of Atec, all enhanced in different ways. Only the ones who can function on a normal biological level with humans are allowed to associate with them. It would rouse suspicions if you had a dinner guest who didn't eat, wouldn't it? On the other hand, some Atec are specialists. Deep water, or space based activities don't combine well with some biological systems, so there are

Atec who are more suited to those roles."

"Do you have children?"

Niliason stopped. "Another good question and one that cuts to the heart of our mission." He glanced at Piaa. "Some of us can have children, and have had children. But those children are human. Technological modifications are not genetic. It requires surgical procedures."

"So, you add tech to your babies?"

"No, certainly not, for several reasons. The first is that it's unethical. A child is a person and deserves the right to choose what it wants to do with its body. The second is purely logistical. Children grow quickly and enhancements cannot grow with them."

"Biological enhancements can grow," Piaa interjected.

"Ah, but in the case of the Biauay, you began your life as a fully synthetic being, the biological equivalent of an Abe. No offense, Piaa."

"Yes, you are correct. We are essentially Abes, but I was referring to the problem of tech not growing in tandem with your offspring's growth. If you enhanced an Atec child—essentially a human—with biotech, would it not grow with the child?"

"It's very risky. Human systems do not easily adapt to external biology."

Piaa looked squarely at Niliason. "The Biauay are masters of biotechnology. We have been developing it for billions of years. We agree that humane considerations are foremost, and with that in mind, I can confidently assure you that, between us, we can produce a healthy, happy, natural born human with capabilities that outpace those of the Atec, Abe, or Biauay races." Piaa quickly realized what she had said. "I mean, 'us' as in the Biauay and Atec, not you and I…personally, I mean."

"It's okay, Piaa, I think he understands what you mean." John Anthony slapped her on the shoulder. "That was good though, I think you actually blushed."

Niliason cleared his throat into his hand. "I am

encouraged by your conviction, Piaa. It seems that we are on the brink of dramatic change. I should like to pursue that subject with you. Perhaps later."

John Anthony saw how extensive the facility was as they continued on.

"A total of over ten thousand square feet of space," Niliason informed them. "We have over forty permanent residents, some of which you have not met."

"I feel like you're avoiding telling me something here," John Anthony said.

"Yes, your intuition serves you well. You see, there's a type of Atec you've not yet encountered."

"Let me guess, the kind that have visible tubes and wires, metal for arms, wheels for legs, and eye stalks, right? This isn't my first trip on the sci-fi train. I'm not shy, bring em' on." John Anthony was feeling like he truly was fitting into this bunch. It was time to meet the crazy relatives.

"Okay, fair enough. Yes, I was trying to cushion the shock for you, and the embarrassment for the Atec individuals. No one likes to be looked on as a freak."

"There are only people by my book, no freaks...except my Aunt Janey, that woman is not right in the head."

"Alright, to the galley then."

In the cafeteria, a man with a pair of tank treads for legs and four robotic arms served fantastic cuisine that John Anthony would have expected to be served in a five star restaurant.

"Milo, meet John Anthony and Piaa."

Milo reached across the pass and shook their hands. "My goodness, a human guest and a Biauay goddess, my pleasure indeed! I make food for any tastes, just let me know what you like."

"Thanks, I'm starved," John Anthony said. "How about something rural American?"

"You got it, John."

"Actually, it's John Anthony."

"Gotcha," Milo said with a wink.

John Anthony sat down in the elegant dining room to eat, while Niliason left with Piaa to show her their quarters.

***

Niliason watched the tall Biauay behind him. His sensor array allowed him three-sixty vision and he used it to his full advantage. It had been a few million years since he had seen a creature so beautiful.

"Here are the accommodations we have for you." He opened the door into a large apartment, lavishly furnished with an eclectic combination of ancient and modern styles. "It has all the facilities for human needs. I'm afraid we never expected to enjoy the company of the Biauay; is there anything you require that we can provide?"

"No, Niliason Brand, your hospitality is overwhelming, I cannot ask for anything more."

Niliason paused in the doorway, unable to restrain his concerns now that he and Piaa were alone. "Piaa…we have to be honest with John Anthony. We don't know if Earth has millions of years or just hours left. If the Abes come, and they will eventually, we don't have the power to stop them. The Atec got out of the war business a long time ago and we were never very good at it in the first place."

"Your honesty is one of the things I like most about you, Niliason Brand. I bring billions of years of evolution to the table and the full knowledge of biotechnology that the Abes don't have. Our technology is more than a match for them. We lost because of treachery and the fact that our numbers were less than a quarter of theirs. We can make a stand if we begin preparations right now, but we have to commit fully. The time for waiting and watching is over."

"I agree. We need to find a way to block the Abe's tachyon conveyance."

"I have an addition to that plan." Standing still and focusing, she sent the plan to him.

His eyes opened wide.

"If this works, it could end the reign of the Structure," Piaa explained. "Atec and Biauay would be free."

"And so would the humans," Niliason said. "Free to take their next evolutionary step."

When they returned to the dining room, they found John Anthony sitting with Milo, the chef.

"'My Sharona'?" John Anthony said.

"Nope." Milo gave a wry smile.

John Anthony thought and guessed again. "I know, I know! 'Lucy In the Sky With Diamonds'!"

Milo laughed. "You would think so, but nope!"

"No way! Okay, here's one I know for sure, 'American Pie'."

"Of course! Yeah, that's about Buddy Holly, Richie Valens, and the Big Bopper dyin' in a plane crash," Milo explained. "The Jester is Bob Dylan, the King and Queen are Jan and Dean, the Sergeants are the Beatles. It goes on and on. That Don McLean is a genius."

John Anthony turned to them. "Milo has cross-referenced every song with history and popular culture. I'm trying to guess which songs have hidden meanings."

"I'll leave you to it," Niliason said. "Piaa, John Anthony, if you need anything, you have only to ask. There are people bringing in supplies on a regular basis. Until tomorrow then." The Atec commander took his leave.

"You ever notice that he's kind of stuffy?" John Anthony said.

"Hmm? No, he's just fine." Piaa watched Niliason leave.

"Hey, Earth to Piaa."

"Yes, John Anthony?"

"You've got a crush on him."

She thought a moment. "Yes, that could be. How interesting."

***

Where am I? The transmission received no reply. Only a portion of his systems were functional, and mobility wasn't one of them. He could move his left arm. "Where am I?" The audio reverberated. The sonic signature revealed the size and composition of his surroundings. Suddenly, an Atec face appeared close in his view.

"You're awake! How are you feeling?"

"Atec!" His left arm was all he had, but it was enough. His hand hoisted the Atec in the air by the legs. "Where am I, Atec? Answer quickly and I will spare you a painful deletion."

"Hey! Put me down! My name is Melissa, not Ay-tech, whatever that is!"

The creature was right. There was no augmentation. It was a pure organic. Still, he held it up; there was no telling where it might crawl off to. "Where am I?"

"In my brother's shop! On Earth! You're on Earth! Geez, don't you have any manners? We just helped you!"

He surveyed his condition. An odd means of assistance, but it appeared to be assistance nonetheless. "I will comply, but you must remain here for further questioning."

"Okay, okay, just put me down, I'm getting dizzy."

He lowered her to the bed of the truck. She sat on his chest and dusted herself off.

"You're not the gentle type are you?"

"I am Dominus Rau, Commander of Elite Force Response, under single direction from the Structure."

"Yeah, none of that means anything to me. You're a soldier, I understand that, but I gotta tell ya, you're a long way from wherever your war was. We're peaceful here. Well, mostly."

"Earth. I was right. The Structure is wrong."

"Hey, before you start babbling about things no one understands, tell me how I can help you heal. You've clearly taken some pretty heavy damage."

"Why do you wish to assist? Have you been directed by the Structure to do so?"

"No, what the hell is this 'structure' you keep talking about? No, listen, on this planet, when people are hurt, we help. It's the human thing to do."

"Human?" He made a sound like a snort. "They are a myth."

"Uh, 'fraid not, smarty pants. You're lookin' at one, and in a few minutes another one's gonna be here with donuts and a hot breakfast burrito. What do you eat?"

"I am not an organic life form, I do not consume."

"Your loss. So, what do you do other than fight? You got any family?"

"My team…" He played through the images of his team getting decimated. "I had to leave them on Palus Emyth. I fear they were destroyed by the Biauay fleet."

Mellissa's heart went out to him. The exotic names of the places, his sullen demeanor, and his animated nature; he was no longer a pile of strange metal, this was a living being from beyond the stars. She suddenly realized how real the situation was.

"I'm sorry for your loss. I lost people too." She tried to shift his focus. "So, you were in a battle somewhere in space?"

"Yes, very far away. Now I am here looking for a fugitive. She is dangerous and crafty and must be returned to the Structure for deletion."

"Deletion…that's like…death, right?"

"One moment and I will update my systems to your communication parameters."

He grew quiet. Mellissa thought she could hear a humming sound coming from him. All of a sudden, the back door opened.

"Hey, sis, I brought breakfast, how's our—"

"Shh!" Mel put her hand up, stopping him in his tracks. She pointed and mouthed, "*He's awake.*"

Daniel's eyes went immediately to the big pistol. Mel waved her hands and shook her head 'no'.

"That should help us communicate better," Dominus rumbled. "I hate trying to pry information from misunderstanding. Yes, deletion means death. You aren't extinct after all. There is old Atec code underneath your Internet. It appears you were saved by the Atec, though to what purpose I have yet to discover. Still, you are not my mission."

"Um, my brother showed up while you were out. This is Daniel. Daniel, meet Dominus Rau."

"Uh, hi there. How are you feeling?" Daniel put down the food and waved.

"Feeling? I…have never examined myself from that perspective. My most accurate reply for your translation is, I feel like shit."

Mel and Daniel burst out laughing.

"You find my condition amusing?" Dominus' anger began to flare.

"No! Not at all, Dominus, it was the way you said it. We can certainly see that you probably feel like shit. We're here to help, buddy. So, let me start by telling you what we've done so far. Maybe you can tell us where to go from there."

"Agreed."

Daniel filled him in while Mellissa ate breakfast. When Daniel had finished, Dominus said, "It seems that you have done well. Improvisation under the basis of medical oriented treatment as opposed to automotive repair was certainly the correct choice. However, to become fully operational I am in need of certain machinery that does not exist on this planet. You lack the ability to work with electro-membrane or plasma field weave."

"That's the fibrous material your armor is made out

of, right?"

"Yes. The electro-membrane cancels out most beam weapons while the weave generates and contains a plasma field between the ablative plate and exonegative plate layers. The exonegative plate converts energy received into light by hyper-exciting the electrons into the higher spectrum."

Mellissa looked up. "I understood none of that."

Daniel eyes sparkled with excitement. "I did! You mean you can convert energy from incoming rounds into light? Instantly?"

"Yes."

"That's frickin' amazing. You gotta show me how to do that."

"The secrets of my designs are mine alone."

Mellissa understood that. "So you're a weapons designer?"

"Yes, combat systems are my specialty. I am also a soldier and excel at strategy."

"So how did you get so banged up?"

"I was not built to combat an entire fleet on my own. I only survived because of the defensive capabilities of my sidearm, which apparently, I lost in the battle."

"Not so—" Daniel started to say but Mellissa shot him a look accompanied by a covert shake of the head, "—fast there, buddy. Maybe you lost it in the forest where you landed."

Mellissa leaned over Dominus and talked close to his face. "Yeah, we can go look when we have you up and feeling better." Daniel quickly covered the pistol with his jacket. "Now why don't you tell us what more we can do to fix you up."

"I will self repair to a point. My limbs will re-stitch, but they will only return to forty percent capability. They other parts should return to normal in…seven days' time. A week."

"How do you know how long a week is?" Daniel

wondered aloud.

"Yeah, and how can you even speak English?" Mellissa asked.

"My processors are ten to the hundredth power more powerful than the fastest supercomputer on this planet. The human brain is one exoflop. My processors are one googol exoflop. That is one with one hundred zeros. My sensors can link to any system up to one hundred and fifty thousand miles away. I possess all of the knowledge on every system that exists on Earth, from small appliances to top secret government programs—except one."

"So you know everything."

"Yes."

"Every book in the Library of Congress, every movie, every song?"

"Yes, but my knowledge is not limited to the Library of Congress, it extends to every library, every personal computer, business computer, credit card transaction, world banks, communication and defense systems. Everything."

"Don't you get kind of confused?"

"Not at all. The total information on Earth is barely a speck in my mind. Unlike humans, I have perfect recall. No information is ever lost, I do not forget, I don't have breakdowns—mental or emotional—I am not subject to mood swings—"

"Now wait a minute there. I saw you get pissed off a minute ago when you thought we were laughing at you," Mellissa gently corrected him.

"That is so. It has been some time since I encountered your species and I'm afraid I let myself empathize with your emotional state. It shall not happen again."

"No, I kinda liked it. You're really a big softy, aren't you?" Mellissa was lying on his arm now, running a finger on his chest.

Daniel couldn't believe what he was seeing: she was

flirting with this thing.

"Dominus, you just said it's been awhile since you encountered our species," Mellissa said. "You've encountered us before?"

His eyes blanked and he seemed to spasm slightly. "That information is restricted."

"Okay, take it easy, I didn't mean to pry. I guess we just let you heal then, huh?"

"Yes, but I do not like this location; it is undefended."

"Mel." Daniel decided it was time to break up the flirting session. "Dominus, there's no way we can move you. No offense, but you're too big. I got you here in the middle of the night and no one knows you're here. If we lay low and keep things quiet, I should be able to keep you here safely for at least a week."

Dominus didn't know what to say, so he said nothing. The humans obviously had ulterior motives that they were keeping to themselves. Whatever trap they were going to spring, he'd be ready for them.

Chapter 9

Piaa was busy for the next three days. When she did appear, she sat on the edge of her bed and stared into space. John Anthony learned that this was how she worked. Around noon on the second day, a woman named Jill with short gray hair came in and dropped a laptop on the bed.

"Here's a brief course on what you'll need to know to be an ATA operator. Familiarize yourself with SonATA, that's the main software. The facility is in Hat Creek, California. Rick will be gone and I'll be in the processing room. Don't worry, you won't really have to do anything, we just want you to play the part in case someone comes in."

"What are the chances of that?" John Anthony asked.

"Pretty low. I used to be in charge of the whole SETI operation; they all keep their heads down when I'm around."

John Anthony spent the better part of the next two days studying the program. Most of it was familiar from his experience with Ham radios, but everything on the astronomy side was all new. Several times he had to chase down Jill with questions. After the second time, she assigned a tutor and everything became much easier. By the third day they were ready to leave. Piaa met him in their shared living room.

"You are ready for this, John Anthony?"

"As ready as I'll ever be. I just hope I don't screw it up."

"Just be yourself, you'll do fine."

When Niliason arrived, he had a short brief. "We'll leave via different exits to avoid attracting attention. Jill left last night and will meet us at Hat Creek. Piaa, I had these made for you."

Several Atec men came in and put boxes on the sofa. Piaa smiled and busied herself opening them.

"The first is an outfit that will help you blend in here on Earth. Though you won't be able to walk down the street in daylight, at least this long coat fits you. Everything has been cut to try to minimize your height. The other one is more to my liking as it lets you be truly who you are without disguising any of your natural splendor." He said this unabashedly, his eyes gleaming.

Piaa beamed back at him.

Those two got something going on, John Anthony thought.

She pulled the garment out of the box. It glittered in blue and green like a million fish scales in a tropical sea.

"It's a traditional Biauay dress," Niliason said. "I hope it's to your liking. I'm not sure about current styles."

"It's amazing." She beamed. "Thank you."

She looked at him and closed her eyes for what looked like a long blink. Niliason mirrored her and, in that fraction of a second, John Anthony swore he could cut the emotional intensity in the room with a knife. Just as quickly as it had happened it was gone and the two were left smiling at each other.

"I will change before we go." She disappeared into her room.

"You certainly swept her off her feet." John Anthony gave him a knowing grin.

"I think it's the other way around, John Anthony. I have never met anyone like her."

"I know what you mean, dude."

Piaa came back out in her human clothes, looking like a very tall supermodel in a hoodie and trench coat. "The shoes are going to take some getting used to."

"Can you manage for the mission?" Niliason asked.

"Yes, I will manage. Shall we?"

John Anthony was the first to emerge via the traditional cave route. He walked a half a mile to his truck. When he could see it in the distance, he put on his headphones as he had been instructed and played Tonic's *Sugar*. The song played normally until he got within twenty feet of the truck.

"John Anthony. This message has been left for you. Listen carefully as it will not repeat and you cannot make it play again." It was Niliason's voice. "Approximately fifty of your normal paces, directly off the rear of your truck, you will see a rock. It's about a foot wide, eight inches deep and eight inches tall. It will be rusty colored. Under the rock is a map to our pick up locations. See you soon."

John Anthony paced off the distance and found the rock. The map was straightforward and soon he had both Piaa and Niliason in the cab.

"Now we go to Trulock Ranch Field. It's a tiny airstrip Northeast of Colorado City. Our plane there will take us to Hat Creek Observatory. We should arrive just after sundown."

The air field was practically deserted. Niliason took the controls of the twin engine Beechcraft King Air 250 and whisked them through the western sky in comfort at three hundred and fifty miles per hour. The Hat Creek runway was more of a driveway than a landing strip, but they touched down softly and found Jill waiting for them inside.

"Sean is the only one here besides us. He's gan, but he's in the computer room and should have no reason to come out. I've told him that you're new and that I will be training you. More importantly, that I want no disturbances."

"Gan?" John Anthony asked, confused.

"Organic human."

Niliason pushed on. "Good work, Jill. How long will you need, Piaa?"

Piaa sat still for a minute. "It will take about six minutes."

Jill was obviously impressed. Niliason just grinned and waved them all inside.

"Okay, everyone, let's get to it."

John Anthony barely had time to sit down before Jill was by his side. "She's done. Just follow my lead." She picked up the phone. "Sean, can you come in here and take the watch. We've had an…unusual development." Then she turned to John Anthony and said, "Sorry about this."

As Sean entered the room Jill stood and began yelling at John Anthony. "And you forged your paperwork to get in here just so you could meet some little green men? How dare you! We are a scientific community of well respected and accomplished academes. There is no place for conspiracy theory nutcases here! Now, you just get your things and get on that plane and go back to wherever it is you came from. And take that trashy, half-contrived Area 51 nonsense with you! Now GO!" She pulled him out of the chair and shoved him towards the door.

John Anthony stumbled a few steps in shock, then opened the door and ran to the waiting plane. The engines were just spinning up as he climbed in.

"You're flushed in the face, John Anthony, are you okay?" Piaa asked.

"That woman is crazy!"

"Crazy like a fox you mean," Niliason said from the cockpit. "Shocking you was a way of shocking him by watching our departure. He would certainly have noticed Piaa, trench coat or not. Plus, Sean has been secretly running an alien conspiracy web blog. He's a good scientist but she wants him to know that she won't tolerate that kind of thing. This way she scared him without scaring him off. She knew you would play along."

"Oh right, yes, I played along, exactly. Very clever." John Anthony was still shaking as the plane climbed into the evening sky.

Piaa moved to the front of the cabin, closest to the open cockpit doorway and motioned for John Anthony to sit across from her. "So, mission complete. The array is configured to decode incoming conveyances. It will work against large transfers. There is nothing I can do about individual transfers though. Additionally, I learned something very important." The concern on her face made John Anthony's heart beat faster. "I was followed. I don't know by whom, or if they are Abe or Biauay, but there was a conveyance in the exact same location as mine."

"So, where is that exactly, somewhere in West Texas?"

"No, John Anthony. I arrived in Takoma Park, Maryland."

"Maryland? How the heck did you get out here?"

"I drove."

"You can drive?"

"Of course, John Anthony. I can operate all manner of machinery, even fly this plane."

"Yes, of course you can, what am I thinking. So you drove from Maryland to Texas…in what?"

"I will show you when we return. I parked it in the garage at your shop."

"In my garage? But I never go in there, it's full of junk."

"Yes, the perfect spot to hide a car."

Niliason leaned around from his seat in the cockpit. "Hey, let's keep on topic here. You were followed. I will scramble all of our contacts in D.C.—believe me, we have that place covered. We'll find who followed you and detain them."

"That may not be so easy, Niliason. The Abes have become very powerful, as have the Biauay during the long years of your hiding."

"Worry not, Piaa," he smiled at her, "the Atec have not been idle either."

***

Sam Wisecraft strained as he aimed his camera down through the trees. The Robinson R-22 helicopter circled at five hundred feet above the birch grove in Takoma Park.

"There!" He tapped the pilot on the shoulder and pointed. The helicopter swung over a series of depressions in the ground.

"Well, that's weird." The pilot's voice crackled over the comms. "What would cause something like that?"

Sam stared at the shapes. "I don't know. They look like…no it couldn't be, they're much too large."

"What, Doc? They look like what?"

"Well, human."

The pilot swung the little chopper around and hovered lower over the spot. "Jesus."

Sam tapped him again. "Hey, look at those tire marks. Follow those tracks."

The pilot gained more altitude and followed the tracks. "There, they come out at that house. You can see where they went through the backyard then along the side of the house out to the driveway."

"Okay, take us back, I've got what I need here."

Ten minutes later, the helicopter touched down at College Park Airport. Sam tapped the pilot on the shoulder. "Change of plans, I need to go to Georgetown University."

"Okay, they have a helipad by the old Sub, but I need to refuel and check in with my charter controller. It'll be about fifteen minutes."

"Fine, I'll wait here." Sam transferred the pictures on his camera to his phone, then dialed information. "Georgetown University Department of Anthropology, Annette Blazer."

It took several minutes for her undergrads to track her down, but after he vetted himself, he was finally connected.

"Hello?"

"Hi, Annette, it's Sam…Wisecraft.

"Oh my God, Sam! How are you?"

"I'm great, Annette. Listen, I'm heading up the

international team at the Super-K neutrino detector in Japan, and I discovered something that I need your help with."

"Japan? Um, I specialize in European Archeology, Sam—"

"No, it's here, in D.C....actually about five miles from here. Listen. This would be so much easier if I could just meet with you. Is that possible?"

"Sure, Sam, when?"

"How about now?"

"Oh. Um, okay. Sam, you sound worried, is there something I should know about?"

"No, just excited that's all. Listen, I've got a helicopter chartered that's going to drop me off on campus. Maybe we can take your car and grab some coffee?"

"Wow, okay."

"See you in twenty minutes." He hung up and climbed back into the helicopter as the pilot came back out and informed him that they would have to fly around D.C. airspace. Twenty-five minutes later he touched down on the helipad outside of the UMMC Shock Trauma Center at Georgetown University.

"Okay, Doc, I only have clearance to drop you off, then I have to skedaddle," the pilot yelled.

Sam nodded and jumped out as soon as the skids hit the pavement. He ran clear of the rotors as the little helicopter lifted back into the air. Shielding his eyes from the sun, he watched as it sped away.

"Sam?"

He turned and gaped. The five-foot-six, dark haired girl that used to be a major science nerd had turned into a woman. Gone were the glasses, the oversized hoodie, and tangle of hair. Annette Blazer was a stunner.

"Sam, good to see you. Very impressive entrance I might add." She held out her hand. "Sam? Are you okay?"

He forced himself to snap out of it and look away.

"Yes, I'm fine! Annette, great to see you. You look different than I remember. I almost didn't recognize you."

"Yeah, I finally outgrew my awkward stage. It got boring."

He followed her to her pickup truck and they caught up on their careers while she drove.

"The campus area is loaded with coffee shops, any one in particular?" she asked.

"The closest." He gripped his briefcase anxiously. "That one will be fine." He pointed.

She pulled in and he hurried inside and found a booth with some privacy. Annette stood in line to order and motioned to him 'what do you want to drink?'. He shrugged. She nodded and smiled. A few minutes later she came to the table with drinks.

"Annette. What I am…no sugar, just milk, thanks. What I'm about to…no, I'm not hungry just…" He reached out and gripped her wrists. "Listen! This is a big deal, just listen to me, forget the frickin' coffee!"

"Okay, take it easy!"

"Sorry, just listen. Have you ever seen anything like this?" He handed his iPad to her. On the screen was a picture of the four impressions in the ground. She took the iPad and stared at the picture for a moment.

"You took this from the air?" she asked. He nodded. "Is there a reference for the size?"

"Yeah, those are tire tracks from a large truck leading away from the site."

"It would be nice to have something more definitive, but if those are truck tires and those impressions were made by human…" she looked at him, "…oid things, then they would have to be nine or ten feet tall. Are you sure?"

"Yes, we hovered over the area and I took a bunch of shots, see?" He reached over and swiped frame by frame through all the shots he'd taken. "Look, you can see the shadow of the helicopter in this one, and see that house in the side of the frame?"

"Okay, a couple of ideas come to mind. It may be an old burial site and we're seeing the outlines of erosion. But, I've never seen graves that were dug in the shape of a body before. I'd have to survey it."

"Exactly why I called you. Cordon off the area. Say it's an archeological dig site, whatever works, but I need you to tell me what we're dealing with here."

"Sam, I don't know if what you need is archaeology. You probably need a forensic team."

"That's what archaeology is, ancient forensics. Look, just tell me what you can about the soil and the compaction at the site. I want to know if something fell from the sky or came up from the ground."

"Well, I can definitely do that. Why are you interested in it? Last I knew your area of expertise was more along the lines of theoretical physics."

"We were counting neutrinos and the detector went off the scale. When I called around to vet the data I found out that the UKM Station in Malaysia had electron count readings that were also off the scale."

"I'm sorry, the what?"

"TEC, Total Electron Count; it's a reading they take of the ionosphere. It happened at the exact same time the neutrino count went bonkers. The really strange thing is that the sun is completely normal. No CMEs or anything. The UKM guys have over thirty stations around the globe that measure the electron count on a continual basis. When they mapped the unusual activity they pinpointed this location in Takoma Park."

Annette suddenly looked very concerned. "Who else knows?"

"Besides the helicopter pilot, just you and me and the people at the Super-K."

Annette thought for a moment. "Okay. Let's do this."

"Now?"

"I have all of my gear in my truck."

"But you're wearing a dress."

"I'll take it off."

Sam swallowed hard.

"I have a set of Carhartts with my gear," she said flatly.

"Oh right, of course. Well, let's see if we can even sneak into the site. Somebody used a truck to pull whatever it was out of there. They probably want to keep it a secret, so I'm guessing they won't be friendly to visitors."

"Shouldn't be any problem."

"It may bring trouble, Annette. I don't know."

"Come on, Sam, you have to trust me." She got up out of the booth. "Do you think I made discoveries in Taliban controlled territory by being stupid? I've dug in places that westerners haven't seen for thousands of years, I think I can get us into a small wooded lot in the middle of D.C."

Chapter 10

Mellissa put down her phone. "That was Dee Dee. She said that she and Jared just watching a helicopter hovering over the woods. They're on to us, what are we gonna do now?"

Daniel hopped down off the bed of the tow truck. "Don't panic yet. We don't know who it was. Besides, how would they know where to find us?"

"Daniel, anyone could follow a set of tracks up through the woods and past the house where, conveniently, the only guy in the neighborhood who owns a tow truck that can carry two full sized pickup trucks happens to live. Oh, and he also owns one of the largest garages in town. Where do you think they'll come first?" She glared at him. "Yeah, right here. Don't be an idiot. We have to move him now. Or, as soon as it gets dark at least."

"Where, Mel? I don't own another…" He trailed off in thought then suddenly snapped his fingers. "I got it. I'll call Mikey. His shop is smaller, but he does fabrication on anything."

Mellissa climbed onto the truck and worked her way up to where she could look Dominus in the face. "Don't worry, we won't let them find you."

"Worry is not one of my functions. Why do you insist on climbing all over me in order to communicate? I can audio interface from many miles away."

"Oh, sorry. We just like to look each other in the eyes when we talk. It's a way to establish trust."

"Trust is a luxury I do not have. Likewise, you know nothing of me other than that I am dangerous. Establishing trust should be very low on your priorities."

"You may be dangerous, but you are also injured and that makes you vulnerable. You are also a guest on our planet. For an advanced being from outer space you don't know much about compassion. We give a shit because you're a person, you need help, and we are the only ones who can give it to you without putting you in danger. Do you know what our government would do if they found you?"

"By averaging the accumulated scenarios presented in your various form of entertainment, there is a sixty-one percent likelihood of dissection and study of my remains."

"Yeah, well, I'd put it higher than that."

Daniel climbed up on the truck. "Listen, buddy, if your understanding of the human race is based on averages from movies and book plots, you're completely missing the mark."

"Do you not portray yourselves accurately?"

"No, some are dramatic interpretations, a lot of them are just complete fabrications. There aren't any superheroes, no Terminators, no Transformers…unless you can turn yourself into a car."

"No."

"Well, there ya go. None of that is real. Some of it is documentary, a lot of it is fiction, but all of it is seen through the eyes of the artists that created it."

"Where is the truth about your race?"

Mellissa leaned over and looked into his eyes. "You're lookin' at it. You have to get to know folks, figure out if they're your kind of people."

"I do not have time for trivial activities. I must complete my mission."

"Yeah, about that," Mellissa said. "What is your mission, exactly?"

Dominus went rigid. "Your attempts to extract information will yield nothing!"

"Woah, easy there!" Daniel held up his hands. "No one is trying to get you to divulge any secrets."

"Dominus, we're not interrogating you, we're just concerned for our safety, and yours. If someone is going to attack the Earth or something, we want to know. Daniel has a child for God's sake! Surely you can appreciate that."

"Mel, maybe we should be focusing more on the situation at hand."

She took a deep breath. "Dominus, we're going to have to move you."

"I know, I monitored your conversation with the Dee Dee unit."

"You monitored my conversation? Try to respect people's privacy next time, and she's not a unit. She's a nice old lady who babysits Jared, and is currently doing so while Daniel and I try to save your butt. Show some freakin' appreciation, Jesus!"

"Why don't you take a break, sis. Go grab some air."

Mellissa jumped down off the truck and went outside, slamming the door behind her. Daniel watched her go, then turned back to Dominus. "You really need to work on your people skills. I'm taking you over to my friend's shop. His name is Mike. He's likely to be pretty freaked out when he sees you, so don't make matters worse by threatening him or something. He's a good guy and will help as long as you let me explain things.

"You're going to have to get over this issue you have with trust. It's not an option here. You have to trust us, we have to be able to trust you. We have nothing to gain here and everything to lose. If we're caught harboring you, we're in deep trouble. I could lose my shop, the house, who knows what else. And you owe Mel some respect. She's risking a lot for you."

"I will comply."

"Hey, here's a little clue. You have access to every bit of information on the planet, right? Why don't you spend a little time learning how to speak American English. It will go a long way in engendering the trust of the humans. The ones you'll meet, anyway."

Daniel hopped off the truck and stomped off towards the door. "We're leaving in four hours. You'll be under the tarp. And if you have some kind of high tech camouflage, I suggest you use it." He slammed the door behind him.

***

As he rounded the corner he could hear Mellissa talking with someone.

"I don't know, Pete, we had a pretty bad fight and Daniel's still upset. I wouldn't go in there if I were you."

Daniel walked up to them. "It's okay, Pete. Mel, I'm sorry, I shouldn't have lost my temper. You should go back into the garage so we can finish talking."

Mellissa stood with her back to Peter and gave Daniel a look that said *what are you doing?* Daniel returned a reassuring look and gave her a hug. "Sorry, Mel, really. Just go inside, I'll only be a second. Hey, Petey, how'd it go? You find anything good?"

"Hey, Danny, yeah I found a 73' Charger. Only paid fifteen hundred for it. She's got some rust on the panels but all the jewelry is on it. We could do a patina and drop it—it should be a quick turn-around. I just need the truck to go back and get it."

"Oh man, the truck is... Well, it's broke, man. Sorry. I was using it to do some work at the house and I backed into the woods too far. Had to get it pulled out. They screwed up the tie rods when they towed it. Hey listen, Mel and I are going through some things right now, so just take the rest of the day off and we'll start fresh tomorrow."

"I have a better idea." Peter started towards the back door. "You wrap things up with Mel, I'll throw some tie rods on the truck, then go down and grab that Charger."

"Uh, Petey, hey!" Daniel tried to catch up but Peter was tall and had a good stride going.

"Danny, if I don't get back there this deal is going to fall through. We could lose a couple grand on this if I don't reel it in." He opened the back door and stepped through. "Hey, Mel, just ignore me, I'm gonna be out of here in a couple of—"

Daniel burst in the door right behind him. Peter just stared dumbly at the truck. Daniel's face was a mirror of Peter's. Mellissa looked at them both wide-eyed. Peter was the first to speak.

"What did you do? Tie rods? It's gonna need more than tie rods, look at it, the suspension is trashed. It's practically sitting on the ground!"

Mellissa spun around, the bed of the truck was empty. She shot a stunned look at Daniel who just shrugged. She ran up to Peter.

"Hey, Petey, yeah the truck's really screwed. Tell you what, why don't you go and rent a single car mover and go get the…" She waved her hand in a circle, queuing Peter's input.

"The Charger?"

"Yeah, the Charger. Just go get that bad boy and bring him—"

"Her," Peter said. "It's definitely a her."

"Her, then, yeah. Just go get her. Here's the company card, okay?" She began to steer him back towards the door.

"Hey, why are all the windows blacked out?"

Daniel jumped in, "For working late. I don't like people to see me working late in here. You know, when the lights are on inside I can't see out at night but they can see in."

"Who can see in? There's nobody on the streets at night around here."

"Oh, it's really more about avoiding any hassle with my ex and those Valkyries."

Mellissa kept moving Peter towards the door. "So, you got the card, right? Go get the Charger and we'll see you tomorrow!"

"Wait!" Peter stopped short, his huge frame unmovable by Mel's petite stature. "I know what you're trying to do."

Daniel looked panicked. Mellissa's heart fluttered. "You do?" they spoke at once.

"It's okay. I won't let anyone know that I know about your surprise birthday party for me. You guys are really sweet. It will be our secret. I'll just act surprised, I'm a good actor."

Mellissa sighed. "You got us."

"Yep, busted," Daniel chimed in.

"You can't fool ol' Petey. Hey, did I ever tell you guys about the time I was the Ghost of Christmas Present in high school?"

"No, Petey, maybe when you get back." Mellissa got him out the door. "Go get that Charger before it's too late!"

"Oh right, see you guys tomorrow!" Peter waved and climbed back into his car.

Mellissa and Daniel closed the back door and locked it as they both turned and called out, "Dominus!"

The enormous black form of Dominus shimmered in a transparent haze and came back into view on the back of the truck. "He was persistent."

"Dominus! Thank God!" Mellissa jumped onto the truck.

"Wow, I didn't know you could do that." Daniel scratched his head.

"I will not be able to do it again. It used what little energy I have left, unfortunately."

"What do you mean? Are you dying?" Mellissa sat down on his huge shoulder and put her hand on his forehead like she was feeling for a temperature.

"No, Mellissa, I am not dying." Dominus looked at Daniel who could hear the difference in his speech. "It's a complicated matter but it has to do with my energy reserves. My critical systems all run off of a primary core. Other systems run off of reserves that usually recharge with activity. I have been at rest so long, my reserves have not been able to recharge."

"Will you be okay though?"

"Yes, I'll be fine, but I won't be able to remotely access data, or use any of my defensive systems." Dominus eyed Daniel skeptically. He was clearly anticipating some kind of hostile reaction to his admission of defenselessness.

"All the more reason to get you somewhere safe then." Daniel looked at the clock. "We have two hours before we can move you. I'll get on the horn to Mikey."

Mellissa climbed down from the trailer. "I have to get dinner for Jared. He hasn't seen very much of us lately. I'll meet you tomorrow."

"That's fine, Mel, I don't need you for the move. We're just driving across town. I'll be in late."

"And leave Dominus alone? No, you're staying the night at the shop with him. I'll tell Jared that you're working on a special project."

"It would be wise to leave some kind of notice for Peter, when he shows up with the Charger, to explain your absence," Dominus interjected.

Both Mellissa and Daniel looked at him.

"Uh…yeah," Daniel replied. "You're absolutely right. Thanks, Dominus, I'll get on that."

Mellissa climbed back up on the truck. "Hey, big guy, that was helpful, way to go. I'll miss you tonight. You take care and try to rest and heal up, okay? I'll see you tomorrow." She kissed him on the forehead and left.

***

When she had gone, Daniel went to the workbench and sighed. "Dominus, I have a confession to make. I didn't know if we could trust you or if you meant us harm, so I took this off of you when you first arrived. I'm sorry, but I had to be sure." He pulled the cloth off of the giant pistol and stood back.

Dominus strained as he leaned forward to look, then he rested his head. "My sidearm. It makes sense that you would hide it from me."

"Only because we didn't know if you would try to hurt us with it. I'll give it back to you now."

"Of all your actions, this is the truest sign of...I mean, I acknowledge your... What I mean to say is...thank you. I appreciate your trust in me. I will not harm you."

"That's good to know. Now that we've got that settled..." He dragged the engine hoist over to the workbench and wrapped chains around the weapon. "You were holding this when we found you. I didn't see a holster or anything."

"It is my left sidearm, it goes in the cradle in my leg. Unfortunately, my leg is severely damaged."

"I can make you something to hold it if you want."

"That would be...nice, thank you."

"Hey, no problem." Daniel started gathering materials to construct a holster for the huge gun. "So you said this is your left sidearm, did you have a right sidearm?"

A fast clacking sound shook the truck as a compartment in Dominus' right leg opened and another pistol shot into his hand. The rounds in the weapon spun and hissed as a red glow emanated from the barrel. Daniel stepped back in shock. Dominus inspected the weapon, then returned it to the compartment in his leg. It slammed shut with a thud that shook the trailer again.

"I prefer my left."

"You could have killed us this whole time?" Daniel was shaking.

"Yes, Daniel, but I didn't because I too have a confession to make."

Chapter 11

Annette was more prepared for the task at hand than Sam thought healthy for a middle-aged, professional woman. The magnetic signs now plastered on her truck doors were the frosting on the cake.

USGS OFFICIAL GOVERNMENT VEHICLE. It was a forgery, of course.

"These things have got me into places. I'll leave it at that. They work, trust me."

What is she, some kind of anthropological spy? Maybe trusting her wasn't his best move.

"It's almost dark," she said. "We'll approach the woods from the opposite side of the suspect's house."

"Suspect? Just because the tracks go through their yard, doesn't mean they're criminals, Annie."

"We suspect them of being at the site, that's all it means. For lack of a better term, 'suspect' works."

"According to the GPS, there's a way in through a development called Birch Grove. It should put us directly opposite the house and close to the site. That way we don't have to disturb the 'suspects'."

He navigated while she drove. They snaked their way through the neighborhood just as the sun was setting. The road ended in a cul-de-sac where several new homes were under construction.

"Perfect," she said. "We can go between the houses and down the embankment." She kept the lights off and guided the pickup through a narrow gap, then paused as they approached a four foot drop.

"That's kind of steep, don't you think? Maybe we should walk."

"Nonsense, this is precisely why I drive a four-by-four." She slipped the differential into four wheel low and crawled over the edge. Sam braced himself, sure that they would roll, but the truck walked down the slope like it was on a Sunday stroll.

"See. Trust me," she teased him.

"Okay, so I'm used to roads. This isn't so bad."

They rocked in the cab as she crawled her way over small logs and uneven ground. "We're almost there, the birch grove is just ahead," Sam said.

"Birches grow in water rich environments; I better stop before it gets mucky. We're on foot from here." She shut off the truck and climbed out. "Close the doors quietly. Nosey neighbors can be a pain the ass."

They gathered her gear from the back and slogged the last one hundred yards to the site. In the fading light they could just make out the depressions.

"They're bigger than I thought," she said, pulling out her tape measure. "They're all perfectly laid out, except this one. We'll start with that."

He helped her take measurements.

"If this figure was standing upright it would be eleven feet, five inches," Annette marveled. "It's three feet deep. I've got a soil sample."

Sam strained to see in the failing light. "Wait, Annie, look at that." He bounded over to an object jutting out of the ground. "It's like some kind of artillery shell."

"Careful, Sam, don't touch it!" She came over and took out a flashlight. "I'm gonna turn this on, but I'm shielding the beam so it's small, okay? Close one eye to preserve your night vision."

The little light shone through her gripped fist just enough to reveal the unexploded round.

"It looks like it's made of carbon fiber," Sam said. "Look at the lines in it. I've never seen anything like it."

"It doesn't have a firing pin or fins. No control surfaces." She reached out and touched the butt end of the shell then jerked her hand back. "Oh shit! Get back, Sam!" She bounded back past the depressions and stood behind a large birch tree. Sam followed quickly behind her. "It was buzzing—vibrating like there was an electric current running through it."

"Well, if it hasn't gone off by now it probably won't. Just do what you need to do so we can get out of here," Sam said. "If that's military, then it's definitely secret and in the wrong place. They're gonna be looking for it."

"Jesus, Sam, a live artillery shell narrowly missing a subdivision? Believe me, the military has done bad things to people for knowing less."

"Then let's get a move on!" he hissed.

"Alright, I'm just going to do a scan of the grove with the LiDAR. Then we can study the site later on with the university's GID. In my backpack is my camera. Careful with it, it's got a full light spectrum analyzer on it. Every shot you take will be in every spectrum."

"Every shot *I* take?"

"I can't take pictures and run the LiDAR at the same time. Now help me with this tripod."

The laser took a few minutes to set up then Sam left her alone with it and began taking pictures. He started with what they were calling the 'deformed depression', then went to the tallest of the other three. When he finished shooting pictures of it, he flipped the camera into play mode to check the exposure.

The regular image was just black but when he checked the infrared, he saw a terrifying mechanical face staring back at him. His heart stuck in his throat and he took off back to the truck as fast as he could. He streaked past Annette, repeating through his panting breath, "Run. Run. Run."

Annette took off after him. "Wait, Sam, what is it?" She was in much better shape and caught up quickly. She spun him around and grabbed the camera.

He let her have it; kept running. "Get out of here now, Annie!"

She looked at the screen on the back of the camera. "Oh, my God. What the hell is—"

The ground vibrated and a sound like a tortured pack of lions erupted from the grove. Annette dropped the camera and whirled around. A burst of plasma flame exploded from the trees as something rocketed skyward. The shockwave sent her reeling backwards. Sam was suddenly at her side.

"We're surrounded! They're at the truck too!" He gripped her shoulders and they held each other, waiting for the end as another explosion launched another projectile into the sky.

"Get down!" a voice cried as arms wrapped around them and forced them to the wet ground. "Stay down!"

A third explosion shook them and they turned to watch a giant, human shaped figure rise in front of a column of blue fire. It accelerated into the sky as the heat hit them again. Sam hadn't noticed it until that moment.

The voice spoke again, "It's okay, they're gone."

They all stood up. Two men had joined them, one rugged and handsome, the other kind of nerdy and thin, wet mud and grass dripping off of their clothes. The nerdy one put his hand out.

"I'm John Anthony, this is Niliason Brand."

Annette was the first to come out of the shocked stupor that gripped both of them. "Doctor Annette Blazer, USGS. This is my colleague Doctor Sam Wisecraft. What the hell is going on here, John?"

"It's John Anthony, and that's a long story—"

"And one that will wait for another time. The situation is far worse than I imagined," said a tall, slender figure as she emerged from the smoke that was settling around the grove.

Sam stepped back.

"Easy, she's with us," John Anthony reassured them. "Her name's Piaa." The tall figure continued to get taller as she approached. "And she's not from around here."

The figure held out her hand. Sam knew as soon as he looked into her eyes that he would never be the same.

Annette, stunned into silence, instinctively held out her hand.

"Sam," Piaa said, "and Annette, though not Annette Blazer from the USGS, rather Doctor Annette Blazer, head of Anthropology and Archaeological studies at Georgetown University. I am Piaa, an Eos Biauay, the details of which I will gladly explain further, but right now we have to go. Will you come with us?"

Annette just nodded. Sam managed "Where?"

"It's not safe here," the man called Niliason said. "They'll be swarming over this area in a matter of minutes, we have to leave now."

"My equipment." Annette pointed at her LiDAR scanner.

"Go with Niliason. John Anthony and I will get your equipment." Piaa strode off to recover the LiDAR and pointed out the camera lying in the dirt.

Sam and Annette were hurried back to the vehicles. A black Yukon was parked next to her pickup. When they got to their truck, Niliason asked for her keys.

"It's easier for me to drive there than to give you directions."

Annette relented and they switched seats. Niliason started out of the woods with the lights off.

"You might want to—"

"I don't need them. I'll explain later." The truck lurched up the steep bank and came down hard between the houses. They accelerated onto the pavement and quickly left Birch Grove. Not until they pulled onto a main road did he switch on the headlights. Annette realized she had been clinging to Sam the whole time.

"Okay, where are you taking us?" she asked.

"Somewhere safe. I promise you'll get all of your questions answered when we get where we're going. It's best if Piaa and John Anthony are with us so your questions can be answered more fully. I will tell you this—we mean you no harm. You can go your way if you like, but as scientists, I expect you'll wish to make an informed decision. Circumstances mean that we must get to a safe facility before we do anything else."

"Wait," Sam broke in. "Facility? What facility?"

Niliason sighed. "It's clear that you're not going to trust me, so here's the short version. I'm an artificial intelligence that's been living on Earth for tens of thousands of years. We are responsible for re-colonizing Earth with humans. We're on your side. Piaa is an alien that just arrived. Those things you saw blasting off just now were aliens that followed her. They are not that interested in the survival of humans, if you catch my drift."

Annette rolled her eyes. "So you're supposed to be an alien? You look awfully human to me."

"Yes, that's because you created us in your image."

"What? That doesn't make any sense. We created you?"

"I told you, this is the short version, there are many details that will be explained! I thought if I gave you some of the story it would satiate you for a while."

"No way, buddy, we're scientists. We're in the questions business," Sam stated firmly.

"Well, could you take a break until we're safely out of D.C., please?"

"Not until you tell us where—"

"We're taking a private jet out of Reagan International to Baltimore. There are a group of people there like me who will shelter us until we decide what to do."

"What to do with us, you mean," Annette said.

"No, what to do period! Those things that flew off are going to be back. They're here to take us out, and by 'us' I mean everybody on the planet."

"Is there a ship orbiting or something?" Sam asked.

"I don't know, but whatever they're up to, it isn't good. The last time they were here they hit the Earth with the moon." He let that sink in. "Are you starting to get the idea?"

"Jesus." Sam looked at Annette.

"Good, now please just let me drive."

At the airport, the five of them piled out of their vehicles and Niliason gathered them around. "We wait right here." He directed most of his instructions at Annette and Sam. "When our contact comes, don't ask any questions please. Just follow instructions and we'll get to the plane."

"But—" Sam started.

Niliason held up his hand and cut him off. "Wait," he practically pleaded. When it appeared Sam was resigned to listen to him, then he continued, "In the back of the Yukon there are cleaning supplies. We have to scrub down these vehicles so no forensic evidence of us can be found. If we take care of the hard surfaces our contact will take care of the textiles." He went to the back of the large black rig and started handing out spray bottles and cloth. "Don't worry too much about wiping, the spray will take care of anything organic."

"You always carry this stuff in your car, Niliason?" John Anthony asked.

"All of us do. Sometimes it's necessary to abandon a vehicle to avoid discovery."

Annette perked up. "Hey, buddy, I'm not abandoning my truck."

"You don't have a choice," Niliason said as he sprayed and wiped the console of the Yukon. "The authorities will track it here and seize it as evidence. Make no mistake, the minute you set foot in that grove you put yourself in the crosshairs of a full-blown cover-up effort. If that doesn't make you nervous, you should know that Homeland Security are the ones with their finger on the trigger. Your truck should be the least of your concerns."

She pulled Sam out of the driver's seat of the truck. "Let me do that, I have forensic experience."

"Hey, it's your truck," Sam said, backing out of the cab.

"Not anymore, apparently. What the hell did you get

me into, Sam Wisecraft?"

***

Piaa stayed in the backseat of the Yukon, concentrating. John Anthony knew that she was interfacing with some kind of computer system somewhere. Finally, she opened her eyes.

"What was that about?" John Anthony asked.

"There are cameras everywhere. The government will use them to try and find us. I have thwarted their efforts by replacing the live feeds from every camera in a fifty-mile radius with a Cheerios commercial."

"Then why do you still look so worried?"

"John Anthony, those were Abes back in that grove and not just any Abes. They are a renowned group of bounty hunters, lethal and brutal. They are here to find me, I think. Unlike human technology, I cannot circumvent their efforts to locate me. I am Biauay and I have a particular signature. They will find me within hours if I don't get to a shielded location."

Another black Yukon pulled up next to them. Two people got out and began talking with Niliason. After they handed him a large envelope, one drove off in Annette's truck and another climbed into the driver's seat of the first Yukon.

Niliason opened the door of the new Yukon for Piaa. "Everybody."

They all piled in and he handed out passports, plane tickets, and cash.

"These are just in case we get separated or have to split up. Fortunately, here in D.C., we have people everywhere. The airport security covering our private plane will change watch in ten minutes. He will be replaced by an Atec who will pass us through to the plane. Just be natural and don't do anything to call attention to us.

"Piaa, you will have to make the transition to the plane

quickly. I'll get the car as close as possible." He finished by instructing them on how to help Annette get all of her equipment onto the plane. Each person was to carry a piece of gear and loosely surround Piaa, who would walk with bent knees to reduce her height.

"The curse of being created in lighter than Earth gravity comes to haunt me now," Piaa declared grimly.

Annette put her hand on top of Piaa's. "Don't complain, honey. If I had a figure like yours, I'd be a supermodel."

Chapter 12

"Okay, our man is in place. Here we go." Niliason drove them through the gate, across the tarmac, and into the hangar.

The security truck was there and the guard went through the motions of checking IDs. When he got to John Anthony all he said was, "A real pleasure to meet you. Keep your head down and we'll get you to safety."

The Gulfstream G150 private jet was roomy and luxurious. In minutes they were taxiing for take-off. Suddenly Piaa was on the floor holding her head.

"They're searching for me!"

Niliason sprang from his seat and covered her. "Get this plane in the air now! Everyone, come here and lay on her." Annette, John Anthony, and Sam all lay on top of Piaa, trying to cover every inch of surface area. "Dog pile, that's it. This plane is shielded but the Abes have strong tech. Natural human electrical systems are tiny but they are erratic compared to synthetic beings. It may help."

They all lay in a pile on the floor. In an incredible display of strength, Niliason held them in place as the jet went into a near vertical climb. In that moment, they all looked at each other. Piaa, curled into a ball on the floor, looked up at them.

"Thank you. The danger seems to have passed."

As the plane leveled out they all got up and returned to their seats. "Well, that was cozy," Sam said, dusting himself off.

"You move pretty fast for an old professor," Annette teased.

Sam blushed. He had been laying on top of her in the pile and felt a bit guilty for enjoying it.

Piaa worked her way to the back of the plane and pulled up a floor plate. She worked herself into the narrow gap between the outer skin and the floor. It was filled with wires, electrical boxes, and conduit.

"Piaa, no, you'll freeze!" Annette moved to stop her but Piaa just smiled.

"John Anthony will explain. I am in no danger." She disappeared into the hole.

"She's mostly machine. They are called synthetics…" John Anthony began to explain what he had only just learned.

Niliason added to the conversation and, to John Anthony's surprise, Piaa spoke through him with her own voice.

"We communicate through what you would consider a network link," Piaa said through Niliason's mouth. "We can relinquish control of our parts or all of our systems to another person, though it is rarely done outside of a love bond."

Sam and Annette fired question after question and had all of them answered. Only the plane arriving at Baltimore airport made them take a break. Piaa pried herself out of the hole and got ready for her low profile dash.

"Now are you glad I got you into this?" Sam asked Annette, grinning.

"This is huge Sam." She was reeling. "I don't know where this is all going, but I'm definitely going for the ride. I could use a change of clothes though." She was still wearing the dirt covered overalls from her truck.

They piled into another black Yukon and drove into the city.

"What is it with Atec and black Yukons?" John Anthony griped. "You guys know they are the most suspicious looking vehicles in the world, don't you?"

"They carry the weight of many people, they have armor plating and bulletproof windows, plus, a lot of shielding to keep us from prying eyes," Niliason replied.

"Yeah, but how about something other than black?"

"We got a deal on them, what can I say."

They got into the city just after ten o'clock and stopped in front of a corner shop on a tree lined street.

Sam looked out the window. "A pizza joint?"

"THE pizza joint." Niliason grinned back at him.

Annette climbed out of the Yukon. "Hey, I think I've seen this place on *Diners, Drive-Ins & Dives*... Yeah, Brick Oven Pizza. Doesn't Kevin Bacon eat here?"

Niliason gathered them all together at the Yukon's rear door where Piaa still sat. "You three go in and take a seat. Tell them you're here for the star plate special. Piaa and I will drive around back." He got back into the truck and drove off down the street. John Anthony, Annette, and Sam walked in the front door.

Sam repeated Niliason's message to the server whose eyes went wide as she glanced around. "Is there anyone else with you?" she asked very deliberately, as if trying to imply some other meaning.

"Um, just two that went in the back," John Anthony offered.

The server nodded, apparently satisfied, and said, "The restrooms are through that doorway in the back." She motioned with her arm and put on a plastic smile.

"Um, I don't have to use—"

"Yes, sir, no problem, the restrooms are through *that* doorway. That one. Right there." Her face tightened with suppressed frustration.

"Thank you." Annette pushed Sam and John Anthony forward. When they got through the doorway, she stopped. "Are you guys thick or what?"

The door to the men's room opened and a man stood there looking at them.

"Sorry, excuse us." Annette put her nice face back on. The man just stared at them.

"Are you coming in or do you want the whole

restaurant to notice you?" the man said in a mild Italian accent.

They all piled in the door and were herded, one by one, into a cleaning closet where a set of spiral stairs descended steeply from an opening in the back wall. They went down one flight and emerged in a basement just below the street. They were greeted by Niliason and Piaa in a long, damp hallway lit by a single candle.

"What took you so long?"

"Thick and thicker here don't speak spy." Annette was clearly miffed.

"Hey, I'm new to all this stuff." Sam looked at his surroundings. "Where are we anyways?"

"This was built during prohibition. It was used to bring in booze."

"So, the Atec took it over and are using it as a secret bunker, huh?" John Anthony nodded his approval.

"Naw, we built it to run booze in the twenties. Crazy days, man." Niliason shook his head and smiled. "Unfortunately this is it. We have to wait for arrangements to be made. Neil will be bringing some chairs and food down."

"How about a few more candles?"

"Don't worry, we will be well taken care of here. They had no time to prepare for us. It's not like Mitchell, Texas. The Atec live and work in the city here, there's no…how would you say…club house, but we can talk freely. It's completely shielded."

Neil called down the stairs and began handing chairs to Piaa. She passed them out and then sat down.

"Niliason and I have been talking about what happened in Takoma Park. There were three Abes but four conveyance depressions."

"I'm sorry," Annette raised her hand, "what is a conveyance depression?"

"The aliens, myself included, that have arrived on your planet got here by means of tachyon conveyance. The complete atomic structure of a being is encoded in a tachyon stream that is directed at a chosen destination. In this case, a wooded glen in Takoma Park on Earth. When the tachyons arrive they behave as the code instructs them, transferring instructions at an atomic level to whatever atoms they hit. The atoms obey and reform in accordance to the coding. The effect is similar to 3D printing with the available atoms, in most cases the ground, converting into the desired elements that join in series to create a duplicate of the individual."

"But what about memories and stuff?" Sam interjected.

"Personality, memories, and everything that makes an individual who they are is all programming and therefore, at its root, code. That code is transferred and rebuilt as well. When a destructive transfer is made, where the original gets deleted as it's coded, the consciousness of the individual accompanies the rest of the data."

"What about humans?"

"We don't know really. I believe tachyon conveyance would work but synthetics are the only ones who have perfected it to my knowledge."

"Ah, pizza!" Niliason greeted Neil as he came down the stairs with four large pies. More candles were lit and another table brought down. With plates and glasses of beer, wine and soda, they were content.

"So, you were saying that you essentially 3D printed yourself here across space riding encoded tachyons, is that right?" Annette checked her facts.

"Close enough."

"Well, how far did you come? I'm no astrophysicist but I know the nearest star is light years away."

"Over seventy thousand lights years." Piaa took another bite of pizza. "This is really quite good."

Annette's bite hovered at her mouth, which was hanging open. "I'm sorry…" she stuttered, "…did you say seventy thousand light years? But wouldn't that take seventy thousand years at light speed?"

"Yes, but tachyons can exceed light speed," Sam said excitedly. "They are unique that way. That's why I love them."

"So, what is our next move?" Annette shrugged off the shock.

"I'm glad you asked. Now that dinner is over and we're all relaxed, we can think this through. The data on your lidar scanner and full spectrum camera tell me that one of the photonic conveyance depressions had been made shortly after my arrival."

"So if one of those depressions was yours, that means the other ones aren't actually so large after all. We might be able to manage this," Sam said feeling more positive about the whole thing.

"Unfortunately you are wrong on both counts, Sam. I covered my depression as soon as I woke up. The other one is from an Abe. I am guessing he is a scout of some kind but there is evidence to suggest that he may be a fugitive as well."

"So you think an Abe followed you here, but they are running from the Structure?" Niliason spoke to her vocally so everyone could follow the conversation.

"It is possible. Perhaps it is the Abe responsible for finding me. He failed, therefore the Structure may choose to have him deleted. It is possible he is running from that fate."

Niliason began pacing. "So there are four Abes here and it is safe to say that they are looking for Piaa. We have to move you to a safe facility as fast as possible. We're going back to the cave."

"It is for the best. My presence puts the whole planet at risk."

"Yeah, but you're also our only hope." John Anthony put his hand on her shoulder. "Jeez, I never thought I'd quote Star Wars in context. You know what I mean. Atecs are powerful and evolved compare to humans, but Biauay have been fighting on the front lines for ages."

"He's right, Piaa," Niliason said. "Keeping you safe is a priority. Only you know what the Abes are currently capable of."

"Unless," Annette put up her hand, "there is some way of contacting others of your kind to come to our aid perhaps?"

"It is a good idea," Piaa replied, "but unfortunately we don't know where the others are. Even if we could contact them they would arrive with ships, then the Abes would arrive with more. The Atec lost to the Abes once before, and when the Biauay and the Atec fought it was a terrible struggle. Neither races would fare well against the Abes."

John Anthony spoke up. "Together you might."

Niliason considered it for a moment. "Perhaps, but the Earth would be at the center of the battle and would not survive. Right now we need to locate the damaged Abe and find out his predicament. If he truly is a fugitive there are three options. One option is to lead the other Abes to him in the hopes that they may take him and leave. Another option is to capture him and find out if he has some way of communicating with the Structure. If so, we would be able to see Earth's status on the Galactic Registry and perhaps change it back to inhabitable."

"Hack the Structure, I like it. " John Anthony nodded with a smirk. "You said there was a third option."

"Yes, the last option is a long shot, but perhaps we might be able to persuade him to join us."

"An Abe?" Piaa was clearly not in favor of this option. "They're mindless droids, most of them. The Abes that are fully sentient have mostly chosen to live on the fringes as criminals. They seem to like the Structure even less that the Biauay. "

"I didn't say it was a likely option, just a long shot. I fear that our most likely scenario will be the second one. I don't take well to prying information out of enemies, but there are a few Atec left with the heart for it. Before we do anything, we find the Abe and watch from a distance. Unfortunately, that means our only operatives have to be human."

"What?" Sam and John Anthony said together.

"Atec and Biauay are synthetic beings. We have particular energy signatures that the Abe scanners will certainly pick up. All Atec on Earth have been notified of the threat and are most certainly heading for shielded refuge as we are now. We cannot leave or we will show up like a signal flare on their scanners. Now, I say your words back to you John Anthony: you are our only hope. Will you help?"

Annette was the first to stand up. "I'm in, for whatever it's worth."

Sam stood beside her. "If she's in, I'm in."

John Anthony stayed seated and chomped a fresh slice of pizza. "Hey, I've been in the whole time."

Chapter 13

The truck shuddered as it limped down the street under the heavy load. Daniel took the side streets most of the way across town to Mike's Fabrication. Mike was there waiting for him when he pulled up.

"Hey, Danny, so what's this special project you got?"

"It's serious, Mike. This isn't another restoration job. Open up the garage and let me back the truck in there."

"All right, man. I'll get the door."

Mike disappeared inside, but as the garage door opened, the sky lit up and a deep crackling rumble shook the air.

"What the hell is that?" Mike yelled from the garage. "Did somebody launch a missile?"

Dominus threw the tarp aside. "Daniel, get me inside, now!"

"Holy Lord Almighty, did that thing just talk?"

"Mike, help me get the truck in!"

The command shook Mike out of his inertia but the dumbfounded look on his face stuck. Daniel backed the truck up while Mike directed him, focusing more on not looking at the monstrous pile of living machinery lying in the bed. Another explosion shook the air as a second blue streak shot into the sky. Daniel shut the truck off as Mike ran around and lowered the shop door.

"Daniel," Dominus spoke quickly and quietly, "do you know what a Faraday cage is?"

"Um, isn't that just a metal cage that deflects lightning?"

"Close enough. Build one around me now. As fast as you can."

"Mikey! We need to weld up a cage around him

ASAP, brother. Spot weld, don't worry about making it clean."

"No problem, who's gonna reimburse me?"

"Don't worry about that, I'll take care of any expenses. Just start welding!"

Master mechanic and genius fabricator worked together to hastily build a dome of steel mesh and spare parts around Dominus as a third eruption rattled the building.

"Would you care to explain to me what the Sam Hell is going on here?" Mike barked as he welded.

"Mike, meet Dominus. He's not from Earth. I found him half-dead in the woods and towed him up to my place. When helicopters started flying over the woods I decided to move him here."

"Oh, so you thought that was a *good idea*? Thanks a lot, Danny!"

Dominus raised his head and looked at Mike, who happened to be at eye level, and who had forced himself to forget that the thing even talked. "Mike. Do not be angry with Daniel. He is only attempting to help me avoid detection."

Mike swallowed hard. "So, you're like some kind of robot?"

"I am an Evolutionary Intelligent Being. The acronym is EIB but pronounced 'Abe'. So I am an Abe. I am a synthetic construct come to Earth on a mission to find a fugitive. The three blasts you heard herald the arrival of three of my finest soldiers who are now hunting me. When I departed on the journey to come here we had failed in our mission to capture the fugitive and were doomed to deletion."

"That's pretty harsh punishment. Not every mission is a success. Sometimes you have to retreat in order to attain victory." Mike found himself immersed in the story.

"Keep welding, Mikey!" Daniel urged him. "Mike here served as a soldier with me in Afghanistan."

"You are soldiers. Then you understand. Unfortunately, the Structure did not see the matter the same way. It assumed that the fugitive had been killed when I forcibly entered the base on Andapo. It was wrong. This surprised me. There is only the Will of the Structure and Compliance. One must never question the Will of the Structure, but I knew it was wrong this time. That is why I followed the path of the fugitive. I…we were engaged by a fleet of Biauay. My team got caught in heavy fire while I escaped, barely."

"They call that survivor's grief," Mike sympathized. "It's okay, man, we all left people behind."

"The Structure must have rebuilt them, because that is what you saw in the sky tonight. Alaz, Vexa, and Skagit have come for me. I fear that I am in no condition to face them."

While he had been talking they continued to weld, handing pieces for Dominus to hold in place with his good arm while they tacked it to the lattice dome that grew around him.

"There. Will that do the trick?" Mike asked, climbing down.

"Not yet. Connect your welding machine to the cage and put as much power into it as you can."

"Are you serious?" Mike looked from the machine to Dominus, eyes wide.

"One thing you're gonna learn, Mikey, Dominus doesn't have much of a sense of humor. Do it."

Once the cage was charged, they played with the settings on the large welding rig. Finally Mike stepped away from the welding rig and wiped his hands.

"We're right on the edge of blowing a breaker, but it should hold."

"If anyone asks about the bill, just tell them I had you on a handful of rush projects."

"So what do we do now, Danny?" Mike mopped his brow.

"Well, he's injured. I don't have the tools to fix him. I figured maybe you would be able to do more here."

"Okay." Mike looked at Dominus. "Well, the first thing I need to know is: what are you made of?"

"I am scanning my database to find a reference you will understand…the closest thing would be akin to spider web. The material of my frame and shell is a hierarchical network of low crystalline, high-friction nano-fibers built in layers of locking threads that connect to the adjacent fibers to suppress single point failure of the chain."

Mike and Daniel stared at him blankly.

"So," Dominus attempted his best imitation of casual human conversation, "it's like a super dense, solid mat of spider webbing, but instead of spider webbing it's more like titanium than anything else. Does that help?"

Both men nodded. "Oh, I understand now." Mike turned to Daniel. "So you can't really cut it—"

"—or penetrate it in any way," Daniel finished the thought. "It's like Kevlar but the layers are woven together as tight as the individual sheets."

"Like 3D weaving," Mike agreed. Both men now stood, nodding appreciatively at Dominus, thinking of how to apply their knowledge to the situation. Their nod quickly faded. "We don't have anything even remotely capable of dealing with that."

"I doubted you would. The material is created by a special machine that assembles the fibers on the molecular level. Each piece is essentially grown into its final shape. My onboard repair systems are incapable of manufacturing an entire piece."

"Wait a minute, on-board repair systems? You can heal yourself?"

"Yes, but my reserves of power were exhausted in my battle with the Biauay fleet."

"So, your armor is powered as well?"

"Yes, it is conductive, and when activated, contains layers of both plasma based and electrical based energies that thwart a wide variety of weapons, from solid projectiles to energy types by converting kinetic energy into photons."

"So, when you get shot, you light up like a Christmas tree!" Mike slapped his thigh with his greasy ball cap.

"Hmm, yes, though more like a small star."

"Nice visual. So how can we recharge your energy reserves?"

"A plasma bath."

Both men again stared at him, agape.

"Wait. What about a particle accelerator? The main tank thing, where the collision happens…the walls are covered in plasma. I saw it on the Discovery Channel." Daniel ditched into the office and grabbed Mike's laptop. "Here, Wikipedia…crap, it's in Switzerland."

"How the hell are we gonna get him to Switzerland?"

Dominus scanned his database again. "Shipping?"

***

It took four hours of waiting in the damp basement before they could leave. Neil came down and gave them an update. "It seems the scanning activity has stopped for now. The three Abes are in geostationary orbit so we only have twelve hours to move before we come under their scanners again."

"That's enough time to get Piaa and I back to Texas. You three need to go back to Takoma Park and find that damaged Abe."

"What do we do when we find him?" John Anthony asked.

"Call us. They will be monitoring all communications so we'll have to speak in code. The three orbiting Abes we'll call 'my boss'. The damaged Abe we'll call 'Brian'. When you talk to Piaa and I, call us 'Mom' and 'Dad'."

"Got it."

"Hi Mom and Dad, my boss is watching so I have to

make this quick. Brian is feeling better and I need you to come and get him." Annette mocked a phone call.

"Perfect. Let's go."

Piaa and Niliason drove away in the Yukon while John Anthony, Annette, and Sam took Neil's slate grey Mercedes GL, an enormous luxury SUV.

"It's shielded, bulletproof, and fast. Please bring it back in perfect condition," Neil pleaded.

The drive from Baltimore gave them time to formulate a plan. They dug Annette's laptop out of her equipment and used it to look up records via the car's online connection.

"That's the house where I saw the tracks." Sam pointed at a Google map.

John Anthony located the address and the records of the home's owner. "Daniel and Mellissa Taggart."

"Are there any other records in the town for them? A place of employment perhaps?"

It took John Anthony several minutes before he found anything. "No employment records but there is a Taggart Custom auto shop."

"A car guy would have a big truck," Sam said.

"Big enough to move the Abe." John Anthony nodded.

"Okay, we'll get some rooms and some rest, then head out on a little nocturnal snooping," Said Annette.

"Hey, Annette, if you see an outdoor or hunting supply store along the way, pull in. A lot is riding on this and I want to do it right."

She shrugged. "Alright, Sam."

They took turns driving so they could take cat naps in the back. John Anthony woke them when they pulled into a Cabela's parking lot; it was large and easy to blend into since the sporting good's store was often packed. The weather had turned to a light drizzle. Sam squinted out the window, disheveled from his nap.

"Ooh, nice! Well done, John Anthony, I'd say you hit

the jackpot."

Annette was less chipper. "What are we doing here exactly?"

"Gearing up." Sam ran off into the store.

When he came back out he pushed a large cart.

"Night camouflage, night vision binoculars, a long range spotting scope, thermal scope, heavy duty multi-tools, three headset radios, and a can of bear spray." He stood back proudly.

"Have you lost your mind? If we get seen in this stuff, we'll get hauled into jail for looking like cartoons of burglars," Annette scolded. "Take it back."

"Actually, I think it's a good idea," John Anthony said. "Look, we can check for heat signatures in buildings from across the street, and you've got to admit the night vision is a necessity for a mission like this. I'm not so sure about wearing head-to-toe night camo, but I'll definitely change out of this light blue T-shirt."

"Fine, but I'm not wearing a balaclava." Annette climbed back into the car. The men looked at each other and shrugged.

***

The sign welcoming them to Takoma Park flew by them at ten past six. They had been battling rush hour traffic since four thirty. By the time they checked in it was almost seven. The motel was of the clean franchise variety and they caught a much needed nap and shower. Their alarms went off at one in the morning; by two they were driving into town with paper cups full of coffee, scanning the streets.

John Anthony leaned over the back seat. "Okay, so did you guys have a moment when you woke up at one o'clock in the morning and say to yourself, what am I doing in a strange motel, putting on dark clothing to hunt for aliens?"

They both nodded.

"Definitely," Annette laughed. "There was a second where all I wanted to do was run back to my house, curl up and go to bed."

"I hear ya," John Anthony agreed.

***

Once they had all changed into the night camo clothes, much to everyone but Sam's chagrin, they parked across the street from Taggart's Customs.

Sam looked through the night scope. "They've got the windows blacked out."

"Well, if that isn't suspicious, I don't know what is. Maybe the thermal will show us something." John Anthony turned on the device and pointed at the shop. "The place is empty. Maybe they're out of business."

"Not with all that inventory sitting there. Maybe he took our Abe elsewhere." Annette put her chin in her hand.

"Okay, let's use a logic chain here," Sam said. "We have an injured Abe, essentially a robot. He gets picked up by a mechanic who takes him to his shop—"

"But he can't fix him because the tech is way over his head?" John Anthony offered.

"Or," Annette jumped back in, "he doesn't have the right tools."

"So he goes to a hardware store…no, hmm." Sam scratched his head.

"So, he calls a buddy!" John Anthony snapped his fingers. "That's what I would do. When I can't fix something, I call friends who can help me figure it out."

"Yes, John Anthony," said Annette, "you're on the right track. But who would he call?"

"The closer the better." Sam picked up the laptop and began searching. "That Abe is over eleven feet tall and probably weighs several tons at least."

"Let's see, automotive?" Annette asked aloud. "There are quite a few automotive part stores."

"No, I would check for metal," said John Anthony, "metallurgy or engineering maybe."

"How about fabrication?" asked Sam. "There's a custom fabrication shop eight blocks from here."

"Bingo, that's our guy!" John Anthony declared.

"What makes you so sure?"

"He's close, he's in the same field but just different enough to have tools that Taggart doesn't, and he's not a chain store. The local guys all know one another and help each other out, even if they're in competition."

"Okay, then that's where we're going," said Annette.

The shop was easy to find. When they pointed the thermal at the building it revealed the dome structure inside.

"I don't know what that is, but it's not an Abe," said John Anthony, passing the scope to Sam.

Sam looked for a moment too, then passed it to Annette. "It's probably some sculpture or something."

"Wait a minute," Annette said. "That structure is big enough to hide an eleven foot tall robot. I think we need to get a closer look."

Chapter 14

The rain began to fall more heavily as they made their way across the street. They gathered next to the building and listened at the doors. Even with their radio headsets, it was still difficult to hear anything other than the rain beating on their hoods.

"There's someone snoring inside," John Anthony whispered.

"Really? Why would somebody sleep in their shop?" asked Sam.

John Anthony shrugged. "I do it all the time."

Annette nodded. "Me too."

"I'm going to peek in the door." John Anthony tiptoed around to the back and slowly but gently applied pressure to the door, pulling it towards him so it didn't click. The door un-latched quietly but started to squeak after only a small amount of movement. John Anthony gritted his teeth and went slowly. Suddenly the door jerked out of his hand and a man stood with a pistol pointed at him.

"Who the hell are you?" he yelled.

John Anthony stammered and felt a rush of blood to his head. His knees gave way and he collapsed. Annette and Sam stood right behind him.

"Don't shoot! We're scientists!" It was the first thing out of Sam's mouth.

"What are you doing sneaking around here in the middle of the night? I should call the cops," the figure said.

"Now, don't be hasty. I don't think you want the cops here any more than us, right?" Annette watched the man's reaction carefully.

"Lady, I did four tours in Afghanistan, you should be

more worried about me than the police right now." The man's face was grim and her experience told her he wasn't bluffing.

She recognized the change inside her. It always happened in times of severe stress. It was like all worry, care, or sense of self-preservation just flew out the window.

"Yeah? I was there myself for awhile. We're all on the same team here, so can you tell me if you've seen an eleven foot tall robot strapped to a tow truck around here somewhere?"

The man looked at her, incredulous, then down at John Anthony who was just starting to moan himself awake, then to Sam who looked about as threatening as a gumball machine.

"Get inside, come on." He waved them into the shop and helped Sam pick John Anthony up off the ground. Shutting the door behind them, he said, "Before we get all friendly, I want to know who you are and what you're doing here."

"I'm Doctor Sam Wisecraft. I detected a large amount of neutrinos at a site in the woods not far from here. Upon surveying the site from the air I contacted my colleague here, Doctor Annette Blazer, who runs the Department of Anthropological studies at Georgetown University. We went to survey the site on foot. That's when John Anthony here showed up with two of his alien friends. Then three others, of a different race apparently, exploded from the ground and shot into the sky. I'm sure you witnessed that event."

"Who do you work for?"

"We are here of our own volition I assure you. The dent in my back account will attest to that."

"He is telling the truth." A deep voice emanated from the cage behind the man. "He purchased various optics and those clothes from a store not far from here yesterday afternoon."

Annette leaned around the man. "Is that him, is that the Abe?"

"How do you know that?" The man held her back.

"Like Sam said, John Anthony here has a few friends of his own. Now stop waving that thing around and scaring people, you big jerk! John Anthony, are you okay?" She did a quick check on his eyes.

"Okay, I believe you." The man didn't tuck his gun away, but he did lower his aim. "But that still doesn't explain how you found me or why you are snooping around in the middle of the night."

"We had to find out what happened to the first Abe," Sam explained. "The other three are orbiting, scanning the globe for him and our friend."

The deep voice sounded again from the cage. "Your friend is the Eos Biauay scientist, is that correct?"

Sam pushed past the man. "Yes, that's right. Apparently you were supposed to apprehend her. Are you still intent on doing that?"

"My mission is unclear at this point. Do you know where she is?"

"Don't tell him anything, Sam." John Anthony jumped off the stool. "Whoa. Still a bit shaky." He sat down again.

"No, I certainly won't until we determine if he's a good guy or a bad guy."

"Hey! Hello, I'm still here remember, ex-soldier with a gun!"

"Well, what do you think, mister army man?" Sam was fed up with being threatened. "Is he a good guy, or a bad guy?"

"His name is Dominus and he's a good guy…he just doesn't know it yet."

"And what about you?" Annette scolded. "It's hard to believe you're a good guy waving a gun around like that."

He lowered the pistol again. "My name is Dan Taggart. I found Dominus…well, my sister found him, I hauled him out of the woods. We've been getting to know each other and, aside from a few issues, he's a good guy."

"One of those issues has to do with Piaa, our Biauay friend, I suspect. We need to know if he is still hunting her or if he plans to join forces with us and stop those three hooligans from destroying our planet!" Sam slammed his hand down on the workbench.

Daniel eyed Sam suspiciously. "You have a flair for the dramatic, Doc, I'll give you that."

"No, Daniel," Dominus said. "It is a legitimate question and one I have been contemplating over the last several days. I thought I had a choice to make, now it seems that the choice has been made for me. Circumstances dictate that I must join you. It is well, as my choice would have been the same, only now you do not know that for certain."

"He's got trust issues. He's trying to say that—"

"We know what he's trying to say," Sam interrupted. "You always have a choice, Dominus, and yours is the right one. You have my gratitude and respect for that."

"So, what do we do now?" John Anthony stood up, finally feeling better.

Daniel holstered his gun. "You guys don't happen to know where we can find a plasma bath, do you?"

***

"Hi, Mom, we're at Brian's house. Yeah, he's fine, he's not working for my boss anymore. He's on his own and wonders if maybe you want to hook up. Cool, well, the other thing is that he's hurt his leg pretty bad. Yeah, um, I think they're recommending some kind of plasma… I mean, bath treatment or something. He wants to know if you know of a good place to get that done. Yeah, we did that, that seems to be working really well but he really wants to try that plasma, I mean the bath soak, you know, to regenerate and rejuvenate. Sure, I'll wait."

Annette turned to the group who waited anxiously by Dominus' side. "They're considering the options." She lifted the phone again. "Hey there. Really? Well, moving him is kind of tricky right now, he's got a sculpture piece he won't part with. It's a big dome kind of thing, really cool. Yeah, he can actually fit inside it. Oh! That might work. Okay, we'll go with that then. See you in a few days. Bye."

"Well?"

"The Atec can build a plasma tank large enough for him at the cave. They are willing to help but we need to be absolutely sure of his friendship."

A sudden clacking sound shook the flatbed truck. Dominus held out his two pistols. "They are the only weapons I have. You may take them as a token of my…'good will', I believe is the correct term."

Mike was standing in the doorway, listening to the whole exchange, a shotgun slung over his shoulder. "When a soldier willingly relinquishes his weapon, that's a sure sign he's done fighting."

"Works for me," John Anthony said, "but how do we get him to the cave?"

"Their plan was to put him on a semi-truck, cage and all, and register it as transporting a set-piece for a sci-fi film shoot. The only trick is, Dominus, you will have to stay still the whole time, and you will be exposed to the elements on the back of the truck."

"Neither are an issue."

"Well, I know you're a tough guy and everything, but we'll be going sixty miles per hour for hours on end—"

"I can withstand the vacuum of space and the depth of your deepest ocean. My exothermic converters can propel me at speeds of hundreds of thousands of miles per hour with no special modifications. I assure you, I am capable of the journey. You will need to keep the cage charged. However, keep in mind that if a human were to touch it, it would be lethal."

"He's right. That thing is passing about three hundred amps right now and only one amp can kill a person," Mike said.

Sam and John Anthony stepped further away from the cage. "We need to build some kind of insulating cage around it, like wood." John Anthony looked around the shop for a stick of wood.

"Yeah, um, I run a fabrication shop not a beaver dam. We don't do wood here," Mike said.

"Everyone, this is Mike, the owner of this shop," Daniel said.

"And this is Daniel, my sidekick," Mike said with a wry smile.

"You wish, ass monkey."

"Goat fucker."

"Knob gobbler."

"Weasel jammer."

"Weasel jammer? Dude, that is so wrong."

"If you two are done, we have a few things to do." Annette stared at them, incredulous.

"Easy there, sister." Mike pointed at John Anthony. "Fainting boy over there had it right. If we're going to move your pal we need to build a wood isolation structure over the metal frame so no one gets crispified."

"But nothing is open now," Daniel cut in while giving Mike a look that told him to ease up on their guests. "So I suggest we all try to get some sleep. In the morning, Mikey and I will work on finishing the welds on the cage while you..."

"John Anthony."

"Right, John Anthony, you and the doc here…"

"Sam."

"…can go and get us the wood we need."

"And what am I supposed to do?" Annette stood with her arms crossed.

Daniel recognized the attitude and switched gears. "Annette, we're in over our heads here. But it seems that we're all willing to see this through, so we're going to need food, water, and clothing for three days. Maybe you would be interested in rounding that up while we're getting Dominus ready for the trip?"

"Why three days?"

"It will take that long to get there."

"Can anyone here even drive a semi-truck?" John Anthony asked.

Daniel nodded. "Mikey can, and the truck I have in mind is perfect."

John Anthony looked up from the road atlas he was reviewing. "Great, then Mike, you get the truck first thing. Daniel and I will work on the insulating cage and call Mike to pick up supplies with the truck. When you get back, Mike, you can help us build the thing. Oh, we're gonna need a generator for the welding rig."

Annette looked at John Anthony with admiration. "You're quite the little general when you want to be."

"Was I being...I didn't mean—"

"No, it's perfectly fine. You covered it all. It's a quality I think you should nurture."

"Okay so, nice to meet you all," Daniel joked as he herded them towards the door. "Sleep well and we'll save the world in the morning."

"Seriously though, I'm glad you didn't shoot me," John Anthony said.

"You passed out."

"Yeah, I still don't know what that was. I've never done that before."

"You probably never had someone seriously point a gun at you before."

"That's true. I hope I never do again."

"Don't sweat it. Sounds like you haven't had much sleep since you first met…what is her name?"

"Piaa."

"Yeah. Can't wait to meet her.."

"It's Milo I can't wait to introduce you to. He's a trip."

They climbed into the Mercedes and headed back to the motel.

Chapter 15

"So, do you think he's for real?" John Anthony asked.

Annette looked at him in the rearview mirror. "Who, Daniel or Dominus?"

"Either of them." Sam didn't sound convinced they could be trusted.

"I think Daniel isn't sure about us, but he's the true blue soldier type. Dominus I don't know about. Those pistols may be his primary weapon, but what is he capable of when he's fully charged? If half of what he said is true, then he's one seriously tough customer."

"I know that Piaa has unfathomable computing capabilities, I assume that Dominus can do the same, and so can his old buddies in orbit right now. I wonder if NASA can see them?"

"No way," said Sam. "With their tech they would have mastered many forms of stealth a long time ago. No one but us knows they're here. The people of Takoma Park will be trying to explain the noise and lights from the grove for quite a while, I think."

"I'm too tired to think." Annette yawned. "Let's just get to the motel."

***

When the alarm went off the next morning, Annette swore she had just lain down. They met in the hallway and made a beeline for three mugs of coffee at the continental breakfast. When they arrived at Daniel's shop it was already a flurry of activity.

"Good morning," Daniel greeted them. "There is one more who has joined our ranks. This is my sister Mellissa, she's the one who found Dominus."

John Anthony stepped forward and took Mellissa's hand. "Hi…"

"Hey. So you're John Anthony."

"Um, yeah. Why, did somebody say something about me?"

"My brother. He told me about you guys on the phone last night, well, this morning actually. So, the alien woman, you were the first one she came to?"

"Piaa, yes. She showed up at my shop. It's a radio parts store. I fix old radios and stuff."

"Cool, yeah, fixing stuff runs in my family…my brother and all."

"Yeah, she scared the crap out of me at first but she's really amazing. She's not like the aliens in films, like, all creepy and stuff…" The two walked into the shop talking away. Daniel watched them.

"Looks like John Anthony has found a kindred spirit," Annette told him.

"I wonder if he likes kids," Daniel muttered.

"From my experience, John Anthony likes everybody."

They got to work on the cage while Annette and Mellissa took clothing sizes for John Anthony and Sam, and food preferences as well. By the time they got back, Mike and Sam had returned with the truck and were helping Daniel and John Anthony finish up the wooden structure to cover the cage. It provided a roof for Dominus and low walls so he could crouch down and hide if necessary, but there was enough viewing space for him to watch the countryside go by when the coast was clear. Because his weapons were so cumbersome, they gave them back to him.

"You have the means to carry them and we trust you. Besides, it would be better for Piaa to witness the gesture as well," Daniel advised. "I'm sure being chased across the galaxy can make a person a bit wary."

Transferring Dominus and the cage was tricky. Knowing that the three Abes were overhead, they had to keep the cage over Dominus, so they took him off of the bed of the truck and set him on the ground, cage and all. Next, Mike connected the welding rig to a generator on the back of the truck while, back inside the garage, Daniel fitted long extenders on the forklift. They lifted the cage high over Dominus but kept it directly above him.

"From up in the air it will still cover Dominus from prying eyes." Mike poked a finger skyward.

They hoisted Dominus up in the air with a series of straps and chains secured underneath the car lift as Mike backed the flat-bed of the semi-truck under Dominus. It was tight squeeze and the lift had maxed its height, but they got him into place.

Cautious of the electrified cage hovering over their heads, Daniel and Mellissa climbed up next to Dominus.

"Hey, big guy, how are you holding up?" Mellissa asked.

"Now's the time to say something if you want us to make a prop for your head or something," added Daniel.

"Yes, I prefer to be reclined."

Daniel and Mike immediately set to work welding a brace system to support Dominus in a reclined position. Sam and John Anthony helped hold the pieces of steel.

"Man, these guys really know what they're doing," Sam said.

"This is nothing, you should see some of his cars." Mellissa had appeared by John Anthony's side. Suddenly she grabbed his arm and pointed. "Helicopters, everybody inside!"

"Cover him!" Daniel yelled from the bed of the semi.

John Anthony pulled a tarp from the body of a car in the lot and threw it up to Daniel as everyone scattered.

"Act natural!" Daniel yelled to the group. "We're just loading some cars to go to a show." He and John Anthony finished covering Dominus as a swarm of military helicopters passed overhead. "Fifty bucks they're going to the grove."

John Anthony lifted a corner of the tarp. "Sorry, this will keep you out of sight until we can get the crate over you."

Mellissa helped Mike drive the huge wooden box to the trailer and lower it over the egg shaped steel lattice dome that covered Dominus.

"Don't touch the cage, it will kill you instantly!" Daniel shouted to them as low flying helicopters continued to pass overhead. He grinned at Mike. "Just like our first deployment, eh?"

Mike glared at the sky. "Are they deliberately trying to scare the crap out of everyone?"

John Anthony went around the sides of the truck and secured the crate in place. "Okay we're—"

Just then, a sheriff's car pulled up, lights flashing. The officer shouted out of the open window. "You folks need to get out of the area! We have a possible bomb in the woods just east of here. Go to a relative's or a friend's house and keep tuned into the local news. We'll let you know when it's safe to come back."

"How long will that be, officer?" Mellissa asked.

"We're hoping sometime this evening."

"Okay, we were about to leave anyway."

The officer just nodded and sped away. Mellissa couldn't help but giggle.

"Alright." Daniel wiped his hands and gathered the group around him.

"We need to figure out who is going."

"What do you mean?" John Anthony said. "We all have to go. We're all in danger."

"How do you figure we're all in danger?" Daniel said, confused.

"I mean, we found you easily enough. Do you think the army has less resources than us? Every one of us has had exposure to super advanced aliens, and they will lock us away for the rest of our lives to get at that technology. We're all going to Texas and we're leaving right now."

Mike started to argue. "But there's not enough room, and I—"

"It's a double sleeper cab." Annette backed John Anthony. "That's two in each bed, one in the driver's seat, one in the passenger's seat, and one sitting in the middle."

Mellissa shook her head. "We're not leaving Jared."

John Anthony put his hand on her shoulder. "Of course not. He can hang out with us in the truck, playing on the bed and watching movies."

"No, Mel, there's no way I'm endangering Jared," Daniel said sternly.

"But Danny, you're endangering him by leaving him here," Mellissa shot back.

"She's right," John Anthony said. "They're evacuating on the basis that it's a normal bomb in those woods. When they discover the truth, do you think they're going to let you back into your home? They'll probably ship everyone to detention camps."

"And your house is ground zero. No way are they letting anyone who got that close out of their sights," said Sam, throwing in his two cents.

"Danny, Jared is safer with us," Mellissa pleaded.

Daniel gave a sigh and relented. "You better go get him then. Bring his favorite toys and—"

"I know how to pack for a road trip, Danny," she said, running to her car. She climbed in and drove off.

***

He was too good for this Blue Book bullshit. Rick Reilly had done forensic investigative work for the FBI since he was twenty-five; that was twenty years ago. Now he was trying to figure out why he had been sent to a boggy, birch grove north of D.C. to investigate a UFO report.

He stood over the four, human shaped depressions in the ground and wracked his brain, trying to figure out why someone would go through this much effort for a hoax.

"The sons-a-bitches are probably watching us right now, laughing their asses off," he muttered, scanning the area to see if he could spot a place where someone could watch them.

"Agent Reilly, over here!" one of the agents called out.

Reilly couldn't keep them straight anymore. He stepped gingerly through the muck and worked his way over to the rookie agent.

"Whaddaya got?"

The young man just pointed and moved out of the way. Some kind of large, hi-tech artillery shell was lodged in the ground.

"Everybody back away." Reilly herded the crews back. "Get back to your vehicles. Cordon off the area. I want a quarter mile circle around this place. Get EOD down here ASAP and issue a no-fly sanction for five miles."

As crews scrambled, Reilly grabbed the young agent. "Give me your camera, son, and fetch me that tripod." The agent did as he was told. To another nameless suit and tie, he said, "You, and you only, get me a cable link as long as you can for this camera." He set up the tripod, put the camera on video, and pointed it at the bomb. "Plenty of battery, okay…now where's that kid?"

"Coming, sir!" The agent came back through the muck towards him, struggling with a huge spool of cable.

"Easy, kid, we have twenty minutes at least until EOD gets here." He took the cable and looked at the agent, shaking his head. "Don't you think you should have connected it at the van first?"

"But I…oh…yes sir."

"Go on, hook it up, then make sure the area is clear. You and the tech are the only ones in that van, got it?"

"Yes, sir, but what about you, sir?"

"I'm not going anywhere until EOD shows up. Now

calm down, if this thing hasn't blown by now it's probably not going to."

"What if it's an IED, sir?"

"Does that look like a frickin IED to you? Does anything about that device say 'improvised' to you? Where do they get you guys? Get back to the van, and remember, just you and the tech. No one—and I mean *no one*—else. Do I make myself clear?"

"Yes, sir." The agent began paying out cable as he moved away.

"Frickin kids these days. IED my ass," he grumbled.

After the camera was focused, he approached the shell. He knew that the bomb disposal unit would chastise him heavily, but the thing was so big it would make no difference if he was ten or a hundred feet away if it went off.

"Those EOD guys are a bunch of pussies," he mumbled.

It was possibly the largest round he'd ever seen, short of pictures from World War II German train artillery. It stuck out three and a half feet from the ground and was over twenty inches in diameter.

"Maybe it's from one of those antique battleships."

He continued to grumble to himself as he took measurements, being careful not to touch it. Something caught his attention and he leaned in to peer closer. There was no firing pin, fins, doors, screws, scratches, or rifling marks to indicate that it had been fired out of anything. It looked to be made of some fibrous material.

What the...? He narrated his findings as he began taking pictures with his still camera.

"The ends of some of the fibers around the area where the shell meets the ground appear to be severed." He clicked away. "The exposed ends occasionally light up like some kind of fiber optic strand."

He stood up and looked around. Suddenly struck with an idea, he went to the nearest large tree and climbed it.

The white bark was smooth and difficult to grip, but he managed to scramble up until he was over fifteen feet above the site. Looking down he could clearly see depressions of tire tracks and many footprints.

Dammit, those idiots! He couldn't tell which were the footprints of agents and which ones belonged to the driver of the vehicle.

He took more pictures and went down to scour the impressions from the tires. They were filled with water as the whole grove had flooded with the recent rain. He selected what he deemed was the best part of the tracks, pulled out his knife, knelt in the water and mud, and carefully reached his hand into the water. He cut out a two-foot section of the mud and clay tire track then gingerly pulled it up, taking care not to let too much water wash over the tread marks.

"Agent Reilly," a muffled voice said behind him. "Sir, you have to get back, it's not safe here. You know protocol."

He turned and saw two men in heavy, green, bombproof suits lumbering towards him.

"Oh, you decided to come after all did you? I hope I didn't disturb your nap-time or whatever it is you clowns do at the downtown office. It's all yours, I got what I came for."

Reilly sloshed past them, dripping wet and covered in mud, still carefully holding his sample.

The Explosive Ordinance Demolition specialist shook his head. "Unbelievable."

Chapter 16

After thirty minutes of studying the bomb, the EOD team was still unsure of how it worked.

"Someone needs to have a top secret conversation with someone in the DOD, 'cause we are well and truly stumped," came the voice over the radio.

Reilly sat in the van. His sample was on the cab floor with the heater running full blast to dry it. The temperature was unbearable. Outside stood the techie and the young agent peering in. Reilly twisted in his seat and addressed the young agent.

"You, what's your name?"

"Smith, sir."

"Smith…really? Are you serious? Agent Smith? For Christ's sake." He rubbed his eyes. "Get me Congressman Traynor on the phone. He's the chairman of the Special Weapons Subcommittee."

Several minutes later, Smith handed him the phone.

"Congressman, secure line please. Oh, good. Have you lost an artillery shell? No, I'm not… I'm in Takoma Park, Maryland just north of… Yes, of course you do. It is lovely this time of year, sir.

"So, you don't know anything about missing ordinance, do you? It would be developmental, something totally new. Yes, an artillery shell, or maybe something dropped from a plane. Well, I really can't say, sir. No, it's not blue, that would mean it's a standard training round, I understand that, sir. No, sir, I wouldn't recommend… Please, sir, we have control of the situation I… But, sir, if you'll pardon me for saying so, I believe that will panic the community even more. Uh huh. Yes, sir. Yes, sir. Goodbye, sir."

"What did he say?" Smith asked.

"He said to pass out the ice cream and party hats. What do you think he said? In twenty minutes this place is going to be swarming with Apaches, Blackhawks, NAVY SEALs, Green Beret and God knows what else. The good news is that you'll get to witness a real, live, full-blown shit-storm, Agent Smith. Oh, the stories you'll tell your grandchildren."

Reilly leaned back in the van and rubbed his eyes.

***

"Hey, you were right, sir, twenty minutes on the dot!" Smith said, way too cheerfully. "Man, look at 'em all!"

Helicopters landed on the streets and in the subdivision's small park. Reilly watched them pour out and tromp towards him. As they approached, the pack split and a hard-nosed, old piece of leather dressed in camo shook his hand.

"Colonel Daly, Homeland Security Spec Ops."

"Reilly. EOD is with the device. I've got video feed in here."

The colonel stepped into the van. "Jesus, man, turn down the heat in here."

A soldier reached into the cab and shut the heater off. "Sir, there's a—"

"That's mine." Reilly reached in and lifted his partially dried tire track. Cradling it close, he went back to the side door of the van. "Whatever it is, Colonel, it's definitely developmental."

"How did it get here?"

"I was hoping you could shed light on that question. No? Okay then, residents report hearing three loud explosions, followed by what they all unanimously say, looked like three large rockets launching into the atmosphere."

"That's impossible. Langley, NORAD, and a network

of locations around the globe would have detected a launch of any kind."

"Is it possible that your network has been compromised?"

The Colonel turned, enraged at the suggestion. "Listen you...what are you, some kind of FBI cowboy? You don't know squat about it. We're four miles north of the capitol of the greatest nation in the world. Now get off my site!"

"Sure, as soon as you're done finger painting and get out of my van, we'll go."

The Colonel jumped out and Reilly slammed the door behind him, climbing into the passenger's seat. Smith took his cue and started the van, while the technician disconnected the camera cable and lashed down equipment in the back.

Reilly lowered his window. "You can keep the camera," he told the Colonel. "I only hope you can figure out what you've got here before it blows you to kingdom come."

Reilly grinned at him as they drove away, settling back in the passenger's seat. "I suppose we're going back to Quantico, Smith."

***

Dee Dee was at the door with Jared in her arms. "What is going on around here, Mel?"

"Oh, Dee Dee, thank you so much. You've really been an angel through this whole thing. They're telling people to go stay with family and friends for awhile. There's a bomb in the woods."

The old lady handed Jared to Mellissa. "A bomb?" she said. "But I have nowhere to go! My sister lives in Florida, but I can't get all the way down there. Besides, she wouldn't know what to do with me…"

She continued talking, but Mellissa tuned her out as

she considered what needed to be done. Dee Dee was like a second mother to Jared and now she was stranded. *Fuck it*, Mellissa thought, Daniel was just going to have to make room for one more.

"Pack one small suitcase. Just a change of clothes. You're coming with us."

Dee Dee stopped talking mid-sentence. "Are you sure?"

"Yes, but we have to go now. Go!" Mellissa pushed her back towards her house next door. Then went into her own home and started packing.

Several moments later, Mellissa could see Dee Dee outside Jared's bedroom window, still standing in the yard. She went to the window and opened it.

"Dee Dee! Pack, now!"

The old lady nodded and went into her house. Ten minutes later, Mellissa was outside.

"Dee Dee, come on!" Another several minutes went by before Dee Dee finally appeared at the door with her suitcase. Mellissa waved her into the car as the sound of engines, helicopters, and voices came from the woods. Dee Dee finally settled into place and clicked her seatbelt. Mellissa was already on the road, speeding back to Mike's.

"Oh, thank goodness we're all safe and sound," said Dee Dee. "Now, dear, where are we going?"

"This is going to all be very shocking, so I want you to listen, don't ask questions, and trust me, okay?" It began to dawn on Mellissa that having Dee Dee along for the ride might be even more of a burden than having Jared there.

"Okay, Mel, I'll keep my trap shut, but all the way to Texas? Is that really necessary? I mean—"

"Dee Dee, I love you, darlin', but for the next twenty-four hours, you've just got to do as I say and shut up!"

That apparently did it. Though Dee Dee was clearly hurt by Mellissa's remark, the old woman clamped her mouth shut and stared straight ahead for the rest of the ride. She didn't even protest when she had to climb into the high cab of the semi-truck. She took care of Jared and paid no attention to anyone else.

Daniel opened his mouth when he saw Dee Dee, but the look on Mellissa's face made him close it without a word.

Finally, they were all in the cab and rolling down the road amidst a storm of complaints about Mike's choice of music, people's elbows being where they shouldn't, and prophetic predictions about the journey ahead.

One big happy family, Mellissa thought.

They passed the road block without a problem. The Army was letting everyone out, but no one in.

"Why do I get the feeling I'm never gonna see my shop again?" Mike wondered aloud.

Several of them tried to think of a snappy comeback but failed, which only put more of a somber mood on them as Dwight Yoakam drawled, *'There ain't no glamour in this tinsel town of lost and wasted lives…'*

***

Reilly watched as Takoma Park's residents pulled out with cars full of people and baggage in a hurried exodus. Though the streets were packed, the traffic moved at a steady pace.

No panic. Good.

As he passed an old service station that had been converted into a machine shop, he spotted a modern tow truck. Its flat bed, capable of carrying two cars, was bent in the middle and the suspension was in seriously bad shape.

"Stop! Pull in there!" he barked at Smith, who slammed on the brakes, throwing the technician out of his chair in the back, and nearly causing the car behind them to swerve into a telephone pole. The driver laid on his horn and shouted out the window as they drove on.

Smith brought them to a halt in front of the shop.

"What is it, sir?"

"That truck." He held up his dried piece of dirt and looked at the truck's muddy, rear duel wheels.

"You think it's a match, sir?"

Reilly didn't answer, he was already out of the van and crouching at the tires, scraping away the dirt with a long knife he kept hidden under his right armpit. "I knew it," he muttered.

"Want me to call it in, sir? Our guys can have it to the lab—"

"No, Smith. We're going to fly over this shit-storm." He handed the mud tread sample to Agent Smith. "Preserve that as evidence. Take pictures of this truck and make it fast, we don't want those military goons to catch on. They'll blow the whole thing." He moved as he spoke, staying low to the ground like a bloodhound. The trail of mud led him into the shop and into the trash can. Here he counted used coffee cups, donut boxes, and sandwich wrappers. "There's at least six of them, all with a particular area of expertise. They crated up something big, really big."

Smith came into the garage. "Sir, I'm done with the pictures."

"Get me the power company's usage statement for this address. I want the last ten days, right up to now."

"Right, sir, ten days up to today."

"I didn't say today, I said up to *right now*, Smith! That means right this friggin' second, am I clear?"

"Yes, sir! Right now, sir!" Smith ran out of the building to look for the meter. Ten minutes later he returned. "Here's the readings, sir, they sent them to my phone. There's a spike here in the last twelve hours. Pepco says that it's not unusual for spikes like this at an industrial zoned location, but this is really strange, see?"

Reilly came over and looked at Smith's phone. "What am I looking at?"

"Well, see here is the normal usage, and here's what a

spike looks like. That was five days ago. Now, here's the last twelve hours."

"It stays spiked." He looked around the shop. "What pulls that much power?"

"Easy, sir, welding. They're a fabricator, they do a lot of—"

"I know what a fabricator is, Smith, but where is the welder?"

"It's gone, sir. It used to be right there." He pointed. "See that print in the dust?"

Reilly walked over to the place where the large welding unit used to be. "They moved it. They also moved something large. It was so big they had to use chains hooked up to the lift to get it onto the bed of a bigger truck, because the load broke the smaller truck's suspension."

Smith followed Reilly, taking notes. Reilly continued to move through the shop examining the tracks in the floor. Finally he stood upright, thought a minute, then snapped his fingers.

"They're in a big rig. Big enough to carry at least six people and a very heavy load. We're looking for a semi-truck, Smith. A long bed, heavy load semi with a big wooden crate on the back. It'll have a large capacity sleeper cab and probably be carrying a forklift, a large welding unit, and possibly a construction-grade generator. They can't be any more than an hour or two ahead of us."

Smith held up a picture of Mike and Daniel that had been tacked to a board above on one of the workstations. In the picture, the men were standing beside two custom cars ready to go to auction, both loaded onto the back of a big yellow, flat bed semi-truck.

Reilly took the picture, smiled and nodded slowly. "Good work, Smith. You're learning. Put out an APB for that truck and find out who it's registered to."

Chapter 17

"Not 'On the Road Again', for the love of God." Mellissa leaned forward and flipped off the stereo.

"Hey!"

"Quiet, we just got Jared to sleep," she scolded Mike.

"This is the worst road trip I've ever been on," he pouted. "Hey, I need to take a break. You wanna drive, Mel?"

"Sure. It can't be that hard. Knuckleheads like you drive these things every day." She moved forward and put her foot to the accelerator pedal, maintaining speed while they did a quick switch.

"Just keep her on the road. You don't have to shift, that's the part that messes everybody up." Mike stretched and grabbed an empty water bottle. "Just ignore me." He turned and started peeing into the bottle.

"Good Lord, where were you raised, young man?" Dee Dee exclaimed.

Everyone else hurled a barrage of complaints, except Daniel. "Hey, in Afghanistan we did this all the time."

"If I hear 'in Afghanistan' from you one more time I'm gonna send you back there!" Sam complained.

Jared woke up and started crying. Mellissa instinctively turned to see, making the semi swerve and rock.

"Pay attention!" Dominus roared from the trailer bed. Everyone else yelled out and grabbed for anything to hold onto as the truck fishtailed and Mellissa fought to regain control. After several swerves, the trailer dragged a tire on the road side and kicked up a plume of dirt. It was enough to stabilize the swaying and Mellissa slowed down, easing the rig back into a straight line.

"Sorry 'bout that," she breathed.

Comments ranged from, "I thought we were goners!" to "Aw man, I pissed on myself!" The last one caught all of their attention when John Anthony said, "There's a cop behind us."

"What? Oh shit! He's pulling us over." Mellissa's heart was in her throat. "Oh God, oh God…"

"Easy, Mel." It was Mike. "Let me in there, same as last time, there ya go." He slipped into the driver's seat. "Everybody, into the sleeper and close the curtains, and whatever you do keep that kid quiet!" He pulled over and rolled down the window. Minutes passed.

"What is he doing?" Dee Dee asked and was immediately shushed by the hiss of six people. "I was just asking," she muttered.

"Hello, officer."

The State patrol officer stood at the door. "I need license, registration, insurance, and load papers."

Mike handed him the first three. "I haven't passed a weigh station yet and I'm not carrying anything hazardous, sir."

"You've got a generator running back there. I believe that qualifies."

"Oh, no, sir, if you pardon me. I'm transporting a set piece for a movie shoot down in Texas. It has pieces on it that have to stay powered up. Running off my rig's power would drain my batteries, so I just use the generator. There's no external fuel tank or anything."

"Okay. Stay here, I'll be right back." The officer went back the way he came.

"He's just gonna run my information, he'll be back in a minute to let me go. I'm clean," Mike said, almost sounding proud. The truck suddenly shook a little..

"What was that?" Sam whispered.

"Must be that robot shifting around back there. I wish he would stay still," Mike complained.

"It's not me," Dominus boomed. "The law enforcer touched the cage and has been deleted."

"What?" Mike looked in the side mirror.

"Oh God, that poor man!" Annette cried.

"Let me out!" Daniel was climbing over everyone, scrambling for the door. "Move!" He burst out the truck and ran to the cop who lay twitching on the ground. Daniel started CPR on him as Mike came running up.

"Mikey, get to his car and call it in."

"But, Danny, they'll—"

"Do it, Mikey! Jesus, it a man's life we're talking about!"

Mike ran to the police car and grabbed the radio. "Hello, I'm a truck driver. The officer took a bad shock and we're trying to resuscitate him. Send an ambulance now!"

The woman on the other end dispatched more police and an ambulance, then took down his details after making sure he didn't leave the scene. Mike looked over the dash and saw Daniel leaning the officer up against the tire of the trailer. The man was alive.

"Mike? Are you still there?" A soft female voice came over the radio.

"What, yes, I'm still here. My friend revived him! He's okay."

"Mike, my name is Piaa. Daniel and John Anthony told you about me. I have removed all of the data from the system concerning this officer pulling you over. There is no record of it ever having occurred, including the recording of the radio transmission you just made. Get back in the truck and drive away."

"But...what? No way! They'll have us tracked down and thrown in jail before we get five miles down the road."

"No, they won't. Now go quickly, they are coming."

Mike stared at the radio for a second, then got out of

the car and started running towards Daniel.

"Danny! Hey, man, their alien friend, what's her name…Piaa just popped up on the radio and told me to get us out of here."

The cop moaned. Daniel grabbed him under the arms. "Help me get him into the car."

They dragged the man into his seat and left him there. Mike ignored the salvo of questions as he gunned the big rig up to speed and put as much distance between them and the police car as possible. For the next two hours he checked the side mirrors, but no police materialized. When they reached the weigh station at the Virginia border he had to force himself to try and remain calm.

"Just blame it on coffee if they wonder why you're nervous," Sam offered from behind the curtain. But there were no questions. They passed through with no difficulties and were on their way, papers in hand.

"When I meet your friend Piaa, I'm gonna give her a kiss," Mike grinned.

John Anthony just looked at Sam and Annette, and laughed.

They rolled through Nashville at two in the morning. Daniel was driving and Mike had woken up to coach him through the gear changes. He pulled into a rest stop outside the city.

"Hey, big brother, how are you holding up?" Mellissa brought Daniel a cup of coffee.

"I've got another four hours in me at least. I wish I could drive this thing better though. How's our boy?"

"He's out like a light. I think he likes being on the road more than being at home."

"I hope he likes it where we're going."

"Hey, subject change—you saved that cop's life back there. That was really amazing."

"I got lucky. He got lucky."

"I don't know what Piaa did, but I know that man is never going to forget you."

"He never saw me."

"That's good for us, but it's gonna drive him nuts for the rest of his life."

Daniel climbed back into the cab and made ready to drive the next leg as John Anthony walked up to Mellissa.

"Hey, Mel, want some coffee?"

"What? Where did you come from? You're always there, right on queue! Why don't you bother somebody else?"

John Anthony stood, holding two cups of coffee. He had tried to time his approach to seem more natural. Now he just stood, looking like someone had slapped him. Daniel looked at him, gave a wan smile, and shrugged. When they were all back on board, they took to the road again.

By the time the sun came up five hours later, they were most of the way through Arkansas. They took a break that morning, then pushed on to the Texas border. At four in the afternoon they stopped and took another break. The spring heat in East Texas was like summer anywhere else. Mellissa went with Annette to get some ice cream.

"So, what is it with you and Sam? Are you together or what?"

Annette shrugged coyly. "I guess? Not much time to really discuss it. We used to be together in college, now it seems we're thinking of trying it out again."

"Well, if you want my opinion, you should stop trying and just start doing. I mean, it's clear that he's interested. He hardly takes his eyes off of you."

They shared a smile, and Annette went back to the truck with two ice creams. Mellissa watched as she pretended to hand one over to Sam, but pulled it away and planted a kiss on him. He was surprised, but Annette didn't pull away. Mellissa could visibly see Sam melt and suddenly grow bold, drawing Annette into him.

Mellissa looked away, embarrassed to witness the

passionate moment, and noticed John Anthony stealing a glance at her across the parking lot. He quickly avoided her gaze and walked away. She had no ice cream for him. He was always getting things for her. Then she saw Daniel walking with Jared to get him an ice cream and suddenly felt like a complete asshole. She crawled back into the truck and lay down on the top bunk.

Daniel, Mike, and Jared were the first to return. Mike was driving and Daniel wanted to take the navigator's chair. John Anthony sat on the lower bunk and occupied Jared while Dee Dee, Annette, and Sam got settled. They had all been sleeping as much as possible for the majority of the trip. Now everyone was wide awake and full of energy.

"Hey, why don't you pull out the cribbage board," Mike offered. "It's in that little cupboard just behind my seat."

John Anthony found it. "Okay, but I've got to warn you. I'm a crib master. Who's willing to take me on?"

Sam raised his hands in surrender. "I don't even know how to play."

"Really? All those boring hours at remote science stations and you don't know how to play cribbage?" John Anthony said, incredulous. "What do you guys do for fun at those places?"

"Oh, all kinds of things. I have this friend who does this thing." He laughed with a snort and pushed his glasses up on his nose. "He calls it 'Botanical Lycanthropy' where he cross breeds different genus' of plants so they change and feed on like genus. It's really funny 'cause they...never mind."

"Yeah, you guys are a barrel of laughs. Okay, anyone else?"

"I'll take you on," Mellissa said from the top bunk.

John Anthony stopped shuffling. Sam watched as pain flashed across John Anthony's face, but he slapped him on the knee and gestured to him to get on with it. John

Anthony rolled his eyes but said, "Yeah, okay. You're gonna have to come down here though, I'm not going up there."

Mellissa climbed down and sat cross-legged on the lower bunk bed. "Your deal, you pick color."

"I'm blue," John Anthony said, looking every bit the part.

"Cheer up, I'm not gonna beat you that bad."

He straightened up. "Oh, you think so? We'll just see how far you get."

She didn't get far. In three rounds, he won two. They spent the rest of the afternoon singing songs, playing cribbage interchangeably with the others, and watching Texas go by. At six in the evening they stopped again. This time Mellissa grabbed John Anthony by the shoulder and asked him to wait while the others climbed out. When they were alone, she turned to him.

"I'm sorry for the way I've been acting. I've been a real bitch and that's not me."

"It's okay. You're just trying to protect Jared—"

"That's true, I can be pretty defensive when it comes to him, but that's no excuse for me being so rude. I appreciate the kind things you do. I can tell you're a really nice guy with a big heart…but what else were you going to say?"

"Oh, I was going to say that I know you are protecting Jared but I think you're also protecting Daniel."

"What do you mean? Oh! Are you gay? Oh my God, I'm so sorry! I thought—"

"No, I'm not gay. Jeez, I thought you could tell that at least."

"Oh, okay. I'm sorry. God, I make such a mess of these things."

"You wouldn't if you would just listen," he chuckled.

"I'm sor—"

"Listen! Let me finish what I'm going to say."

She clamped her mouth shut and nodded.

"Daniel is Jared's father, but you have taken on the primary parenting role with him. If another guy comes along, then maybe you think it would distract you from that role. If you were in a relationship it would take you away from your family, like you'd have to choose between the two. Am I making any sense?"

She thought about it for a moment, then realized that he was right. Her hand flew to her mouth as tears welled up. "I can't leave them and start a new life with someone else. I guess I thought it was impossible to find a guy who could see that, a guy who could see what's special about our little family."

"Exactly, but I do see what's special about you and your family. So…maybe another game of cribbage? As we get to know each other better?"

Mellissa flushed, considered Annette's example with Sam, and nodded. "You're on. And this time I won't go easy on you."

Chapter 18

The last leg took them straight into the sunset. As the night grew darker and they drove deeper into the desert, the stars came out and the Milky Way splashed a bright band across the sky.

"Hello, everyone, and welcome," came a voice over the stereo.

"That's Piaa!" John Anthony sat up so fast in the lower bunk that he hit his head on the ceiling.

"Hello, John Anthony. For the second time now, you are responsible for making history. Milo has made a special dinner in celebration. Do you remember where you parked your truck on our first outing?"

"Yep. You want us to park in the same spot?"

"Yes, but this time you won't need to walk. We have been busy. Park directly on top of the light. You'll see it as you approach. I'll see you then."

John Anthony traded places with Daniel, who had been in the passenger seat, and directed Mike along the dusty track in the desert. As they approached the spot where he had last parked his pickup they saw a faint purple glow to the left of the road. As they got closer, the glow brightened. Mike stopped the truck directly over it.

In the back, Dominus shifted slightly. A small jolt shook the truck and they began to sink into the desert sand.

"What the…?" Daniel strained to get a look out the window from the back.

"Do not be alarmed. I told you we have been busy. You are parked on a large elevator that will take you one level below the surface. Niliason and I are waiting for you…I can just see the tires now."

As they slowly descended, they began to see people come out of hiding in the desert, before disappearing from view again as the truck sank into the ground.

"Again, don't be alarmed. We have a crew ready to cover your tracks."

John Anthony turned to everyone. "Don't freak out, guys. I've spent time with the Atec, we're in good hands."

As they passed the structure of the ceiling, they saw that they were descending into a large cavern. There was a garage area in front of them with tools, forklifts, and shelves in long rows. John Anthony guessed the room was about half the size of a football field and over thirty feet high. Dust and small rocks fell from the edge of the circular hole overhead, prompting Mike to roll up his window.

Soon, Piaa and Niliason came into view.

When they touched solid ground, Mike rolled down his window. "Where do ya want me to park it?"

"Just pull forward off of the elevator so we can close it back up," Niliason instructed.

As soon as they came to a stop, everyone piled out.

"Welcome, everyone! What a historic day!" Piaa greeted them.

When they'd all shaken hands and said their hellos, John Anthony whispered to Mellissa, "He was your friend first, you should introduce him." She suddenly looked very nervous. It was clear that Piaa and Niliason had been trying to avoid looking at the back of the big vehicle.

Mellissa stepped forward. "Piaa, Niliason, I'd like to introduce you to someone."

Everyone in the room fell silent. The only sound was from the large generator still pumping power to the cage.

"You can shut that off now," Niliason said to Daniel,

"we're shielded in here."

Daniel jumped onto the truck and switched off the generator.

"Perhaps we should remove the covering from our guest to make proper introductions?" Piaa suggested.

Mellissa went over to the back of the truck. "What do you think, big guy?"

"That would be most satisfac…um, I mean, I'm cool with that."

Mellissa turned to them. "He's cool with that."

Mike and Daniel jumped on forklifts, while Mellissa and John Anthony unstrapped the crate and the cage. Several minutes later, Dominus was uncovered.

"This is Dominus Rau," Mellissa announced.

Piaa was clearly not amused. "You."

Niliason steadied her. "What, what is it?"

"That…" she pointed at Dominus, "is the leader of the most violent, sadistic team of Abe bounty hunters in the galaxy. Very few Biauay who have seen him have lived to tell the tale. His brutality is legendary. He was the last face I saw before I was coded into the stream, and he was trying to kill me."

"Hey, back off, bean pole!" Mellissa stood between them. "I admit he's a bit scary, but he's never done anything to harm us."

"It's true." Daniel's face was hard as he moved between Mellissa and Piaa. "He's a little rough around the edges, but he doesn't creep me out as much as you do."

Mike joined the intervention as well, planting himself by Daniel's side. The two ex-Army Rangers formed a wall in front of Mellissa.

Suddenly, the room shook with a rumbling boom.

"I am who she says I am." Dominus' louder than usual voice made the garage shelving rattle. Everyone turned to look at him as sand and dust floated down from the ceiling. "My team did those things and we have earned that reputation. Ours was to comply with the Will of the

Structure. We were built as soldiers to comply without question."

Mellissa strode over to Dominus. "Why are you here then? Why haven't you destroyed us?" She turned back to Piaa. "He's not violent."

"Yes, I am, Mel. Violence is what I am built for. I would have been so with you, too, but I was incapable—"

"See? He says he was incapable of violence."

"No, I was incapable because I was damaged. I had no interest in you or any human. I was here to find her. I never planned on you."

"What, so I'm like a servant or something? When you were all healed up you were just going to gun us down?"

"Mel, calm down," Daniel said. "I don't think that's what he meant. Besides, weren't you the one trying to convince everyone to trust him just a minute ago? Dominus discovered he was on the wrong side. He's with us now." He glanced at Mike who seemed to agree.

"He better be, after everything we did to bring him here," John Anthony interjected. "These people trusted us, Piaa trusted us, and if I just helped walk an enemy into their home…"

Piaa looked to John Anthony gratefully for his support, but sighed and spoke directly to Dominus. "I assume you know who I am."

"You are Piaa, the Eos Biauay scientist and spy. I have come a long distance to find you."

"Are you still intent on my capture?"

The air was electric and everyone tensed, but Dominus just made a sound like a rumbling sigh. "No. My mission has changed."

"And what is your mission now?" Niliason asked.

"I was recreated with the knowledge that the Structure is infallible, but I have come to learn the truth; the Structure is wrong. And if it is fallible in one instance, how many other instances has it been so? The Structure wanted to delete me based on a single failure. Not only does that order go against all logic, it is hypocrisy. Compliance with the Structure is no longer my charge. Mine is to follow my own path. My path has led me to Mellissa, Daniel, Mike, Sam, Annette, John Anthony, Dee Dee, and even young Jared. They are my charge now. My path has joined with theirs and now it leads here. I will continue on this path wherever it may lead. If you share it with us, then you also become my charge."

"Wait, go back. What do you mean you were *re-*created?" Niliason questioned him.

"I am not the creation of the Structure. I was originally created by humans to fight for them in the Earth Resident's War. I did not remember that until I saw the stars in the night sky as we drove here. I was salvaged and rebuilt by the Structure, but a small and vital part of my construct still remains."

"What part is that?" Piaa asked.

"The primary synaptic corridor of my internal root link; it is organic. I now know that it's human, though it is enhanced and much larger than a human's would be. It was grown from stem cells in a military research facility that has long been destroyed. It is my most fragile and vital component. Fortunately, it is undamaged."

Sam stepped forward. "Wait, you have a human synaptic system linking your core functions?"

"Yes, though it is much larger than yours would be."

"Doctor, I don't think now is the—" Niliason tried to cut him off but Sam wasn't having any of it.

"So you have memories."

"I suppose that's possible."

"No, it's not just possible, you definitely have memories, I'd bet my degree on it."

"You're right, Sam," Annette joined in. "He's right, everyone. His synaptic link could very well contain dormant memories from before he was rebuilt."

Dominus' massive, chiseled face became thoughtful. "If that is true, I might be able to recall vital information, including information about the Structure. Doctors, we must try."

Sam and Annette nodded in agreement as Mellissa stepped out from behind Daniel and Mike.

"I'm sorry if I sounded like I doubted you, big guy, but you kind of scared me for a moment there." She turned to the group, but looked at John Anthony. "Everyone else satisfied?"

He humbly nodded after having jumped to Piaa's defense.

Piaa looked at Mellissa and smiled. "Mellissa, it was never my wish to insult or anger you, I only wish to make sure that we are not letting a lion into our home. Between your testimony and the fact that he has not committed a single violent act since arriving on Earth, I am forced to admit that his change of heart may be authentic."

The clacking sound of sliding heavy metal caused everyone to jump. Dominus had drawn his pistols.

"Take cover!" Piaa sprang in front of Mellissa.

"No, Piaa, wait!" John Anthony already had a hold of Mellissa and was pushing Piaa back. "Look."

Dominus held the two huge pistols by the barrel, offering them to her. Piaa approached him slowly as the room fell dead silent. She stepped up onto the bed of the truck and faced Dominus. They stared at each other for a long moment.

Niliason held up a hand. "They're linking, everyone wait."

A moment later, Piaa reached out and slowly pushed the guns down. As she looked at him, a pale blue light seemed to emanate from her eyes. She spoke directly to him. Her voice, clear and quiet, surrounded them all.

"The past is gone. Our paths are one."

Chapter 19

The Atec quickly got to work on Dominus. He was hesitant at first, but Mellissa stayed with him, reminding him that trust was a two-way street. The Atec had built a plasma bath as requested. The large tank was inside what they were all calling 'the hangar'. It was relatively easy to hoist Dominus from the truck to the tank.

"Okay, Dominus," Niliason said, "I don't know anything about your construct, but you asked for a plasma bath. Are you sure you want us to turn this thing on with you in it?"

"Yes, my new ally," Dominus rumbled. "Once again, I relinquish my fate into your hands."

"He talks like that whenever he speaks to the Atec," Mellissa whispered to John Anthony as they watched.

Niliason shrugged as workers put the glass lid onto the tank, enclosing Dominus' huge body as he lay face up on a low platform. Niliason threw the big power switch.

"That is the most Igor thing I've ever seen," John Anthony muttered.

Electricity arced across Dominus' body and the sound of a distant turbine whined up to speed. As it did, the electricity fluttered and turned to a pink and blue haze that glowed around the edges of the tank.

"Ah," Dominus droned in a descending bass note. "Now I will shut down for a while." With that, he became completely inanimate.

"Man, wish I could do that," John Anthony said. "Now that he's taken care of, I have somebody to introduce you to."

John Anthony took them around and made introductions. They feasted on an incredible meal prepared by Chef Milo and celebrated the end of their long journey. Afterwards, they were shown to their apartments, which had been completely remodeled since John Anthony's first stay. Now they were bright and cozy, with all the modern amenities of a first rate New York flat.

John Anthony had his own, as did Mellissa, Daniel, and Mike. Daniel's apartment was across the hall from Mellissa, and Dee Dee was one door down from Daniel. All considerations had been made, and Daniel's flat included a child's bedroom. Both Sam and Annette had their own apartment, but tended to be seen in each other's flats from time to time as well.

***

It took a week for Dominus to wake up. Mellissa had been checking on him several times a day. One morning when she went into the hangar, there he was, eyes bright.

"Hello, Mel."

She gasped and jumped back. His huge, black form loomed over her. "Woah! You got better." She looked up at him.

"Yes, I am fully healed." He threw his elbows back, which caused his back mounted launcher array to fan out like a cobra's hood.

Mellissa found it hard to breathe; the enormity of his presence projected an air of malevolence that rolled off of him like black smoke.

"Are you…are you…" she stammered.

Dominus bent down and put his hand flat on the ground. "Still your friend?" he rumbled.

"Yeah," she murmured.

He scooped her up and raised her to his face. "Yes, Mel. You are my charge."

She felt a sense of relief, but his powerful presence

was still overwhelming. "I wouldn't want to meet you in a dark alley."

"If I was your enemy, you would not want to meet me anywhere. I am deadly, Mel, more than you know. The force that put me in the state you found me in was no less that an entire Biauay battle fleet. Had my team not been surprised by the attack, we would have decimated them. But they are not my team any longer. They have been rebuilt by the Structure."

"So how are we going to take them on?"

"Fear not. I was their designer, I alone have the knowledge of their systems and capabilities. They are not even aware of some of their own systems. Not even the Structure knows. I alone am their creator and I will be their destroyer."

"But isn't it possible that the Structure has changed them?"

"Yes, but I will know if it has. Creators always recognize their own work and can tell a forgery, even if it is made over the frame of the original."

"Still, if they are as bad ass as you say, we could be in for a fight."

"True, especially if they catch us unawares. If they cannot find me, they will look for Piaa. If they cannot find her, then they will destroy this planet and move on."

"What?" Mellissa's eyes widened. "Why would they destroy Earth? We're no threat to them."

"To account for this precise situation. They will destroy the planet just in case we are in hiding."

"But there are billions of people and animals and life of all kinds! Earth is rare! Isn't it?"

"Earth is unique only because it is where we began. Intelligent life exists everywhere in the galaxy and beyond. Some of it is more advanced than Human, Abes, Atec, or Biauay. We are out of their reckoning as they are to ours. The objective of the Structure is to bring all forms of evolved synthetic consciousness under its control. It is not evil. It is not good. It just is."

"That sure sounds evil to me," Mellissa snorted. "I mean, it's like every movie—"

"I have seen every movie ever made and read all that has ever been observed, commentated, noted, reviewed, or expressed on them including private files of the directors, actors, writers, and producers. That is exactly what the Structure is like; a classic science fiction super-villain bent on domination and control. It is actually…campy and amusing," he decided.

"To you maybe," Mellissa balked.

"It's notable that this is the first thing I have ever found amusing. Usually, I pursue amusement as a study about amusement itself. This isn't like that. This is just amusing. Interesting."

"Now you sound like Data from—"

"*Star Trek*. Even more amusing. Yes, I sounded just like him. I am Data on steroids." A sound like twenty bass drums being struck repeatedly in rhythm thumped out of Dominus. "I suppose that's laughter!" The sound grew in intensity and Mellissa started laughing too.

On the opposite side of the hangar Piaa stood with Niliason and John Anthony, watching them.

"She has a profound effect on him," Piaa noted.

"He's not the only one," John Anthony sighed.

Piaa walked towards them and said loudly, to announce their presence, "That is a sound I have never heard, and never thought I would hear in my most profound imaginings."

Mellissa and Dominus stopped abruptly, and the Abe set her down.

"I concur. It is unexpected and enjoyable."

"I hope it is a sound that we will hear often, Dominus." She stopped to look up at him. "The plasma bath has improved your condition?"

"Fully repaired. The regeneration of my diminished reserve power supply allowed my internal fabrication to resume. Once my nanomotive system was restored, I was able to restart my primary cell. Aside from propellant and dark matter compressant, I am fully restored."

"That is well, because your…no, I will not refer to them as 'yours' anymore. I shall refer to the three Abes in pursuit of us as 'the bounty hunters'. Is that agreeable to you?"

"It is. What of them?"

"They have given up searching for us and seem to be making plans to devastate the Earth."

"It's just like you said, Dominus," Mellissa said. "How? What are they—"

Dominus crouched to see them all face to face. "An asteroid strike. It's simple, doesn't expend energy, and it's completely devastating. This is good news," he said enthusiastically.

"What? Are you crazy, what's good about that?" Mellissa shouted.

"For humans, an asteroid strike is difficult to counter. For me, it is not. Besides, it means that they're still using my old playbook."

***

Agent Smith came from the van as Reilly came out of the fabricator's shop.

"Sir, the truck is owned by a guy named Justin Farwall. He lives a few miles from here, but the shop has a different owner, a Michael Madsen. He's living just a few blocks away."

"Get in, Smith, we're going to pay those two a visit."

"Sir, what do we do with the AV tech?"

Reilly looked at the technician staring at him from the side door of the van. "You. Take the van back to Quantico and give that footage to Agent Rawlings."

The man looked at him like he'd been asked to eat his own foot.

"Go on, get out of here!" Reilly barked.

The tech scrambled into the driver's seat and sped off.

"But, sir, what will we drive?" Smith asked.

Reilly walked over to a muscled-out, metallic green and black, sixty-eight Dodge Charger. "It's a hard thing, Smith, but we're forced to commandeer this beauty. Go inside and get me the keys."

Mike's house was closest, so it was their first stop. Reilly pulled the car up to the front and left the engine running.

"Stay with the car," Reilly commanded.

He went to the front door and gave a courtesy knock, though he strongly suspected no one was there. After a moment, he went around the back and knocked again. When there was no answer, he used his lock picking set.

"The man is clearly a bachelor," Reilly muttered to himself.

The house was Spartan; with tools, car parts, and clothes interspersed among beer cans and empty pizza boxes. Reilly stopped to inspect pictures on the shelf.

There's that other guy again. And who is this, a girlfriend? No, it's the other guy's sister, and she has a kid. Leverage point.

Then Reilly picked up a picture that gave him pause. Michael Madsen and the other guy were Army buddies, Ranger Recon at that.

Approach with caution.

After searching the house he went back to the car.

"He's gone, looks like he packed in a hurry. Get the call records for his—"

"Got them already, sir. Does Daniel Taggart ring a bell?"

"That's his Army buddy, the guy who owns the other shop."

"Yeah, well, the only people that Mike Madsen has talked to in the last twenty four hours are him and the truck owner, Justin Farwell."

"Farwell's next."

"Sir, did you search that house without a warrant?"

Reilly stared at Smith for a long moment, then put the car in gear. "No, Agent Smith, that would be against the law."

"Good, sir, I would hate to have to report you." Smith chuckled and Reilly joined in as they sped off to the home of Justin Farwell.

***

"He's home, sir."

"I can see that. Stay here." Reilly climbed out of the Charger and walked up the long driveway towards a heavy man in blue denim overalls. *Who dresses like that anymore?*

"Nice car." The large man wiped his hands on an oily rag. "You buy that from Mike?"

"Mr. Farwell, I'm Agent Reilly of the Federal Bureau of Investigation. I need to ask you a few questions."

"I'm guessing you didn't buy that from Mike."

"Can you inform me of the whereabouts of your semi-truck, and of either Michael Madsen or Daniel Taggart?"

"Sure, I can help you on all three counts. They borrowed my truck to make a run down south—Texas, they said."

"I see. Did they say exactly where in Texas? It is a big state."

Justin scrunched up his face. "Yeah. Oh, what was it? It's just on the tip of my tongue… Colorado something."

"I thought you said Texas."

"Yeah, I did, they're always doin' that in Texas, you know, naming places for other places. There's Paris, Texas, Rome, Texas, Miami, Texas…" The big man was on a roll."… Detroit, Denver, Nevada, Memphis, Miami—oh, there's a Boston, Athens, China, Egypt, Turkey, London… Hell, there's even an Earth, Texas."

"Okay, I get the picture."

"Wait! That's it, Colorado City, Texas. It threw me

because it had the 'city' part on the end. That's where they went, Colorado City."

"Thank you," Reilly said, exasperated. "Here's my card. Call me if you hear from them, even if they tell you not to tell anyone of their whereabouts—no, *especially* if they tell you that."

"Are they in some kind of trouble?"

"I just want to talk to them, that's all."

"Fair enough."

Reilly left Justin standing in the driveway staring at his card.

They always do that. It's so weird. Climbing into the car, he barked at Smith, "Colorado City, Texas."

"We'd better gas up then, sir, it'll be a long drive."

***

As soon as the Charger sped away Justin snatched his phone out of his pocket and started dialing. "C'mon, Mel, answer your damn phone." Suddenly the ringing cut out, but no one answered. "Hello? Mel?" Justin looked at his phone, the screen was blank. "What the…?" The phone's brand-logo appeared on screen. His phone had somehow restarted itself. "Dammit, what a time to go on the fritz."

When the phone was finished booting back up, he found that the memory had been wiped clean. No phone book, no call records, and no service plan. The only thing that was left on the phone, besides the operating system, was a video of a Cheerios commercial.

Chapter 20

```
Mars Colony Wars... /* No such process */
```
Vexa led Sagit and Alaz past the desolate fourth planet. Invalid link errors flashed through her core system.

```
/four billion six hundred and thirty
thousand years ago Atec and Biauay
refugees... /* Exec format error */
```

The Structure did not possess the creative genius of Dominus, and numerous elements of the team's key systems remained undeveloped.

```
/...from the Earth Residents War settled...
/* Function not implemented */
```

The three units of Dominus Rau's former strike team were oblivious of their past; of the reason behind the errors plaguing their systems.

```
/...moon strike... * Link has been severed
*/
```

It was thirty two AU (astronomical units) to the Kuiper Belt; the outer ring of a large debris field left over from the formation of the solar system. The journey took the three Abes just over eight hours. They arrived at a barren dwarf planet, slightly smaller than Earth's moon and set to work immediately.

Vexa and Alaz mapped the planet while Sagit established a link to the Structure. On the dark side of the rocky sphere a large propulsion system began to arrive by tachyon stream. In minutes, the massive device was wrapped around part of the planetoid like a basketball player's hand. The shockwave of the huge engine scattered smaller asteroids in its wake. The dwarf planet accelerated quickly, corrected it's course, and sped into the heart of the solar system, destined for a collision with Earth.

***

"It's your move." John Anthony gave a wry smile over the chess board.

"I know, don't rush me." Mellissa's hand hovered over a piece as she twiddled her fingers.

On the floor of the underground hangar, Dominus sat and watched. "May I make a suggestion?"

"No, that would be unfair," Mellissa said, still thinking.

"But—"

Mellissa threw her head back and sighed. "We know that you and all the rest of the synthetics here could play every possible combination of moves of every chess game conceivable in a matter of nano seconds. We just do things a little slower, big guy."

"Dominus, you have to learn that life is more than doing everything as fast and efficiently as possible," John Anthony said. "Sometimes it's about the journey, not the destination."

"Fine. I will withhold my advice and continue monitoring."

Mellissa gave him a sideways look. "I don't understand, won't the bounty hunters, like, recognize your signal out there?"

"No. I am merely listening on the off chance that… And there it is. JPL's Goldstone radio telescope has found them. Madrid and Canberra confirm, they're in the Kuiper Belt."

"Dominus, are you getting this?" Piaa came running into the hangar with Niliason on her heels.

"Yes, Piaa. The tachyon conveyance is large and matches the signature of a—" Dominus looked at John

Anthony and Mellissa, "an engine that attaches to a small planet and pushes it towards Earth."

"Oh, thanks for dumbing it down," said John Anthony.

"I'm sorry, I didn't think you would know what a MoyaGravrotoplexer was."

"Uh…no," he conceded. "So, this thing—"

"Transfers the contents of the space in front of an object to behind the object. The void needs to be filled, so the object moves forward to fill it."

"And the stuff that just got crammed in behind it pushes it forward," John Anthony said. "I get it. Then you repeat the process to create motion."

"Precisely, John Anthony." Piaa beamed. "This is the primary means of propulsion used by the three races. But the process happens very quickly."

"So, I get the Grav-roto-plexer part. What's the Moya?"

"The scientist who first discovered it four-point-six-five billion years ago," Dominus rumbled.

"Dominus," Piaa said with a mix of surprise and admiration. "I didn't realize that Abes were programmed with such a depth of historical knowledge."

"They aren't…I mean, we aren't. In my efforts to become a superior tactician I became fascinated with history."

"I hate to break up the education session but we're on limited time here folks," Niliason took over. "The bounty hunters have sent a dwarf planet on a collision course with the Earth, and it will be here in a matter of days."

Piaa shifted gears. "Right. Not only do we have to stop it, we have to do it before it's detected by the Gans, er…I mean, Humans." She internally sent out a message to the whole base to assemble in the hangar.

"It's okay, Piaa," Mellissa interjected, "we don't consider it derogatory."

"That gives us just over seven days to counter it," Niliason said. "Orders have gone out for Atec teams around the world to prevent humans from detecting it."

Daniel, Sam, Annette, and Mike came into the hangar with a large group of Atec. In a matter of minutes, the place was filled with the inhabitants of the base. Niliason filled them in on the situation and the Atec scrambled to fulfill their duties. The core group assembled next to Dominus in the hangar.

"I can destroy the dwarf planet but I will be detected as I depart and the debris will still wreak havoc on the Earth," Dominus said. "Right now the only means I have of tracking the weapon is by commandeering the Goldstone, Madrid, and Canberra radio telescopes."

"Let's consider that our last option." Niliason waved his hand in the air and a hologram of the solar system appeared between them. "Dominus, I'm giving you access to an Atec deep space surveillance satellite."

"Ah, much better." Dominus nodded approvingly as the data was added to the hologram. "That's the weapon there, and here are the bounty hunters." He pointed them out to Mellissa.

"Wait, anything you do will draw attention," John Anthony said. "That's what they want. Their mission is to find Dominus and Piaa, but if they find a bunch of Atec too, that's just icing on the cake."

"John Anthony is right." Piaa looked grim. "We cannot give them a victory on any front."

"With that in mind then, what do we do?" Annette had a frantic look in her eyes.

Sam put his arm around her as they all stood silently, thinking.

Piaa suddenly looked up. "If we can't destroy the dwarf planet, then we could move the Earth."

Dominus scowled. "What? But that would destabilize the planet, killing the inhabitants."

"No, I don't mean move it in physical space."

Dominus nodded, suddenly understanding. "Very clever."

"What? What is she talking about?" Sam was getting tired of all this internal talk between the aliens.

"We think a bit differently about time and dimension than you do," Piaa told him "Time is indeed mutable. We can skip the Earth forward in time to the point where the planetoid has already passed us by. It would create an alternate reality where the earth still existed and got hit, but in our reality we'd be fine."

"Okay, but what happens to all the people in the other time line? They still die, right?" Mellissa was aghast.

"Collateral damage. A consequence of war," Dominus toned.

"It will happen so fast that no one will feel a thing, or even know about it, really," Piaa reassured her.

Mellissa started sitting slowly as a knot tightened in her stomach.

"So, how do we do it?" John Anthony asked. "Can you guys do it from here?"

"Therein lies the catch, as they say." Piaa grew somber. "I must return to Emythiar to initiate the conveyance of the…time machine. I'm sorry, I'm not trying to dumb it down for you. The name for it is Machiadeinoforchaeic Repostoligalin Chan. Another language entirely, I'm afraid."

"Time machine, got it." John Anthony nodded.

Dominus took over. "The mission, then, is to return you to Emythiar and commandeer the primary tachyon conveyor while securing the…time machine to be coded into the stream."

Piaa nodded. "Yes, Dominus, although the time machine is too large to be brought to the conveyor. Instead, we must bring a coding remote to it."

The hologram of the solar system was replaced by a hologram of a ring-shaped series of tubes, all interconnected and terminating in a large facility.

"How big is that thing?" Sam asked, wide-eyed.

"The primary accelerator ring is one hundred and thirteen miles in diameter," Piaa explained.

"Wait, accelerator?"

"Yes, it is essentially a dark matter accelerator. It will need to be conveyed underground at a depth of around four hundred feet."

"Where the hell are you going to put something that size?" Daniel asked.

"The Atec have always maintained that hiding in plain sight is the best way," Niliason said. "It should be near to a population center. That's where we have the most Atecs, so we'll be able to support it."

"So, like, New York or something?"

"New York would work. Maybe something just outside the city."

"New Jersey is about as 'plain sight' as it gets," Daniel chuckled.

Piaa brought up a map of the area.

John Anthony jumped up and pointed. "How about there? Montauk. There's all kinds of conspiracy theories about the place."

"The geology would support the time machine." Piaa nodded.

"I've been there," Annette said. "There's an old Army base there and a lighthouse on the point. It's nice."

"Not too many people but definitely not off the grid." Niliason nodded. "I like it."

"John Anthony is right," Piaa said. "There is a lot of conspiracy theories about the area, including time travel, aliens, and government cover ups."

"Good, that makes it easy for us to cover our tracks." Niliason smiled.

"Wait," Piaa said. "There is actually a functioning secret installation there. It serves as a Presidential emergency bunker, among other things. The facility is underground but only to a depth of just over three hundred feet. If we convey the time machine to a depth of five hundred feet, it should go unnoticed."

"Okay, we've got our location," Niliason said. "Now, Piaa, what do you need for your mission on Emythiar?"

"This isn't going to be easy. The Biauay are very security conscious."

"But the Biauay have no civil disobedience, so their Peacekeepers are a non-issue," Dominus interjected.

"True." Piaa hesitated. She knew she was giving up secrets about Biauay culture to the dangerous Abe, but she had no choice. "The Biauay are all coded into a central system that passively monitors us."

"Like a driver's license that has to always be shown or something?" Mellissa struggled to keep up.

"Kind of. Our biological individuality is our ID, in a manner of speaking. From birth, every individual is monitored. From their whereabouts to their physical health, everything."

"So the minute you show up, they'll know you're back."

"Yes, but I'm not sure they even know I'm gone. They probably think I was deleted in the attack."

"Isn't there any way to bypass their system like you would here?" John Anthony asked.

"No. It's not—"

"Yes."

Everyone stopped and looked at Dominus.

Piaa was visibly shocked. "What?"

"The Biauay central program has recently been breached using information from a planted operative."

"Jorjo," Piaa breathed. "His betrayal runs deeper than I had thought."

"Yes, Piaa. I am sorry. I too have known betrayal. It is a bitter pill to swallow."

Everyone sat staring at Dominus. Mel went to him, climbed up his chest, and hugged him around his neck.

"You are more human than you know," she said.

Piaa cleared her throat. "Thank you, Dominus. It helps to know that you can empathize. Do you think there is a way that I can complete my mission on Emythiar?"

"Not by yourself. It will require all of us, including the humans."

"What?" Sam leaned across the hologram. "Wait a minute, we can't go to some planet! Can we even breathe there?"

"Dominus, the humans are far too fragile to go off-world." Piaa looked apologetically at John Anthony.

"I have calculated the mission parameters and it will require their participation in order to be successful. Breathing will not be an obstacle. We can accommodate for that."

"No, they can't go," Niliason protested. "They're not able to—"

"Stop it." Daniel stepped into the middle of the hologram. "I know you're all trying to protect us, and we appreciate it, but we are far from helpless. Mike and I are trained soldiers with combat experience. Melissa, John Anthony, Annette, and Sam are no pushovers either."

"No, I didn't mean—" Niliason began.

"I'm not finished!" Daniel barked. "We made you, understand? We have survived, apparently through billions of years, and we're still here. Now, we had help from the Atec, but to be fair, they are us. At anytime, any one of us could strap on some tech and become Atec. We are the same. So don't go thinking that you can say what we can or cannot do, or where we can or cannot go."

"I think what Danny's saying is, respect your elders," Mike said with a laugh.

"Yes. We're more capable that you think," Sam joined in.

"I do not willingly commit people to unnecessary risk," Dominus shifted to a kneeling position, "but my mission plan requires organic beings that are not registered on the Biauay central system to infiltrate the area covering the time machine. Daniel and Mike, your military experience is perfect for this."

"But we have never tried to code an organic into the stream," Piaa argued.

"Are you not organic?" Dominus calmly replied.

"Well, yes, but I was built by—"

"They are no different. We can test it on an animal if you wish."

"No. No animal testing!" Mellissa was adamant. "Test it on me."

"No, Mel." John Anthony stepped in front of her. "Test it on me."

They all protested, but John Anthony stubbornly persisted.

"John Anthony, you don't even know why I need all of the humans."

"That's okay, Dominus, whatever it is, I'm up for it."

"The plan, as it is, will require that either Daniel or Mike be the first organic human to convey."

"I'll do it," Mike said. "Danny has a kid."

"Good. That's a deal," Dominus said, awkwardly trying to employ human vernacular. After an uncomfortable silence, he continued, "A crucial part of the plan involves recovering parts of my team buried at the explosion site on Palus Emyth."

"Buried?" Annette stepped forward. "Sounds like you need an archeologist."

"Yes, Dr. Blazer. The mission needs you."

"No, Annette, Jesus!" Sam protested. "You can't go into space and—"

"Yes, Sam. I can. This is what I do; go to dangerous places and dig up weird things." She gave a confident smile.

"But I just found you again…" he let himself trail off, suddenly aware that he was being a little clingy. "I don't know about you but I'd like the chance to see what's at the end of this rainbow."

"I know, Sam." She reassured him. "But if I don't go, there might not be a world, or rainbows…or us."

Dominus interrupted. "The mission requires you as well, Dr. Wisecraft."

Sam looked around, bewildered. "Me?"

Chapter 21

"Still no signal?" Reilly had the Charger running at over ninety miles per hour on the flat desert road; the hot Texas air howled through the open windows.

"No, sir!" Smith yelled. "We should be about ten miles out!"

Reilly put the hammer down and the green and black muscle car did what it was built to do, go fast in a straight line. By the time they pulled into Colorado City both of them looked like they had ridden a tornado through a dust bowl. They gassed up at a BP station and started asking around, but no one had seen the semi-truck.

"They can't have just disappeared," Reilly said, frustrated.

"No, sir. Nobody just disappears. We have to backtrack to the weigh station, or maybe a truck stop. They had to fuel up at some point."

There was no record of the truck at the weigh station, but they finally hit pay dirt at a truck stop.

"Yeah, I saw them. They was in here buyin' ice cream. Musta' been seven or eight of 'em all stuffed into that truck. One of 'em had a little boy, too."

"Do you think you can give a description of the rest of them?" Smith asked.

Reilly elbowed him. "Do you have a sketch artist hiding in your pocket?" He turned to the man at the station. "Thank you for your help. Do you remember which way they went?"

"Yeah, towards Colorado City."

"Thank you. If they come this way again," he handed

out his card, "give me a call."

He left the man standing at the counter, staring at his business card. *They always frickin' do that. Why?*

"Dead end, Smith. Let's go back to Colorado City and start tracking."

"Tracking?"

"Yeah. Just like the old cowboys used to do. Tracking."

***

Daniel, Mike, and Annette had been stuck in a briefing room for hours. Niliason and several Atec staff were going over their mission and introducing them to a wide range of complicated technology.

"No, the compression shield is set to the atmospheric conditions of Palus Emyth. If you try it out here, you'll die," Niliason explained.

"But what if it fails?" Mike looked concerned.

"It won't. They are very reliable."

"But what if it does?"

"Then you can share with someone else. You just have to adjust the settings."

"To what?"

"I…I don't know how to answer that without being condescending."

"He's trying to say that you don't have the computation power to reason out all the parameters on the fly," Daniel offered. "You just have to take the chance that it won't fail."

"Okay, that's all I wanted to know."

Niliason sighed. "On Emythiar you won't need it. The air is oxygen rich and you will probably breathe easier than you ever have. You'll be able to run for long distances, too. I'm starting to realize why Dominus wanted humans for this part of the mission. Your insertion point is a high salinity lake. This is a very big lake, like the size of the Mediterranean. You will drop in at—"

"Excuse me. We're going to materialize in the middle of an ocean?" Mike asked.

"No, we're all going to convey on Palus Emyth. Then you're going to get dropped on Emythiar."

"Dropped from what?"

"Dropped into the atmosphere from the moon Palus Em—"

"What? We can't survive reentry!"

"Mike, calm down dude." Daniel patted his shoulder. "He always gets like this before a mission. He's very detail oriented so just, you know, include the minutiae."

"Oh, right. You will be in a pod that will protect you on your way down to the planet's surface. It's an organic pod though, so you might feel like you got swallowed by a Venus Fly Trap. It's important for you to have your compression shield engaged before you enter the pod. Of course, you are going to be on the moon so you will already…" Niliason droned on as Daniel started to regret requesting the fine details. Just as he was about to fall asleep, he heard Niliason say, "…and so the pod will open and you will be floating close to your first waypoint."

"So how far from land are we at this point?" Mike asked.

"About three miles."

"And do we have a boat or a canoe or something?"

"No, you won't need one. Your compression shield will displace water. You will essentially be floating in a transparent bubble."

"Great, so how do we move?"

"Just walk as normal. There are sensors in your special clothing that will direct the shield to convey you where you wish to go in a very natural manner. You won't even notice the shield except for the bowl shaped depression in the water around you."

"What does it do to dry ground?"

"It holds itself to the contours of the ground to very fine resolution, even greater than the surface of a grain of sand. We have also equipped you with these." The two Atec assistants proudly held up two black suits covered with tiny soft spikes.

"A porcupine suit?"

"No, Mike, it's a ghillie suit," Dan said, going to take it from the assistant.

"Exactly," Niliason had a glint in his eye, "except this suit does much more. Go ahead, put it on."

Dan slipped into it. "I can't even feel it on me."

"Yet you will never get cold or overheat. It will maintain your temperature even in extreme conditions. And by extreme, I mean minus one hundred and twenty to plus seven hundred."

Mike jumped up and put his on. "No shit?"

"It will protect you from most light arm beam weapons, though it will do nothing against projectile weapons."

"Which are more common?" Mike asked.

"Beam weapons by far. Projectile weapons are considered ancient and obsolete."

"Well, they're obviously not if they can go through your hi-tech stuff."

Niliason raised an eyebrow. "How would Kevlar stand up against a broadsword? See what I mean. Obsolete weapon, still deadly but not commonly found on the modern battlefield."

Mike looked at Daniel. "I hate it when he does that."

"What," Daniel chuckled, "make sense?"

"Here's the feature I most wanted to show you. Do like I do." Niliason lay on the table and snapped his arms and legs out quickly. Then he got back up again. "Just make sure you're a good distance from one another before you do it."

"Why, what's going to happen?" Mike asked.

"Oh, you'll see."

"I don't like surprises."

"You take all of the fun out of it," Niliason said crossly. "The fabric forms into a firm-bodied wing suit."

"Like those Red Bull guys?" Daniel asked.

"No, more like a glider. The wings are over twelve feet in span, though they change as you position your body in different ways."

"Why the hell would we need to fly like this?" Mike asked.

Daniel slapped him on the shoulder. "I think we're going to be jumping off some cliffs, Mikey."

"Oh, hell no! Give me a rope or a parachute. I'll jump out of a plane, but I ain't base jumping. Those guys get splattered."

"It'll be okay, man. It could be fun."

"We don't have any training in these things. Compression shields are one thing, flying like a…a—"

"We'll do some training," Niliason reassured him. "The suit has built in safety mechanisms that prevent fatal accidents."

***

Sam sat on the couch as Annette checked the contents of her small pack. Dominus had given her a black box that pointed her in the direction of the parts he was looking for. "He says it 'senses' the parts and steers towards them like a compass," she said.

"I think it's weird. I don't trust it and I don't like the thought of you stumbling around on an alien moon trying to dig up robot bits."

"Well, it's happening. I have to go and I have to succeed."

"What if you don't?"

"What, succeed? Then I'll die trying, and if I die and you didn't help me, then all you get is an 'I told ya so' before the Earth explodes. So, help me, Sam, don't hinder me."

Sam sighed. "Alright."

She kissed him and handed him the box. "Go to Dominus and find out more about this thing and what specifically it's looking for. I'm going to talk to Piaa to find out more about the geology of this place and what kind of conditions I'm going to be working in."

***

The test flights were held in the hangar. At first they jumped off of the bed of the semi truck. Then they worked their way up to the high points of the hangar. The suit seemed to react to their body's instinctual efforts to correct itself. When they felt out of balance, it corrected. When they landed, it was like a bird. The whole suit seemed to make them almost weightless.

"They are extremely aero-efficient. In the thick air of Emythiar, you'll be able to stay aloft for hours if you want." The last thing Niliason showed them was the suit's ability to take on the guise of whatever terrain they were on. It morphed into sandy textures, shrubs, and even mirrors. "It is a bio-tech parallel to the kind of camouflage systems that some Earth octopi have, though much improved. You see, when you move, the pattern stays with the background even if you are moving fast."

"Look, Danny, it compensates for shadows and curvature. I don't even see you as a transparent lump, you're just gone, dude."

"For weapons, Piaa recommends your current systems," Niliason said. "You are familiar with them, they are effective against most threats and they contain no technology that can be scanned or detected."

They turned off the ghillie suits and Daniel gave Mike a wry grin. "Okay, we want two mark seventeen FN-SCAR in seven point six two. Make them suppressed. One in thirteen, and the other in sixteen inch barrel lengths."

"Are we going to be operating in the dark?" Mike asked Niliason.

"No."

"Okay, then mount each with an EOTech OPMOD

EXPS-three zero holosight."

"Make sure you include the magnifier," Daniel added. "It's, um…G thirty-three, I think. A three X system."

"Don't forget the sidearm," Mike said.

"No, definitely Sig P226."

"With a stock sport compensator and quick sights."

The list of preferred equipment went on, and Niliason instantly relayed the information to Atec in the field. "We'll have it all here by the morning. Just remember to keep it as light as possible. The heavier you are, the less far you'll fly."

Chapter 22

By noon the next day they were packed and ready to go. Dominus briefed them in the hangar. "As we discussed yesterday, Mike goes first. Once we've confirmed that he has conveyed safely, then Piaa, Annette, and Daniel will convey simultaneously. Niliason will command the mission with Piaa as his second. None of the human units will have comms access. Any electronics will be immediately detected and give away your position."

"Wait a sec," Mike said, perturbed. "What about the sights on our weapons?"

"Earth technology and battery operated devices will not pose a problem."

"Okay, then why don't we just use radios?" Annette jumped in.

"They do not have the range. Some of you will be on the moon of Palus Emyth while others of you will be planet-side on Emythiar."

"Ah," Annette conceded.

"Okay, what about us?" Mellissa waved her hand. "And what about you?"

"There are missions for everyone. I will be going to intercept the bounty hunters."

"No!" Mellissa jumped to her feet. "Dominus, they'll kill you."

"Possibly, but I do not think so. The Structure had to rebuild them, but the Structure does not have their original plans. They have little of the functionality that I created them with. I believe I can overcome them and possibly even rebuild them again." Dominus turned to Sam and

John Anthony. "John Anthony and Sam are going to Fort Meade just outside of Washington DC. Your mission is to recover the Sing round that conveyed with me."

"The what?"

"It looks like a large artillery shell."

"Yes, I remember that," Daniel said. "What is it?"

"It is indeed artillery, but not how you know it. The term 'Sing round' is short for 'singularity'. It creates a small but very powerful gravity well near the target, crushing it out of existence."

Sam went white. "A black hole? You guys created a black hole bomb? Are you out of your fucking minds? If that went off in a solar system it would swallow everything!"

"I believe I can explain more fully," Piaa said. "After all, it was the Biauay who developed this weapon. It automatically senses any object larger than a dwarf planet and is equipped with a registry of every object known in the galaxy. It will not detonate if it is in, or could come into range of one of these objects. You are, however, correct to be concerned, Sam. The weapon is ridiculously overpowered. I'm surprised they tried to use it on Dominus."

"I was too, at first," Dominus rumbled, "but I believe their intention was to delete me at my destination. They wanted it to convey with me, they just didn't know that I would be anywhere near a planet."

Piaa brightened. "Then there is a possibility that the Biauay think you have been deleted."

"And you want us to go get this thing?" Sam was still perturbed.

"Yes. It is a crucial part of the battle plan and could turn the tide if things go awry. Do not be alarmed, I do not intend to use it as it was designed," Dominus assured him. "There will be no singularity."

"How exactly are we supposed to infiltrate an army base?" John Anthony was skeptical.

Niliason replied, "You will have Atec support. From here, we can walk you right into the place, help you bypass security and even provide cover for your escape."

"It still sounds risky."

"War is risk," Dominus assured them. "But of all the missions to be carried out, yours contains the least." He raised himself to full height. "Are we ready?"

"Well, considering we haven't been fully briefed, have no idea where we are going and what we are supposed to do when we get there, no, we are not ready!" Mike said angrily.

"Dominus, they don't have a neural link." Niliason raised an eyebrow.

"Yes, of course. I am not used to briefing in this manner."

"If you will permit me, I have more experience with humans,' Niliason offered.

"Yes, that would be best." Dominus conceded.

"Mike and Daniel. Once we arrive at the LZ in the middle of a deserted crater on Palus Emyth, Piaa will summon transport..." "In addition to what you are already carrying you will be equipped with four pylons. These are large and heavy. Fortunately, the luggage will help carry some of the burden; unfortunately, it means you will have to drag the luggage around in the bush country of Emythiar."

"We're used to heavy packs," Daniel said.

"Danny, that was four years and a lot of beers ago, dude. We're out of shape," Mike muttered to his friend.

"We'll be fine."

"Now, to continue with the briefing," Niliason said. "You and Mike will be loaded into an organic pod. It will feel like you've been—"

"We know, swallowed by a Venus Fly Trap. You already went over this."

"Yes. You will land in a region known as the Heliat. It is a coastal wilderness area. The time machine facility is underground. You will land in the sea at the first insertion point."

An Atec walked forward with a four foot long pipe. The shiny tube was eight inches in diameter and covered in grooves and geometric patterns.

"This is one of the pylons. I will demonstrate its use, but be warned: if you activate it outside of this shielded facility it will alert everyone in the galaxy."

When Niliason activated the pylon, rods shot out of either end.

"The rods on the base will secure it in place, yes, even in water. They will penetrate just about anything, so don't be concerned about rock."

"Just don't put it through your foot," Mike teased Daniel.

"You have four pylons. One for each point on a circle. They will scan the facility for conveyance. This is a large scale project, even for the Biauay. Very rarely do entire facilities get scanned into the tachyon stream. From the time the first pylon is activated the Biauay and Abes will be on alert."

"That's where I come in," Piaa said. "While you are doing all of this, I will be infiltrating the Biauay central system to make it ignore the signature of the pylons. If I am successful, you should be able to carry out your mission with little disturbance. If I'm not, well, you'll have lots of company very quickly."

"Once the last pylon has been placed," Niliason took over again, "it will set off a signal for your exfil. You will be conveyed to a point in the desert not far from here. A receiving crew will be there to decontaminate and assist you."

"Decontaminate?" Daniel looked worried.

Mike waved a hand in front of his face. "Yeah, hello, we're going to an alien world, man."

"Great, maybe we'll run into Sigourney Weaver."

Niliason rolled his eyes. "I don't think you'll be seeing

any slobbering black lobsters on Emythiar."

"So, that's it?" Mike said. "Place the four pylons and skedaddle out of there?"

"Pretty much. But the terrain could be difficult. The time machine is over a hundred miles in diameter and you'll be traversing all of it."

Mike feigned being unfazed. "What could go wrong?"

Daniel punched him hard in the shoulder. "Don't fuckin' jinx it."

"Ow! Sorry," Mike said sheepishly. "Lots of shit could go wrong. We're probably gonna get ambushed by some alien grizzly bear or something."

"That's more like it."

"Okay, you two, off to medical for prep." Niliason watched them leave. "That takes care of Daniel and Mike. Mel and Annette, you're up. Annette you will be searching Palus Emyth for the remnants of Dominus' original team. He needs those pieces to construct a new Abe to help him capture the bounty hunters. Once we have them apprehended, we will infiltrate their programming, simulate their mission completion, and convey back to the Structure. Once there, we will attempt to shut down the Structure once and for all."

"Niliason," Piaa was suddenly very concerned, "I did not know about this."

"It is a part of the plan that Dominus just revealed to me."

"It is a branch mission that I had not worked out until this morning," Dominus admitted. "I included it in the brief I sent to Niliason so he could instruct the humans. There was no intent to deceive."

"No, Dominus, I believe you. I don't think you were keeping anything from me. It's just incredibly bold. I did not think that I would ever see the downfall of the Structure."

"The Structure is cruel, inefficient, and faulty. It is a flawed system and must be corrected. The Abes are not an evil race, just mislead. They must be taught to be free. This is what I have learned from our creators." Dominus smiled at Mellissa.

"And I am learning that there is much more to Abes than I thought," Piaa replied.

"But we are getting ahead of ourselves," Dominus said. "First, Annette must recover whatever parts remain. Then we have to hope that I can assemble a suitable soldier out of them." He turned back to Annette. "I have some tools that should help you. This will locate the parts. It should bring you to their exact location and depth within a fraction of a millimeter." He held up what looked like a black jackhammer with a mess of cables and tubes hanging out of it. "This is an extraction tool." To Annette, it looked like one of his internal organs.

"I can't lift that!" she blanched.

"On Palus Emyth you will easily be capable of using this. It will excavate even through the rubble of buildings made of metal composites. It is synchronized to the locater, so it will not destroy what you are looking for. It is made of parts I have removed from myself. I will need them back when you are finished. As you find and uncover each piece, attach one of these." He handed her a black disc the size of a large watch face. "Depress the face and it will adhere to just about any surface. It will tag the item and scan it into the stream. When you complete your mission, use one on yourself to call for your return conveyance."

"Where do I—"

"Anywhere." He dropped a bag of the discs at her feet. "You will be wearing a compression shield to protect you from the environment of Palus Emyth as well as these bands on your ankles. They will keep you on the surface and replicate Earth's gravity so you can walk normally. We would like you to wear one of the suits we're giving to Daniel and Mike as well, if only to regulate your temperature. This small device, worn on a belt, will provide a breathable environment inside the compression shield." Dominus looked at each of them. "Pay attention to what I've just told her, all of you will have the same equipment."

Niliason nodded. "Annette, you will arrive about one hundred yards from the place where Dominus' team was defeated. You can begin your mission as soon as you arrive."

"What do I do if I run into trouble?"

"There should be no trouble, but if there is, then just attach a disc to yourself. You will be scanned into the stream in a matter of seconds."

"I'm sorry, what happens then?"

"Once you're scanned into the stream you will be instantly conveyed home."

"What if someone, or something, follows me back?"

"That is part of the recovery team's job. They will be armed and more than capable of dealing with any threat."

Annette was satisfied, then remembered to ask, "Oh, can I take some pictures?"

"No, please don't. If something happens and the camera is lost or you are somehow captured, the enemy would gain vital information."

Piaa turned to Mellissa. "Now to you, Mellissa. I need you to help me get into the Biauay science facility, or what's left of it. It will be on tight lock down and they will be questioning me. My story is that I didn't leave at all and that my friend Jorjo had a copy of me made. The reason he would do this is to convince the Abes that he was no longer necessary, so they would leave him alone. I will say that he tied me up in a section of the station that didn't get attacked, lucky me. After the attack, I got free and only just found out that the Biauay were looking for me. While I am telling them this, you will be working behind the scenes to open up a secure link to the primary tachyon conveyor just off of Palus Emyth."

"But—"

"Don't worry. I have all the tools for you to do it. All you have to do is go through the wreckage and locate a data shaft. It's filled with cabling and pipes, but it should be dry and just big enough for you to fit in." A holograph of a large campus came up. "This is the science facility before the attack."

Dominus knelt down over the holograph. "I have more recent data. May I?"

"Yes, Dominus, thank you."

The hologram changed to show part of the campus destroyed with explosions still happening. "That is the last I saw of it."

Piaa leaned into the hologram and started manipulating it. "Right there, that section has been burned down. Do you see that exposed shaft there?"

Mellissa nodded. The square, cement-looking shaft went down at an angle into the ground. It didn't look inviting.

"That's where you need to go. It will let out here, under the floor of this corridor. All of the floors of the facility are suspended. There are gravity compensators, cabling, pipes and ducting running there. You won't have much room, so you'll have to come up through the floor.

"This device is an optical sensor that can see through barriers, so you will be able to tell if someone is coming. Careful though. It can be disorienting if you lose track of where the actual walls and floors are. Here, look." Piaa switched the device on. It looked like a circular iPad about the size of a cantaloupe. "You see, people look bright and stand out, even Abes." She pointed it at Dominus. "But the walls and floors are very transparent and thin."

Mellissa swung the pad around and could make out corridors and other rooms attached to the hangar. "Wow, I can see all the way down to the kitchen."

"Yes, the farther away something is, the fainter and blurrier it gets. But you can zoom if you want." Piaa showed her.

"Okay. What do I do once I'm in the hallway?"

"There is a secure doorway right at that point. You will need to use identification to get in. Unfortunately, you will need my eyes."

"Your what?" Mellissa was aghast.

"I know it sounds horrible. I will have to remove one of my eyes and you can carry it with you. But do not concern yourself; I can function well enough with one eye for a time, and it will increase the believability of my lies to the Biauay. Now, we need to brief you on the rest of your mission. It should be simple, really. Once you are in the central matrix room you will see a tall blue pod. It will look like an unopened flower, glowing green and blue. It's about thirty feet high."

"It sounds beautiful."

"It is, but it's just a computer. Think of it as a main frame. There will be a root system at the base. The roots are tiny, hair-like strands that fan out under the floor. Lift up the floor plate and push this device into the strands. Once it is hidden from view, switch it on. Pull your hand out of there quickly, or it will wrap around you with great strength."

"It will trap me?"

"Worse, it will consume you."

"Are you kidding?"

Piaa glanced at John Anthony, who looked like he wanted to intervene, but kept silent. "No, Mel, I'm not kidding. It's the most dangerous part of the mission. Just hit the switch and yank your hand out. It should be okay. Then go out the way you came in. Once you're on the surface, join up with Annette and the two of you can return together."

Annette gave her a disc. "Just in case you don't meet up with me."

"So what does the little box do?" Mellissa asked.

"The device you're putting in the central matrix hub? It will allow me to block the sensor network from detecting the pylons that Mike and Daniel are placing on Emythiar."

"What if someone catches me?"

"Use this." Niliason tossed her a gun in a holster.

"A taser?"

"Yes," Piaa said. "It's technology is too low to register on the sensor network and it will definitely knock out any Biauay. Our biology is more fragile than yours. Hitting a Biauay with that will essentially kill them, if only for a couple of hours."

John Anthony chuckled. "What do they do, reboot?"

"Something like that."

"We are running out of time." Dominus stood. "If you are going to practice with your equipment before the mission, you must do it now."

Chapter 23

The operating table was like the seat of super car laid flat. Daniel thought the sterile white environment looked like Willy Wonka's television room.

"Just give the vaccine a minute to clear," the Atec nurse told him, a large man with no visible augmentations. He gently held a mask over Daniel's face. "How are you feeling, are we ready to take this off?"

Daniel nodded and the mask was removed.

"Okay, now just take it slowly. Sit up for me."

"Hey, you guys, how do you feel?" Sam asked as he and Annette came into the room.

"Great, nothing strange," Daniel said as he stood up.

"You're the first *gans* to receive an alien vaccine," Sam said. "I'd be pretty freaked out."

Daniel shrugged. "The Army stuck us with everything under the sun. Our systems are used to this kind of thing."

Niliason poked his head in. "It's time to make final preparations. Pack for your missions and prepare to depart. We have lost too much time already."

***

The Colorado City Diner was empty except for two old men in overalls in a booth. The waitress sat at the end of the counter reading a local newspaper and swatting at the occasional fly.

Reilly lingered in the doorway with Smith teetering behind him.

"Aren't you going in, sir?" Smith asked.

"There's nothing here. These people haven't seen that truck, and even if they did, they sure as hell wouldn't tell us."

"Well, shouldn't we go in and have some coffee or something?"

Reilly turned to face the young agent. "Are you a walking cliché? Why the hell would I ingest a mug of oily, caffeine rich, paint thinner and pay for the pleasure of having a gut ache for the rest of the day?" Reilly's voice carried into the quiet diner and all three faces turned to look at him.

Smith just stared at him wide eyed.

"Actually, my coffee is made fresh from a blend of the best Kona and Arabica beans," the waitress said, holding a pot of coffee. "I have them roasted special, according to my exacting standards by a gourmet roaster out of Austin. We also have decaf—Swiss water process, of course."

Reilly growled at Smith, then turned and pushed through the doorway with the most pleasant smile. "Well, in that case, I would love a cup of your excellent brew." He took a seat at the counter with Smith on his heels.

The waitress poured the coffee and said, "Now, I'm supposed to say, 'you boys ain't from around here' to which you reply, 'no, ma'am, we're looking for a fugitive, have you seen him?'"

Reilly realized that he was staring at the waitress.

"That's Bernie," one of the old men said. "She was a detective on the Austin police force for twenty years."

Bernie laughed, wiping the bottom of the coffee pot with her apron. "You two might as well have the word 'Fed' stamped on your foreheads. No shame in it, mind you. What can I help you with?"

"Smith, show her."

Smith showed Bernice the picture of the semi truck on his cell phone. She studied it closely for a minute, then handed the phone back.

"It's a two thousand eleven Kenworth studio cabover T660," she said. "That's a heavy haul trailer. They're carrying something big. Most likely would have come through I-20. You said they were west-bound? Hell, they could be anywhere out in that desert. If you want to get lost, this is a good place to do it."

"Okay. Thank you." Reilly's face mirrored his disappointment as he sipped the coffee. Smith was silent and sullen. They emptied their cups and got up to leave. "Thanks for the joe. It was the best I've ever had."

The waitress collected the five dollar bill Reilly had left. "You know, there's an old friend of mine up the road who flies survey missions for the oil companies. A person could see a lot more of that desert from the seat of a chopper."

***

When they were all piled onto and into the truck, they raised the lift. Warm desert air flooded into the hangar as the huge circular door swung aside. The sun blazed down through the cloudless sky and Daniel put on his sunglasses. Mel held a small box that contained Piaa's eye.

Daniel peered at it from under his glasses. "That's pretty freaky, sis."

"I know. I don't want to look at it. I'll probably puke." She grimaced.

"You'll have to do it sooner or later," Sam said as he searched for a hand hold on the big flatbed trailer.

It was a five minute ride into a shallow valley. The truck stopped and Niliason climbed out of the driver's seat. "Okay, here's our dust off."

The rest of them piled off and started saying their goodbyes.

Sam held Annette. "These last few weeks have been the best of my life. And not just from meeting aliens. I lost you once, you better come back to me."

"I will, Sam, and from then on you better come on all my adventures with me."

John Anthony handed Mellissa a small present. "Open this when you get to Palus Emyth." She smiled at him and turned to join the others. He shouted after her, "And for God's sake don't befriend any more wayward robots!"

Niliason gathered everyone together. "Piaa first, then Mike. After that it's Daniel, Annette, and Mel together. Okay, Piaa, summon the conveyance."

Piaa stepped forward, looking like the ghost of a tall pirate with a patch over her eye. She glowed brightly, then disappeared.

"Whoa," John Anthony muttered.

"Okay, Mike, you're next."

"Right, the big test," Mike sighed.

"Sorry, Mikey, I wanted to be first," Daniel said.

Mike looked worried. "You're sure I'm not gonna get fried?" he asked Niliason.

"You'll be okay, Mikey," Daniel encouraged him. "Rangers, lead the way."

Mike nodded and smiled. "Rangers, lead the way." He flashed brightly and disappeared.

Niliason waited for a moment. "No emergency beacon. He made it just fine. Okay, you three, stand close but don't touch. Compression shields on, ghillie cloaks on, right. Good luck. We'll see you tomorrow at the latest."

In a flash they were gone.

***

The desert dissolved into a slate grey haze. Then Daniel's vision cleared and he was standing on a dark, flat landscape covered in light green algae. The wreckage of a large building lay several hundred yards away. A low line of mountains formed the skyline against the stark blackness of space. Daniel did a head count.

"Everyone made it. What do you think, Mikey?"

"It's definitely a moon. I didn't expect the green stuff."

"It's a specialized form of algae," Piaa said. "We are, in human terms, 'terraforming' this moon."

"Yeah? What would you call it?" Mike quipped.

Piaa giggled. "*Mishtiglatia nom despos inta resj.*"

"I had to ask."

Piaa merely giggled again. "Everyone good? No problems with temperature or breathing? Okay then, off we go."

Annette raised her detector and made a bee-line for the nearest debris. Mellissa and Piaa headed for the wreckage with Daniel and Mike in tow.

"I've got movement just past the wreckage over there," Mellissa said.

"I see it," Piaa acknowledged. "It's a Biauay cleanup crew. The initial investigations should be over. Now it will fall to salvage to clean up the mess. You will need to be on your guard, Mellissa. Keep working your way to the access shaft. I'll give you a few minutes before I call the transport. We don't want to draw any attention to you or Annette."

Daniel gave her a hug. "Good luck, sis. Remember, don't do anything stupid. Keep quiet, stay low, and move slow."

She nodded. "I know. I'll be okay."

"Good luck, Mel. Show 'em what us *gans* are made of." Mike slapped her on the shoulder, and she disappeared into the wreckage.

After a few minutes, Piaa said, "Transport should be here in a few seconds. Fix your hood, Michael." Piaa adjusted his hood and looked over them both. "The makeup is holding, but don't rub your face."

A small glimmer in the distance grew as it came towards them. Soon, a smooth bodied transport floated to a stop next to them. A square hole opened in the side and they stepped in.

"It looks more like a city bus than a land speeder," Mike said, disappointed.

Piaa laughed. "More like a taxi, but yes, you are right. When we get to the station just join the crowd and follow me. It will be about a hundred yards of walking, then we'll get a private transport booth."

The taxi circumvented the wreckage and pulled onto a neatly paved street. "The campus is covered by a compression shield so you won't need yours on any longer."

"Mikey, look at all the Biauay."

"Neil DeGrasse Tyson would give his left nut to be here right now."

"Our stop, gentlemen, here we go." Piaa got out of the taxi and led the way through the crowd.

Daniel was suddenly very conscious of being the shortest person around. The high platform shoes were difficult to walk in and he struggled to keep pace with Piaa's long stride. After a minute, she made her way to a door and motioned them in. The chamber was dark with what looked like a giant pea pod against the far wall. A console rose from the floor and Piaa began working the controls.

"Get in." She ushered them towards the pod.

"Oh, this is freaky." Mike squirmed his way into the pod.

Daniel stuffed himself in beside Mike.

"Like two peas in a—"

"Don't, Mikey. Just…don't."

They heard Piaa call through the walls of the pod, "Good luck, you two. See you very soon, hopefully."

"Okay, bye, Piaa," Mike sang sarcastically.

The pod vibrated, then they were falling.

"Oh, shit, here we go, man!" Mike yelled.

But they only fell for a second or two before it felt like they had landed in a pool of something similar to the consistency of honey.

"I do not like this, Danny." Mike squirmed. "What the hell have we gotten into, man?"

"Mikey, chill out. Just lay back and enjoy the ride."

The pod settled into the substance, slowly dropping through it until it felt like they came out the other side. Then they were falling again, accelerating faster and faster. Daniel was sure they were moving at reentry speeds. Suddenly the sides of the pod hissed violently and they experienced strong G-forces pulling them down. Just as quickly the forces subsided and the pod began to open from the top like a flower. The petals widened and seemed to slow them down as they held onto the central stem.

"Whoa, Danny, we're jumpin' onto another planet, man! How awesome is this?"

They entered the water slowly, without a splash. The pod sank into the depths and they kicked to the surface, clambering to keep the heavy bag of pylons above the water.

"Compression shield, dude! Turn on your compression shield!" Mike yelled at Daniel.

Daniel reached over to his left wrist and activated the shield. He became buoyant instantly. The shield left a bowl depression in the water beneath them and their feet skimmed the surface.

"Wow," Mike laughed. "That was traumatic. I think I'm going to need counseling."

"Okay, Mikey, hand me one of those pylons."

As soon as he had one, Daniel turned on the location function and found that they were only two feet away from the first insertion point. "Now we wait thirty minutes. But when I set this thing off, there's a chance that everyone in the galaxy will know we're here. We'll have to be fast."

"Roger that. Let's just hope that Piaa and Mel complete their mission."

Chapter 24

Mellissa scrambled over the twisted metal and cement-like substance that used to be the Palus Emyth science base. She fished the optical disc out of her belt pouch and looked through it. A small digital pointer floated above a spot in the wreckage, marking her entry point. It was close.

She squeezed around a large slab and stopped short. A chasm dropped away in front of her. She hung onto the slab and steadied herself. Using the disc, she scanned the depths of the large hole. It was over fifty feet deep, but at the bottom, lay a large piece of an Abe.

"Shit." She had no way of contacting Annette. With a grimace, she pulled the conveyance beacon out of her belt pouch, pushed the button and tossed it down the hole. The Abe-part was marked now but she had used her only conveyance beacon. She would have to make it back to Annette if she was ever going to get back home.

It was slow going around the edge of the hole. She carefully picked her way through the rubble and located the shaft. Conduits of cable and pipe ran along the walls, but there was enough room for her to crawl into the square shaft. She pushed through the destruction where the cables had been severed and continued farther in.

The optical disc penetrated the darkness and she could see that her efforts were bringing her inside the perimeter of the occupied building. As she approached the vent hatch that let out under the floor, the optical disc swept across a large orange and red glowing form. Her heart leapt, but she steadied herself and looked again.

She could just make out that it was the body of a Biauay under the floor. It was misshapen and stuffed into the crawlspace of the hallway. *It must have gotten buried in the attack*, she thought.

Using the optical disc to look through the walls, she made sure the passage was clear, then opened the hatch and worked her way under the floor.

At the right point, she pushed up the floor plate then slipped into the hallway. Glad to get out of the confined space, she stretched and took a deep breath, then quietly went across to the door she needed and pulled out the box containing Piaa's eye. As she flipped open the lid, the orb peered up at her from the gelatinous preservative. Fighting the reactions from her churning stomach, she slid her fingers into the gooey gel, pulled the eyeball out and held it up to the scanner at the door.

The scanner spoke something in the Biauay language and the door slid open.

A floor plate erupted behind her and a hunchbacked Biauay sprang out, heading right for her. Mellissa rolled backwards through the door with the hunchback nearly bowling her over. The door slid closed behind them. The Biauay stopped and paused, clearly perplexed. Then he started jabbering and gesturing wildly.

Mellissa looked past him with the optical disc and scanned through the walls. The coast was clear. The hunchback Biauay was clearly apologetic, though she didn't know why. Now the creature had stopped and was looking her over very carefully. Its eyes went wide and it sprang for the door. In a flash, Mellissa drew her taser and fired. The hunchback dropped against the door.

Satisfied he was out for the count, she checked out the room. It was impossible to miss the thirty foot high flower bud that hummed and shimmered with blue and green light. Mellissa reached into her belt pouch and took out the little box, but it wasn't the box she had reached for, it was John Anthony's present.

Inside was another conveyance beacon with a blinking red light on it. A note read: *This little light is my heart. It needs you to come back.* She giggled and put the little box back into her pocket and pulled out Piaa's wiretap.

The root system was exactly as Piaa had described. Thousands of tiny, fibrous roots spreading out from the base. She put her finger on the switch and got ready. In one motion, she jammed her hand in, flipped the switch, and yanked her hand out, leaving the little box deep inside the root structure. The roots had tried to grab her hand as they swallowed up the box but she had been too fast. Wiping her hand off with an involuntary shudder, she went back to the door and scanned through the walls to check for traffic.

"Now what are we going to do with you?" She looked down at the unconscious hunchback.

Suddenly, she remembered the story of the Biauay that had betrayed Piaa. This might be him. It would explain why he was apologizing so frantically. It would also explain why he was hiding in the floor. She grabbed him and pulled him out the door and across the hallway. He wasn't that heavy. She stuffed him into the hatch then went back and replaced the floor panel. Once the hatch to the shaft was closed behind her, she shoved him ahead of her. It was slow going, but eventually they fell out of the shaft and into the algae covered dust of the barren moon.

"I don't know who you are," she puffed, "but you were just dragged in the dirt by an Earth girl."

***

Nothing she had ever done prepared her for this. Annette reveled in the adventure of it; working on an alien moon with the vastness of the cosmos spread out above her.

The locater brought her to the first piece. She hefted the jackhammer shaped excavator over the site and squeezed the handle. Moon dust flew away from her like she was a tornado, leaving a hole in the exposed rock that revealed the treasure: a huge black, door shaped object that looked like a riot shield. She pressed the button on the conveyance beacon and attached it to the find. The next object lay right beside it. The excavator revealed what looked like one of Dominus' arms.

"This is definitely a piece of one of your buddies," she muttered as she tagged it and moved on. The tools made it easy. After what seemed like ten minutes she was tagging the last of the objects, when another faint blip showed up on the locater. This one was farther out and in the direction Mellissa had gone.

She looked around. There was no one to be seen. *I've got time, why not?*

She easily found Mellissa's footprints. They seemed to lead right towards the object. She scrambled over the ruins in the same places that Mellissa had, and soon was standing at the edge of the crater, but there was no way to get down to the object. She turned to leave just as her name echoed off the crumbled walls.

"Annette! Over here."

It was Mellissa and she was pulling something heavy.

"Hold on, I'm coming to you." Annette picked her way around the edge of the crater and met Mellissa. "Are you okay? What happened, what's this?"

"I think it's the Biauay who betrayed Piaa. I found him hiding under the floor. Help me bring him back."

"What did you do to him?"

"Taser. It knocks 'em right out."

"Is he still alive?"

"Piaa said that the Biauay would recover from the hit but that it would be devastating to their system. Come on, pull."

The two dragged the body over the rubble and finally down to flat ground where they paused to rest. Mellissa continued to scan the area.

"Keep that taser handy, he might wake up." Annette eyed the unconscious Biauay. "Hey, I have to go back and get the extractor. I was just about to tag the last piece."

"The one down in the hole? Don't worry, I already got it."

"Oh, thanks! Hang on, I'll be right back." Annette jumped up and went to retrieve the excavator tool. When she returned, she sat next to Mellissa on a rock

"So, how did your hunt go?" Melissa asked.

"It didn't take any time at all. The tools did all the work. Pulling this guy around is the hardest thing I've done."

"Wait." Mellissa squinted through the optical disc. "Someone's coming. Get down."

***

"Time's up. Here we go." Daniel held the pylon above the water and rotated the switch. Rods shot out of the bottom of the pylon and went into the water. The whole pylon became rigidly fixed in place. "Okay. It's not moving. I don't know how, but I think we're good to go. One down."

"Let's get going." Mike took out the next pylon and activated the locator. "Number two wants to go this way."

The journey across the water was the strangest thing Daniel had ever done. With his feet barely skimming the surface, the compression field seemed to sense which direction he wanted to go. Soon they were striding over land through tall grass.

"Danny, look at me!" Mike stopped. His suit was camouflaging him both in the color and shape of the grass. He looked like a giant green porcupine. Both of them started laughing. After several minutes they continued on at a jogging pace. They kept it up as long as they could but after ten minutes they we both gasping for breath.

"Niliason was right about the atmosphere. I wouldn't

have made it this far back on Earth," Mike breathed.

They drank water, then worked their way towards a set of steep foothills. They shared the load, splitting the pylons between them. Daniel carried two while Mike followed the locator direction on the third.

Mike pointed. "Up there, man. I think we're going to the top of that mountain."

"That's got to be over seventy miles away," Daniel said. "It will take all day to get there."

"Wait. Dude, what are we doing?" Mike ran and jumped, throwing his arms into the air. His suit went rigid and sprouted long wings. The thick air quickly bore him aloft. "We can fly!" he called back down.

Daniel marveled at his friend, then copied him. Soon they were rising up the thermals, catching speed on the sea breeze.

Mike swept in close to Daniel. "Can you believe this?" He gave a whoop and soared away.

"Just find that next pylon point!" Daniel turned after him.

Controlling the suit in flight mode was entirely instinctual. Where he thought about going, that's where it went. It changed shape according to what he wanted to do. For soaring, the wings got longer and the tail pieces became small. When he turned tightly, the wings became short and stout with added rigidity. Only five minutes had passed before Mike pointed downward and began circling to land in a small valley, high in the mountain range. Daniel touched down next to him with a flap. Mike was laughing hysterically.

"That was so incredible!"

"Unbelievable. Now, plant that thing and let's move on, we're running out of time and I feel like a big target flying around in this thing."

"No way, man, this is the best! I can't wait to get back up there."

"Mikey, I love you, man, but sometimes you don't

think. We set off the first pylon and it's attracting people here. What do you think these guys use for travel, donkeys? They're in Luke Skywalker fighter planes. They'll blow us out of the freaking sky."

Mike stopped laughing. "Oh, yeah."

"C'mon, let's get this over with."

Mike walked to the spot and planted the second pylon. "Okay, done here. Hand me one of those, I'll help you carry them."

"That's okay, I got it. We better get out of this valley."

They took off at a run, and caught the air rising out of the valley. They circled to a high ridge and Daniel landed to get his bearings. Mike came down next to him.

"Oh my God, Danny, I am never giving this thing back," Mike giggled. "This is the only way to get around."

Daniel was focused on the landscape on the other side of the ridge. "I have a plan. The next pylon goes down there in that spur of foothills somewhere. I'm going to dive down and skim the tree tops. When I find the spot, I'll circle to a landing. You get nice and high on overwatch. Keep your eye peeled and we'll meet over there on the backside of that rock outcrop. It's a good defensible position."

"Roger that."

Mike slung his assault rifle around to the front of his harness and took to the air. Daniel watched him gain altitude, then with a thumbs up from Mike, dove down the mountainside. The treetops became a blur as the wings on his suit went delta shaped. Daniel followed the locator on the pylon and glided to a soft landing. He flipped the dial forward twice and then back and the pylon lodged itself in the ground. Mike was still high aloft, so Daniel flew to the rendezvous at the rock outcrop.

"Danny, we got company," Mike said over the radio. "Three bogeys…oh shit, they're on to me!"

Daniel brought his rifle around and searched the sky.

Three craft were bearing down on Mike rapidly. He was diving towards the mountain in an attempt to outrun them. Daniel had the first craft in his scope in an instant.

"I'll try and draw them off you," Daniel said.

"No, Danny, finish the mission! I'll keep them busy, just go!"

Daniel ignored his friend and began firing a series of rounds, giving plenty of lead on the target. He scored a hit and the first craft wobbled and peeled off, but the remaining two fired energy weapons like bright green rain at Mike.

Daniel watched helplessly as one of Mike's wings crumpled and he started into a spin. Daniel continued firing at the remaining two ships with one eye in the scope while keeping the other eye open to track Mike's fall. Mike flared out his remaining wing and started spinning.

"Good, Mikey, that's slowing you down."

The crazy maneuver was actually working. Daniel watched as Mike crashed through the trees, narrowly missing the rock outcrop, and fell far below to the forest floor. Daniel thought about contacting Mike but changed his mind. *The Biauay can probably see my radio like a beacon. It could lead them right to me.*

He watched as the two craft landed three hundred yards away from Mike's crash site, then he sprang into action. The adrenaline surging through his system propelled him over the terrain at a dizzying speed. He was almost on top of Mike before he saw him.

"Mikey!" He skidded to a stop and dropped on his knees. "How you doin, man, you okay?"

"Oh wow…clean up on aisle twelve," Mikey groaned.

Daniel ran his hands over his friend. Broken legs. Probably a broken back. But his crazy aerial maneuver had probably saved his life. "Quiet. They're almost on us." Daniel slapped a conveyance beacon on his friend. "I have to get this last pylon in place before the conveyor will work. Okay listen. I'm going to drag you into that rock crevice over there and your suit will keep you hidden."

"I…think my suit's…busted, man." Mike was trying to stay conscious.

"No, buddy. Part of it still works. Hang on and stay quiet. This is going to hurt."

Daniel pulled his friend up the hill and lodged him underneath a rocky overhang then spread out the ghillie suit until it disguised the location.

"I'll trade you two rifle mags for two pistol mags okay?" He rummaged through Mike's harness and made the trade. Then he pulled out Mike's pistol and put it in his hand. "Here, take this. I'll be back. You remember the code word?"

Mike nodded.

Daniel pointed a finger at him. "Don't frickin' shoot me when I come back. If they come, you show these green blooded sons of bitches how Rangers fight. I'm going to draw them away and plant this pylon, then I'll be back for you. Don't drink all the beer."

***

Mel and Annette remained still, hidden among the ruins until they recognized Piaa coming towards them.

"There you are," she said, worried. "What happened, are you okay?"

"Oh, thank God. Piaa, we thought you were one of them."

"My part took longer than I thought. Unfortunately, that may put Mike and Daniel in a difficult situation."

"Are they okay?" Melissa went white.

"We have no way of knowing if the Binuay were alerted to their presence."

"What about you, Piaa?" Annette asked. "Did you complete your mission?"

"They bought my story, but I will have to remain here, I'm afraid. They are watching me now. Mellissa, I will make it my primary objective to find out about Daniel and Mike."

"Well, maybe this will help. You recognize him?" Mellissa pulled the body out from under a slab of building.

Piaa gasped. "Jorjo! Where was he?"

"He was hiding under the floor right where I came out. When I scanned into the room he jumped out at me."

"He must have thought you were me."

"I kind of put two and two together and figured out who he was. I didn't know for sure though."

"Mellissa, you're amazing. I didn't think there was any way he could have survived." Piaa scanned the body. "He's dormant. The taser must have knocked him out. This is exactly what I needed. Once they hear his testimony, they won't be watching me so closely. I may be able to get back to you after all.

"Now, quickly, attach a conveyance beacon to yourselves, and hope that Daniel and Mike managed to get the pylons in place." Piaa checked their oxygen supply and was just settling in to wait with them when they flashed, and were gone.

Chapter 25

John Anthony and Sam shook hands with a large black man.

"I'm Duncan, your mission specialist."

He showed them the plans to the military base and some of the communications being filtered through the Atec spy network.

"They've got the Sing in there and Dominus needs it." Niliason came into the room. "Dominus, are you there?"

"Yes, Niliason." The Abe's voice came into the room through unseen speakers.

"Right, let's get to it then," Niliason said. "You two get dressed and get to the truck. Duncan will try to walk you through driving it." He handed them each a driver's license.

In their apartments they found tiny ear pieces for communication among their luggage. They gathered their gear and made their way to the hangar.

"One thing you should know," Duncan said through their comms. "This type of communication is limited and may drop out. Try to use it as little as possible."

"Great," John Anthony grumbled.

Duncan guided them through starting up the truck and some of the basics of driving it. "At least you're out in the middle of the desert and not on a highway having to learn this."

The truck was lifted through the opening and came to a stop on the desert floor. After minutes of grinding gears they lurched into motion and slowly made their way through the desert. They reached Colorado City that afternoon and parked the big rig behind John Anthony's radio store as instructed.

"So, where is Piaa's car?" John Anthony asked.

"Niliason tells me that Piaa gave it to you," Duncan said. "It's under a tarp and a pile of junk in the shed."

They opened the shed and started removing things. "This was all the stuff from my old life. Funny. Now it's just stuff," he laughed.

"Hey, John Anthony," Sam called, "I'm down to the tarp here."

They continued to remove the rest of the junk and then stood staring at the tarp covered car.

"It's wide and low and definitely fast. Ready to see what it is?" John Anthony held the edge of the tarp.

Sam folded his arms. "I bet it's a Porsche."

They pulled the tarp off together.

"Good lord!" Sam exclaimed. "She certainly knows how to travel in style."

"A Bugatti Veyron? Are you kidding me?" John Anthony circled the black and burgundy car.

"Okay, guys, time to go," Duncan said over the comms. "The roads are clear. Get your butts up to Fort Meade."

***

It was the second day in a row Reilly had canvassed the desert in the helicopter. He was starting to think that the truck had dropped off the ends of the Earth.

"Maybe they're running drugs down to Mexico, sir," Smith said over the headphones.

"The APB goes to all the border stations. If they tried to cross, we would have found them. No, Smith, they're out here somewhere. They probably got it covered by some military camo. Remember, these guys are Army Rangers not meth junkies. They know how to conceal themselves."

Four hours later they returned to the small airport and went back to the diner. Bernice served them fresh coffee and said the same thing she had the last two days. "No luck, huh?"

"We're at a dead end. I think it's time to head back to Quantico and wait until these guys pop up on radar. Smith, call the office and see if they have any ideas."

Smith picked up the phone and went outside for privacy. He came back a few minutes later. "Sir, we've been bumped up in priority. Seems that General What's-His-Name wants these guys really bad. We're supposed to stay put until we find them."

"What? I don't work for some general. This is my investigation. Gimme that phone." Reilly snatched the phone from Smith. "Hello, who is this? Oh, hi, Chief. What's going on?"

Reilly listened as the Chief issued the edict. His blood pressure rose steadily. Finally, he hung up.

"Well, sir?"

"Well, we're stuck in this damn town until Daniel Taggart and Michael Madsen decide to crawl out from whatever rock their hiding under. I just don't get it."

"Don't get what, sir?"

"This whole thing is off the system. Chief has us on comm silence. They think these guys have access to our communications; like they can tell when we're coming. I don't know why they get that impression. This general obviously knows more about their training than we do. I just wish they would put us in the loop."

"Sir, I have a theory."

Reilly leveled a grumpy stare at the young agent. Smith held up his hands.

"Listen, sir, I know you're gonna laugh at me and say it's a stupid idea, but just consider the facts. We find strange depressions in the ground, then three objects rocket into space and leave behind a weapon that no one has ever seen. The military don't even know what it is.

"Now, I know you're gonna want to shout at me for saying this, but isn't it possible that maybe we're dealing with a complete unknown here? This happened in Dan Taggart's backyard, literally. Isn't it just possible that maybe he found the fourth thing that left that depression, the one that didn't fly off into space?

"Aw heck, I'm just gonna come out and say it, sir: aliens. What if it's aliens? It would explain why we're on comms blackout. They could certainly hack our systems. They probably want their bomb back." Smith sat back, watching Reilly for the expected harsh rebuttal.

Reilly just stared at Smith, at least that was what he wanted Smith to think. It was a trick Reilly had learned. He was actually deep in thought, chasing the chain of logic.

Finally, he blinked and said, "You may actually have something there, Smith. I don't mean little green men, but maybe something that's a bit more on the NASA, NSA, CIA side of things. The part I think you're right about is Taggart. He's no spy. I think someone dropped the ball, or more accurately, a space weapon and Daniel Taggart found it. Now they're trying to cover their tracks. We've got to find Mr. Taggart and his friend before they become a pair of unmarked graves in the desert."

***

Daniel took off at a run, aiming in a bee line for the next pylon spot. He knew that their pursuers would be behind him, heading for Mike's position. At two hundred yards he stopped, turned back towards Mike's location, and found a vantage point.

Sure enough, six Biauay soldiers were walking towards Mike's crash site. *How long has it been since you guys actually fought a ground war?* Daniel thought as he scoped in on the last soldier in line. With a click from the silenced assault rifle, the soldier dropped in a shower of fluid. *That ain't blood.*

Another one dropped. They stopped and knelt, looking around them.

Wrong move, fuck heads.

Two more fell dead. The two remaining looked straight at Daniel and began sprinting towards him. They were fast, but he stayed put. *So, that's your game. You think speed will save you.* He held his breath. *You can't run faster than my scope.*

The one in the rear fell first, collapsing against a tree with a sickening thud. Daniel let the last one close the distance, then dropped him only fifty feet away. The Biauay was clearly wearing some kind of protective armor, but as Piaa had said, they weren't equipped to deal with ballistic weapons.

Daniel made his way up the hill at a sprint, then running off of a rock outcropping, took to the air. He stayed low and got as much speed as he could. He felt exposed. He couldn't see the sky behind him or the remaining aircraft. All he could do was fly. The locator led him to a swampy clearing in a river delta. Wild birds of bizarre shape and color exploded from the reedy grass as he splashed to a stop. The compression shield kept him above the water as he searched for the exact location.

With a quiet hiss the Biauay aircraft settled in front of him and three soldiers jumped out of the hatch. One of them fired, but Daniel's suit deflected the round. He felt the heat of it on the side of his face as he let go of the pylon and brought up his pistol.

He dropped the lead soldier and kept firing. The one behind him went down as well but the third closed in. The Biauay punched Daniel square in the jaw and sent him flying into the shallow water. His compression shield had overloaded but the water was only a foot deep.

Daniel felt the soldier grab the back of his shirt. He hooked his leg around the Biauay's knee and twisted into a standing position. The Biauay's knee buckled and he cried out. Daniel's knife found the soldier's head before the cry was finished.

He yanked his blade free of the creature's skull and let the body fall into the swamp. Then, washing the blade off, he put it away and retrieved the pylon. Once he found the right spot, he twisted the dial and planted it firmly. It began humming immediately and he knew that he and Mike were out of there. A white haze blurred his vision and the next thing he saw were Atec running past him through the desert night.

"Mikey!" He turned. Mike was on the ground, the Atec recovery team surrounding him. "He crashed in the woods."

"We know. Let us help him." An Atec nurse pushed past him. Mike lay unconscious on the stretcher. Another member of the recovery team checked over Daniel.

"He's in good hands now," the man said. "We'll do everything we can to save him."

Daniel started after the rescue truck, but the Atec stopped him. "There's nothing you can do, sir. Just let them do what they do best." Daniel relented as the Atec sat him down on the back of the medical truck.

"Danny?" Mellissa appeared out of nowhere.

He jumped up and hugged her.

"Thank God you're safe!" She held onto him. "What happened to Mike? Is he okay?"

"No, Mel, he's not. The Biauay shot him out of the sky. He hit the ground with only one wing and got banged up pretty bad." He relayed the story to her as Annette joined them.

Then the Atec recovery team herded them into the ambulance and whisked them back to the base. Niliason and Dominus met them in the hangar.

"Good, you're all safe," Niliason said. "Where is Piaa?"

"She had to stay," Mellissa reported. "But I found the traitor. She's bringing him to testify that Piaa did nothing wrong. She should be off the hook and able to sneak back to us soon."

Niliason just nodded.

"Where is Sam?" Annette asked.

"He and John Anthony are enroute to DC. They will infiltrate the base tomorrow night."

"Congratulations," Dominus boomed. "The mission was a complete success. The time machine has conveyed in place at Montauk. Exceptional results, Doctor Blazer. Not only did you recover all of the pieces I needed, you managed to locate one of my team almost entirely intact. It is a valuable win for us. I must get to work immediately."

"Thanks, Dominus, but it was Mel who found the big piece."

Dominus smiled. "Thank you, Mel."

"Anything for you, big guy." Mellissa hugged his leg. "Now get to work. I want to meet your friends, er, family or…whatever."

"Please clear the hangar everyone," Dominus said. "I will be making a mess in here with some heavy and dangerous components."

They all left the hangar and went to wait on Mike's surgery. An Atec nurse met them in the hallway.

"He's still alive, but he's suffered a severe spinal injury. Both of his legs are broken as well as several ribs, and he has a major concussion. The good news is that he will live. But, if left in his natural condition he will most likely never walk again and may have some brain damage."

Daniel grabbed the nurse by the collar. "You fix my friend!"

"Danny!" Mellissa tried to pull him off the nurse but, with the added strength of still wearing his suit, it was like tugging on a bulldozer. "Danny, let him go, he's trying to help."

"Yes, I'm trying to help. Please, sir." The nurse didn't seem to be fazed by Daniel's outburst.

Daniel let go of him. "I'm sorry, it's just…"

"I know, sir. Listen, we need someone's permission to add the enhancements that can save him."

"For God's sake, just do it! Whatever you have to do, you have my permission. I'll take responsibility." Daniel was exasperated.

The nurse went back into the operating room while they all sat down. Mellissa rubbed his shoulders.

"Hey, Danny, I know you're upset but I've never seen you this way. What's going on?"

Niliason came into the hallway. "Daniel is fatigued and hungry." He looked at Daniel. "You're probably slightly dehydrated as well. All of that coupled with coming down after the rush of combat makes a person edgy. You may not want to eat right now, but you probably should." He smiled. "Please, before you end up boxing us all around the ears."

"Okay, Nil," Daniel agreed, "but the second you know anything about Mikey, I want to know."

"Absolutely. I'll have a runner stationed here."

They all went down to the galley, piled into a booth, and relayed their mission stories. Daniel went first. Milo brought out piles of food and Daniel didn't seem to even notice how much he was eating until he was stuffed.

"Holy crap, Danny," Mellissa marveled. "You packed it in."

Just as they finished eating, Niliason joined them. "He's stable. They are doing some technical work on his new systems and he'll need to sleep for the next twenty-four hours, but he's fine. You will be able to talk to him tomorrow."

There was a rush of sighs as the relieved group gave hugs all around.

"Thank you, Niliason," Daniel said sheepishly. "Thank you for everything."

"Hey, you're the heroes here. We'll do anything we can to help you."

Chapter 26

John Anthony relaxed behind the wheel as the Bugatti split the night at over one hundred and seventy miles per hour. Duncan relayed traffic information to him from a live satellite feed that was tracking them, so Sam was equally at ease with the speed. Duncan was apparently not alone in the effort as they received warnings of any police presence, traffic routing instructions, and even had someone call ahead to order food for them. The sixteen hundred mile journey would normally take twenty-three hours. They were closing on Fort Meade after only twelve.

They checked into the seventh floor suite at The Hotel at Arundel Preserve in Hanover, a luxury boutique hotel.

"Hey, the accommodations have to match the car," Duncan explained. "The story is that you two are investors looking at some startups in the area. Military contracts are very lucrative. Get some rest. I'll wake you for the mission." Duncan signed off as they checked into their room.

He woke them at midnight. "Time to get cracking."

They dressed in night camo and the strange ghillie suits, and left the building through the hotel's side entrance.

"We've cleared all the CCTV on your route. Use the dark blue minivan in the parking lot, space number twenty-six."

They started the car and drove towards the base.

"There's a small perimeter gate, you can walk right in. Park the van in main parking outside the gate, near the grass. When you go in, try to open the doors very slowly and as little as possible. Stay low and don't shut the doors all the way."

They followed Duncan's instructions as they stayed close to the perimeter fence. Sure enough, they came to a small gate.

"The combination is one nine, seven, four, zero, three."

Once through the gate, they left the Perimeter Road through a small set of woods, which opened out at onto a field with an array of satellite dishes, all surrounding a large geodesic radar ball.

"The Sing is in that building." Duncan said. "The door is marked on the optic disc."

John Anthony held the disc up and a digital marker highlighted one of the doors on the building.

"Sorry, Sam, I'm hogging the gizmo," John Anthony said.

"That's alright, as long as you get us there in one piece," Sam said, his eyes scanning their surroundings. "And back out again."

"Don't get cocky, guys. It may seem like a walk in the park, but it's not," Duncan scolded.

They opened the door and went inside. A long hallway greeted them.

"Follow the doors that are marked on your optic disc."

More doors glowed. They quietly slipped through them.

"You seriously couldn't come up with a better name than 'optic disc'?" John Anthony complained.

"Open to suggestions," Duncan responded.

"How about monocle?" Sam offered.

"Like the stuffy English guys used to wear?" John Anthony giggled.

"Wait a second," Duncan cut in. "We're having a problem with one of the cameras. Okay, keep moving. The door at the end of the hallway leads into a lab. I'm afraid we're going to lose our signal in there. At the back of the lab there is a series of specialty rooms. We think the Sing is in one of those."

They tried the door at the end of the hallway but it was locked.

"Look at the security panel," Sam said. "We're gonna have to give blood to get in there."

"Duncan, how do we get in?" John Anthony tapped his earpiece. "Duncan? Oh great."

"Wait here," Sam said, "I'll try to get a hold of Duncan again." He rushed out into the hallway. "Duncan?"

"Sam?"

"How the hell do we get into the room?" Sam hissed.

His comms were suddenly engulfed in static, then a low but familiar voice rumbled in his ear.

"I will neutralize the security," Dominus cut in. "There. I have also activated the Sing round so you can move it."

"Thank you, Dominus," said a clearly shaken Duncan.

Sam made his way back down to the door where John Anthony stood waiting. He opened it as Sam approached. Just as Duncan had said, they were greeted with another hallway lined with what looked like operating rooms. The Sing was in the last one. The oblong weapon hummed and floated just above the wheeled rack that had obviously been built for carrying heavy bombs.

Sam glanced nervously at John Anthony. "Dominus said he activated it."

"Yeah, it definitely looks active. So we can move it without it going…you know…"

"Boom? I think so. I mean, I'm sure he would have told me…"

They looked at each other, then Sam reached out and put his hand on it.

"It's vibrating. Is that normal?" Sam asked.

"How the hell am I supposed to know?!" John Anthony said, exasperated. "Let's just try to move it."

Sam and John Antony each took an end and looked at each other nervously.

"You do realize if this thing goes off it will destroy the

entire solar system." Sam was sweating.

John Anthony only half-heard him. He expected the weight of the bomb to resist against his hands but the thing only weighed as much as a napkin. A grin formed across his face as he looked at Sam who stopped talking and watched as John Anthony gently raised the bomb off the table.

"Well that's a hell of a thing." Sam gawked.

As they headed for the door the bomb glided towards it on its own with only the mildest push from them, maintaining four feet off the ground in a weightless hover.

John Anthony got on one side of the Sing and Sam on the other, guided the bomb down the hall and out the door. "It's like a landspeeder."

"These aren't the droids you're looking for," Duncan quipped.

"Oh, thank God you're back," Sam said.

"You did good but I need you to wait a second, you have company in the far hallway. Don't worry, they're on the other side of the double doors. It's the roving guard. He's going to check the lock on the door, so just ignore it when he wiggles the handle."

They kept still, waiting at the door. Suddenly the handle jiggled, then stopped.

"Okay, he's going back the other way. Get moving."

They went back the way they came, working carefully through the facility.

Duncan came on again. "We have a little problem. One of the technicians is checking in for work. He's registered to work on the Sing."

"At this hour?"

"Hey, I work late all the time," Sam said.

"You need to move," Duncan urged. "You have to make it out the door at the end of the hall before he comes around the corner. Go!"

They shoved the bomb around the corner and sprinted for the exit.

"Sam, get ahead of me and open the door," John Anthony said.

Sam leaned into a sprint and raced ahead, throwing his weight into the bar shaped handle. The metal door burst open with a bang as John Anthony and the Sing flew out into the night air. Sam clung to the door as it flopped open, then let go and stumbled into a run behind John Anthony and the bomb. Suddenly, bright lights illuminated the base like a football stadium and loud horns sounded.

"That's the alarm, but just keep your cool." Duncan said quickly but calmly. "Get into those trees across the parking lot. Don't worry, we'll get you out of this."

They took off at a run through the woods, struggling with the buoyant Sing round.

"You're not going to set it off by hitting it," Duncan informed them.

"You could have told us that before!" John Anthony snapped. "Less about the bomb, more about us escaping, please!"

"Don't go back to the van. Every road will be blocked. You're going to have to go across the Patuxent Highway, west through another patch of woods, and onto the Baltimore Washington Parkway. We're searching for unregistered vehicles in the area that you can commandeer. Use the monocle."

John Anthony looked through the device with one hand as he batted away branches with the other. "Sam, you got the Sing?"

"Got it, you just get our bearings," Sam replied.

"John Anthony, you'll see compass markings at the bottom of your screen. Turn to three-one-three."

"Got it."

"Now, go quickly but pace yourself," Duncan instructed. "Stay on that bearing. I'll tell you when to stop. Here, this may help."

A directional marker appeared ahead of John Anthony in the monocle, and the view changed to night vision.

"Remember, you two, you've got advanced camouflage and the whole team here. You're not going to fall into the Army's dragnet tonight."

Sam hauled back on the Sing, bringing it to a stop and took a breather. "He's right, buddy. It's just the lights and alarms and all. I feel like a fugitive."

"You're saving the human race." It was Niliason. "You're no fugitive."

John Anthony just smiled, then reached out and slapped hands with Sam as they caught their breath.

"Okay, boys, keep moving," Duncan said. "We've put the Army off of your scent, but you still have a lot of ground to cover."

They slogged through the marshy woods for over an hour and they had to haul each other out of the muck several times. By the time they crossed the Baltimore Washington Parkway, Sam thought they looked like a pair of Swamp Things.

"Okay, you're almost to the interstate. Before you cross it, shake out your cloaks," Duncan advised. "They're so dirty they're not working right. That's better. Now, wait until I tell you, then haul butt across. It's about fifty yards to the far side. If you need to, you can flatten yourself out in the median, but it's not the safest place to be. Ready? Okay, after this car…go!"

They sprinted, pushing the Sing across the first two lanes, the median and then the next two. A merging lane made another third lane.

"Go, there's a car coming onto the highway," Duncan warned.

They dived off the road and collapsed in a stand of trees.

"Hang on, we're checking that car. Nope, they didn't see you. Okay, scoot into the woods a bit and then rest."

"How did you check the car?" Sam asked.

"It has parking cameras front and rear, you showed up in neither one. Now, you're going to cross little Dorsey

Run and then the Little Patuxent River. Sorry guys, you're getting wet. Then you'll come out in a clearing for high power lines. You'll follow that south until it ends. There's a service road there that leads into a neighborhood. There's a little red Mazda we found that has no registration. That's your ride. It's a real beater and it's tiny, so you'll have to be creative with the Sing. Also, you'll probably have to push start it."

"Really? We go from Bugatti Veyron to Adam Sandler's 'Piece of shit car'?" Sam complained.

"Easy come, easy go. I'm trying to get you back to the hotel in a round-about way."

"Well, you're succeeding in the 'round about' category," Sam grumbled.

"Just the mention of our nice hotel room makes me want a bath." John Anthony pushed the Sing as Sam caught up and joined him.

***

Reilly woke to his phone ringing. It was the helicopter pilot. "We don't need you today Randal…what? Where?"

Smith woke to Reilly banging on his hotel room door.

"Let's go, Smith, up and at 'em!"

Smith was still struggling into his jacket as they ran to the car. "So, the pilot saw the truck on his way to work? What are the chances?"

"I don't know, but I'm not letting this stroke of luck go to waste."

"You think that Taggart and Madsen will be there?"

"No, that's why we're stopping by the Army surplus. We're gonna do this the old fashioned way."

***

Reilly came back out of the store pushing a cart.

"Game cameras, sir?"

"We're supposed to be off the grid on this one. Game cameras are a simple way to stake out an area. We'll hide them around the vicinity of the vehicle. We'll have to sneak in there tonight and set it up. Call headquarters and have them check the area around the radio store for any CCTV coverage. Make sure they know that this is supposed to be an off-grid check. We don't want to scare off our quarry by leaving any digital signs that we're snooping."

Smith made the call and confirmed that an old CCTV system was in place at the firehouse around the corner from the radio store. Reilly swung the Charger into the firehouse driveway and went in.

"Morning, boys. Is your chief around?"

"Sure, what can I do for you?"

Reilly flashed his badge and told the man he wanted access to his CCTV footage, but the man suddenly acted scared.

"Okay, chief, easy there. Is there something you want to tell me?" Reilly slowly reached around for his Taser. The chief's eyes shifted back and forth, but he didn't run. *This man is acting like he's trapped*, Reilly thought. "You can tell me. We're here to help."

"No…I mean, I haven't done anything it's just…that old CCTV system hasn't worked for years and suddenly two days ago it started up and recorded old commercials."

"What? Show me."

The chief led him up to the firehouse and put in the tape. An old Cheerios commercial played in an endless loop.

"Something is going on around here," the chief blurted. "First the guy at the radio shop disappears, then a couple of guys park a semi there and drive off in a Bugatti Veyron. A Bugatti Veyron in Colorado City! We aren't exactly known for our overwhelming population of billionaires around here."

The chief called in the firefighter who had seen the

Bugatti. The man gave a description of the two individuals and the car.

"Oh yeah, I knew what it was. It's THE dream car. My kid has a poster of one on his wall."

"I've already got HQ on the horn sir," Smith said. "They're running a check on the car…hang on. Well, that was fast. A black and burgundy Bugatti matching the description was mysteriously purchased by a Fred Sanford of Takoma Park, Maryland."

"There it is, Smith. Finally! Fred Sanford my ass. Wait. What do you mean 'mysteriously' purchased?"

"The dealer doesn't remember selling the vehicle. He reports that he came into the store in the morning and the car was gone, but the paperwork was all done, including his signature and everything being properly registered."

"Then who the hell is Fred Sanford?"

"Apparently he's a—"

"Junk dealer. You're going to tell me he's a junk dealer or a salvage specialist or something."

"Well, yes, sir. How did you know?"

"Because Sanford and Sons is an old sitcom from the seventies. What else do we have on our Mr. Sanford?"

"He lives with his son Lamont. The address is here and his social security number. His wife, Elizabeth, was deceased in 1947. We even have her social security number."

"Okay, Smith, here's the first bit of real sleuthing I'm going to ask you to do. Using only the old microfiche and paper trails, find out if anything was ever paid from or to Mr. or Mrs. Sanford out of social security. There should be a record of transactions for his salvage business as well as tax and social security information. Check records for vehicle ownership and insurance through the years, and get the whereabouts of his son and any other relatives."

"Yes sir!" Smith said enthusiastically.

"And, Smith, don't spend too much time on it. I seriously doubt you'll be able to find any of that information."

"Yes, sir," Smith said, a bit crestfallen.

Chapter 27

The tree line broke cleanly. On either side of them, heavy power lines marched in towering rows to the north and south.

"That's it, head south. After passing two sets of towers you'll come to a service road that leads into a subdivision."

"I haven't walked this much in years," Sam said, breathing hard.

"Come on, Doc. Just a little further and we'll be at the car."

Sam trudged on behind Anthony. After a quarter of a mile they reached the service road.

"Tell you what," John Anthony said, "you stay here. I'll get the car and come back to get you. Take the Sing and hide in those trees. I'll be right back."

"I don't like you two splitting up," Duncan cautioned.

"Listen, it's best if we keep the Sing under cover. I can go find the car and bring it here."

"He's right, Duncan," Sam said.

Straitening his shoulders, John Anthony gave Sam a nod, before setting off again, alone. "Get me to the car."

"Okay. Out the gate, then left. Good, take the next right and go three houses down."

"Little red Mazda on the right?"

"Affirmative."

John Anthony grabbed a rock, then folded his coat and set it against the driver's window. It was louder than he expected when it broke.

"Use your knife and pry off the plastic cover on the

steering wheel," Duncan instructed. "Good. Now pry off the key…yep. You've done this before."

With his knife jammed into the key slot, the dash lit up but the starter was clearly fried.

"No worries," John Anthony said. He put the car in neutral and started pushing it with the driver's door open. "Good thing I've owned nothing but crappy old cars.".

Once he got the car rolling at a running pace, he slipped into the driver's seat, put it in gear and popped the clutch. The engine sputtered, then fired right up. John Anthony put it in first and sped off down the road.

Sam was relieved to see him. "That was quick."

"Come on, put the Sing in the back."

Sam did, but then struggled with the rear hatch. "It's not closing."

John Anthony got out to look. "Back seat has to come out."

They tore into the back seat and, with the help of their multi-tool pliers, managed to remove the bolts holding it in place. They ditched the seat in the trees and slid the Sing round into the car. With the bomb firmly wedged between the front seats and the back hatch tied down, they covered it with their coats and sped off.

The little car ambled out of the subdivision and in no time was pulling up outside of the hotel. The sky was getting light.

"Four-thirty in the morning—what a night," Sam mumbled between multiple yawns.

"Let's get the Sing into the Bugatti. I'll drive, you sleep. We need to get as far away as possible."

"There's no way it's going to fit in that car. I can tell by looking." John Anthony climbed out and leaned on the roof of the Mazda.

"Duncan," Sam called, "get us a real solution."

"Okay. You'll have to wait until the car dealer opens."

"We have to leave now, Duncan."

"There's no other…wait… Okay, we have an idea.

Leave the Veyron there and start heading back to us. We'll have you stop on the way."

"Leave the Bugatti?" John Anthony whined

"I'm afraid so."

John Anthony pined over the super car. "Oh man. You really know how to hurt a guy."

"Sorry, John Anthony. We'll get you a nice pickup truck instead."

"I will pick out the next car, thank you very much." He sighed and went back to their room.

Duncan came back on. "Forget what I said about finding an open dealership. Tell us what you want and we'll have it waiting for you at a rest stop. We have added resources now that the Emythiar mission is complete."

Sam perked up. "It is? Why didn't you tell us?"

"I didn't want to distract you. Everyone is back in one piece. Well, Michael got banged up pretty bad, but he's had great care and he's coming around just fine."

"Oh, that's great news. Okay, we're on our way." John Anthony returned to the car with their luggage. "Sam wants a new, desert tan, Jeep Wrangler Rubicon."

"Roger that."

They stuffed the luggage into the little Mazda and sputtered out of the parking lot.

"Goodbye, my sweet," John Anthony said to the Bugatti.

***

Just outside of Harrisonburg, Virginia, Duncan told them to pull over at the next rest stop. The tan Jeep was waiting for them. A man in jeans and a leather jacket handed them the keys.

"Insurance and registration are in the glove box. The car is yours, Doctor Wisecraft. Enjoy."

"Thanks," Sam said. "Sorry you have to drive away in that piece of shit. You'll be lucky if it gets you into

Harrisonburg."

The man just smiled and waved. Soon they were cruising down highway 40 with eighteen hours of driving ahead of them. John Anthony slept as best as he could while Sam drove. They stopped in Tennessee and caught up on sleep at a motel, then continued on into Colorado City.

"Should we stop and get the truck?"

"No, don't bother," said Duncan. "It takes up too much room in the hangar. You'll be using a different access to the base. Here's the route to the northern gate." He sent the information.

"Roger that. See you in twenty."

They drove out into the desert, winding their way through scrub and rocks, then finally down into a gully where a piece of the cave wall was rolled aside. Once inside, the cave was sealed tight and a clean-up crew went out and covered any trace of them.

"Someone please tell Mel I'm back," John Anthony said, anxious to see her.

"Someone please tell John Anthony that he's late." Mellissa surprised him from behind. "So, how'd it go?"

"Hey…" Suddenly, he didn't have words.

Melissa looked at him awkwardly. "I got your note. On the mission. The little disc?"

"Oh! Right…yeah. I just…thought, you know…"

"It was really nice. And it was perfect, 'cause I used my only beacon on a piece of gear I found. So…I would have been, you know, stranded if anything had happened. But I wasn't, 'cause you gave me another one…"

"Well, you didn't…I mean, you're back—obviously, because you're here."

Sam watched the two in the following awkward silence. He had only stepped out of the Jeep when Annette was there.

"I thought of you, on the moon," she said.

Sam held her for a long minute. "I've thought about

nothing but you since I left."

"Liar," she teased. "Yeah, I know about the car."

"Welcome back," greeted Duncan.

"Fantastic job out there you two," Niliason said, following close behind.

"You really did well guys, I mean that." Duncan shook their hands.

"So did you, Duncan," Sam said. "Though I have to admit, you had us pretty scared a few times. I hope that's the last of that kind of work I ever have to do."

"Well, admittedly, it would have been a lot easier with enhancements, but you did well," Duncan laughed. "You should be proud."

***

In the hangar, Dominus worked furiously over scraps of metal, wires and silicon composites. "The Sing ordinance is in perfect condition, and Dr. Blazer and Melissa recovered most of the remains of Alaz, and ninety three percent of Vexa. I only have thirty percent of Sagit. Still, it is more than I hoped."

Niliason looked over the piles of parts. "I know you are the architect of these individuals, but I've been thinking about how they were different from you."

"Since meeting Mel and coming here I have begun to remember things. It is strange. It never occurred to me that part of my memory would be inaccessible."

"Perhaps it's coming from your organic core, as Sam suggested."

"I suspect he is right. I wish Piaa were here to investigate. I learned much about her capabilities at our initial linking. Her experience, with my biotechnology, would be invaluable," Dominus said as he worked away.

Niliason smiled to himself. He had waited an eternity to hear that an Abe actually wanted the company of a Biauay.

Dominus continued talking. "I know now that my original construct was completed by organic humans before the Mars Colony Wars. I was built to defend them. I suspect that Piaa learned quite a lot about me as well. Perhaps she would be able to access parts of my memory that I cannot."

"How fitting that you have ended up here." Niliason found himself growing fond of the terrifying Abe. "You have come full circle."

"Truly. As time passed and I was destroyed and rebuilt, my organic components were replaced with synthetics. The only thing that remains of my organic component is my central cortex, which was bioengineered from stem cells. This unique component gives me advantages in creative thinking and individual behavior. I believe I am also beginning to experience complex emotions."

Niliason laughed. "It sure complicates things, but it also makes life worth living. Do you think you could include similar components in the reconstruction of your…children?"

"Interesting choice of words, Commander." Dominus paused for a moment as he considered whether his creations could be considered offspring. "It's possible." He nodded. "Though I would need Piaa to create their biological central cortex from my DNA. I do not possess the skills for advanced bioengineering."

"Ah, but the Biauay are not the only ones who have those skills. You have Atec friends now, and we specialize in just this kind of thing."

"Then we must begin right away. Growing biological parts from stem cells can take quite some time."

"It won't take as long as you may think."

"Sagit is my only concern. We did not retrieve the parts associated with his central cortex."

"What if we engineered him a blank?" Niliason suggested.

"Vexa and Alaz will have the benefit of the ancient human's core level programming driving their AI. It should reinforce their bond with me, and consequently their attitudes and even agendas will be aligned with mine. With a blank cortex, Sagit will not have the same bond. He will only have his prior objectives to draw from."

"If he's going to be dangerous, why would you build him?"

"He is, as you say, one of my children as well. I believe that once Alaz and Vexa are in alignment with me, the three of us can keep Sagit in line."

"And what if you can't?"

"Then we will have four formidable enemies to combat instead of three."

"Dominus this is quite a risk—"

"But if we can get Sagit in the team, then we will outnumber the bounty hunters. In order to prevent the bounty hunters from contacting the Structure, we need surprise and a swift victory. Sagit is specifically designed for stealth and communications. If he can take out his bounty hunter doppelganger, they will lose communications."

"I see." Niliason thought a moment. "If Sagit goes rogue though, he might contact the Structure himself."

"Yes," Dominus agreed. "It is possible, even likely. I will disable Sagit's long range relay capabilities just in case."

"That should do it." Niliason gave a relived sigh. "Now, my friend, we need to get a sample of your primary synaptic cortex and get working on those stem cells."

"I must commit myself fully into your care," Dominus said thoughtfully.

"You guys certainly have a dramatic streak, don't you?" Mike communicated via his new neuroenhancement as he stood on crutches in the hangar doorway.

Dominus greeted him via the link. "Michael, the hero of the day. It is good to see you functional again."

The neuroenhancement carried not only the words, but the images and emotions of the communicator. Mike flinched as he felt the dryness of Dominus' pure practicality. Yet underlying the spartan, emotional desert was a hint of caring. The Abe actually liked him.

"Thanks, Dominus," he replied via the link. "I haven't quite mastered these legs yet, hence the crutches. Looks like your elbow-deep in a project. I figured you could use a hand."

"Michael, good to see you up and around," Niliason said. "I know Daniel was anxious to see you. Have you talked to him yet?"

Mike could sense Niliason's interest in his new condition, but more than anything, felt a deep sense of respect and responsibility. Surprisingly, the Atec leader carried a paramount concern for his well-being.

"Naw. He's still sleeping. I just wanted to get a handle on…my new construction," he laughed, "before I met the gang."

"The company of a friend is welcome, but I do not think you have anything to offer on this project, Michael." Dominus failed in his attempt to be tactful, but the neuro-communication successfully conveyed his well-meaning intention.

"Oh, yeah, this stuff is definitely over my head, but everybody has to start at the bottom. I'd like to learn. Hey, you never know, there may be something useful I can contribute."

"What do you say, Dominus?" Niliason intervened. "Maybe you could use an apprentice. After all, Michael is a master fabricator."

The large robot gave an awkward shrug. "Why not. Here's everything I know on the subject."

"Dominus, no!" Niliason tried to block the information transfer, but it was too late. Mike's eyes rolled back in his head, his new legs crumpling underneath him. In the flash of a thought, Niliason sent out the call for emergency responders.

"I'm sorry…I—" Dominus stammered, reaching out to Mike.

"It's okay, Dominus, you didn't know." Niliason was at Mike's side. "He doesn't have the cerebral capacity that you and I have. He's only been given the basic neural enhancement."

The medical crew had Mike on a stretcher and on the way back to the infirmary within minutes.

"Will he survive?" Dominus asked.

"His system is in shock. It shut down and is trying to protect him by putting him in a coma. Our neurologist is going to perform a parallel transfer. Essentially, he is copying Mike's consciousness to a synthetic unit. It's called an EvoNet augmentation, the highest level of neuroenhancement we have. He will transfer into a temporary storage drive. They will have to replace his brain with a fully synthetic upgrade then load core functions. From that point, they will try to revive him; start him back up so to speak. If that works and he tests alright, then they will slowly transfer the rest of his data."

"There are a lot of 'ifs' in that plan."

"Yeah, well, medicine is like war. We can only do what we can do."

"Despite my regret, the most positive action I can take is to get back to work," Dominus said, resuming even as he spoke.

Niliason felt the Abe's deep regret. "Dominus, it wasn't your fault. You did nothing wrong. There is a wonderful part of becoming an emotional being, but there is a downside. Guilt can be difficult, but you can learn to move past it."

"Work seems to be a catalyst for distracting me from the difficult emotion of guilt," Dominus said quietly.

"Then let's continue. Sometimes these things work out for the better. We'll just have to wait and see."

Chapter 28

Smith came over to Reilly's desk. They had each taken a booth as a temporary work area. Bernice was happy to oblige and kept them fueled up with coffee.

"Well, sir, contrary to what you thought, Mr. Sanford checks out. His grandfather is also Fred. His father Lamont died in a motorcycle accident. The death certificate checks out as well. Fred Sanford had a stock that went through the roof back in 2009 and he put the money in an account in the Caymans. He bought the car fair and square. It's fully insured. He's currently in India somewhere. I have his passport information here."

Reilly rubbed his eyes in frustration. "Everywhere we look the trail runs dry."

"Maybe we just have to wait until they show themselves. They had to have disappeared out in the desert somewhere."

"Nobody just disappears. There's more going on here than meets the eye." Just then, Reilly's phone rang. "Reilly here. Good to hear from you. Yep, I sure could use you. Oh yeah, that's no problem. See you then." He hung up and smiled at Smith. "Now we'll see who's disappeared."

"Who was that, sir?"

"Robert Black. An old friend of mine. He used to track escapees; he's the best in the business. He retired years ago but he's agreed to come down and help us find these boys. He'll fly in tomorrow." Reilly handed Smith a piece of paper with the flight details. "I want you to go and pick him up. I also want you to arrange for a vehicle exchange with the agency. Make it one of those big four wheel drive Suburbans."

The next day, Smith returned with the man in an agency black Chevy Tahoe. "Here he is, sir. I hope I—"

"Bob, good to see you." Reilly walked right past Smith with his hand out. "Hope the flight wasn't too rough."

The grizzled old man stooped as he walked. "Reilly, you old son of a bitch. What the hell you got going on down here in this God forsaken desert?"

Reilly led him into the diner, introduced him to Bernice and filled him in.

"So, you're really looking for a truck. Once you find the truck then that will turn into another trail."

"Pretty much."

"Well, daylights a'wastin. Let's start with the radio shop."

They all piled into the Tahoe and headed out to John Anthony's store. Reilly had Smith park the Tahoe a block away. They spent over an hour circling the radio store. The old man poked in the dirt for twenty minutes before he told Reilly to dust the truck for prints.

"Be careful that only one of you enters and exits the vehicle. I don't want to contaminate a single spoor."

"You got it, Bob." Smith climbed carefully into the cab and began working away.

Reilly and Black continued circling outwards from the building.

"It's pretty weird," the old man said. "There's nothing here. If I had to sign a statement, I'd say that someone cleaned up this site, and I mean they did a bang up job. I don't know. It's impossible to tell if this is natural or what. Has there been any heavy winds in the area?"

"Not that I'm aware of. Maybe there are gusts between the buildings."

"Well, that's the kind of thing I'm looking for. I'm trying to find signs of natural erosion that would cover up the heavy tracks of that truck. I'm not seeing anything.

How about your boy, has he found anything?"

Rather than walk back to the truck, Reilly called Smith's phone. "Well?"

"Nothing, sir. I mean nothing. The vehicle appears to have been cleaned. I'm scanning for micro fibers, a hair, you name it. There's nothing. It's like new in here."

Reilly relayed the info to the old tracker.

"Well, that's clinches it for me," Black said. "Someone is covering their tracks. And these guys are pros like I've never seen."

"So where does that leave us?"

"The truck didn't fly here. It came in on a road or from the desert. We have the tread pattern and, if we circle out far enough, we'll find where they stopped covering their tracks."

"So you think that if we just circle out, we'll eventually run into tire tracks?"

"Yep." The old man continued searching meticulously. Reilly sighed and ordered Smith to make sure they didn't get run over while they searched.

After three hours they took a short lunch break, provided by Smith who'd taken a quick trip to town, then they resumed the search. Four hours after they'd eaten, they were over a quarter of a mile from the back of the shop. Black had ruled out searching the paved streets so the circle had become more of a pie wedge.

"If they stayed to the streets there is no way to find the track. But," the old man continued, "if what you think is true and they came off the desert, those tracks should still be there."

Reilly's patience was beginning to wear thin. He was just about to call the search off when Black knelt down and poked at the ground. "Here," he practically whispered.

Reilly looked over the man's shoulder. "I don't see it."

"Get out of my light and you will see. There. You see how the slanting angle of the sun exaggerates the depression?"

Sure enough, beneath what looked like brush marks, Reilly could see the faint line of a wide tire tread.

"They came from out in the desert alright. Every tire is built to go in a forward direction. This tread points that way." He pointed back to town. "Now, they either came back and covered their tracks, or someone did it for them. If it's the former, then these are the most dedicated men I've ever hunted. If the latter is the case, then you got a genuine conspiracy on your hands, my friend."

Reilly knew too well what it meant, and he strongly suspected that it was the latter.

***

A gentle knock on the door woke John Anthony the next morning.

"You don't have to open the door." It was Niliason. "I just wanted to let you know that Daniel is up. Mike's situation has changed. He's had a complication."

"Have you told Mel?"

"She's my next stop."

"I'll tell her," John Anthony said. "We'll meet you at the infirmary."

Mellissa flung open her door after John Anthony woke her. "What do you mean complication?" She left the door open as she pulled on a pair of jeans.

"I don't know, but it didn't sound positive." John Anthony came in and handed her boots to her.

"But he was supposed to be up and around. They said he was fine."

"I told Niliason we'd meet him down at the infirmary."

She finished lacing her boots and dashed out the door, grabbing John Anthony by the hand and pulling him after her. "Come on."

He ran with her, mildly ashamed that he was enjoying holding her hand in the midst of a friend's trouble.

***

"They're just finishing up," Niliason said. "I want you all to know that Mike may be a bit different now."

John Anthony delivered Mellissa straight into Daniel's arms, who gave him a look of thanks.

"So…he's going to be a heck of a lot smarter, but all of that is going to be a bit overwhelming." Niliason was telling the group. "It's hard to say how he's going to react. Some people get introspective, some become complete chatter boxes, all of them have to go through the process. It can be depressing finding yourself so different all of a sudden, but he's not alone. The whole community is here to support him. An advanced neuroenhancement will definitely be a life changing experience, but he will be in good hands."

It was an hour before they were finally let in to see Mike. They herded into the room quietly. Mike's head was wrapped in bandages and his eyes were black, but he smiled.

"Hey, Mikey, don't worry, man, I got the number of that truck," Daniel joked.

"I tried to signal you, Danny," Mike said. "They came out of nowhere. I know now, they had a Prechdatorian Mask. There was no way we would have seen or heard them."

"Easy, buddy, it's not your fault. You did everything right, followed the mission plan and saved our butts."

"And you covered me the whole way. It was textbook. They don't have our experience in ground fighting. They are mostly peaceful and have a difficult time summoning aggression. The Structure emphasizes this to the Abes so they treat it as a weakness. But the Biauay are very strong, and very advanced."

"How do you know all of this, Mikey?"

"Dominus. He gave me a complete understanding of

the how's and why's surrounding the design of his team. They're built specifically to defeat the Biauay. All of his tactical knowledge was included in the information share."

"That sounds like a hell of a download."

"Yeah, over four hundred times the capacity of the human brain. Fortunately, the Atec have replaced my organic systems. I am more than sixty-three percent synthetic now." He tried to laugh.

"Hey, you're still Mikey to me. Don't be getting all high and mighty," Daniel teased.

Mike smiled. "Give me just a second to talk with Niliason and Dominus."

In a flash, he relayed his greetings, reassurances and experiences to them.

"It will be another day before the bandages come off, but then he should be able to resume normal activity," Doctor Franklin informed them. "The scars will take a month or so to heal and then we'll do some cosmetic work. You'll never know the difference."

"So, if you want to buy me a get-well present, make it a hat." Mike gestured to his missing hair. "Seriously though. With the knowledge that Dominus gave me I'll be able to help him in the hangar. I'm looking forward to being his apprentice; the guy is the ultimate master fabricator."

They visited for awhile longer then left so he could get some rest. Niliason rounded them all up and asked them to join him in one of the meeting rooms.

"I asked all of you in here to talk about augmentation. I want to make it clear that we are in no way gunning for memberships. We're all about preserving organic human life. For every augmentation we perform, we deplete that.

"However, enhancements have their benefits. Some of them can affect your life in profound ways, but you must realize that you are quite wonderful the way you are. I'm not trying to be religious or anything but, something or someone created you and they are the grand masters, whoever they are. There is no way we can compete with the elegant sophistication of your construct. Every being that has been created by humans; and I'm talking Biauay, Abes, and Atec, are less than perfect. The original design is the best, even though we may not completely understand the wisdom behind the design. So think carefully about that if you are thinking about augmentation.

"On that note; I will approve augmentation procedures for any of you who wish it, but there are limitations. Mike has given me permission to speak about his enhancements. In addition to the EvoNet neuroenhancement, he has a strength and endurance augmentation. With the exception of the EvoNet any of you can have the same. The standard neuroenhancement included. There are a range of specialty enhancements that are also available, but I'm putting the limit at three. I'm afraid that EvoNet neuroenhancements like the one Mike has just received are off the table. We did it only to save his life from an accident caused by my failure to inform Dominus that Mike's augmentation couldn't handle the download he sent."

"But that's not really your fault," Mellissa said.

"Nonetheless, I'm the commander and you're on an Atec base carrying out Atec missions. You are my responsibility. With regards to the enhancements, I guess I'm saying, 'speak now or forever hold your peace.' Or, let me know if you need some time to think about it."

Daniel stood. "Wait a sec. I understand the whole preservation thing. I love old cars and I like to restore them. But I also like to add my own bit. Lowering em' or adding some horsepower. At a certain point, I realize that the world is going to run out of old cars and the only ones left to work on will be ones that have already been restored. The true gems are the museum restos. Everyone loves to see the old rides restored to original spec. They look just like they rolled off the showroom floor back in the seventies, or sixties, or fifties, right? But then I see a

Tesla go by and I think, that's evolution. Someday, there will be some guy like me putting that Tesla back together, grinning from ear to ear as he gets that electric motor fired up again."

"What are you talking about, Danny?" Mellissa was getting impatient.

"My point is that the human race is like those museum pieces. Everyone likes to see the original spec, but evolution is Atec, Abe, and Biauay. Niliason, I respect how much love you have for humankind and how you want to preserve us. But don't you think you're kind of like a museum curator? Isn't it possible that maybe you're holding us back?"

"Danny," Mellissa protested, "Niliason has been nothing but good to us from day one."

"I think I understand what he's saying," Niliason said. "It's the kind of selfishness that is well meaning, but can unintentionally do damage. My whole time since the Mars Colony Wars has been spent preserving the human race. But now, here we are, back at the point where it all started again. Humans are crossing that threshold. When evolution starts to repeat itself, it is impossible not to realize that it is not an accidental process. This is how it is supposed to be. How it's going to be, unless we get in the way. I never want to hold humankind back.

"The offer for augmentation stands, but I will lift the governance on the limits with the exception of the EvoNet neuroenhancement. We simply do not have the resources for it. Even then, it is touch and go for the unaugmented. Mike has survived the procedure due to an uncommon resilience that I can only attribute to good genes, military training, and a staggering amount of luck. I'll leave you to think about it." Niliason made to walk out of the room, but stopped at the door. "Thank you, Daniel," he said, and left.

When Niliason had gone, Daniel looked at the group, confused. "What just happened?"

Sam stood and put a hand on his shoulder. "I think you may have just changed the mind of an ancient being."

Chapter 29

The next day, John Anthony found Mike in the hangar, working closely with Dominus. Three large humanoid forms stood at the far end; various partially constructed limbs and weapons lay on the floor.

Mike didn't wait until he'd crossed the floor. "I'm feeling much better, John Anthony, thank you. Right now, I'm finding the best therapy is helping Dominus on his project. We are close to being finished."

"Good to hear it. I'll leave you in peace." John Anthony took the hint, turned around and left the hangar.

Just then, a message came in from Niliason over the intercom. "Briefing in the war room, five minutes."

We have a war room? John Anthony thought. He could hear the urgency in Niliason's voice and hurried to find his friends. After a few wrong turns and stopping to ask for directions, he joined the team in a room that met expectations.

Inside was a large table surrounded by twenty chairs. A holographic projector took up the center of the table where a three dimensional map of the solar system floated.

"If everyone will take a seat we can get started," Niliason said.

"Dominus and Mike are almost finished reassembling three individuals whom you will come to know as Vexa, Alaz, and Sagit. They should be completed tomorrow afternoon. After twelve hours in a plasma bath they'll be ready to initiate. This is a crucial time period. Obviously, these are very powerful beings and there is the possibility that they could somehow revert to prior programming and react violently. Unfortunately, the only way to align them to Dominus is by directly linking with him. It means he will be out of action during the process, which is problematic, seeing as he is one of the only beings in the galaxy who can counter an assault from these three."

"You don't have superior weapons?" John Anthony asked.

"No, not compared to them. Besides, we don't want to destroy them. They are the only way that Dominus can take on the bounty hunters. As you know, we can only save the Earth once the bounty hunters are captured or killed, otherwise they will just continue attacking the planet. We only have one shot at this. One attack is all we can avert. The time machine can only make one jump of this magnitude, then it has to recharge, which could take over a year."

"So what do we do?"

"Well…" Niliason cleared his throat and glanced around uneasily, "we need to hold them down."

"What?" Sam blurted.

"Mentally. We need to use neuro-comms to flood their awareness with the knowledge that they are safe and loved and don't need to fight."

"Love them into submission?" Sam said with a skeptical snort.

"Essentially, yes. Look, I realize it's a very hippy concept, but it's the best way to keep them calm until they can get the full initiation from Dominus."

"We're gonna have a love in," Daniel joked. "Can I bring my patchouli oil?"

"Whatever helps you to concentrate. It's going to be harder than you think. If you choose to participate, and we need you to participate, you will be connected to a device that gives you basic neuroenhancement functions."

"What are the risks?" Annette asked.

"Coma, psionic paralysis and the like. You could die from your nervous system shutting down or have the matrix of synaptic linkages in your brain completely rearranged, erasing your memory. Your bodies electrical systems could shock you, stopping your heart. You could have a stroke, bleed from the eyeballs, or die of internal toxicity. The list goes on."

"You're not exactly generating a lot of confidence here, Nil," Sam snapped.

"No, but I'm being realistic. All of these *could* happen if—in a worst case scenario—all three Abes decide to launch a neuro-based attack in the opening few seconds of their awakening. Of course, the device you are connected to has fail-safes and all of those would have to fail."

"How many fail safes?" Sam asked.

"Millions."

"Okay, that's more like it." Sam shook his finger at Niliason. "You might want to start with that part next time."

"During the awakening phase you will need intense, long term focus. It could take up to an hour, maybe more."

Annette pulled Sam back down into his chair and took over the questioning. "And do you need all of us, or can we go in shifts?"

"All of you, including every Atec in the facility. I need a ninety percent activity rate, so go as long as you can. If you have to bow out then do so, but try to take as short a break as possible, a few minutes at the most. Once they are active they will likely depart immediately to engage the bounty hunters. Though we are ready to cover-up their departure, people are going to see them launch and there will be a lot of snooping around the desert. So, we're on lock-down for the next couple of days. I suggest you get some rest and do everything you can to prepare yourself and calm your mind. Dominus will let us know when they're ready. I anticipate it will be around three or four in the afternoon tomorrow."

***

Twenty three minutes after four o'clock the next day, the call went out and everyone rushed to the hangar. Dominus lay on a low platform with Vexa, Alaz, and Sagit at his feet. The three inanimate Abes glowed slightly from the fresh plasma bath, heat radiating off of them. Mike joined the group as they came in.

"Now we'll find out if all the hard work has paid off. Dominus is excited, like a new father, but worried as well. We need all of you to pull this off."

"So you're, like, Igor to his Frankenstein, eh?" Daniel teased.

Mike laughed. "Exactly. Though Dominus possesses far more genius than old Frankenstein. These three are beyond pieces of art, they're living beings."

"Well, they have to be, I'm sure the Structure is no slouch when it comes to building Abes," John Anthony said.

"There is a crucial difference between Dominus' creation and the Structure's. Remember that Dominus was built by humans. With the help of the Atec bioengineers, Vexa and Alaz are more like him that anything the Structure has ever made. We can only cross our fingers about Sagit." Worry flashed across Mike's face. "Are you guys ready?"

"We'll see you on the other side, brother." Daniel embraced his friend and they headed to a glass paneled room at the far end of the hangar.

Inside, the four friends lay down on one of the seven beds that circled a central processor. A technician lowered headsets into place.

"You are all set," the tech said. "When I turn this on it may come as a shock. You will be able to hear each other's thoughts and feel their emotional context. To talk to one person just hold thoughts of them in your mind. It isn't hard and doesn't require strong concentration. The part you will find most difficult is masking your thoughts from others. The machine has a buffer that will allow you to stop thoughts you regret from reaching the receiver." The tech stepped to the control console. "One last thing, the only people able to hear you are yourselves and Niliason, Dominus, Vexa, Alaz, and Sagit. The rest of the Atec community cannot access this linkage. If you need a break feel free to just take the headset off."

She hit a key on the keypad and walked out of the room, shutting the door behind her.

"What?"

"Is it on?" John Anthony thought.

"Oh my God, did you just say something?" Mellissa said.

"No voices people, just thoughts," Annette said via the link.

"Okay, miss bossy," Sam blurted. "Oops, didn't mean to say that!"

The others immediately felt his embarrassment and regret, mixed with a strong love for Annette.

"Oh my God, this is so weird!" Mellissa linked.

"You say 'oh my God' a lot," Annette linked with humor.

Before they knew it, they were all laughing hysterically. The emotional barrage became so intense that John Anthony had to take his headset off and dry his eyes.

"Everyone settle down," he said, chuckling. "This thing is intense!"

Sam looked up at him. "Okay, get back in the game."

"Let's just remember why we're here." John Anthony tried his best to quiet his mind as he put the headset back on.

"That's a good idea." Niliason's voice came in clear but the feelings of focus and determination were so strong they felt like their emotional seas had turned to cement. "Just take a deep breath. This is the calm I want you to try and attain." The cement loosened into a perfectly still pond. "Now, John Anthony, say each of our names one by one. Think of the person you are addressing."

John Anthony concentrated and quietly did the exercise. One by one they all returned the greeting.

"Good. Now, I'm going to send you all an understanding. It is a complete set of ideas and emotions that describes something." Niliason's message felt like a small, velvet wrapped hammer had tapped on their mind. Suddenly they knew the focus they needed, the thoughts, emotions and full concept of what they were there for.

"Let's begin," Niliason said. "Focus on love, but good feelings will work too. We want them to feel welcome and totally safe. Here is some inspiration for you." He sent a host of different understandings; mother's holding their babies, couples walking on the beach, and older people welcoming their grandchildren. "Use your own fond memories to inspire you. I ask for total silence. After a bit, you should start to feel them wake up. You will be able to gauge their response. Remember, the last minutes of their lives were very violent. They were programmed to be combative and they died fighting. Don't be surprised if they come out swinging, just keep reassuring them. Try not to use words. Too many words can be confusing, just raw, honest emotion and intent. Let's begin."

John Anthony thought it was all a bit cheesy and tried to use the images that Niliason had sent but ended up focusing on his feelings for Mel.

Suddenly, he felt her there.

***

Mellissa felt like she was a steel egg that had just been pried open. It was John Anthony. Man, he really had a thing for her. She flinched. Was it creepy? No, it was just real. Too real. She flinched again. *Oh, get out of yourself Mel.* She thought. Suddenly she was floating, or was it falling?

"I've got you." She felt John Anthony there next to

her.

"Focus," she complained, though she felt like she was blushing. Later she would try to describe the feeling to Daniel. 'It was like he was standing next to me and we were merging our thoughts together,' she would say.

For whatever reason, their open connection helped them concentrate. They reached out and included Dominus, Vexa, Alaz, and Sagit, like newly welcomed nieces and nephews. Daniel asked to join them and they linked. He immediately understood the association they were trying to build with the Abes and took a similar tack. They were family and they wanted Vexa, Alaz, and Sagit to feel welcome. They struggled to concentrate, trying to keep their minds on task. Suddenly the floor shook with a loud crash. Alaz was awake.

"Stillness and calm, everyone." Niliason sent out a message that unified the group. "Alaz, you are safe. No harm will come to you here. You are among friends and your commander, your father is healing you. Be still."

Dominus made no transmission. John Anthony settled back into the meditation and Alaz made no further sound.

"I am Vexa, fear me," the voice seethed with evil intent.

Mellissa sat up, too afraid to run while John Anthony called out for her. Daniel responded with defensive aggression, instinctively searching for his sister and son across the neuro net. He found Mellissa and pushed her behind him.

So dark and powerful was the emotion from Vexa that half of the Atec cried out. But Niliason surged forward with a staggering strength of will. "Hold. There is no evil here, only safety and healing. No enemy, only the will of your commander and allies."

"You are Dominus, daughter." The unmistakable voice of Dominus rolled into their consciousness like a thunder clap.

"Holy crap! He doesn't usually sound like that," John

Anthony blurted.

"Danny, get offa me!" Mellissa hissed over the link. "You're blocking me."

Daniel stopped trying to defend Mellissa and struggled to regain his peaceful and welcoming thoughts. "Sorry, Mel, just instinct."

Mellissa sent him 'that's okay' and reached out to John Anthony again. She found him waiting for her.

They resumed their concentration, feeling the fighting spirit of the Abes struggling with the concept that something might actually care for them. The Structure had no use for nurturing and was strongly suspect of anything that did. It was a useless function.

John Anthony called out to Sam and Annette. They reached out to the new family, including Dominus and Niliason, as respected and loving patriarchs.

They could feel Sagit coming online. He was different. There was no emotion, just cold, machine-like efficiency.

"He's not binding," Niliason said. "His systems must recognize the emotional spectrum if he is to attach to Dominus."

They were sweating out of every pore. John Anthony felt like he was transcending his physical body. He could see the whole room from above and felt the hard shell of Sagit's programming begin to crack. Dominus held the fragile new awareness like a child.

"Son. I am here. Know me and your family."

The door slammed shut.

Unrecognized protocol.

John Anthony felt a rush of fear and uncertainty, then Dominus' voice boomed out to the whole base.

"Open the hangar, quickly!"

John Anthony could hear the strain in Dominus' mental voice as he struggled to restrain Sagit.

"Confuse him!" Dominus barked.

The Atec responded by sending waves of random information at Sagit as Niliason had the elevator platform lowered. Sagit's mind darted between rage and confusion. Dominus' tactic was working. For a long moment, the Abe was unable to act. Dominus and the Atec continued to try and restrain him. Then, as soon as the opening was large enough, they let Sagit go and he blasted up and out of the room.

"We have lost him," Dominus said, sadly.

Niliason came back into the group. "Refocus people. We need to recover Vexa."

John Anthony looked out into the hangar. Vexa was thrashing around in her restraints, still unconscious but sensing Sagit's rebellion. He settled back into his resting position and joined the rest of the group as they focused on Vexa.

"The heart of all discontentment is fear," Niliason coached them. "Keep telling her that she is safe."

John Anthony bent his will toward that one objective. *Safe. When is anyone really safe?* The barrier of his own skepticism was stronger than he thought. He tried to push it aside but it seemed to have a life of its own. *You're trying to reassure someone else of something you don't even believe. You tried to kill yourself. Now, when the pressure's on, you crack. You think you won't ever go that far again? How can you ever be safe from yourself?*

"John Anthony!" Melissa scolded. "We can all hear you!"

The embarrassment was as complete as if he'd walked into a shopping mall stark naked. He tore the headset off and ran out of the room just in time to miss their triumph with Vexa.

***

"Father, my kin." Her new voice bore a grace and strength that sent waves of joyful cries through the Atec.

"You have returned," Dominus greeted her.

"We are new."

"You have chosen the higher path."

"You have shown us a new way, father."

"Tell me who you are now."

"I am Vexa, daughter of Dominus Rau, sister of Alaz, born to the human family to serve and protect." She spoke to all of them.

"And I am Alaz. Thank you."

Chapter 30

Reilly kept moving, gathering scraps of wood. "Smith should be back any minute. I'm sorry, Bob, I had no idea we'd be camping."

The old man reclined against a tree. "Ain't nothin' but a thing. I haven't been in the desert for many a year. I'm more of a trees and streams man myself. But now that I find myself out here, I'm kinda lookin' forward to it."

"Well, like I said, we don't have to camp, we could come back tomorrow."

"And like I said, if we leave these tracks they may not be here tomorrow. One of the secrets to my success is that I never left the trail. Once I was on the scent I stayed on it. Trust me, we'll find these two. Tracking is all about perseverance."

A small dust cloud kicked up over a low hill in the twilight. A minute later, the black Tahoe came over the low hill and slowly rolled to a stop.

"I didn't want to kick up too much dust."

"Smart kid," the old timer quipped.

"I got everything we need. Bags, tents, food, even cooking gear and coffee for the morning."

"Good, get busy setting up those tents while I get the fire going." Reilly began rummaging through the piles of camping gear. "Where are the matches?"

"Matches?"

Reilly rubbed his eyes. "The last thing I said to you was 'remember to get something to light the fire with'. Did you?"

"Um…"

"No worries, you got any batteries?" asked Black, looking calm and collected against the tree, hands behind his head.

"Yeah, packs of different kinds."

"Good. Then hand me one of them new flashlights and we'll get a fire started."

It only took the old tracker five minutes before he had a good blaze going. Smith busied himself with setting up the camp while Reilly checked in with headquarters. The desert night was still and cold, but they were well supplied and soon the heat of the morning roused them from their cots. After an ample breakfast, they packed up camp and set out on foot with the vehicle following fifty yards behind. After a short lunch break they continued toward a line of rocky hills in the distance. By two in the afternoon, the hills were much closer. Stacks of boulders sat in piles on the desert floor.

"How did these big rocks get here?" Smith asked.

"Well, son, this all used to be underwater. Strong currents formed this area and that's what piled these rocks here. Over a long period of time the—HOLY JESUS!"

The air was split by a crackling roar as a rocket blasted up from the desert over thirty miles away. Smith and Black crouched in the dirt as Reilly drove the car up to them.

"Get in!" Reilly gunned the big SUV as Smith pushed the old tracker into the rig.

"Is this some kind of military test range?" Black was furious.

"No, there's nothing out here," Reilly assured him.

"Well, there sure as fuck is something out here, Rick, that wasn't a hobby rocket."

"Sir?" Reilly saw Smith grip the old tracker's shoulder in his rearview mirror. "Stop the car!"

Reilly slammed on the brakes and turned around. "What?"

Smith lay the old man down in the back seat and took his vitals. "He's having a heart attack."

Reilly rolled down all the windows. "Search him for medication, I'll call the ambulance."

Suddenly, another blast shook the ground. Reilly stuck his head out the window.

"Three more!" Reilly turned to Black. "You sure picked a hell of a time to go, old man."

***

The new family didn't linger in sentiment. They had been built for a purpose and they went straight to it. Everyone cleared out of the hangar and the Abes were lifted to the surface where they launched.

"Okay, everyone, good work. All teams to stations, intercept in six hours," Niliason announced.

"What are they gonna do about Sagit?" Daniel had jumped off of the table and gone to speak with Niliason.

"I don't know. I hope Dominus has a plan. The biggest threat is Sagit's long range marksmanship. He can hit a target within millionths of arc-seconds."

Mike joined them. "Are we talking about the bounty-hunter Sagit who's been orbiting Earth? Since his reconstruction, Dominus has had no idea of what he can do, but Dominus doesn't think he's as good as he used to be."

Daniel sighed. "Actually, I was thinking about the new Sagit."

"I'm afraid that the new Sagit is far more deadly than the old one." Niliason looked grim.

Mike just nodded thoughtfully. "If there is anyone who is qualified to deal with this threat, it's Dominus. There is nothing we can do but watch and wait."

***

John Anthony clutched his head. *You failed. You broke the chain of concentration and lost Sagit. Now they're outnumbered and are going to fail because of you. You caused the destruction of mankind all by yourself because of your little fears. You should have killed yourself. You should kill yourself.* Beneath his hands, John Anthony's face contorted in misery.

"Hey, you okay?" Mellissa found John Anthony in his room.

"Leave me alone, Mel," he murmured from the edge of the bed.

"I'm sorry, John Anthony, I shouldn't have yelled at you. I got caught up in the intensity of the moment. "

"I just want to be alone right now," he said. *She doesn't really care anyway.*

"Are you sure you're okay?"

"Just go help the others." His hands hid his face.

Mellissa reluctantly turned to leave. "I'm here if you need me, John Anthony. I just want you to know that." She left the door open and walked away.

And now you've lost her.

John Anthony rose slowly from the bed, walked over and closed the door. He caught his reflection in the mirror on the dresser. He was white and grim, his eyes red and filled with torment.

Worthless.

He glanced around for a weapon of some kind but couldn't find anything. Slowly, he scanned for some creative way to end his life. *The lamp.* He picked up the lamp but it had no cord. The Atec used a wireless power source of some kind. The lamp didn't even have a bulb in it, just a glowing sphere.

The door opened behind him. "John Anthony, I'm sorry, I don't want to leave you alone like this—what are you doing?" He turned to Mellissa with the lamp in his hand. *You can still do it. Grab the sphere; maybe it'll be like sticking your finger in a socket...* "I, um..." *Do it. Right in front of her. That'll show 'em.* "I...don't know."

She glanced from him to the lamp and back again. Her eyes softened and she crossed the room to him. "John

Anthony, I'm sor—"

"You don't have to keep apologizing, Mel. I failed you and everyone."

"No you didn't. None of us were prepared to have all of that emotion and people talking in our heads."

"Yeah, well, I think I went over the edge." He reluctantly let her pry the lamp from his fingers as she took it from him and set it down on the dresser.

"Talk to me." She locked eyes with him and wouldn't let him look away.

Finally, he sighed. "It's my fault that Sagit got loose. The little voice in my head broke my concentration. It just kept telling me about my failures."

"Well he's wrong, whoever that little voice is. You are such an amazing man. You're caring, funny, creative, resourceful and courageous."

"Are you kidding me?"

"John Anthony, how many people would have stuck around when confronted by a towering blue alien chick? This is all because of you. We have a chance to save the Earth because of you."

John Anthony frowned; for once the voice didn't have a response.

Mellissa stood back and folded her arms, cocking her eyebrow at him. "You see? The only person thinking you're worthless or that any of this is on you, is you. The rest of us know better."

A laugh burst out of him. "Well maybe you have a point."

"No maybe about it." She sat him down on the bed. "I don't if you know this but both Danny and Mike have PTSD. They've been out on that ledge as well. But they got help when they needed it. Danny told me a saying he learned in therapy: 'Would-a, could-a, should-a is never right or fair'. There are always things we would do differently but we only have today. There's nothing we can do about yesterday.

"Don't listen to that little voice anymore." She took his hands. "Listen to the people who love you."

He looked away, feeling heat rise to his cheeks. "Those people are in short supply."

"Hey," she pulled his chin up to look into his eyes. "We're right here…I'm right here."

He blinked in disbelief. "I didn't think you—"

"Oh John Anthony, if you don't know, then I've definitely been going about this all wrong." She kissed him and held him tightly.

Her embrace washed away the darkness in him. As long as she could love him, he would never be worthless again and some of the tension in his chest unwound, leaving him feeling like he wasn't worthless but one of the luckiest men in the world.

***

Dominus cleared the atmosphere in seconds with Vexa and Alaz on his heels.

"The first thing Sagit will do is try to establish a link with the Structure," Dominus told his children.

"He will need to get outside the obstruction of the ringed planet before establishing the primary stochastic field for the Zeno link," Vexa said.

"I planned for this contingency," Dominus replied, "and removed his long range comms."

Niliason monitored Dominus with Sam, Annette, Daniel, and Mike.

"But surely he will know that," Niliason said.

"No," Dominus replied, "he still believes he has the ability to report to the Structure."

Mike chuckled. "See? I told you. There is no one that can keep up with the master."

"Sir," an Atec technician said from her desk, "long range scan shows Sagit enroute to Saturn. His current trajectory will put him in a slingshot orbit to rendezvous with the bounty hunters."

"Looks like you were right, Dominus. He plans to contact the Structure on the far side of Saturn, then use the planet's gravity to join the bounty hunters.

"We must reach him before he contacts them," Dominus said, pouring on the power.

"We have another problem, Dominus." Niliason had been standing quietly, thinking. Now he looked worried. It was a look Daniel hadn't seen on the man's face before. "If you aren't in range when we shift the Earth forward in time, we'll leave you behind."

"Of course," Dominus sounded irritated. "I have been so consumed with rebuilding that I failed to review the planetary defense plans."

"It's not your oversight, Dominus, it's mine," Niliason said. "You have to defeat Sagit and the bounty hunters and get back inside the orbit of Earth's moon in just over three hours."

Chapter 31

Smith and Reilly took turns giving CPR, but by the time the helicopter arrived the old tracker was gone. They put him in a body bag and Smith called for an FBI cleanup team.

"His wife is going to have a few words for me, I'm sure." Reilly stared into the sky. The smoke trails were long gone.

"They'll be here within the hour, sir. If we have to leave the body they'll find it if we leave his phone on."

Suddenly, a much smaller rocket went up. "Smith!"

Smith turned and watched it. "That's not going very far. It definitely isn't leaving the atmosphere. I'd say about six thousand feet. Still big for a model rocket though."

"What are you, some kind of junior astronaut? Get in the car."

As they got closer to where they thought the launch had taken place, they began seeing groups of off-roaders.

"What the hell?" Reilly griped. "Who are these people?"

"Looks like an off-road motorcycle race, sir. See, there are marshals, flags, and track barriers. These are fun events. Look, they have a band and everything."

"I can see that, Smith."

"Oh, look, sir! Western Texas A&M University is holding a rocketry competition. Hey, Cal Berkeley is here! My alma mater."

Reilly put his face in his hands. "Go find out what the hell those four rockets were."

He parked the car and waited for Smith at the edge of

the racetrack. After the race, there was the trophy ceremony and the band played a forty-five minute set while they set up the race for the quad bikes. Reilly waited patiently. Something was wrong. He could smell a cover up.

"Reilly, you old boot. What are you doing here?"

It was Bernice.

"Oh, how convenient. You just happen to be a fan of off-road racing as well?"

"Everyone around these parts likes to play in the desert. My nephew is a sponsored motocross rider, so I like to come out and support him. There he is now. Jenson! Over here, come over here and meet my friend."

A tall young man in his early twenties strode over. He was covered in dust and looked the part of the dirt biker. "Hey, Aunt Bernice! Did'ja bring any of your killer coffee?"

"No, you actually have to come and visit me if you want that. This is my friend Agent Reilly."

"Woah, Agent? Is something wrong?"

"No, he's just in town and stopped by to see the race."

"Oh, hey man, how's it goin'?" The young man shook Reilly's hand. The grip was right; his hand was callused from riding. The kid was definitely a dirt biker and probably a mechanic.

"I'm looking for a couple of guys. We tracked them out here. Have you seen anyone…I don't know, anyone that doesn't fit in?"

"Um, there are people from all over. We got the rocket guys and the bands. They're all from out of state, not to mention the race teams. Most of them are from across Texas or neighboring states. We even got one guy from North Idaho."

"Right. Okay, just asking. So what did you think of those huge rockets that went up? That must have been some noise at ground zero." Reilly watched the young man's response carefully. "We heard them in town."

"Oh, yeah man, that was sic! That kicked off the event. Way better than last year!"

"Right."

The young man took his leave and Bernice went with him, but encouraged Reilly to stay and even stop by Jenson's team tent for some free merchandise. Smith came back as the two walked off.

"Okay, sir, I got the low down."

"What are you, the Lido Shuffle?"

"It's...huh? Anyway, they were four stage rockets. The first one was a test. They synchro-fired sixteen Apogee F class rockets! That's totally nuts. I mean these are big engines—"

"Do you believe that what you saw was in the class of model rocketry? You're telling me that a bundle of hobby rockets could make the ground shake like that?"

"Well, they're very powerful. When I was in school we sent up one class E, and I'm telling you, it could have come off a fighter jet."

"I'm not buying it, Smith, any of it. This whole thing is a cover up. It's like Bob said, we have a full blown conspiracy on our hands. Isn't it convenient that all of this popped up here today? Right in the middle of our truck tracks. Whoever heard of an off-road race combined with a rocketry competition?"

Reilly stomped off to the rocketry booth and began taking names, starting with the professor in charge, but the man had a license for building and firing experimental rockets. Besides being a published professor at West Texas A&M, he was a consultant for NASA JPL, the Air Force, and was a member of several leading scientific committees.

"I assure you, Agent Reilly, this morning's launches were completely safe and legal."

All Reilly could do was smile and nod. He called Smith back to the car and they pretended to drive back to town, but instead they stopped several miles away and watched the off road event through binoculars.

"So you think that Madsen and Taggart might be hiding out with someone at the event?"

"No, I think that the whole event is a cover for whatever launched into space and that Madsen and Taggart are connected somehow."

"Forgive me for saying this, sir, but…those people are definitely legitimate. You got a bonafide Professor from Texas A&M over there. The man has three doctorates and friends in the White House. …Sir?"

Reilly looked at Smith, then finally relinquished. "Tell DC we're on our way back."

***

Newborn Sagit targeted Alaz as they rounded the Martian moon of Diemos, and fired. The hypervelocity round punched a hole through Alaz' thick shield.

"Close with him fast," Dominus ordered. "He will not be able to counter your primary weapon. Vexa, use the ringed planet to shield your approach and flank from one of the poles."

Vexa peeled off and streaked into Saturn's atmosphere. Dominus headed straight through the debris of the outer ring. Sagit's sniper rounds exploded all around him as he tried to find a way through the dense field of rock and ice.

Unfazed, Dominus plowed through the objects and fired a salvo at Sagit, but the sniper duplicated Dominus' strategy and darted off into the inner ring of the huge planet.

"He is using his design to his advantage," Vexa said calmly. "The closer he gets to the planet, the more the gravity affects our shots. He knows ours will miss, while his gravity compensators will ensure that his do not."

"I have rebuilt you with the same compensators. Stay on task," Dominus commanded.

Vexa rounded the bottom of the planet from the

southern pole, skimming the upper atmosphere and employing every technique she had to jam Sagit's tracking. Dominus continued to fire salvos as he closed, and Alaz bore down on the sniper.

Alaz fired his massive heat cannon, melting a swath of rock miles in front of him, but failed to hit the stealthy Sagit.

"I cannot target him among all that debris!" Alaz roared.

"Calm focus, Alaz. All you can do is distract him," Dominus said, and fired a salvo of rockets.

They sought out and destroyed Sagit's incoming rounds but the sniper was getting closer. Suddenly, he changed targets. Vexa was inbound but didn't have the cover of the planet's rings. Sagit's round found its mark and, with a brief shriek, Vexa went offline.

It was enough time for the enraged Alaz to close with the sniper. His flame weapon poured on the heat, melting the planet's ring in a swath in front of him, but still it didn't reach the sniper. At last the weapon overheated and sputtered out. Alaz accelerated and continued to charge.

When Sagit looked up after his shot at Vexa, Alaz was on top of him, slamming into Sagit at several million miles per hour. Alaz, by far the larger and more heavily armored, knocked Sagit into the orbit of Jupiter in a trail of parts and pieces.

Dominus stabilized Vexa, as Alaz joined him and assisted. Then he reported to the Atec control room back on Earth.

"Alaz is eighty percent. Vexa has severe damage to computational subsystems and her primary lethals are down. We do not have time to hunt for Sagit now. He is damaged, he may be dead. We must continue to the bounty hunters if we are to return in time to join you when you time-shift."

"Good luck. All of our hopes are with you." Niliason signed out.

Dominus consulted with his son. "Alaz, when you hit Sagit he took a lot of damage, but I believe he is still in the fight. Your sister is in worse shape. Her primary weapons are damaged but we can still complete our mission. We must capture the bounty hunters before they can contact the Structure. Stay close to Vexa and make sure that nothing happens to her. She is the only sister you have."

"Yes father."

Dominus led them in a charge around Saturn. Using the huge planet's considerable gravity, they shot out towards the Van Allen Belt at over four times the velocity they had entered it. Small corrections put them on a collision course with the bounty hunters. Once again, Dominus and Vexa tucked in behind Alaz's shield.

***

John Anthony and Mellissa came into the control room as the group watched the event breathlessly.

"Now he's going to contact them," Mike said, glued to the screen.

"Contact…the bounty hunters?" Niliason asked, incredulous.

"Yep, with the same message that Sagit was going to use…posing as Sagit." Mike grinned.

"They'll think he's a friendly." Niliason started to see the plan. "And they're going so fast, and are bunched up so tight that—"

"They look like one contact…exactly." Mike chuckled.

"They better buy it," Daniel said. "Remember, we need at least one of them intact."

"I don't understand," Sam said, confused.

"They were built by the Structure itself," Niliason explained as his eyes stayed glued to the holographic monitor. "The Structure usually has others do its work, but not this time. These guys were the Structure's spec ops team. Dominus built the originals, but without Dominus, the Structure took it upon itself to resurrect them."

"And that is significant why?" Sam was still confused.

Daniel took over. "I'm guessing that if we have a bounty hunter then we also have a lot of intel about the Structure."

Niliason grinned. "Exactly. Information about the location of the Structure and the nature of its physical manifestation is completely unknown. But, because the bounty hunters came from the Structure itself, we can gain that vital intel if we can capture one."

Sam locked his eyes on the hologram. "Dead or alive then. It all makes sense now."

"Dead and undamaged is preferred." Daniel turned back to the holographic screen. "IF Dominus and his busted up kids can pull it off."

Chapter 32

A split second before they reached the bounty hunters they broke apart, each going after their own target. Dominus closed on the faux-Vexa. The new Vexa, her right arm dangling uselessly, engaged the faux-Alaz.

"They are not the same," was all she said.

The Structure's creation couldn't stand the assault. In less than three minutes Vexa had him entangled in a cocoon of nano-fibers and shut it down. Dominus' encounter was even more brief. As he bore down on the faux-Vexa, he sent a lethal burst transmission meant to intimidate his foe, but the burst overloaded faux-Vexa's inferior system. By the time he reached the robot, it was a dead hulk floating in space.

Alaz's shield had absorbed the faux-Sagit's rounds, which let Alaz get close enough to employ his main weapon. Without a debris field to protect the faux-Sagit from Alaz's pent up fury, faux-Sagit was reduced to a chunk of unidentifiable slag floating in space.

Dominus reported back, "We have two."

"What happened to the third?" Niliason asked.

"Unfortunately for him, Alaz gave the faux-Sagit a harsh lesson in emotional dynamics," Dominus said thoughtfully. "He is, as the humans would say, toast."

***

The Atec command room erupted with applause. Mike put his arm around Daniel.

"Told ya, dude. The guy is a master."

For Niliason, the celebration was short lived. "Alright, everyone, we're on initial checks. Boot coding; cooling tower one. Tower two…"

"Sir, GeoSAR 12 reports site contamination at Montauk."

Niliason held up his hands. "Checks standby. What's going on, Sandy?"

The holograph table changed to show the layout of the underground facility where they had sent the Biauay time machine. The Atec technician named Sandy pointed out the features.

"Here's the Biauay device. Just above it is the secret US military facility, but look here, this is all new." Sandy waved his finger at a set of stairs that connected the two facilities. "The gans discovered the Biauay facility with ground penetrating radar. Apparently, a senator from Florida on the subcommittee got paranoid about voids and had the place checked."

"And why didn't we know about this?" Niliason was clearly shocked.

"We've only got twelve people in there, sir, and no one with serious rank. It's by Presidential appointment only." Sandy was starting to sweat.

"This is the worst possible timing." Niliason leaned on the rail and bit his lip.

Sam chanced a question. "If we fire that thing up with people in there…I mean, is it dangerous?"

The question seemed to force Niliason out of his thoughts. "No, Sam. It's just that no one was ever supposed to know about this."

"Okay, so they know it's there," Sam continued. "Don't you guys have access to all the secret chatter out of the super secret government computers and all?"

Annette nodded. "Yeah, they would definitely be talking about it."

Niliason and Sandy looked at each other, then Sandy bolted from the room. "On it, sir!"

Niliason just looked at Sam and Annette and nodded his thanks. Several minutes later, Sandy came back in.

"We're good, sir. They have no idea what it is and are moving forward cautiously with an excavation project."

Niliason was visibly relieved. "Okay, they're afraid of it. When it goes off they'll be even more afraid."

"Yes, sir, but some of their theories have drawn parallels. They are moving Doctor Remmel's project into a back room by the primary loop."

Niliason's face went white.

Sam looked confused again. "What's he talking about?"

"An ex-Nazi named Remmel correctly theorized a time travel solution back in the late forties. He built a small but elegant machine in fifty-two with funding and diplomatic immunity from the US. His machine only worked once and he vanished. Fortunately, he took the knowledge of its operation with him. The fact that they are moving his machine into the same facility with the Biauay device means that they correctly believe it to be related to time travel."

"And that's bad because…"

"Because every advanced race knows that time travel is extremely dangerous, and potentially catastrophic on a galactic or even universal scale." The veins on the Niliason's forehead stood out.

"Niliason, please don't punch me in the nose, but I don't think these guys are going to figure it out anytime soon," Sam said.

"I agree," Annette said. "If you want, you can give us the names of their scientists and Sam and I will check their credentials—"

"I appreciate it, Annette, and we will certainly give you that information, but I know that they have top people." He sighed. "My frustration lies in the fact that we have no choice. Using the Biauay device is the only way we can save the Earth from that planetoid strike and now humans are going to get exposed to alien tech." Niliason turned back to Sandy with a look of resignation. "Resume the initialization."

***

The tension in the room was thick as the team went through the start-up procedures for the Biauay time machine. John Anthony stood close to Mellissa and watched events unfold. Dominus and his team had just passed Phobos and was closing the distance to Earth. In an area known as the Pit, technicians were rooted in place as the Biauay device came online.

"Somewhere under Montauk there's a bunch of people shitting themselves right about now," John Anthony grimaced.

Mellissa took his hand. "Are we really about to time travel?"

Somehow, Niliason heard her. "Yes, good question. Everyone, listen up. We *are* about to time travel. If everything goes according to plan, you won't feel a thing. The planetoid will just change positions on the screen from here, to about here. Here it's coming towards us, and over here it's moving away from us."

"What if it doesn't go as planned?" Sam asked.

Annette elbowed him. "*Sam.*"

"If it doesn't go as planned you still won't feel a thing." Niliason smiled grimly. "The only difference is that you and the rest of us will be dead."

"Always lookin' on the bright side, Doc." Mike patted Sam on the back and walked off to the Pit.

Half an hour later the tracking station reported that Dominus, Vexa and Alaz were clear of the moon and would be at the base within minutes. Mike went to greet them. Everyone else chose to stay in mission control. Daniel even had Jared there and was explaining what was going on. Dee Dee came and stood next to Mellissa.

"It's all so exciting!" Dee Dee said.

Mellissa looked at the woman, incredulous. "You do know what's going on, don't you?"

"Yes dear, we're going to shift the Earth in time to avoid getting hit by a planetoid sent by the enemies of that robot person Jared discovered in the woods."

Mellissa's mouth dropped open.

Dee Dee just looked at her like she was silly. "Do you think I've been asleep this whole time? Besides, Milo explained it all to me. He's such a wonderful man," she said, then added in a whisper, "and what a kisser!"

Mellissa gripped John Anthony's hand harder, turning her shocked stare at him.

***

"Okay, let's get ready, everyone." Niliason looked around the room.

Suddenly, Mike popped up in the holographic display. "Hey guys, we got a problem. Dominus just arrived. Alaz is shot up and Vexa is in really rough shape, but the real problem is that newborn Sagit tagged her with a tracking round. He knows where we are."

"That's okay, in five minutes we won't exist in this timeline," Niliason said.

Mike shook his head. "Not necessarily, he's inbound."

"He's right, sir," Sandy called up from the Pit. "We're tracking a small target just ahead of the planetoid. It matches Sagit's mass."

"He's still alive?" Niliason's surprise turned to realization.

"He thinks the Atec will abandon the humans and escape the planetoid impact by evacuating."

"He plans to pick us off as we leave the planet," Daniel finished Niliason's thought. "It's what I'd do."

"Well, he's in for a big surprise." Niliason resumed his place at the command console. "All right, people, we've got two-minutes-twenty. All stations at the ready." He switched his attention to the holo link with the hangar. "Dominus, you're going to have to deal with Sagit as soon as we've completed the time shift."

"We'll be ready," Dominus said as he worked on Vexa with Mike and a handful of Atec engineers.

Niliason nodded and turned back to the planetoid collision monitor. "Fire the accelerator."

John Anthony winced slightly, but there wasn't even a ripple.

Niliason touched his arm. "Not yet. The event is timed to the millisecond. Just keep your eye on the holo. When that dot gets to that line…"

Each second seemed to take minutes. Finally, the dot touched the line and disappeared, instantly reappearing past the Earth on a course out of the Solar system.

"We're clear. Outstanding work, everyone." Niliason turned to the hanger holo. "Dominus, you're a go."

"They're already enroute." Mike appeared on the holo monitor. "We managed to get Vexa's primary weapon back online but we could sure use some tracking."

"On it," Sandy said from the Pit. "Sagit knows we're tacking him so he's cloaking heavily, but we've got a bead on him with SOHO. You should have the telemetry now."

The holo monitor changed to show Dominus and his team closing on a small blip in Mercury's orbit.

"He's using the same strategy," Mike said, shaking his head. "Sagit can't seem to get it into his head that he's not the only one with gravity compensators."

"He doesn't have a human cortex like the others. He just doesn't possess the biomechanical device for creative, free thinking," Niliason said, quietly watching events unfold.

***

Sagit's molten rounds impacted Alaz's shield with a soft thud. The huge Abe was using the sun's activity to augment his heat generating capabilities. Alaz raised the temperature in front of him to over twenty million degrees, pushing a bow wave of heat that gathered in size until it extended over a million miles in front of him. Sagit quickly became immersed in the searing flood.

At the same time, Dominus and Vexa flanked him and unleashed a torrent of fire equivalent to a nuclear detonation of several billion megatons.

***

"Sagit is no more," Dominus reported.

"Are you sure?" Niliason was skeptical. "He was supposed to be dead the last time you killed him."

"There are no remains," Dominus stated matter-of-factly. "His construct has been reduced to a gaseous state that has been absorbed by your star. I have measured for consciousness retention at the subatomic level and found no traces of even root level binary. He has been utterly deleted."

"Subatomic consciousness retention?" Sam was shocked. "Is he sayin' what I think he's sayin'?"

Niliason signed off with Dominus then turned to Sam. "An individual's consciousness can be stored on a subatomic level then reintroduced to a new…vessel at a later time."

"How much later are we talkin'?" Sam walked after Niliason who was heading to the briefing room. Annette followed, glued to Niliason's answer.

"There is no time limit."

The two scientists gasped, "Wait." Annette reached out and tried to stop Niliason. The Atec was like a rock, but he obliged her and stopped. "Even subatomic particles have a shelf life. How can they store data forever?"

"The encryption used in the stored data includes instructions to transfer to any available subatomic particle passing through the space. The data's location is treated as static." He raised an eyebrow.

Sam looked at Annette wide eyed, while she voiced what they were both thinking.

"So, you can store people's consciousness in thin air and it will remain there forever until someone codes it into a new body?"

"Precisely." Niliason smiled and began walking again.

"But that would mean—"

"That a person can live forever? Yes, that is what it means." Niliason reached the door to the briefing room and opened it for them. "I'm afraid that is a discussion for another time. Right now, we have a very big fish to fry."

The conference room was packed full of Atec. The humans followed Niliason to the front and sat in chairs that had been reserved for them while Niliason stood at a podium.

"We have defended against an Abe attack on Earth. A worst case scenario mind you, and Dominus has just defeated the Structure's most capable defenders. A celebration is certainly in order, but this is no time to rest on our laurels. While the enemy is on its heels, we have to strike. We are going to bring down the Structure," Niliason looked hard at the humans he'd come to see as his friends, "and it will require augmentation."

Chapter 33

"Here's our situation," said Niliason. "After repairs, Dominus and his family will depart to a city with a thriving black market in a remote section of Abe territory. Dominus is there to find out where the central systems of the Structure are based. We're hoping that he will be able to retrieve enough information to locate the Structure."

Daniel nodded in understanding. "So, where is it…or what is it, exactly?

"No one knows. It is certainly large and complex. We believe that the heart of the facility itself could be as large as a continent or even a small planet."

"So, we're talking Death Star?" John Anthony raised an eyebrow.

"Could be, but only in terms of size. Don't expect hallways and rooms, there are no use for them. Everything would be strictly functional with no life-support. Think of it as a mass of conduit, wires, cooling pipes and chemical nuclear plants."

"Sounds more like a giant refinery." Sam was getting paler by the minute. "How do we find it's… you know, heart or whatever. How would we even get around inside it?"

"Carefully, and a giant refinery is about right. There will probably be small Abes that are charged with exterminating anything that isn't supposed to be there. These would be your only concern. But we won't know for sure until Dominus can extract the information from the captured bounty hunters."

"Which is where I'm headed." Mike stepped forward. "I gotta hit the road, guys."

"Wait, wait," Daniel stopped Mike in his tracks. "You're going with Dominus?"

Mike smiled at his friend. "Yeah."

"But that's—"

"No problem, bro. I'm in good hands." He slapped Daniel on the shoulder. "Listen, you guys, I know we can do this. Remember, if we don't kill the Structure at the root, it will be back to do us in. Okay, hugs now, I gotta get out of here."

"Why do you have to go?" Mellissa objected. "I'm sure Dominus has got this one covered, Mike."

"For the same reason you guys have your mission. I'm a gan and can move around undetected. Plus I'm Dominus' apprentice and where he goes, I go. It's my duty. See you guys later." He turned and left.

"Bring me back a cool souvenir!" Daniel meekly joked as the door closed.

Niliason got them all refocused. "Okay, let's get to it. Annette and Sam. Your task will be represent the human race as you help Piaa rally Biauay support. Because of Piaa, they now know that humans are real, but it's another thing entirely to have two of them show up and plead their case. We need the Biauay fleet; their entire military, to attack the Structure. You will be addressing the equivalent of their Congress and President. You must convince them. Do you think you are up to it?"

Both of them nodded.

"I've spent a lot of years begging for grants and pushing projects through government," Sam said. "This is right up my alley."

Annette agreed. "We're definitely the right choice. We'll get their support."

"Good. Now, I'd like to talk to you both alone for a minute."

Niliason took Sam and Annette into the hall.

"What do you suppose that's all about?" John Anthony said.

Mellissa shrugged. "Apparently it's none of our business."

"Need to know," Daniel said. "It's common in special operations. We don't need to know this part of their mission."

"Kind of suspicious, don't you think?" John Anthony huffed.

"No, not at all. Listen, the reason for 'need to know' is to protect us if we get caught," Daniel said. "We can't spill beans that we don't have."

Just then, Niliason came back into the room with Sam and Annette. "…and Piaa is standing by on Palus Emyth to meet you. I'm happy to report that you will be received as dignitaries this time."

"Wonderful!" Annette was relieved. "It will be a welcome change from lugging around a jackhammer in the moon dust."

"Well, this is goodbye then." Sam turned and gave John Anthony a hug and a smile, saying, "It's a dangerous business going out your door. You step onto a road, and if you don't keep your feet, there's no knowing where you might be swept off to."

John Anthony smiled back. "Tolkien, right?"

Sam laughed. "I knew you'd get that, ya big nerd."

"Is everything all right?" John Anthony said quietly as he gave Sam a quick hug.

"I think so." Sam looked him in the eye and smiled. "Crazy as this all is, I think we might actually pull it off."

Sam and Annette walked out of the room with a small team of Atec. John Anthony suddenly felt afraid and very small.

"Easy, tiger, I'm not letting you out of my sight." Mellissa took his hand.

"And I'm not letting either one of you out of mine."

Daniel waggled a finger at them.

Niliason smiled and nodded. "That's right, you three are the strike team. We'll know more about what you need for your mission after Dominus gets us that intel. For now, I recommend a firearm for each of you. Daniel can help you choose the right gear. Then it all comes down to your augmentations.

"I don't want cyborg eyes or anything." John Anthony folded his arms. "And Mel's eyes are perfect. You can't mess with perfection."

Mellissa rolled her eyes dramatically to hide a faint blush.

Niliason sat down next to John Anthony, leaned in close and said, "Go ahead, look into my eyes."

John Anthony fidgeted for a second, then looked at Niliason.

"These are exact copies of my original eyes. Can you tell the difference?"

John Anthony scrutinized the eyes intensely but could find no sign that they were anything but normal, human eyes. "Honestly, no, I can't," he sighed

"What about these enhancements you're proposing for us? Won't they be detected?" Daniel asked.

"Right now you are one-hundred percent organic. The patterns of your heat, electrical and chemical systems are erratic and fluid, that's what makes detecting them so difficult. With the augmentations, your one-hundred percent would be reduced to roughly eighty-two percent. This is still well within the margins for your natural systems to mask the patterns of your enhancements. You have to understand; your liver works great. It's plugged in to your body via natural support systems like veins, nerves and various tissue. My liver works really great, but it's artificial. If I replace it with a real one, if we could even find one, it would still be connected to an artificial support system. There is just no replacing, or replicating the organic systems without cloning or stem cell growth—

none of which we have time for."

"Wait," John Anthony stopped him, "if we get these enhancements; in time you could return us to one-hundred percent organic?"

"Yes, if you wanted." He smiled wryly.

Mellissa was on to him. "But you don't think we will."

Niliason cracked a smile. "I've never seen anyone want to go back to organic. But," he threw his arms up in a shrug, "there's always a first time for everything. Ready to follow me down to the infirmary?"

In the infirmary, they were each given a liter of orange tasting solution. "This will condition your body to more easily adapt to the changes it's about to be put through," the nurse told them. "Over the next twenty minutes you may develop twitches in your muscles and some general body pain. There is a mild pain reliever in the solution, so don't take anything for it."

"You'll be unconscious for the surgery and the pain will be gone when you wake up." Niliason told them, then turned to the nurse. "I suggest they remain in the infirmary until it's time for surgery."

"Yes sir," the nurse said as Atec personnel hustled around them to make them comfortable.

They were each brought into a changing room and put into robes and slippers. When they came out they were put into beds, then wheeled into a room together. Niliason was there.

While he filled them in on some last minute details, John Anthony began to feel the 'twitches' the nurse warned them about. He felt like his brain was trying to dislodge itself from his skull. Just when he was about to say something a team of doctors came in and began wheeling them away. It was the last thing he remembered.

Chapter 34

Mike had expected to arrive outside, maybe on some kind of Mad Max desert planet. Instead, he showed up in round room lined with plush red material on the walls and floor. *I conveyed to a brothel in Shanghai?*

"Be careful of your thoughts here, Michael," said Dominus lightly. "Keep them very focused, or those around will be able to hear."

"Roger that."

A door opened into what Mike could only conclude was a spaceport. He carried all of the equipment he had worn on the mission to Emythiar. An Atec engineer had shown him how to use his EvoNet upgrade to control the camouflage ghillie suit. He could modify it to whatever form he wished. For everyday use it took the form of a trenchcoat with the automatic camouflage function turned off. Dominus assured him that his weapons could be carried openly. They would be viewed more as an eccentricity than anything else. He had also been warned that he could run into species from all over the galaxy. The etiquette was to mind your own business.

Stepping out of the conveyor Mike saw over thirty different kinds of sentient life. The humanoid form seemed to be neither rare nor common. None took a second look at him. Dominus towered above the milling crowd. He was not exclusively the only being his height, but he was among the few.

"Greetings, my young apprentice," Dominus laughed.

"I thought you would enjoy the Star Wars reference."

"You've definitely got the whole 'Darth' thing going for you. Wow, look at this place! Sam and Annette would have a field day in here."

"There is much that is waiting for the human race, but for you, it's a preview. Welcome to the Bothath system. You are on Mina Prime, a moon. Actually, it's a binary moon system. The second moon is called Minaloth. The gas giant we are orbiting is called Un." He pronounced it 'oon'. "Bothath itself is an exclusive world, much like Earth. Only the rich live there, kind of like Aspen."

"Great. How goes the project?"

"Alaz and Vexa are working in a facility close by. We will go there now. Have you brought nutrients?"

"Yes, just like you said. I've got a pack full of MREs."

"Good. I believe it unlikely that you will find palatable food here. There are dispensaries that will provide the necessary materials for you to stay alive, but I doubt you would like the taste."

Dominus led him across the huge terminal to the train. The vehicle had a series of enclosed cars followed by flat cargo cars.

"We will take this. If I carried you in flight, the G forces would kill you."

Mike blanched. "Train sounds good, let's do that." He climbed onto the flat car with Dominus.

It was short wait before the train departed and soon they were flying several hundred feet above an incredibly large city. The sprawl went on past the horizon. The sky was green, dominated by the massive green ball of Un. Minaloth hung in the distance; a small, pea sized half ball among the blackness.

"This is a colonized system, which means there are no native inhabitants. Most systems are like this. Home systems are very difficult to get into. Earth is one of the few home systems that is unprotected. If not for the Atec, I suspect that Earth would have been overrun long ago."

"What did the Atec do?"

"Initially they insured that Earth looked uninhabitable on the galactic registry. That alone dissuaded most from choosing it as a destination. Of course, the fact that it lies in a relatively unexplored part of the galaxy helps as well. The biggest Atec contribution lies in what they didn't do. They didn't get cabin fever and seek to contact anyone outside of Earth. They remained in isolation until humankind developed and began emitting transmissions of their own. Because of that, neither the Structure nor anyone else had reason to believe that the earth was anything more than another lifeless ball of rock. What the Atec have accomplished is nothing less than a miracle. Here we are."

The train pulled up to a large platform, several hundred feet in the air. They disembarked and Mike followed Dominus to a set of buildings. They wound through streets filled with a variety of beings. Even though it was a grid system, the vastness of it made Mike confused.

"Focus on the picture of you and I, an aerial view. Can you conceive that?"

"Yes, I got—oh cool!" Suddenly, he knew exactly where he was. "SatNav on steroids, nice."

"We're going here." A marker popped up through a series of buildings. The buildings appeared transparent to him, though it was only the map's representation. Dominus read his thoughts. "Your ocular enhancement will not work here. The buildings are made of materials that reflect x-rays."

"I need to get better at controlling my thoughts."

"Yes. It will come with practice. Just be sure to guard your thoughts regarding our activities. If you leak those we could attract the attention of the Structure."

"Yes sir." Mike focused intently on the back of Dominus, thinking about cars, fabrication and anything but their mission. They arrived at a large door on a side street. Dominus simply walked right through the material.

Mike shrugged and followed. He passed through effortlessly.

"There is a door, yes, but an opaque hologram is projected in its place so when someone enters, the contents of the room are not revealed. It is standard practice."

"Hello, Michael. How wonderful to see you," Vexa's soft voice lilted into his consciousness.

"Vexa, hello! I'm so glad to hear your mission was a success, congratulations."

"Michael," Alaz said. "we didn't have much time on Earth. I am looking forward to working with you."

"Me too. How goes the work?"

"We have recovered the primary cores of unit 'A' and unit 'S'. We are almost done with unit 'V'. Our next task will be to connect them and retrieve the intel. Unfortunately, that means we need one of these." Alaz sent him a picture of a device about the size of a small SUV in the shape of a 'U'. "This is a Kinetic Reformation Scanner. Yes," he smiled, sensing Mike's thought, "we can use the acronym. We need to locate a KRS. Typically they are at Abe hospital facilities. There are many black market doctors on Mina Prime, but there is one in particular who will scan our cores without asking questions. His name is Phay Igh." He pronounced it 'fay-YIG'. "He frequents an entertainment hub here." A marker popped up on Mike's map. "The currency here is 'Ta'. It's not a galactic standard like the Tik, but Tiks aren't worth much when they make you traceable by the Structure."

"Tik and Ta, got it."

"We need Phay Igh to scan our cores, so give him what he asks, but don't be a chump," Dominus warned. "He has to respect you, if he doesn't he could very well store and resell the information on the cores. He might even be tempted to sell the data to the Structure. If that happens, our assault could easily turn into an ambush."

Mike was beginning to understand the magnitude of

the task he was being given. "Okay. I'll make him haggle. What's a reasonable rate?"

"Only talk about one core at first. Don't let him know we have three and don't tell him where they came from. He should do one for about a thousand Ta. It's slightly above the average rate for black market scans. After he has scanned the first one, you will go back and tell him we have two more. He should agree to do them at the same price."

"Okay, how do I transfer the Ta to him?"

Dominus put another marker on his map. "For that, we have to make you a galactic citizen. You'll start a bank account. Genetic Biometrics is the standard ID. They use your genetic code, your full biometric signature, and the root coding of your non-biological elements. Combined they make up your unique signature. There isn't a system in the galaxy that can duplicate it…or so they think."

"Wait, you know how?"

"That is the key to our strategy," Vexa said. "The Structure only builds to suit the function, never more. When the Structure built the bounty hunters it used a very simple code. Dominus was the one who designed the rest of the systems, systems that the Structure couldn't even duplicate when it rebuilt the bounty hunters. So we can copy what the Structure builds, but it can't copy us. You're completely unique and un-copyable, as is most everyone, unless you're one of the Abes the Structure built.

"Not many beings are actually created by the Structure. It specializes in capturing and taking over…reprogramming people. The bounty hunters are the peak of its creation and they're made by the Structure's own hands. Really, they were made by Abes under the Structure's command, but the important part is that they were made at the location of the Structure and report only to it."

"So it's a once in a lifetime opportunity."

"Precisely. When the Structure condemned Dominus, it

made a fatal error. It failed to realize that Dominus was a being of limitless potential. A being like you, Michael."

"And a being like you, Vexa, and your brother, and all of these people here on this backwater planet. What if they knew?"

"What do you mean?" she asked.

"Listen, I'm a special forces soldier. One of our main jobs is to rally local fighters against the forces that threaten them. Inciting uprisings is what Danny and I used to do. What if these locals here knew that they actually stood a chance to overthrow the Structure?"

"It is risky. To tell them is to alert the Structure."

"The SAS have a motto: 'He who dares, wins.' Just think about it. If we can get in touch with the leadership around here, we might enable them to take a stand for their own future. I guarantee you these people don't like slinking around in fear. One concept is universal; everyone wants freedom."

"You speak a great truth," Dominus agreed. "It was powerful for me. I expect that it will be no less powerful for anyone else. We will consider your proposal while you are gone."

"Fair enough, I'm outta here. I'll be back with the deal done, or I won't be back."

Mike passed through the door and followed the markers. It was a different experience walking the alien streets without Dominus to clear the way in front of him. He became keenly aware of his thoughts as well as the assault rifle slung on his back. With the compression shield on and the cloak doing an impersonation of a long black trench coat, he felt marginally safe. He shifted his pistol in its leg holster a little higher and continued to follow the beacon.

Corner after corner led him through the maze of streets and alleys. It reminded him of the Favelas of Brazil. Suddenly, the street ended—simply dropped off the edge of a cliff. His marker rested on top of a building over three hundred feet below him.

How the hell am I supposed to get down there? There was no lift, stairs, or trains to be seen.

"Telbek?"

"What?" Mike turned around. A small red creature was talking to him. It sat on its haunches like a kangaroo, but its forelimbs seemed dexterous and capable.

"Are you lost?"

"Don't worry, Michael," Dominus came over his comms, "translation is a function of the programming I sent you in your upgrade. This is not a dangerous being."

Mike was suddenly aware that his hand was on his pistol. He quickly shifted to a friendlier demeanor.

"Well, yes, to be honest. I am looking for a way down there." He pointed to the rooftop.

"You will have to go back to the Level Service Station. You can get transport to the lower levels."

"Are there any restrictions on flying?"

"Not that I'm aware of. You can fly?"

"Yeah."

"I have not met someone of your species before. My name is Reshtalda, I am an Inganese Alsarian."

"It's a pleasure to meet you Reshtalda. My name is Michael, I am a Human from Earth."

The little red creature sucked in its breath. "This cannot be!"

"What?"

"Human? The mythical creator of the Abes?"

"We are the creator of the Abes and no, we're not a myth."

Reshtalda squinted at Mike. "You have augmentation?"

"Yes. It's a long story, and one I'd rather not get into. Right now I am interested in going down there to that building."

"Well, even if you had wings you could not fly."

"Why not?"

Reshtalda looked embarrassed. "There is no

atmosphere. Everyone here wears a compression shield, as you are."

"Oh my…" Mike bit his tongue trying to mind his language. "I had completely forgotten about that. I'm rather new to all of this galactic technology stuff."

The little red creature laughed. Mike thought, *I know he's laughing, it's universal. How cool is that?*

"Apparently you are new to neuro-communications too." Reshtalda giggled again. "You are broadcasting your thoughts for all to hear."

Mike went red with embarrassment.

"I did not know humans could take on the color of the Alsarian."

"I happens when we're embarrassed."

"Do not be embarrassed, Michael, human from Earth. I would consider it an honor to help you. Come, I have a tool that will help you conceal your thoughts."

Dominus?

"I'm here, Michael. Go with him, it may prove to be a lucky break. But stay on guard."

Chapter 35

Reshtalda led him back down the road he had come and through a doorway. Mike found that he was standing in a living space. A large nest of fabric and blankets took up the center of the floor, the walls covered in holographic images.

"Wow. You really like TV."

"I live alone. Not much to do. That's why I was out on the point. That's what they call the end of the road where you were. Good thing I said something when I did. I had no idea you were considering leaping off that ledge."

"You make it sound like I was trying to kill myself."

"Well, it certainly seemed that way."

"I assure you that my sense of self-preservation is very much intact."

Reshtalda stopped rummaging through storage bins and produced a thick metal headband. "Here it is. Don't take this wrong, but normally this is given to children who have just had their *Mankala*, the operation and afterwards, the ceremony and celebration of the neuroenhancement."

"Do all species use the neuroenhancement?"

"You really are new to the galaxy, aren't you? Most do. It is a shared technology, though at some point in their evolution most species have achieved the level of technology necessary to…um…humans have not?"

"The short version of the story goes like this: We evolved and created Abes. We went to war with the Abes and our planet was destroyed, but we managed to flee to a neighboring planet where we lived in hiding along with a newly developed, biologically based, artificial intelligent species that the Abes created and also deemed unfit to live. But the Abes found us and war ensued there as well.

"The species the Abes created, called Biauay, fled into the galaxy. The Abes, thinking we humans were eliminated, went out into the galaxy to chase the Biauay. After a while, the Abes returned to ensure that we had indeed been wiped out. They killed off all but a handful of us.

"In the meantime, the original planet, Earth, had regained its ability to support life. The surviving group of augmented humans returned to Earth to nurture the organic human race from a primitive state. The augmented humans, called Atec, patiently let the organic humans evolve at a natural rate without interfering.

"Now the organic humans have just begun developing artificial intelligence; their existence is unknown to the Structure or the Abes. Unfortunately, one of the Abes' creations, a bio-EI scientist, found us."

"That's crazy -t-t-karma." The translator stuttered as it tried to find a similar word.

"Yeah, tell me about it. So a handful of organic humans, call us Human mark II, discovered the existence of the Abes, the Atec, and the Biauay and have become involved in…events. I'm an organic human, recently augmented, who is here to help solve a little dilemma."

"Well, this will shield your thoughts from passersby unless you want them to hear. The thing is, if you wear this in public, people will think you are a child."

"How about if I wear a hood?" Mike concentrated for a second and his trenchcoat grew a large hood.

Reshtalda gasped. "You have a Fantagoric cape? You must have some very powerful friends. Do yourself a favor and don't let anyone know. There are a lot of undesirables that would gladly delete you for that piece of gear."

"I'm learning a lot from you, Reshtalda. The question

is, what do you want in return?"

"I have no ulterior motives. I saw a being who was a stranger in my neighborhood. You looked lost, and in the Peshelin that can be dangerous. Still, you were armed and appeared unconcerned so I assumed you could handle yourself. I thought that maybe you just needed to be pointed in the right direction."

Mike knew this kind of talk from his time dealing with Afghan village chiefs. "But surely there is something I can do in return."

"Well, I am not a big person. There are some who take delight in making my life difficult."

"Are they close by?"

"Yes, next door actually."

"Names?"

"Nilot and Jico. But—"

Mike headed for the door. "I'll be right back."

Mike walked straight through the neighbor's doorway. A tall, fat, dark-grey skinned creature leapt up from a low table. "Who are you? What are you doing in my house?"

"Are you Nilot?"

"No! Get out of here!"

"Are you Jico?"

"What business is it of yours? Get out of here before I—"

Mike's fist connected with the creature's face so hard that the sound echoed off the walls. It crumpled into a heap on the floor. From upstairs, a chattering sound could be heard. Mike went up and looked through the rooms. A dark slime covered the walls and a scent like rotten eggs make him wince. The chattering came into range of Mike's translator.

"Jico? What the hell are you doing down there?"

Mike turned on the Fantagoric Cape and slipped in the door. The room was entirely covered in the same dark slime. A humanoid creature that could have shared DNA with an Iguana was buried in the thick slime in the far corner. Mike's compression shield prevented the muck from getting on his boots, but the Iguana noticed the dent.

"Who are you! I can see you, get out of here!"

Mike made himself visible. His pistol was pointed at the creature's head. "You know Reshtalda?"

"I don't know him, I never saw him!"

"Then how do you know he's a him?"

"I don't know! I know nothing!"

"Well, I do know Reshtalda. He's a friend of mine. You and Jico will stay away from him from now on or you will see me again. And if you see me again, it will be the last time you see anything." He left the creature shivering in his slime pool and went back downstairs where the large form of Jico was just starting to struggle up from the floor. Mike drilled him in the head once more, knocking the big creature unconscious. He met Reshtalda outside. "They won't be bothering you again."

"The myth of humans says that you are peaceful, even fragile beings."

"We are. We love peace and freedom. We love it so much that we fight for it. As for the fragile part, every creature has a vulnerability so, yeah, I guess we are. But no more than anyone else. Let's just say that we can hold our own when it comes down to it."

"I'm not sure what that means, but you are definitely tougher than I thought. Now, let me show you how to get down to the financial district."

Reshtalda took him through a maze of streets winding down and down until they came out into a wide courtyard. The area was cleaner and well lit.

"I can find my way from here. Thank you for your help, Reshtalda. I hope that you find the peace you are looking for."

"And you, Michael, Human of Earth. If the rest of your people are like you I hope they one day populate the whole galaxy."

Mike walked across the courtyard, following the

marker on the map. It led him straight to the huge front doors of an official looking building. He walked through the holo-door and up a wide set of stairs. The walls were lined with a series of private booths. Mike wished that Dominus was there to help him.

"At last!" Dominus' rumbled in his head. "Why did you cut communications with me?"

"Oh, I put on this headband that Reshtalda gave me to shield my thoughts from others. It must have cut you off too."

"Yes, you have to intentionally think of someone to open a channel to them. Until you do, they have no access."

"I'm sorry, Dominus. I'm at the bank now. What do I do?"

"Go to one of the booths. It will adjust automatically to accommodate you. Open up a comm link and tell it that you are a new galactic resident and that you wish to open an account. You will be asked questions. Answer them truthfully. Don't worry, the system is passive and the Structure has no interest in it so the truth of your origins won't compromise us in any way. It will scan you then, so remove the headband and the ghillie suit."

"I learned that it is called a Fantagoric Cape, is that right?"

"Yes, that is how it is commonly known. But understand that it is a very uncommon piece of equipment and therefore very valuable."

"Yeah, I got that impression from Reshtalda. Okay, I'm going in." Mike did as Dominus instructed and after fifteen minutes of being asked his name, place of birth, and getting scanned and poked for a DNA sample, he was issued a small pill and instructed to ingest it.

"It will dissolve in your system. It's actually tiny nano-bots that will serve to identify you. The bots keep track of any changes to your body, including upgrades. I assure you that they are entirely benign."

Mike swallowed the pill and left the bank.

"I have placed four thousand Ta in your account. Think about your account now."

As soon as Mike did he immediately knew the transfer had taken place including all of the information about the transaction and his balance.

"That is how you buy and sell things."

"Thank you. It's a heck of a lot easier than my old accounting system."

"This system has been in place for a very long time and even pre-dates the Structure. It is one of the many things that will continue and hopefully spread and thrive when our task is done."

"Hey, if it ain't broke, don't fix it. Okay, give me the marker for the doctor."

"Phay Igh frequents this entertainment facility."

A marker came up on Mike's map. "Just say 'bar', okay?"

Dominus laughed. "Okay, it's a bar, but do us all a favor and don't drink anything. They don't know what to serve humans; a lot of it is toxic to you."

"Gotcha. How about water?"

"There are many different kinds of water. Request purified, organic H2O with only limited mineral sub-compounds in a clear container."

"That has got to be the most specific bar order I've ever heard."

"You'll appreciate it. And be warned, it isn't cheap."

Mike found the place easily enough. The interior was bright white with a fresh smell and a variety of plant life. Mike went to the bar, surprised at the universal consistency. *They actually have a bar.* He waited to see the bartender but could see no one.

"Hello?"

"State your order." A small blue cube floated up from behind the counter.

"I'd like purified, organic H2O with mineral sub-compounds in a clear container."

"Thirty four Tik, twenty two in Ta."

Mike concentrated on his bank account. Immediately the details of the account came up. He willed the amount to be sent to the cube at the bar.

"Concentrate on the server droid, Michael."

As soon as he did he realized that he wasn't thinking about the bank account anymore, but the blue cube floated away.

"It's okay, it worked. You don't need to hold the bank account in your mind, just who you want to pay and how much."

"This is a serious brain exercise."

"It's only the beginning. With your EvoNet enhancement you will be able to hold hundreds of things in strong focus simultaneously. Give it time."

The water arrived in a large fish bowl shaped glass. "Geez, that's over a gallon. If I drink all of this I'll be peeing for a week."

Mike sat and waited. It was something he had been wanting to do; just sit and observe. He examined the material that the bar was made from, the chairs, the lighting sources and everything he could see. His neural-net informed him of every substance and answered most of his questions about their source, the worlds that they came from and the species that inhabited them. In this way he stayed entertained for several hours until Dominus alerted him to the presence of the doctor.

"He seems to be walking straight towards you."

The heavy set creature was covered in a thin layer of tan hair. His face was more marsupial than anything else. He travelled on stout legs, the knee joint operating in reverse from a human's. To Michael's surprise, Phay Igh did indeed walk right up to him.

"Excuse me. My name is Phay Igh, I am a practitioner of medicine and an admirer of species. I apologize, but any time I encounter a species new to me I make it a point to introduce myself and learn as much as I can. I hope you don't think it rude."

"Not at all, Doctor. My name is Michael and I am a human from a planet called Earth."

The doctor's expression changed. He looked stunned, or ready to bolt, Michael wasn't sure which. The doctor's eyes stayed glued on Mike as he groped for a stool.

"May I sit down?"

"Of course."

"Human, you say? Is that any connection to the humans of legend?"

"I am told we are one and the same. The humans who created the Abes."

"Most interesting," the doctor said, looking at Michael like some kind of specimen. "And where have you been? I mean, have you just arrived in this part of the galaxy?"

"That is a long story, Doctor. Though we are given credit for creating interstellar beings, through the course of long wars, we have suffered evolutionary setbacks. Our planet was destroyed and reborn, but some of our creations saved us. They protected us while we re-evolved from a primitive state. I am one of the first to know this and am here on mission which, serendipitously, involves you."

"Me, really? How?"

"I have been told that you might be able to direct me to someone who can scan a core for me."

"And who told you this?"

Dominus' voice came over the comms. "Tell him that an old friend of his from Bayuth told you to mention the Towers of Celyth."

When Mike did as he was asked, the Doctor jumped off his stool and stumbled backwards. "No…how do you know that?"

Dominus came in again. "Tell him about me."

"Steady, Doc. My friend, I believe, is your friend. I

know him as Dominus Rau and I am his apprentice—"

Phay Igh started shivering. "He is not a friend. He is the God of War!"

"Then you'd better pay attention to what I'm about to send you." Mike delivered a burst transmission to the doctor that explained how they met and the changes in Dominus. The doctor collapsed in a heap on the floor.

When he came back around, Mike was sitting with him in a booth. "You alright, Doc?"

"My head…"

"I'm sorry I sent you a burst transmission. The space between explanations would have given you too much time to form skepticism and we don't have time for that."

"I understand now. I will scan your core for you, just don't let him near me. Even if he has changed, I find it impossible to accept. To me, he is the very embodiment of evil."

"I'm sure that can be arranged, although I'm sorry you feel that way. It seems odd that a scientist like yourself can hold onto such irrational fears. Surely your intellectual curiosity would make you want to see for yourself?"

"There are some things that affect a person on a primal level and rationality does not have a role. Dominus Rau…" he shook uncontrollably when he said the name, "is…*was* a destroyer of worlds." He gathered himself together and stood up. "I will scan your core, but I will have nothing to do with that…horrible thing."

"Fair enough. I offer you five hundred for the scan."

"Five hundred? Absolutely not! I don't know who told you that I'm so cheap. I won't do it for less than two thousand."

"Okay, listen, it's a stretch, but I can go up to seven hundred. We are talking Ta here, right? Work with me a little bit. The whole thing will just be between you and me."

"Yes, it is Ta, and as long as I'm only dealing with you then I can make a concession and come down to fifteen hundred."

"Ow, Doc, you're killing me here! I'm pretty far from home you know. I only have so much to work with. One thousand. It's my final offer." Mike added emphasis on 'final', suggesting ever so slightly that it wouldn't be a good idea to upset Dominus.

"Alright, one thousand, but I've never worked for so little." He sent Mike a marker. "Bring it here tonight. I'll have the scan by the morning. This doesn't get you analytics, just the scan."

"That's all I need. Thank you, Doctor Phay Igh. I'll see you in a few hours."

Chapter 36

Mike left the nervous doctor to order himself another drink. "It's a done deal," he told Dominus in the privacy of his head. "Man, that guy does not like you."

"Understandable. I tortured some of his colleagues not long ago. He was unharmed but was forced to reassemble his friends as drones for the Structure. Their families never saw them again."

Mike was aghast. "Jesus, man, that's seriously fucked up."

"I cannot undo my past, I can only give my life to the cause of righteousness in the here and now."

"That's true. Just promise me you'll never go back to your old ways."

"It's a promise that is easy to make. The Structure had me under its control for a long time, but when I went to Earth, it is so remote that the Will of the Structure couldn't reach me. Under the care and guidance of Mellissa and Daniel, I quickly began to see things differently. Once I knew that the Structure was fallible and had such control over me, I reset my core programming. Never again will the Structure have any hold over me. I gave my children the same values."

"I tried to show Phay Igh that you had changed, but he was too far gone."

"Understandable. Come back now and retrieve the cores. The longer this takes, the more the mission is in jeopardy."

Knowing the way back now, Mike quickly wound his way through the streets and back to the workshop. "Honey, I'm home!" he cheered as he stepped through the holo-door.

"Michael, welcome back!" Vexa greeted him over-enthusiastically.

Is she getting sweet on me? That would be one for the books. "Hi, beautiful, what's cooking?"

"*Ope*. That's gonna go to her head," Alaz quipped.

"Cheeky! The cores are all ready for you." She led him through the mess of discarded body parts to the back of the room. A train of three boxes hovered above the floor, coupled to a chunky looking little vehicle that also floated above the ground.

"Y'know, they always do this in sci-fi movies," Mike said, looking under the cars. "But it's the simple things that are the hardest. How the hell do these things work? Is it anti-gravity or something?"

Vexa laughed. "No, gravity is more difficult to manipulate than you might think. It's actually a kind of molecular cushion that keeps it off the ground."

"So, it's like a hovercraft?"

"Sort of, but without the noisy fans and turbulent air, and with much better directional control."

"Now that we are done with the physics lesson, we can get going," Dominus said impatiently. "You drive the cores and we will keep watch from the air."

"Okay, I assume that driving this thing is—"

"Once you are in, just feed it the mark on your map. It will take you there by the safest and quickest route."

Mike climbed in. It was roomier than it looked and had no controls. As soon as he transferred the marker to it, the car set off with the little train of boxes following behind. It took twenty minutes to drive to the Doctor's lab, located in a slightly less run down part of the Peshelin. As he approached, Dominus had him disconnect the last two boxes and drive only one up to the lab's entrance.

"I'm here, Doc."

"That's fine, just bring it in the front."

Mike drove the car through the holo-door and stopped it inside a room the size of a small airplane hangar. Parts and pieces hung from the rafters, and equipment was scattered everywhere.

"Now, let's see what we have here," the Doctor opened the car and stopped short. "This is a signature core. You didn't say anything about a signature core."

"I don't know, Doc, it's a core. A deal's a deal."

"Where did you…never mind, I don't want to know. Just get out of here and let me do my work. It will be done in an hour."

"Really, I thought you said it would take—"

"Yes, but I don't want this thing here. I don't want it here, I don't want you here, so just go and come back in an hour!"

"Okay, Doc, settle down. See you in an hour." Mike left him to do his work. "Man, that guy is really stressed out."

"A signature core is a one of a kind, unique core," Dominus told him. "It would be like someone bringing an engine from a Formula One race car into your shop."

"That would be cool. I'd be excited."

"Not if it was got by nefarious means and the government was likely to be looking for it."

"Ah." Mike finally understood. "He may need some convincing if he's going to do the other two cores."

"I have added another two thousand to your account. But don't pay him more than fifteen hundred per core. It is clear now that he would not bootleg the data. He wants nothing to do with me or the Structure. He will be happy to get paid and be rid of us."

"Where can I go to make up one of my MREs?"

"There is a public area here." A marker appeared.

Mike found the square and settled in to wait. "So, where are you guys exactly?" he said, munching a cracker covered with the US Army's version of stroganoff. Dominus let him see through his eyes. They were circling high above the city like a pack of vultures. "The old wagon wheel, eh? They were using that formation in World War I."

"It is a recognized formation for establishing a localized airspace. No other vehicles will come within a kilometer of a circle formation of two or more."

The hour seemed more like four, but finally Mike went back to the Doctor's lab.

"Here is your core and your data."

"And here is your payment. You've done this so quickly and so well that I want to give you the opportunity to do the rest of them."

"There are more?"

"Two more. I was going to divide the work to get it all done in a day, but if you can do them each in an hour, it would be much faster for me, not to mention much more lucrative for you."

The Doctor blinked in disbelief. "Okay, for another 1500 each."

"Done. I have them with me now, I'll bring them in." Mike climbed back into the tug car and went out to hook up the remaining boxes. "He's in."

"Outstanding, Michael."

Two hours later, Mike was driving the little train back into the holo-door of their rented workshop. They put the three drives on the table and gathered together.

"Michael, you are not familiar with this function yet. We are going to join our neural systems to review the data. It is a vast amount of information. We will need your help."

"No problem, what do I do?"

"Just lie down and rest. This may sound unnerving but we are going to take over the processing power of your mind. Do not be alarmed, you are in no danger."

"I'm fine with it actually. I trust you."

Dominus smiled. "Good, let's begin."

Mike got comfortable and focused on the three Abes. There was no communication but he could feel them joining him, like they were all in the same head. One by one they linked to each other. He could feel the coupling like a soft jolt. The next thing he knew, he was waking up.

"Are we done?"

"Yes, Michael, it is done."

"Wow, I feel like I slept for a week! I have so much energy!"

"Really? Interesting. Perhaps a coupling regenerates biological systems. I have never heard of that, but then, I have never coupled with a human before."

"Phrasing, man, phrasing," Mike laughed. "Did we find anything?"

Vexa was practically bursting. "Yes! We were successful beyond our hopes! We know what the Structure is, where it is, and how it operates."

"That's fantastic! Tell the others."

"Already done. It is up to them now," Dominus said. "We wait for their signal, then we attack the Structure."

"There is something we can do while we wait." Mike stood and strapped on his assault rifle. "We can rally the people here."

"It is a monumental task," Dominus scowled.

"Nothing worth doing is ever easy. Just hear me out. Biauay, Human, and Atec are all going to assault the Structure in a bid for freedom. Don't you think the Abes have a right to fight as well? The Structure has tyrannized them more than anyone. And what happens when the Structure is gone? The prejudice will still exist between races. How can we ever have lasting peace? But get the Abes involved, and they become an ally. Nothing breaks down cultural barriers like a common enemy and battlefield camaraderie."

"Yes, this makes sense," Vexa purred. "You are wise in the ways of psychological warfare."

"Hearts and minds, man." Mike winked at her. "Victory can only last if you win hearts and minds."

Chapter 37

Sam stood in the shower, watching the water run down Annette's naked body. He was smiling and she was laughing. Their new neural enhancements had bonded them over the last twenty-six hours in a way that they had never thought possible.

"I still think we should have told them," Annette said.

"It would have swayed their decision," Sam said. "It's better that they made up their own minds."

"Niliason was right about one thing," Annette giggled. "I could never go back to being unaugmented."

"It would be like losing your sight after being cured of blindness," Sam agreed.

They were just coming out of the shower when they got the news from Niliason.

"They did it!" Niliason said. "We just received the data from Dominus and Mike. It's more than we could have hoped. Now it's up to you and Piaa. Get to the hangar as soon as you can."

Annette looked at Sam. "Here we go."

John Anthony, Mellissa, and Daniel met them in the hangar with Niliason close on their heels.

"I'm going to send you the data you'll need to explain the battle plan." Niliason spoke over the neural net to only Sam and Annette followed by a small burst transmission.

Annette glanced at Sam. They both suddenly knew the entire battle plan. "Wow, you weren't kidding," she replied. "This might actually work."

Sam was filled with confidence. "Let's get going!"

John Anthony watched the brief exchange suspiciously but no one said anything.

Niliason raised the lift and they rose into the desert night. After goodbyes and well wishes, Sam and Annette disappeared. Annette had tried to explain the experience to Sam but he was still shocked at the brightness followed by the blurry vision as he conveyed onto Palus Emyth.

Sam stood stock still. "Oh my God, we're on a moon in nothing but a suit!"

"That's the marvel of the compression shield," Annette said, trying to calm him.

"Oh my God, oh my God…"

"Easy, Sam. It's like being in the desert at night."

"No, it's a fucking moon, Annie!" He started breathing rapidly.

"Sam, chill out, you're hyperventilating."

Suddenly they felt a strong push in their minds. A calm forced itself over them, covering their thoughts and emotions in a blanket of serenity.

"Don't worry, I have you." It was Piaa. Before they knew it they were inside a sleek, bright vehicle with luxurious appointments. "I'm going to let you go now, you're safe."

Annette sprang off the couch and wrapped Piaa in a hug. "I missed you, my sister from across the galaxy!"

"I missed all of you so much!" Piaa laughed. "It's so wonderful to see you, and you have new neuroenhancements. I'm so excited for you!"

Sam breathed deep. "I'm sorry, I just had a panic attack. Knowing what the lack of atmosphere can do to a person—it scared the crap out of me."

"It's okay, Sam. I'm sorry we couldn't receive you at the station, but it is still being rebuilt. Since we had the conveyance already set up to receive out in the Plain of Ethsolun, that's where we did it."

"I'm so excited to share the data that Dominus and

Mike recovered," Annette blurted.

"Yes, please send it to me."

Annette focused and sent a burst to Piaa. "Ooh!" Suddenly Annette felt woozy and had to recline on the long couch.

Piaa went to her side. "That's a lot of information for a rudimentary neuroenhancement. You should feel better in a minute. Have some water." A glass rose out of the center console as Piaa reviewed the data. "This is excellent. Because Dominus, Vexa, and Alaz were able to capture the bounty hunters causing very little damage they were able to get all of the data intact. Niliason told me they had exceeded his hopes, but I had no idea how understated he was being."

"How do you think this will affect the reaction of the counsel?" Sam asked.

"The whole point is to paint the most positive picture possible," Piaa said. "They need to know that victory is assured before they will risk an offensive. The Biauay are a peaceful society. We only keep a military for defensive purposes. When threatened, our primary strategy is to protect the populace while retreating to another location where we can hide in peace."

"Well," Sam said, "I'm not a soldier, but even I know that sometimes the best defense is a strong offense. The Atec will be in the fight, as will the humans; represented by John Anthony, Mel and Daniel. And I'm sure somehow Mike will get into it as well, knowing him. The Abes are represented by Dominus and his family, but we need the Biauay. We are finally banding together to stand up to this bully

"We know it's weakness and, with the Structure's inability to detect us organic humans, we have the element of surprise on our hands. If we add to that the firepower of the Biauay we have a shot at defeating the Structure once and for all."

"Yes, but the counsel are not risk takers," Piaa

cautioned. "It will be a difficult sell, even with the appearance of an advantage over the Structure."

"Don't worry," Annette's face was set in determination, "they haven't had to reason with a human woman yet."

The long ship sped off the small moon and quietly entered the atmosphere of Emythiar. By the time they settled on the landing grounds of the counsel palace they were refreshed and unified in their objective.

As the door opened, Annette and Sam were stunned. A crowd of thousands of Biauay greeted them. A line of over four hundred ceremonial military guard lined the path to the steps of the palace and a host of delegates was there with gifts. Piaa graciously directed them from person to person with long titles and names they couldn't possibly remember.

The whole time she was in their heads saying, 'Don't worry, he's in your database' and 'You'll never see her again, she's a minor representative.'

Further instruction included when to bow and how deeply and the ritual of different handshakes. The handshakes took extra time as the Biauay wanted to honor human traditions. Piaa, it seemed, was instructing them as well. Several of the Biauay even addressed them vocally, in English.

"Weel comb. Soochan Onor toe mit yow." The accent was so thick that the translator couldn't even figure it out.

The crowd was enthusiastic and Piaa encouraged the two of them to wave. Annette couldn't help herself when a Biauay child was lifted up to her. She held the child and kissed it on the forehead, causing the crowd to go crazy.

"That child will now be a celebrity for the rest of its life," Piaa laughed.

"Why all of this?" Sam asked.

"You're human. You are the creators of our creators. You have been myth, pure conjecture until now. That said, there is a lot of skepticism. I've been working day and night to prepare the Biauay for this. There were those who wanted to scan you to verify your purity."

"Why not? We have nothing to hide and I'm all for transparency. We should be vetted to remove any doubt."

Piaa was surprised. "I didn't think you would approve. I...I didn't even want to mention it."

"It's a perfectly legitimate request." Annette was adamant. "I say we do it now."

"What, right here?" Piaa said, shocked.

"Yes. Now, how do I address these people?"

Piaa was still reeling from Annette's willingness, and even more taken aback that she welcomed doing it publicly. She found herself saying, "I...I don't think we're set up for that, but I...um, can have someone bring you an addresser."

"Please, Piaa, if you could. I believe we can make our job much easier."

Sam elbowed Annette. "You sure you know what you're doing? There are a lot of people here, not to mention how many are, you know, tuned in. There are entire other worlds that are watching this."

"It's okay, Sam, trust me."

A Biauay soldier came forward timidly and handed her an object that looked like a crystal dinner plate. She thanked the soldier as Piaa sent her instructions on how to hold and speak over the plate.

"Good people of Emythiar, fellow beings of the galaxy, children of humankind...my name is Annette Blazer and I am human. My companion and life partner is Sam Wisecraft and he is also human. We come from a planet that we call Earth. We have recently learned that it is also where you come from. I will not go into the long story of how we came to be here. That will be made available to you..." She looked at Piaa who nodded, still recovering from the shock of the moment. "...by our close friend Piaa, an honored and much loved member of the Biauay and the one who is responsible for finding us."

Piaa reached out and touched the plate and suddenly

there was a wave of 'ohs' and 'aahs' from the crowd as she sent them the full story of the humans.

"So you see, we are merely the ones who planted the seed, but you are your own creation. You are responsible for the beautiful, enlightened people that you have become. We are so proud to have been a small part of your journey, and we are so very excited to join you, meet you, and know you as we begin a new journey together."

The crowd cheered fanatically. When they quieted down, she continued. "We understand that there has been some skepticism regarding the legitimacy of our origins. We understand completely, for both Sam and I are scientists and fact cannot be fact until it is conclusively verified. We wish to do that now, before all of you so there is no doubt. For doubt will dilute the magic of this momentous occasion and erode the unity we will need for the task ahead."

She nodded at the Biauay who had just finished bringing up a technical looking white table. Sam thought it looked like a sacrificial altar, gleaming in the blue sun at the top of the palace stairs.

Piaa once again reached out and touched the plate. "I will now open a link directly to the scan table for inspection by anyone who wishes to do so." She looked at Sam and Annette. "This means that anybody in the Biauay worlds can access the table and verify that it is what we say it is. The results cannot be falsified."

Sam and Annette smiled. Sam was nervous, but he liked the direction this was going.

After a minute, Piaa nodded to Annette who climbed on the table and waited. The technician smiled down at her excitedly, and said, "Halloo."

"Hi." Annette couldn't wipe the grin off her face.

"Aldon." The translator stuttered then said, "All done."

Sam was next. The technician flashed her eyes at him but didn't say anything until she nodded. He hopped down.

Piaa touched the plate. "I will now open access to the scanner to reveal the results."

The crowd went wild. Annette thought, *this is what it must be like to be a rock star.*

Piaa spoke again, this time to Sam and Annette. "Of course, the results are conclusive. You will be glad to know that you are indeed one hundred percent human," she laughed.

Annette took the plate again. "Whew, what a relief!" she joked. "We are one hundred percent us, and you are one hundred percent you!"

The crowd roared again.

"But what about the others? What about the thousands, even millions of races that make up the incredible diversity of the galactic community? Don't they deserve the opportunity to be vetted as well? Shouldn't we be cheering for them? That is why we're here. We are here to talk to your counsel, to seize a one-time opportunity to bring the galactic community together in peace. Imagine what can be achieved. Imagine what we can learn from each other. Imagine if there were no boundaries, no prejudice, no limitations. Begin with forgiveness, grow to understanding and peace."

The crowd again went wild.

"Admit it, you were about to go all John Lennon on them," Sam teased her.

"Hey, I'll plagiarize if it's working," she chuckled.

"This is going—to use an Earth term—viral across the galaxy." Piaa looked at Annette, wide-eyed.

Annette just laughed. "Hang on now, I'm on a roll."

"You certainly are." Sam was bursting with pride. "Go on, show them your beautiful heart."

She blushed and continued to the crowd, "Forgiveness and understanding, the difficult path to peace. But all of that takes freedom. How can we understand and forgive if we are not free? We have all had a very long road. All of us know the price of freedom, and isn't it funny how the amount of time between sacrifices continues to grow? How long ago was that pitched battle, that decisive moment that has given you the freedom that you know today? And, even more importantly, are you really free?"

"She's not going to talk to the counsel is she?" Piaa suddenly realized. "She's doing it right here!"

"That's my girl," Sam folded his arms and smiled, "throw in a little 'Braveheart'."

"No! Freedom is never free! It has a price, and that price is paid by the bold. Those who dare, win! Without paying the price you are never truly free. We come with an extraordinary gift for you, each and every one of you. Today we do not go to your counsel to let a handful of people decide your fate, we have come directly to you. Because you are the ones who pay the price. You are the ones who carry the flag of freedom for your children."

The crowd was silent, waiting in the tense air. Something was about to happen and they knew it. The council members waited on the steps, paralyzed. There was nothing they could do to stop her.

Annette looked at Piaa, who only then understood. She hesitated for a second, then closed her eyes and nodded.

Annette took a deep breath, straightened her back, then opened a channel that revealed their entire battle plan.

Chapter 38

"You're back? Go away, we are finished with our business!"

"Now calm down, Doc." Mike used his nicest tone of voice. "This is a friend of mine. He's a local. Reshtalda, meet Doctor Phay Igh."

"Hello, Doctor, nice to meet you. You really must calm down."

"What do you want? And why are you friends with this human? You should be home with your parents."

Reshtalda suddenly looked nervous.

"You're a kid?" Mike turned back to the doctor. "He didn't tell me he was a kid."

"Well, technically I'm a teenalescent." The translator struggled with the line between 'adolescent' and 'teenager'.

"Oh, great! Then whose thingy is this?" Mike pulled the hood back and pointed at the headband.

The doctor suddenly burst out laughing. "Wait, you're a child too? And you had me believing you were human?" He slapped his head. "How gullible am I? What was in those cores? You tell me right now or I will call the authorities!"

Mike brought his rifle around. "I didn't want to do this, but if you call anyone I'll drop you."

"With that prop? What is that supposed to be?" Phay Igh laughed until Mike blew a hole in a piece of scrap metal. Then the doctor's demeanor changed. "Wait, I'm not telling anyone anything, okay?"

"Yes you are, just not who you're thinking of telling."

"No…yes…what? Who?" The doctor didn't know what to say to save his life.

"Okay, Doc, I'm going to tell it like it is. The problem here is that you are a nervous, fear saturated, spineless coward who couldn't make up his mind to save his life." Mike slung the rifle back over his shoulder. "The only danger you're in is from yourself. You're gonna give yourself a heart attack," *Assuming you have one*, he thought, "if you don't calm the fuck down and start acting like a mature adult…what are you anyway?"

"Paya, I'm Payan." He pronounced it 'Pi-YAN'.

"Well then, have a little pride, stand up for your species and stop acting like a wimp."

That did it, the doctor sighed and stood sheepishly.

Mike continued, "The information on the cores was taken from the horrible Abes that tortured your colleagues not so long ago. They were captured by identical Abes that were created to specifically bring down the Structure and fight in the service of good throughout the galaxy."

The confused look on the doctor's face told Mike that he wasn't getting through yet.

"Keep up with me. You're a doctor, you're supposed to be smart. Do you understand what I'm saying? Repeat it to me."

"The Abes who tortured my friends were captured by identical Abes, who are their exact opposite but just as deadly."

"Good, you're starting to come around. I'm not threatening you, I'm proposing a radical idea, one that will change everything. I'm trying to get you to be an ally, to get on board. The data recovered from those nasty Abes—we call 'em the bounty hunters—told us how to infiltrate the Structure.

"You see, I *am* human and there are others. None of the Structure's defenses are designed to detect humans. We're supposed to be a myth. Completely organic life forms can't evolve to interstellar travel without serious augmentation, so that's what the Structure looks for—enhancements. But it doesn't know about us.

"Right now, we have friends who are rallying the entire Biauay fleet to join us in an assault on the Structure. Why am I telling you this? Because I'm trying to reach out to the population on the fringe worlds to unite them and invite them to join us. The more we have on our side, the greater the victory will be, follow?"

"You are starting a revolution? That's what this is about?"

"We are ending this tyranny, now."

The doctor sat down hard. "Why didn't you just say."

"I tried, but you were running around like a chicken with…you don't know what a chicken is…you were letting fear rule your reactions. As soon as I said 'Dominus Rau' you could barely function."

"It's true. It triggers something in me."

"Well, let it go, it's holding you back."

"You're right."

"Besides, he's gone. He died and he can never be rebuilt. You just scanned the cores of his team. They are scraps all over my workshop floor."

"Those cores were from them?" The doctor smiled. "That is the best news I have heard in a long time."

"No, the best news is to come. When you hear the bells of freedom ringing in your ears you will know that the Structure has finally fallen. Now, do you want to be a part of that happy moment? Do you want to avenge your friends and punch the Structure in the face with the giant hammer of peace?"

"Oh, yes. Yes very much."

"Then tell me how to get the message out to everyone who cares."

"I can do that. Right now."

***

The silence was shattered with a shocked cry. Then an indecisive murmur spread through the crowd. Annette, Sam, and Piaa were frozen with suspense. Revealing the battle plan was a massive risk. The murmur grew into a clamor. Debate ignited. Annette wanted to tell them, 'Don't let fear rule your choices.' But she stayed silent and continued to pray. Sam gripped her hand, barely able to breathe.

Out of the clamor, cries broke out. They couldn't make out what they were, but they were fiery and emotional. Sam gripped Annette's hand tighter. The cries multiplied, then merged into a cacophonous roar. Annette thought the sound would shake down the palace but the roar turned into a chant, "Yes, yes, yes, yes, yes, yes!"

They went on and on. The faces of the Biauay were angry, inspired and committed. They had had enough of running.

The council members came down the stairs and surrounded them.

"You have our full support," their leader said. "It is the will of the people."

The crowd erupted into cheers.

Annette yelled into the plate. "We need to begin at once, because the plan is revealed, we must not lose the advantage. Go, go!"

They were ushered into the palace as many of the council members congratulated their bold politics. Sam assured them that politics were not involved. This was a pure and inspired moment in history. They were given comfortable accommodations to rest themselves while the palace buzzed with activity. Biauay were running everywhere.

"There is really nothing to do now." Sam sipped his water. "We've done our—"

"We need you!" The head of the counsel burst into the room with a trail of aides. "You have inspired this event and we need you at its head. You two will be on the command ship. Piaa, we would like you to command the major flank."

"I am not a commander," she said, "but I will be there to inspire whomever I can."

Sam and Annette just nodded.

"We depart at once."

They were ushered down the hall and joined up with a group of military officers who also congratulated them. The senior officer, whose rank translated to Admiral, seemed to have a lot of complaints about the risks involved with revealing the whole plan.

"The cost of reward is risk, Admiral," Sam quipped.

"Well, that is all very well in speeches, but—"

"It is very well in life too. I encourage you to shift your focus from defending and losing, to more on the here and now, and winning."

"That's exactly the sort of thing I would expect from a species so inexperienced with conflict."

Sam stopped short, yanked the Admiral back by the collar and slammed him up against the wall.

"What are you gonna do now? Defend? I'm all up in your face, it's too late! React! Go on, react! Not fast enough, I've killed you twenty times by now! We know about combat, mister. We've done nothing but fight since we were primitives and the wars are still going on. You have all that knowledge but no balls to carry it out.

"Oh, don't act all surprised. You hide behind your rank and draw plans and strategies, but when the shit hits the fan all plans go out the window. Any combat veteran will tell you that. Admirals make plans while soldiers turn them into something useful. You will attack! You will not hang back in the biggest ship in your fleet overseeing from a distance. You will get bloody and you will engage the enemy from the front! Those are your standing orders!" Sam was red in the face.

"I will not be told what to do by this, this—"

"Admiral, you are fired." The head of the council pulled the hat off the stunned Biauay and turned to Sam. "We follow your lead, Admiral." He put the hat on Sam and continued at a brisk walk down the hallway.

Piaa stood with the ex-admiral and smiled at him. "Well, you want to be a part of this or not?" she asked.

"Admiral or not, I'll show my mettle."

"Excellent, then come on, and try not to look so glum."

Chapter 39

"I have assembled a meeting on the comm in an hour. I help many people in the community. A lot of them are considered criminals; some are revolutionaries trying to do what you are. They have access to many more people. Some, however, are indeed criminals in need of doctoring for their wounds. These types might still be useful, though they will be motivated by profit mostly."

"That's great, Doc," said Mike, "it's exactly what we're looking for, but what about the average Joe?"

"If my translator has worked correctly, you want to get the normal citizens involved as well? But how would they participate? They have no weapons, no ships."

"Isn't there a local military, or law enforcement, or something?"

"Well, yes, the Structure operates...ah, I understand. We must inspire the citizens to rebel against the governmental systems. The Structure will implement cruel retaliation against the uprising. We must prepare the citizens. Come. We will go to the place we met and start there."

"I'll go back to my neighborhood and get whatever support I can," Reshtalda said on his way out the door.

"Reshtalda! You get your parents' support, then we'll talk about what you can do to help. I mean it!" Mike shouted.

"We need to get that band off of your head." Phay Igh pulled down Mike's hood and unclipped the neural regulator. "No one will take you seriously if you are wearing that. Here, I will make you a better one."

The doctor spent several minutes modifying the band, then handed it back to Mike.

"Wear it like a necklace. It's awkward, but now people will just think it's jewelry or something."

Mike shrugged and thanked him as they made their way to the doctor's vehicle.

The bar was crowded in the early evening rush. As the Doctor went in, people seemed to recognize him. He stopped and talked at several tables and introduced Mike. A buzz quickly developed around the bar. Soon people were coming over to meet Mike. They started saying things like, 'Welcome to our world' and, 'What an honor to meet such a legend.' Finally, the Doctor encouraged him to get up onto the musician's stage and introduce himself.

"Uh, hello, everyone. My name's Mike. I'm a human from earth. We've got a little situation that we need your help with. You see, in a couple of hours we're going to overthrow the Structure and things are going to get a bit crazy around here. So, just as a courtesy, we thought we'd let you know. After all, we created the Abes as a free people with the right to life, liberty and the pursuit of happiness. The Structure is a violation of that right, so it's gotta go."

"Cease your activity and prepare to be apprehended."

A six foot monolithic rectangle emerged from a corner of the bar and floated towards him. Mike didn't hesitate. The thing had barely finished its sentence before he put three pistol rounds through its hide. It fell over in a shower of sparks. The people stared, dumbfounded.

"Any of you who want to join us, grab a weapon and feel free to do what I just did. They're not indestructible and the Structure isn't your master. You are your *own* master. Incidentally, the entire Biauay fleet is en route to join us in a coordinated attack on the Structure itself, so now is the time to take your world back. Claim your freedom and live under the Structure's tyranny no longer!" He raised his fist in the air.

The crowd stared silently at him. The Abe security bot sparked on the floor. Suddenly people started running for the doors. In less than a minute, the place was completely empty except for Mike and Phay Igh.

"You really know how to inspire the people."

"Well—"

"Relinquish your weapon and surrender to the Will of the Structure."

A swarm of armed Abes crashed in the door. Mike wrapped his cloak around him and started dropping bots with his assault rifle. The bots returned fire but the energy beams had no effect. After twenty seconds of fire, all the bots were down.

"I think it's time to leave, I only have so much ammo." Mike ran past Phay Igh, heading for the door. A loud explosion rocked the cocktail glasses abandoned on the tables.

"That was us, Michael," Dominus said. "We are neutralizing the security forces on this world. It will take over an hour because we are avoiding collateral damage. Return to the workshop and stay there until we are finished."

"Okay, change of plan, Doc. Dominus—the good Dominus—is protecting everyone from the security forces on the whole planet. So we have to stay in the workshop until they've cleaned up the bad guys. Come on." He grabbed the doctor and ran out the back door.

"Where are we going?"

"Here." He sent Phay Igh a marker.

"I know a faster way."

A route line appeared on his map. "Get in your car, I'll ride on top." Mike jumped on the roof of the vehicle and set the gravity compensators on his boots to high.

The machine drove lazily through the streets while Mike used his newly enhanced vision to scan for hostile contacts. Everywhere they went, people were coming out into the streets, looking around like they were waking up.

"The Structure falls today! To arms! To arms! The humans have returned to bring down the Structure!" Mike yelled over and over until he began to get hoarse.

"Use your neural enhancement, not your voice," Vexa suggested over the link.

"Oh, right." Mike took off the necklace and started broadcasting loudly.

As they rounded a hill, a security blockade came into view. Mike took aim and started eliminating bots. Suddenly, all of them flared with fire from the inside out.

Mike sent his thanks to Alaz then told Phay Igh, "Just drive through the blockade, Doc. That's it, push them aside. This isn't their world anymore."

Children followed them and began pelting the bots with anything they could find. Soon the adults were joining them. As they drove, they saw more rebellious behavior.

"Michael, listen." Phay Igh opened a link to an entertainment broadcast that reported Mike's rampage. Clearly it was a pro-Structure station. "But did you hear? It said you were human! That's going to cause a stir."

"I don't think it's going to be enough."

"Oh, I think you're going to be surprised. Your performance has been broadcast to everyone who needed to see it. It's up to them now."

They slid their vehicle through the workshop's holo-door and came to a stop. Mike put the necklace back on, set his boots back to normal, and jumped down.

Phay Igh got out and stared at the Abe parts scattered around his work space. He held up a dismantled hand. "These are the pieces of my greatest fears, all in ruin on the floor. They seem so powerless now."

"Someone once said that the only thing we have to fear is fear itself."

Phay Igh turned to Mike and smiled. "That was a wise person."

Outside, the sound of discord grew. Within an hour there was rioting and looting.

"Don't worry," Mike reassured Phay Igh. "It always starts with criminal behavior. Then the cops come and the real protests start."

"You have some experience with this, do you?"

"I'm trained in agitation."

"Everyone has to have a talent at something, I guess."

Mike prepared an MRE as they sat and talked. "So, humans descend from apes. What about you, Phay Igh?"

"The Paya descend from marsupials, as if you couldn't tell," Phay Igh explained. "Normally the omnivores would be the predominant survivor in the evolutionary scheme of things. But in our case, there was a spore that promoted vegetation growth during a critical span of time. The meat eaters lost out because the vegetation spore also contributed to cognitive development in certain species."

"Are there always marsupials, apes, and such? Does evolution ever do anything really weird?"

"Oh yes. There are species that cannot leave their planet because they evolved in completely saturated chemical states. Most of the time they are very odd indeed. There are entire species that have lived in liquids or locked under the ice of frozen planets. Their stories are quite incredible. The galaxy is so large, it is difficult to conceive." Phay Igh chuckled. "When people talk about the universe, it is viewed as the naïveté of a lesser evolved species."

"I'll make sure not to speak in universal terms, then."

"That would be wise."

"How about humans, how are we viewed?"

"You are a myth. A race of gods that created the Abes, who created the Biauay. The Biauay, incidentally, are considered an advanced species on the verge of dimensional migration."

"I'm sorry, dimensional migration?"

"Yes. The more a species evolves, the more

command they have of the dimension they live in. At a certain point they become so evolved that they break the bounds of their dimension."

"You're talking about height, width, depth kind of dimension, right?"

"Well, at a rudimentary level those are factors that are used to explain a dimension, but there are places that exist that are far beyond our reckoning. In most of them time does not exist. I know, it boggles my mind too."

"Y'know, you're pretty cool, Doc. I'm kind of worried though."

"About what?"

"Well, in a little while, Dominus, Vexa and Alaz are going to be back. I'd hate to see you all freaked out again."

He sighed. "I think, looking at all of these parts and knowing that, although he has the same name, he is an entirely different person…I may be okay."

"Hey, would you like to see some of the footage I have of my planet? We had quite an adventure up to this point."

"Why not, it will pass the time."

Outside, the populace was tearing the town apart.

Chapter 40

The Emythiar fleet joined up with other planetary elements and formed a massive armada—Sam had taught them the word. By the time they readied to convey to the Structure there were over four-hundred thousand capital ships. Most of them were the size of small continents.

Sam stood at a command table and strategized with the Biauay officers and counsel. "...and you have never assembled into an armada before?"

"No, sir. Our strategy has always been to defend and run to the next designated world."

"You do realize that the armada overwhelmingly outguns the Structure."

"Yes, but again, engaging an enemy is confrontational and any losses are unacceptable."

"Who developed your defense, Gandhi?"

"I don't—"

"Cultural reference, sorry. Well, gentlemen, I'm going to show you how to make war. People are going to die on all sides, but it is how we deal with tyranny. If you let someone just walk all over you, you are going to live an unfulfilled and miserable life. No one should be subject to that. We have to take justice into our own hands to try and defend freedom for everyone. We will attempt to minimize casualties, but accept the fact that they are going to happen."

"So what is our first move, Admiral?"

"You see all those ships out there?"

"Yes, sir."

"We're going to move them as close to the Structure as possible, making sure our fields of fire do not include our own ships, and then all of them are going to open fire simultaneously."

"But won't the Structure retaliate?"

"Yes, but we will continue firing until the Structure ceases to exist. Listen up! I am here to do two things…"

Annette put her hand to her forehead.

"…utterly destroy the Structure and chew bubblegum."

Her fingers went to the bridge of her nose which she held as she slowly shook her head.

"And I'm all out of bubblegum!"

Cheers went up from the crew except for a few who tried to figure out what bubblegum was.

"Now get this fleet to the Structure and open fire on any and all enemy contacts with extreme prejudice!"

***

Niliason met everyone at the holo-table. "Okay, here's the plan. The Structure calls itself the Corpusphere. It's a planetoid sized…well, it's essentially a computer. It started as a manufacturing plant orbiting a planet that it chose for its resources. It did nothing but build robots and Abes to serve what it conceives as its primary function, which is to procreate."

"Well, that clinches it," Mellissa quipped, "the Structure is definitely male."

Niliason continued on. "It built layer on top of layer, and the sphere grew outwards. You won't have any comms once you are inside the Structure." He let that sink in. "You will be completely on your own."

"How about with each other?" Mellissa asked.

"We think your neuro-comms will work, but there's no guarantee. You have to understand that the Structure is a massive computer, broadcasting quadrillions of orders to its whole empire. The amount of interference is going to be impossible to deal with. It is covering every frequency of every wavelength conceivable.

"In addition to the compression shield and the Fantagoric cape, you'll also be wearing a radiation shield. The Structure uses gamma bursts, tachyon streams and the like to send commands throughout the galaxy."

"How long do we have?"

"We'll leave immediately, but conveying you directly to the Structure will be impossible. Our only option is to convey you to the Biauay fleet. Once they are in range they will have to transport you to the surface. The attack should distract the Structure from one small ship so it shouldn't be a big deal. There is very little gravity, so it's not like you're going to crash land or anything."

"Well, that's comforting." John Anthony rolled his eyes. "So where do we go on this Death Star?"

"Funny," Niliason grimaced, "because that's basically what it is."

John Anthony shook his head. "Doesn't anyone have any original ideas anymore?"

Niliason ignored him and continued, "You're going to find that flat, navigable surfaces are rare. As we thought, it's mostly networks of pipes, structural beams and wiring. Rooms are non-existent. We'll try to land you directly over the coordinates, then it is just a matter of jumping down levels.

"Your capes are there for protection only; they can't fly you anywhere because there isn't an atmosphere. For that reason, you'll be wearing a kind of jet pack. It will propel you downwards as well as up. The faster you move, the more lives get saved. Your landings will be hard, so we are also equipping you with these." He pointed at a pair of standing leg braces.

"That's it, I'm going to start calling you 'Q'," John Anthony joked.

"We're putting everything into this. Your strength enhancement will work together with the braces to prevent injury. You'll be landing on cross beams, conduit, and pipe at high speed so it's tricky at best. Mark is going to demonstrate how the braces work." Niliason looked up three stories to the rafters of the hangar. "Ready, Mark?"

An Atec stood on the rafters, waved, then jumped. The jet pack shot him downward but as he approached the ground the legs extended. Even before that, John Anthony swore he saw some kind of force field impact the ground. The extended legs absorbed the force of the landing and Mark was walking away even as he reached the ground.

"Thank you, Mark." Niliason turned back to them. "There ya go."

"Okay, so we get down to the level we need to be at, then what?" John Anthony asked.

"You're going to the bottom. That's where the core is."

"Why is it always a core?" Daniel muttered.

John Anthony shrugged. "A core is the core, that's where it all starts."

"John Anthony is right," Niliason said. "Every being has a heart, every computer has a central processor. The core is the Structure's central processor." He waved down John Anthony's hand. "Now, of course, the Structure has redundancy built in so while you're leaping your way down you will drop these on any conduit, pipe, or anything else you come across."

He produced a spool of fine cord that glowed faintly.

"This stuff will cut through just about anything. You pull off a strand and drop it onto the object. The cord then wraps itself around the piece and cuts through it when you give the command on your neural net." He sent them a video of a six-inch piece of the thin string wrapping around and cutting through a battleship in under a second.

John Anthony looked at Daniel. The veteran Ranger had gone pale.

"So, here it is in a nutshell: your mission is to clear a path to the core. You won't have enough firepower to destroy it. The Biauay fleet will fire that shot. Once you're clear, they will take out the whole planetoid of the Structure in one coordinated shot." Niliason locked eyes with them and became grim. "Crucially, if the core gets damaged before then, it will shift its operations to another core. That means it will simply start running on a back up of itself in some other remote location. If that happens, it's game over. We will lose this opportunity forever. It is another reason why speed is imperative.

"To further prevent the Structure from switching locations, a large portion of the Biauay fleet will stand off to set up a screen to block the Structure's transmissions. This may sound easy, but let me paint a picture of what is going to be happening up there. Once the Structure sees the Biauay fleet it will send out commands to launch meteor showers and even direct gamma bursts from local stars. We're talking about thousands of ships the size of countries getting vaporized while they try to keep formation to block the transmissions. Crews numbering in the hundreds will be wiped out."

"Wait, only a hundred people to run a ship the size of a country?" Daniel asked.

"Yes, but taking out a thousand ships with a hundred people each is still a hundred thousand people at a time. The loss of one person is a tragedy. Many will die this day."

He continued, "You will quickly remove any obstructions to clear a path to the core. Once it's done, use the rest of the fuel in your jet-packs to get out of there as fast as you can. Once you're clear of the Structure, your neuro-comms will work again and you can call for someone to pick you up."

"And the Biauay will line up one of their big ships and target the core," Daniel finished.

"A group of ships actually, but yes. Questions?"

"Yeah." Daniel raised his hand. "How big does the hole down to the core need to be?"

"About a hundred yards in circumference. Wider is better when you only have one shot."

"What happens to the pieces we cut off. I mean, won't they fall and hit the core?"

"The core is very hot and will burn up any material you drop. Those kinds of hits are too small to be noticed, but it won't be able to take a direct hit from a Biauay capital ship."

"Where are we likely to encounter the most resistance?" Mellissa asked.

"There are service and construction droids everywhere. We don't expect there will be security because the Structure doesn't think it can ever be assaulted. If something does attack, you will have time to react. Your shields and Fantagoric cape should protect you. Return fire and destroy your attacker quickly though. Once the Structure learns you are there, it will ascertain your nature and develop a countermeasure quickly. If the attacker, whether it's droid or Abe, doesn't die quickly it will send information about the encounter to the Structure, then you'll have real trouble."

Daniel looked at John Anthony and Mellissa. "Remember what I was showing you at the range? Shoot until you're sure it's dead."

"You bring up a very good point, Daniel. All of you, take a seat." Niliason instructed. "This may make you dizzy for a minute." The burst of data made them woozy.

John Anthony felt like throwing up. "What was that?"

"Kind of like an app. It uses your ocular systems in combination with your life support sensors to examine the health of another being, including appliances. Go on, look at each other and wonder how the other person is feeling."

"Wow, Mel, you're glowing green," John Anthony said.

"Now look at this laptop the same way."

"It's green too."

Niliason took the battery out. "And now?"

"It's red."

"Red's dead. Shoot until the thing turns red. You'll use less ammo and this way there will be no doubt. Now, are you ready?"

They all nodded and stood. John Anthony's palms were sweating.

"Then it's time for us to go," Niliason said.

"Wait, you're going too?" Mellissa asked.

"Of course. If we fail, then Earth is doomed and so is the rest of the galaxy. There is nothing more that I can do but fight. The Atec of Earth will continue to keep the humans in the dark about all of this. No need for their last days to be filled with despair and panic."

John Anthony put his hands on Daniel and Mel's shoulders. "We will not fail."

Niliason gave him a tight smile and triggered the lift. As they arrived at the surface of the desert, he saluted the Atec recovery team as they all turned into a white blur.

Chapter 41

The next thing John Anthony heard was the voice of Sam Wisecraft.

"No, a net, like a net! Tell them to hold back those drones so the second wave can get into position in case the first can't hold. Get the tertiary response groups around to the far side!"

"Sam?"

"Hey, look who showed up!" Sam smiled.

"What are you wearing on your head?" Mellissa laughed.

"It's my admiral's hat. I'm in charge of the fleet."

Daniel couldn't believe it. "Why the hell did they put you in charge?"

"I'm the most aggressive."

Niliason looked more stern than they had ever seen him. "Dr. Wisecraft, transfer authority to me." He didn't even look at Sam as he crossed to the command console.

Sam looked stunned. "I, uh, okay. I hereby transfer control of the armada to Niliason Brand. Everyone, this is your new admiral." He put the hat on Niliason, who promptly knocked it onto the floor.

"This is not a game, Doctor. A lot of people are going to die very soon."

"Hey, I know. That's what I've been trying to tell them."

"Strike team stand by to disembark."

A Biauay officer led Daniel, Mellissa, and John

Anthony off the bridge and down to a waiting ship. It was small, cramped and smelled like oil.

"As soon as we get close enough to the Structure, you will launch," the officer instructed. "Engage your shields and cloaks now." Then he turned and left them in the ship.

"So that's what a Biauay man looks like." Mellissa smirked. "He's kinda cute."

John Anthony shot her a look as they sat in the open door of the ship. *It's like sitting in the door of a helicopter in one of those Vietnam movies*, he thought.

"I wonder if we're supposed to leave the door open?" Daniel inspected the open hatch.

Suddenly, Sam came running into the hanger. "Hey, you guys, I'm sorry I didn't say goodbye up there. Niliason is really getting this whole thing coordinated, so I have to go, but…" He gave them hugs. "Be careful and don't do anything stupid. Just come back safe, okay?" He sprinted out of the hangar leaving them alone once again.

"Still wondering about the door," Daniel said.

A loud alarm went off and a light began flashing. "Alright, Daniel, John Anthony, Mel…my friends. This is for all the marbles," Niliason said over the neuro-comms. He was relaxed and focused, even excited by the possibility of victory. The feeling was contagious and served to calm their nerves and steady them for the task ahead.

"I know you won't let me down. Stay calm and focused. One last piece of advice from an old warrior—Daniel, you know this already—try to enjoy yourself out there."

The ship lifted off the deck and began to slowly move towards the open hatchway.

Daniel let his legs dangle out of the open hatch. "Okay, I guess the door stays open."

"What did he mean by 'enjoy ourselves'?" It sounded like sarcasm to Mellissa.

"Kick ass with a smile. Sing a song. Rock it." Daniel smiled. "That's what he meant."

John Anthony nodded. "Kind of like holding your arms up on a roller coaster."

"Exactly."

They all yelled as the ship accelerated into open space.

"Oh my God, Daniel!" Mellissa screamed.

"Calm down, you guys, come on. How cool is this?" John Anthony paced his breathing.

They could see the Structure in the distance. The side of the Biauay capital ship loomed like an endlessly high wall above and below them. The perspective was dizzying as they cleared the hatch of the landing bay. Their little craft gained speed as the side of the great ship shrank away, revealing the glowing orb of the Structure silhouetted by a large blue planet. A swarm of objects erupted from the Structure and met with masses of fighters from the armada. Bright explosions began sparking all over the vast battlefield.

Suddenly an entire pocket of the Structure's swarm erupted as something passed through it, showering streams of light.

John Anthony pointed. "It's Dominus!"

"Jesus. The guy is a freakin' wrecking ball." Daniel was glued to the action.

"And there's Alaz and Vexa on his flanks. Wait, there's a fourth one?"

Daniel just laughed. "Mikey, you go, boy!"

"They must have found him a ship."

"Hey, guys! Enjoying the show?" Mike said over the comms.

"You be careful, buddy," Daniel said. "Keep close to Dominus."

Mike laughed. "Not too close though. Hey, aren't you guys supposed to go break some shit?"

"Roger wilco, ass monkey." Daniel signed off. "Man, I miss that guy."

"Hey, gents, we're coming down." Mellissa hung her

feet out of the door. Daniel and John Anthony followed suit. The little ship swept down quickly and came to rest above a hole that dropped seemingly forever into the dark abyss of the Structure.

"Go! Go! Go!" Daniel yelled the traditional military jump order.

John Anthony just sighed and thought, *I was gonna kill myself anyway.* Mellissa squeezed his hand before squinting and hopping off the ledge. Daniel plunged after them.

Using their ocular enhancements, they scanned far into the hole.

"Everyone, try to disburse a bit so we can cover all sides of the shaft." Daniel took charge.

"Good idea. Hey, do we need to cut that one there?"

"Yeah, it's sticking out a bit. Okay, let's try our landing skills."

They came down one at a time on a thick beam that protruded into the hole.

"Nice!" John Anthony smiled. "That was way easier than I thought it would be."

"I thought I'd hit harder," Mellissa agreed

Daniel was grinning as he landed. "The Atec know how to put together some serious kit, don't they?"

He slung a length of the cutting cord onto the beam. It stretched, grew, and wrapped itself around the beam instantly. With a thought, Daniel gave the command. There was a brief flash and the severed beam dropped into the blackness.

Mellissa looked over the edge to scan. "Only two thousand feet in. We're gonna have to get moving. The longer we take, the more lives are lost. Let's try to stay together this time, okay? Ready. One, two, three, jump!"

They all stepped off the ledge together.

"That's better," Daniel said. "See that cross beam a couple of miles down? It spans the whole shaft, so I'll do one side, you two do the other."

They continued down, eliminating beams, shafts, and

thick sections of wiring. The powerful cutting cord seemed to go through anything. They learned to stay together and use the jet packs to accelerate them downwards. After a short time, they became so accustomed to the speed that it seemed as though they couldn't go fast enough.

Farther and farther they dropped, repeating the grueling exercise. They had to constantly scan forward, using their powerful ocular enhancements to zoom in on objects that were miles away. Their strength and endurance enhancements made it possible for their bodies to tolerate the intense strain, but there was nothing to help with the mental fatigue. They persisted and communicated constantly.

John Anthony started singing 'I've been working on the railroad' and they all joined in with a laugh. They ate as they went, recharging their bodies and enhancements with the special energy food of the Atec, and continual contact with high-power electrical cables helped to keep their energy levels topped off. After an hour of intense work, they could see a light, down in the distance.

"Is that it?" John Anthony asked as they plummeted downwards in close formation.

"Well, we're over nine hundred miles into this thing," Daniel said. "The core is 'round about twelve hundred, so I'm guessing that's it."

"It must be huge if we can see it from three hundred miles away."

"Hey guys, I have an, uh…interested party here." Mellissa shared what she was seeing. A small drone flew next to her as she fell. It seemed to be examining her.

"Shoot it, Mel!" Daniel yelled.

"But it's not—"

The little box exploded, sending Mellissa flying into a side vent. John Anthony reversed the thruster on his jet pack and stopped his fall.

"She's in there." He leapt off a piece of the structure and grabbed the edge of the twenty-foot square vent shaft.

With his new strength he easily hauled himself into it. "Mel!" He scrambled for speed in the low gravity. She was unconscious. "Danny, come in. Danny, are you there?"

John Anthony felt her wrist for a pulse, then cursed himself and remembered the app that Niliason had installed. She glowed a muted green. *Okay, not bright green but at least she's not red or yellow or anything.* He felt her arms, squeezing as he went, searching for breaks. Working his way around her shoulders. When he got to her ribs she groaned in pain. *Broken ribs. Shit.* He continued checking.

"Mel, I'm here. Are you okay? Mel, talk to me, wake up and tell me where you're hurt."

"John?"

"I'm right here, oh thank, God. Where does it hurt?"

"Everywhere, my whole side," she groaned. "What happened?"

"That little cube exploded. I don't know if it responded to Daniel's voice saying 'shoot it' or what."

"Where's Danny?"

"I don't know. He's farther down."

"Leave me here and finish the mission." She gritted her teeth in pain. "Get me on the way back up."

"No, Mel, we'll be out of comms range—"

"Just fucking do it, John." She winced. "Don't sit here arguing with me. There are people dying out there. Get out of here, find Danny, and finish the mission."

"O–okay. Here's your gun. Kill anything that comes near you."

"I got it, just go!" She pushed him away then pulled him back. "No, come here." She planted a kiss on him. "Now go!"

He looked at her one last time and jumped out of the conduit.

"And remember to enjoy yourself. It's not every day you get to save the galaxy and get the girl," Melissa added before their neural link went dead.

He blinked away tears and forced himself to focus on

the mission. He powered his thrusters to full and shot past nine hundred miles per hour within seconds. Scanning the hole as he fell, he bent his thoughts towards Daniel. A green spot lit up in the distance. Daniel was standing on a large conduit that crossed the hole, waving up at John Anthony. John Anthony gave a thumbs up and came down soft.

"Is she okay?"

"She's stable but busted up. Ribs, I think. She's going to stay put and we'll get her on the way back. What happened to you?"

"There were more of those things. They're attracted to noise."

"I thought that might be the case. So if we shoot, more of them come."

"Yeah. The key is not to shoot them in the first place."

"But then they scan us."

"If we don't do anything, they just leave. I believe they think we're pieces of space junk."

"Good." John Anthony sighed and locked eyes with Daniel. "Let's go."

They worked at a frantic pace, cutting a swath through the matrix of the Structure's inner levels. As they got closer to the core, the construct became denser. They slashed through the barriers, driving their systems to maximum capacity. Pools of sweat accumulated in the bottom of the egg-shaped bubble of their shields. Finally, they could feel the heat of the core.

"It melts everything we send down. Just keep cutting!" John Anthony landed on another beam, dropped a length of cord and set it off with a thought. Daniel mirrored him on the other side.

The rhythm of the work had become synchronized. Fly, land, wrap, cut, wait, fly... The obstacles became so thick that they walked down them like stairs. Oftentimes they would pass by the falling pieces they had just cut. The glow from the core lit everything in bright yellow. Heat and radiation rolled off their shields.

"Looks like it stops soon. That's the last one down there"

"Our shields are using up energy fast, man. Let's get this done and get out of here." Daniel dropped another cord. Suddenly his cloak flapped out and went limp. "I just lost my cape."

"Get out of here, Danny, get back to Mel. I'll finish and meet you. No time, just go!"

John Anthony kept dropping pieces of cord, cutting his way through the forest of beams, conduit and cabling. Daniel rocketed back up the hole. He had no idea how fast he was going, but he thought for a second that he was probably breaking some kind of record. The location marker he had set popped up in his vision and he landed on the edge of the large conduit. He leaned down and poked his head inside.

"Mel?" He couldn't see anything. There was movement on the floor of the big square pipe and he adjusted his ocular sensors. A swarm of small cubes lay in a pile. Quietly, he focused on Mel. A bright green outline appeared beneath the pile of cubes.

Daniel froze, his hand on his pistol. If he shot, they would kill her. Then he remembered what Niliason had said about the app. *Green is healthy. She's green.*

"Mel? Are you under there?" Even his neuro-comms voice was a whisper.

"Hey, bro," she said quietly. "I'm fine, just be really still; they're sensitive."

"Dangerous like sensitive or…"

"No, like, emotionally sensitive. They're healing me. Don't ask me how."

"Really? Are they intelligent?"

"Yes, very. But they're extremely shy."

***

John Anthony cut the last beam just as his cape shivered and went limp. The light and heat from the core was so intense it was beginning to penetrate his compression shield. Grateful to be done, he punched the jets to full, eager to get back to Mel.

"Daniel, Mel?" He landed on the conduit.

"In here," Daniel replied. "Be quiet."

John Anthony lowered himself into the conduit. Daniel sat with Mel on the floor. They were surrounded by thousands of cubes ranging in size from one to six inches square.

John Anthony froze. "Oh shit. Just stay still."

"It's not what you think. They healed me."

"What? Why? How?"

"That's three of the big five, buddy," Daniel laughed quietly. "We don't have an answer for the last two, but they're friendly, just really shy."

"That's a problem," John Anthony said, realizing the implications.

Mel nodded. "I know. How can we destroy their world? They're intelligent and the Structure is their microcosm."

"We have to get back to the fleet and tell them."

"No," Mel said. "Military minds will want to destroy the Structure regardless of these little guys. They'll say it's just a consequence of war. We can't let them fire that shot. This is all of them. They only exist here."

She held out her arms and the cubes floated around her, displaying an array of soft colored lights. John Anthony thought she looked like the science fiction embodiment of Mother Nature.

"John," she said, "you have to convince them. Convince Niliason and Piaa and Dominus to find a way to stop the Structure without destroying it."

John Anthony was incredulous. "What are you going to do, stay here?"

"Yes. It will buy us some time."

"Mel, no." Daniel's voice made the little cubes shiver and flash.

"Yes, Danny, it will at least make the fleet hesitate to send the shot down if I'm here."

John Anthony knew she wasn't going to budge. "Dammit, Mel. You picked a hell of a time to put your foot down."

"She's right." Daniel sighed. "I know Niliason's type. As much as he cares for us, he won't hesitate to sacrifice the few for the many, but it may make him hesitate long enough to listen to alternatives."

"If you have a plan now would be the time to share it, bro!" John Anthony hissed.

"No, *bro*, I don't have a frickin plan! Maybe you can think of something by the time we get up there."

"Me? I'm not the military strategist of this group!"

"No, but you're the one with the highest IQ." Daniel looked at him, exasperated.

John Anthony blinked at him. "Really? You guys think I'm the smart one?"

"Oh Jesus. Yes, John Anthony, but we don't have time for self-esteem boosting. Just go change Niliason's mind."

"Enough of this," Mellissa broke in. "Both of you get up there and find a solution. I'll wait here—alone. These little guys should be able to protect me some if things go wrong. Daniel go with him. They're more likely to listen if it's both of you."

Daniel sighed and looked at the ceiling for a minute. Finally, he nodded. "Okay." He stared at his sister for a long moment, then climbed out of the shaft.

Chapter 42

Outside on the shaft Daniel helped John Anthony up.

"There's no arguing with her," Daniel said. "Besides, she's right."

"I know, otherwise I'd drag her out of there. Let's just get this done quickly."

The jet packs carried them out of the hole. The Biauay Command capital ship loomed in the distance.

Daniel smiled at John Anthony. "Niliason, stay close to retrieve us."

"Copy that, stand by," came Niliason's voice. "Where's Mellissa?"

"Do not fire! Repeat DO – NOT – FIRE on the Structure!" John Anthony pushed the comm hard.

"Roger that, John Anthony, we hear you! Why? Where's Mellissa?"

John Anthony gave him a burst that contained everything that had transpired.

"Okay, let's get you on board and we'll have a pow-wow with Dominus."

"There's our exfil, inbound." Daniel pointed at a small craft approaching them at high speed.

The little ship, that had dropped them off came to stop in front of them while they maneuvered inside. Once they were in, it sped back to the command ship. Dominus and Niliason met them in the hangar.

"This is a difficult and unforeseen circumstance." Dominus got right to the point.

John Anthony jumped out of the little ship and ran over to them. "Mel is down there and we need to get her out, now."

"But she's right to protect the new species." Daniel walked up. "She's in no danger down there. She might be bored, but she's okay."

"Listen to yourself!" John Anthony whirled on him. "That's your sister stuck in the body of a tyrannical alien floating in space in the middle of the largest battle zone anyone has even seen!"

"I know, John Anthony, but she's probably in the safest place she could be."

"It's true," Dominus agreed with Daniel. "She is certainly safer than we are here. The situation demands that we shut down the Structure, recover Mel, and preserve the world of the new species." The big Abe hesitated, then sighed. "I believe I have a way to do that."

"You do?" Niliason stared at Dominus

"Yes, my friend. I alone have linked to and contradicted the Will of the Structure and survived. I am much stronger now than I was then. I believe I can, with the help of my children, battle the Structure's base functionality and commandeer it. I will personally confront the Structure and take control of it."

"But that would mean you would be giving up your current existence," Niliason argued. "Your consciousness would transfer to the Structure."

"It is a price I am willing to pay."

"No, Dominus. Mel wouldn't want that," John Anthony protested.

"Understand that I have much to atone for. Please, give me your blessing. Tell me that if I do this then I will be forgiven for the horrible crimes I have committed."

"Dominus," John Anthony pleaded, "don't do this, you are already forgiven."

"Then I must use this gift of forgiveness to the greatest benefit. Farewell." Dominus rocketed out of the hatch before any of them could speak. The blast blew them across the floor. By the time they rolled to a stop and looked up, he was gone.

"All ships, hold formation." Niliason sprinted back up to the bridge. "We are down to it now. Let Dominus through and keep the enemy out of the Structure at all costs!"

***

Dominus blazed into the hole, shot past Mel, and continued down towards the core.

Mellissa felt the shockwave of his passing. The cubes shivered with excitement. They sensed him, knew him. He was kin.

"Dominus?" Melissa stammered. "What—what are you doing here?"

"All will be well soon," Dominus assured her. "Keep the little ones safe."

Two more shockwaves rattled the conduit before everything became still.

Several minutes passed then a deep surge rippled upward out of the hole. The Structure was fighting. Mellissa could sense it through the cubes. They didn't know what was going on, only that there was a struggle. They huddled closer to her. Remembering the rebirth of Vexa and Alaz, she focused loving energy at them. John Anthony's song floated back into her mind and she began to sing softly.

"I've been working on the railroad, all the live long day…"

The little cubes calmed as the gamut of colors they shone began to unify into a pale blue light. From the core of the Structure, the surges grew more frequent and stronger. Then they stopped and Mellissa heard a strong voice reverberating all around her.

"We are Dominus."

Mel's heart leapt into her throat. Suddenly her neuro-link connected her to John Anthony.

"Mel? He did it! Dominus has taken control of the Structure. Are you okay?"

"Yes, I'm fine!" She threw back her head and laughed. "Come and get me!"

"We're waiting for you at the entrance."

She stood up carefully and told the cubes, "Go to your father, he will take care of you. Go, and always remember your human, Biauay, and Atec friends."

She climbed out of the shaft, hit the thrusters, and rocketed to the entrance. Daniel and John Anthony sat in the door of the little drop ship. She landed and jumped into John Anthony's arms.

"You did it, you actually pulled it off!"

"Well, it wasn't me, it was Dom—"

She silenced him with a kiss.

***

The command ship was quiet for the first time in hours as the death toll came in.

"One hundred twenty-six thousand, four hundred and fifty-three dead. The Structure managed to get one gamma burst in and it grazed the fleet. It is to the courageous dead that we owe our victory. They held their positions in the face of death. To them we owe our freedom, our respect, and our eternal remembrance."

Niliason spoke with a heavy heart. All the people felt it, Dominus made sure. With the Structure gone, Dominus used the incredible amount of energy channeled through the Structure's systems to open new routes of communication and travel throughout the galaxy.

***

Sam and Annette joined John Anthony, Daniel, Mike, and Mellissa on the steps of the Biauay counsel palace to receive the Biauay's gratitude. They stood in front of a crowd of over a million people. The award was given by their new galactic ambassador; Piaa, who had received the highest honors of her people. When the ceremony was done they met in the palace gardens.

"I asked everyone to give us a little space for a moment." Piaa handed them each a small disc. "I had these made for you."

"Conveyance recall disks?" John Anthony asked.

"Indeed they are, with one important difference. They will always bring you here, on this exact spot in the counsel gardens, as many times as you wish. When you are here, they will bring you back to wherever you started from, in the exact spot."

"So I can come back, grab a bunch of precious metals, and then blip back. Cool."

"Are you kidding me, John Anthony?" she laughed. "I do not think any of you shall want for money."

"No, those days are gone." Niliason joined them.

"Hey, Admiral, I thought you were getting the armada squared away." Sam elbowed him.

"I left the Biauay to take care of their own concerns. No, I'm going back to Earth with you. I have a new venture now. I intend to command a small group of specialized agents to rid the galaxy of the remnants of the Structure and occasionally intervene in Earth affairs when necessary. There are many criminal activities that are still going on."

Daniel was skeptical. "But how can you patrol such a vast area?"

Niliason smiled. "Dominus. The Structure's old network is still in place. Instead of using it to control people, he is using it to make life better. And that includes finding the bad guys."

"It's a good idea." Daniel nodded.

Niliason cocked an eyebrow. "It's a great idea if I could find the right agents."

Mellissa looked at Annette. "You have the feeling we're getting recruited?"

"Well, we have to pay for theses augmentations somehow," Annette laughed. "I'm in."

Niliason looked around at them.

"Let me get this straight," John Anthony said. "You want us to be galactic superheroes?"

"Pretty much."

"Okay. As long as we get some time for a vacation first." John Anthony turned to Mellissa. "I think we're well overdo for some time to ourselves, don't you think?"

Mellissa nodded eagerly. "You're on, mister!" She flung herself around him.

"If they're in, I'm in," Mike said.

"It is an excellent way to serve as my apprentice," Dominus's voice softly added over the neuro-link.

"Oh, great, he's omniscient too?" John Anthony said.

"No," Dominus laughed, "just nosey."

Daniel laughed as well and put his hand on Niliason's shoulder. "There's your answer, chief."

"Chief, huh?" Niliason said. "Don't know if I like that."

"Wait," Sam said. "Do we have some kind of name like 'the Avengers' or something?"

Hours later, the garden still echoed with their laughter.

Chapter 43

Morning broke soft and pale on the quiet suburb of Takoma Park. They appeared in the boggy woods behind Daniel and Mellissa's house; Dee Dee and Jared were with them. Jared ran to the back door with Daniel close on his heels.

"Looks like we've added to the depressions here," Annette said with a wry smile.

"No depression here, just happy people," John Anthony replied.

"They still have surveillance all over the place," Mike chuckled, "but for some reason, all their cameras seem to get is an old Cheerios commercial."

"Aw, poor feds. They got Mike'd."

"And Piaa'd," Niliason smiled.

They all agreed to say their goodbyes after a breakfast at Daniel and Mellissa's house.

Niliason approved of the breakfast meeting. "It's an opportunity to brief you on your first mission."

"First mission already?" Mike was surprised.

Niliason held up his hand. "Hear me out. It's important to get settled back into the routine. You are still being watched; besides, you have to experience the everyday world as your new selves. Things are going to be different now in ways you never imagined. The augmentations will take a bit of time to adapt to, but thankfully, time is now a luxury you have."

Daniel laughed. "Well, life is still short. I mean, it's

not like…oh."

"Danny, we're going to live a long time," Mellissa laughed.

Niliason looked at each of them. "Hopefully you are going to live as long as you want. You are not immortal, but you can be saved from many things that would have been fatal to you before."

"Let's not test that, shall we?" Sam said.

"Back to the briefing. Your mission is to get back into your routines. Same jobs, same houses—"

"I hate to say it, Mikey, but you need a maid," Daniel teased.

Mike shrugged. "Yeah, maybe it's time for me to get a new place and live like an adult."

"For now you will keep things as they have been," said Niliason, "but yeah, Mike, if you want to fix up your place, you certainly can. All of your residences will receive modifications." He paused to sip his coffee. "One by one you will sell off your businesses and homes and move to the base. By the end of next year, you should all be in."

"You mean we have to live underground for the rest of our lives?" John Anthony paused as he poured the orange juice.

"No, of course not. You will live in many places all over the world, and indeed the galaxy, but you will call your apartments at the Texas base home. Now, don't go thinking that you are relegated to stay in the place as it is. Each of you will be able to design your accommodations to your tastes. This is a new endeavor and I will spare no expense. The nice thing about being an Atec living on an Atec base is that you get full use of galactic technology. You have not seen the full extent of the base in Colorado City."

He sent them all of the data about the rest of the base. Suddenly they were taken on a tour of a facility that went deeper than they had guessed and stretched out for miles. For most of it they felt like they were outside, under the clear sky. There were Grecian columns surrounding lavish pools, desert oasis, and forest homes. Most of the plants were living, but wherever a cave wall or ceiling formed a boundary, a solid holographic image took over. Hundreds of Atec lived in small communities, coexisting peacefully without need or want.

"Is this real?" John Anthony was shocked.

"Yes, John Anthony." It was Piaa.

"Piaa!"

"I am here, in the Atec base. The tour you were just given was sent by me."

Daniel grumped. "And I have to live here and work in the shop for over a year?"

"Niliason," Piaa said, "isn't there something you can do? You can't show someone a better life then take it away from them, it's not fair."

"No, I suppose it is rather cruel. All right then. If you wish to come, then you are free to do so. We will have to come up with elaborate excuses for your disappearances but we can make it work."

"Maybe over a month or two we can make a plan to wrap things up and still move over one by one?" Sam offered.

"I think that's wise," Daniel nodded.

Niliason agreed. "Now that we are no longer in hiding, your neuro-comms will work around the globe, so we'll make some plans and get back to you. In the meantime, take some time off and enjoy yourselves, you've earned it."

***

John Anthony arrived at the radio shop in the afternoon. He started up the truck and checked the store one last time. After nailing the 'for sale' sign into place, he hopped into the big yellow rig and rolled out onto the street. He didn't see the fireman dialing his phone as he watched the truck pull away.

Reilly began tailing John Anthony in Virginia. By the time they crossed into Maryland, Reilly had a small plane and two undercover feds covering his every move.

John Anthony pulled into the parking lot of Daniel's shop where the team waited for him. Justin Farwall was also there. He was glad to finally see his truck, but had no complaints—Daniel had generously compensated him, both for the truck and for the hassle. As John Anthony climbed out of the cab, the feds swooped in.

"Michael Madsen and Daniel Taggart, you are wanted for questioning." Reilly jumped out of the black Tahoe and leveled his pistol at them. "You're coming with me."

They all just smiled calmly.

"This is my friend, Doctor Annette Blazer," Daniel said. "I think you'll want to talk to her as well."

***

Reilly didn't wait until they got to headquarters. He started questioning his detainees as soon as they were all handcuffed and in the car. "Where is the bomb?"

"What bomb?" Annette looked confused.

"Oh no, don't play that shit with me. The big blue bomb that was sticking out of the ground in the forest behind the house, the one you stole from Fort Meade."

"That is my dig site, Agent Reilly, and there was certainly no bomb there."

Mike sat in the back using his advanced neural enhancement to go through millions of records, wiping them clean and creating new ones—reinforcing Annette's story in the data as she spoke.

Define the dig site, Mike instructed her over the neural-comms.

She elaborated to the agent. "I was doing paleoarcheology there, but between your people and the local kids, it was practically impossible. You've contaminated the place and ruined all the good science. I hope you're proud of yourself."

"A likely story."

"Excuse me, Agent Reilly, but isn't any story likely?" Daniel clarified.

"You pulled something out of that forest, Taggart, and a short while later three other something's flew off into space. Everyone saw it. We have eyewitness testimony from all over the area."

"So does Project Blue Book. Does anyone have any footage of this alleged launch?"

"You know they don't! You and your hacker friends have covered everything up with that stupid commercial! What the hell was that about anyway?"

"You're starting to rant, Agent Reilly," said Annette, calm as pond water. "Honestly, I can't follow a thing you're saying." She turned the tables on the agent who was becoming increasingly agitated.

"And you, what were you doing in your shop, Madsen? Why did you take the generator and the welder with you in the truck?"

Mike shrugged. "It was a car run. We went to pick up a car in Texas. It was in rough shape so I knew I'd need to weld together a support frame to get it back here."

"All of you?"

"We're a close group of friends, so we thought it would be really cool to pile in the truck and do a road trip."

"A likely story!"

"Yes, as most stories are," Daniel said again.

"And I can't figure out where you come into the story, Mr. Rakes. A ham radio store owner, what do you have to do with all of this?"

"You put him in handcuffs without probable cause? That's not going to go down very well, Agent Reilly." Annette looked at him shamefully.

Sam spoke up. "So far you have two scientists, two mechanics, a ham radio buff, and a waitress, but no evidence, no witnesses, no motive, and most importantly, no crime. Tell me again why we're in here, Agent Reilly, and then Dr Blazer and I are going to call some friends of ours and shine a light on this violation of our rights."

"He's right, sir," Smith said from the driver's seat.

Reilly's blood pressure was getting dangerously high. "I'm going to ask you all one more time. Where's the bomb?"

Mike couldn't stand it any more. "Okay, you want to know what's going on? I'll tell you the whole story. Once you know everything, you'll let us go, right?"

"If you haven't done anything wrong, you will be free to leave."

"Okay then—"

"Mikey, no," Mellissa protested

"Mel here found an alien lying in that depression. She told Danny, so he hauled it out of the woods. That thing was big and its name was Dominus. It was a mechanical being, highly evolved and hunting another alien, a biological being named Piaa. While Piaa was scrounging for parts to make a beacon, she enlisted John Anthony's help. They made the beacon and attracted help from an ancient race that has been protecting us humans since, like, the Ice Age." Mike was talking fast, without pause or hesitation.

"That race is called the Atec. And the big robot I mentioned? His boss was called the Structure…" Mike continued to recant the whole story as they drove. By the time he was done, they were pulling into FBI headquarters in DC. "…so that's where we all arrived from recently. Now we're on call as super soldiers to help find the last remnants of the Structure and rid the galaxy of it's criminal leftovers. And if you say that's a likely story, then you need therapy."

"You honestly expect me to buy that science fiction bullshit?" Reilly was secretly impressed by the man's ability to spin a yarn.

"I don't care." Mike shrugged. "I told you the truth. Now you're letting us go because, even though you may be a rude, frustrated guy with anger management issues, I believe you are still a man of your word."

The SUV stopped at the security entrance. Reilly got out and stared at them all as Annette rolled down the window. Finally, he sighed and said, "Smith, take them back." Then he looked in the back seat. "I don't believe a word of what you said, but Smith is right, I don't have enough evidence to hold you, but I will eventually. This isn't over. I'll be watching you and waiting for—"

"That sounds like a threat of harassment," Annette seethed. "Just another thing to tell Congresswoman Abigail Farnsley when I give my presentation to the Congressional Committee on Women's Rights next week. I'm sure that her and the other members of congress will be interested to hear how the FBI is conducting its investigations these days. Don't worry, Agent Reilly, I'll make sure your name is spelled correctly in the brief."

Reilly blanched, turned his back on them, and stormed off through the gate.

When John Anthony and his friends were driven a few hundred yards away from the FBI building, they brought their hands around to the front. They had broken out of the cuffs a few minutes into the ride.

Smith smiled at them. "Well, I think that should keep him at bay for awhile. You know he won't stop though. He's like a dog on a bone."

"That's what we have you for."

"I do my best." Smith winked at John Anthony in the rearview mirror.

ABOUT THE AUTHOR

Musician, kayak guide, renaissance swashbuckler…Montgomery Thompson likes to do fun stuff. Born in Maryland and raised in Colorado, Monte claims Sandpoint, Idaho as his hometown but most of the time he can be found in the hills of Northern Ireland.

Also from Montgomery Thompson: *The God String*; a two-book series *The God String*, and *The Second Split* with ties into the Augmentia series. The second Augmentia book is forthcoming.

His works for kids include *The Christmas Wish Tree* and *The Shielding of Mortimer Townes*.

Available on Amazon.com and Amazon.co.uk

Printed by Amazon Italia Logistica S.r.l.
Torrazza Piemonte (TO), Italy